The Winds
that Blow
Before
the Rains

The Winds
that Blow
Before
the Rains

Michael Anthony

Matador
9 Priory Business Park,
Wistow Road, Kibworth Beauchamp,
Leicestershire. LE8 0RX
Tel: (+44) 116 279 2299
Fax: (+44) 116 279 2277
Email: books@troubador.co.uk
Web: www.troubador.co.uk/matador

ISBN 978 1780883 625

British Library Cataloguing in Publication Data.
A catalogue record for this book is available from the British Library.

Cover design: Terry Compton

Front cover illustration: Neeltje Luyendyk

Cover artwork and back cover illustration: Jane Leadham

Typeset by Troubador Publishing Ltd, Leicester, UK

Matador is an imprint of Troubador Publishing Ltd

Printed and bound in the UK by TJ International, Padstow, Cornwall

This book is for Angie,
who believed in the story and helped me bring it to life.

And to all Zimbabweans,
who believed there was a tomorrow.

And finally to my mother,
who called me Michael Anthony because she believed I
would be a writer.

Belief: the feeling that something is real and true –
trust.

Oxford English Dictionary

AUTHOR'S NOTE

This novel is an unbiased account of a people I once knew and a place I loved. It does not intend to practise or preach but rather to show the reader how it once was.

Although it is a work of fiction, it charts lives and places that are real but to identify with them would be folly because unambiguous characters or places are not necessarily based on real people or events. Neither is there any aim to make concessions in fiction on the actions of any living person.

PREFACE

This novel is Zimbabwe come to life, an unforgettable story told not by a scholar of Africa looking from the outside in, but by an ex-soldier who was there at the beginning of the troubles. I was one of only three young men, from an intake of sixty volunteers, to be selected for the SAS and given the honour of wearing the 'winged dagger'. As such, I have a unique perspective of this country: a white man living in Rhodesia during some of its most turbulent changes. Like Sengamo, the African tracker in the book, I lived through that chaotic period in history and I came to know the hidden paths through the mountains, and to recognise the animals and their nightly calls. I witnessed the Africans' way of life and the terrible suffering they endured at the hands of aggressors from both sides of the divide.

And the fight for freedom continues, with the waves of revolution threatening to wipe out oppressive governments all over the world. Yet almost thirty years since Robert Mugabe came to power, he remains one of the last dictators standing. However, age is one enemy he cannot defeat, and his death will signal an uncertain future for Zimbabwe, leaving a power vacuum that has the potential to instigate a renewed level of violence that may plunge the country into war once more. As such, this book is more vital than ever in its telling of the experience of

Africans in this tumultuous region.

While this story does not shy away from the violence that characterises Zimbabwe's history, it also tells of a beautiful love affair, a chance to start anew and a friendship that survives and flourishes against all odds. My inspiration for writing this novel is Mandela, who showed me that we are all one people. If my book can impart this simple fact to those who read it, then I have achieved what I set out to do.

Michael Anthony 2012

A PEOPLE'S STRUGGLE FOR INDEPENDENCE

For nearly a hundred years the territory known as 'Rhodesia', an unrecognised landlocked country in Southern Africa, was under the sway of the British Empire. In 1888 Cecil John Rhodes and his British South Africa Company had negotiated a territorial treaty with the Ndebele king, Lobengula, which led to Rhodes acquiring the land from the Matabele tribe. By 1923, the territory had become a self-governing British colony.

But all was not as it seemed.

Thirty years later, there was growing opposition to the occupation of African lands, and Britain's colonies began to fall like dominoes. In 1965, the white-minority Rhodesian government, led by Ian Smith, joined the fray when it signed the Unilateral Declaration of Independence (UDI). The document – which the UK government considered to be illegal – put an end to any suggestion that Rhodesia should become a multi-racial democracy, effectively isolating the black man from involvement in the government of his own country.

Incensed, the majority black population formed the Zimbabwe African National Liberation Army (ZANLA) to overthrow republican rule in Rhodesia. Supported by the Chinese and operating from bases in Mozambique, ZANLA adopted the Maoist guerrilla tactics that had proved so successful for FRELIMO freedom fighters in that same country.

The white Rhodesians would come to call the conflict the 'Bush War'. To the guerrilla supporters it was the 'Second Chimurenga', a direct descendant of the First Chimurenga, or the First War of Independence against British rule, which had taken place in 1896.

The war was nothing short of brutal. It saw thousands of casualties on both sides, brought large-scale destruction to the land and the country's innocent tribespeople, and came to define a generation of Rhodesians – both black and white.

Following the Bush War's culmination in 1980, there was a transition to black majority rule and the country finally gained the independence it had sought for nearly a century. Rhodesia became Zimbabwe, and Robert Mugabe its notorious leader.

But history books can never tell the whole story.

PROLOGUE

Last night I had a dream.

I am sitting alone beside a campfire.

Standing on the edge of the darkness are five men, but I am unable to recognise their faces in the faint glow of the embers.

There is no wood to revive the fire and the figures remain anonymous. And when the last of the flames die, the dream is obliterated.

It is the summer of 1982: a part of the bleak years, the days of drought and hardship. Shadows have fallen over the valleys and the mountains of Nyanga.

The Shona people call it 'the winds that blow before the rains'. And until the rains of equality come, Zimbabwe – my beloved country – will continue to suffer.

Isabella

1

In the stillness of the day the silence was mythical. The tracker lay in the long grass and watched the enemy slowly approaching from the west, a string of soldiers snaking along the narrow path that stretched through the bush. High above him a solitary vulture drifted lazily on a thermal. The *makhote* was bad luck. It was waiting for death.

Glancing to his right, he could just make out the shadow of his platoon leader, Nyati, crouched behind a low rock. Scattered to the east of the path were seven of his fellow guerrillas, which left just the *madala*, the old man of the troop, on the opposite side of the track. He had little chance of escape from that position. But then he was cursed with the sickness and, as such, had volunteered to sacrifice himself in order for his comrades to make their escape.

The tracker's eyes returned to the advancing foe and its lead soldier, a *mzungu*, the only white man amongst a regiment of African traitors. As the officer passed the old baobab tree he turned his sun-burnt face towards where the tracker lay concealed and for just a moment the young freedom fighter thought his cover had been compromised. He pressed his body further into the softness of the earth; his mouth was dry and tiny beads of perspiration covered his forehead. Although they aggravated him, he remained completely motionless, his right eye glued to the cross-sight of the Draginov rifle, which was centred on the chest of the first African in the enemy line. Waiting for Nyati's signal to attack, he watched the soldier apprehensively, like a lion targeting a wildebeest.

Still nothing happened.

'Relax man,' he said to himself, easing his finger slightly off the trigger. The patrol was so close now that he could see, magnified in the sights of the Draginov, a button missing on the pocket of the African's jacket.

Suddenly the *mzungu* stopped, like a gazelle when it senses a predator, and he raised his left hand high above his head, signalling for the patrol to halt.

In the brief interlude the young tracker could feel his heart beating wildly.

Then the blast of Nyati's AK-47 shattered the silence and the *mzungu*, his arm still clutching the air, collapsed to the ground. Instinctively, the tracker squeezed the trigger of his sniper rifle and the bullet found its mark on his target's pocket, just below the missing button.

The deafening sound of gunfire from both sides of the divide thickened the air as the enemy went to ground. In the aftermath of the initial contact, acrid smoke drifted slowly across the *veld*, occasionally fuelled by a burst of fire when a soldier broke cover.

The tracker inched his way forward. Six feet to his right he could see the shape of his friend Jiwe, the boy he had trained with in the mountains. His adolescent body hugged the earth. 'Jiwe, Jiwe – are you all right?' he called out softly, aware that any movement in the tall grass would be dangerous.

There was no reply.

A cold shiver crept down the tracker's back and before he reached his comrade he knew he was dead. He turned the body over. Surprise was etched clearly across Jiwe's face, which was frozen in the moment the bullet had taken his young life. The tracker reached across and gently closed his eyes and, as he did so, rage engulfed him. Although he had orders to vacate the area after initial contact, his only thought now was to kill.

Behind a small acacia bush the red beret of an African soldier moved and then disappeared. The tracker forced the stock of the Draginov back against his shoulder to minimise the recoil and tightened his finger on the trigger, waiting for the streak of crimson to reappear. Then he heard a low whistle. It was Nyati, his hand barely visible in the dense grass, frantically beckoning him to withdraw. Reluctantly, he lowered his weapon and moved cautiously away from the ambush site just as the machine gun opened fire. That would be the *madala*, he thought as he retreated.

Elephant grass covered the savannah all the way back to the rendezvous point, a lone tamboti tree that stood below the *kopje*, like a stranger amidst the sea of acacia bushes. It was here, beneath the shadow of a large overhanging rock, that the tracker waited, the heat of the sun reflecting the warmth from the stone onto his body.

Suddenly he heard the blast of a rifle grenade exploding. A shrill scream followed and then a deathly silence covered the battlefield. And in the stillness the tracker realised the *madala's* light machine gun had stopped firing. He looked up. Two more *makhote* had arrived, flying in ever decreasing circles above him, awaiting their turn to feed. More vultures would soon be on their way and he shuddered at the thought of what they would do to Jiwe.

Less than a minute later Nyati appeared with four

soldiers, the only survivors of the skirmish. The *madala* was not amongst them.

'Where is Baba?' the tracker asked. From the look on the guerrillas' faces he knew the answer.

Nyati placed his arm around the young tracker's shoulder. 'He did not make it Sengamo, but he has given us a chance to escape – let us not waste it!'

There were tears in the tracker's eyes. The old man had been like a father to him since he'd arrived in Mozambique and, as such, he'd found it easy to call him 'Baba'. Today he had lost not only his young friend, Jiwe, but also his teacher. Anguish overcame him when he thought of them lying alone on the *veld*. Soon their bodies would turn purple and the stomachs would bloat. Then the scavengers would move in, first the hyenas and then the vultures, attracted by the putrid smell of rotting carcasses; corpses that were once comrades. But he could not dwell on such matters. The safety of the survivors was paramount and it was his responsibility to lead them back to the safety of Mozambique. Without him, this dangerous route across the mountains would be impossible.

Slowly, Sengamo moved ahead of the troop into the bush, signalling to the freedom fighters to follow. Traversing the *kopje*, the six survivors cautiously made their way down to the stream that wended its way across the *veld*. Two hours of sunlight remained in the day when they entered the water and, turning to his right, the tracker followed the flow uphill, using the wet rocks as stepping stones to prevent detection. When the troop reached the forest on the edge of the mountain they stopped to rest and fill their bottles with the cool water. Then, ensuring there was no trace of their footprints on the muddy bank, Sengamo led the tired men out of the stream and up into the hills. It was dusk and with the Draginov slung over his back, he had both hands free to forge a way through the undergrowth that strangled the mountain pass.

The light was dying and a new moon cast a faint outline on the horizon when the weary band reached a small clearing high in the mountains. In the distance they could hear the helicopters. Removing his field glasses from their canvas case, Nyati focussed them on the low-lying ground where the ambush had taken place. The enemy patrol had disappeared, as though it had never existed. They had taken with them their dead and wounded, leaving just the fallen freedom fighters to the scavengers of the bush.

And now, in the quiet of the evening, only the barking of distant hyenas disturbed the tranquillity that had descended across the *veld*.

2

Shadows had covered the mountains when the troop finally burst through the heavily wooded forest and into the camp nestled in the valley. It was a good place for a base, well camouflaged and invisible from the mountain path, even in the daylight. At night, without an accomplished tracker, it would be impossible to find.

Sengamo hesitated and waved his hand in the air, signalling caution.

Suddenly a harsh challenge manifested from the darkness. 'Stop! Who is it?'

'Duma troop – it is Nyati,' the guerrilla leader said, still breathless from the climb through the mountains, his bleached khaki shirt wet through with sweat. Behind him the remainder of the troop removed their rucksacks and rifles, relieved to have escaped the killing ground.

The voice from the dark immediately softened. 'Ah, welcome home *nkozi!*'

'You must have the eyes of a leopard, Sengamo,' Nyati said, turning to the tracker. Sengamo acknowledged the compliment with a smile, but in the dim light Nyati did not see it. 'Come and sit with me by the fire – it's been a long day.'

The compound was almost indistinguishable from the surrounding bush. In the small clearing flames from the campfire highlighted three Africans. '*Molo* Nyati!' shouted the older soldier, upon seeing his superior.

'*Molo* Lembo. Is there *chibuku?*'

'*Yebo nkozi*, also *chakula*,' he said, departing with his friends to summon the cook boy.

Nyati sat down on a freshly sawn tree stump and indicated to the tracker to do the same. 'I am sorry about the old man,' he said in a kindly voice. 'I know you were close to him, but understand it was for the best – the sickness is a bad way to die.'

Sengamo nodded, his mind back with the *makhote*. Although he had grown up with the vultures, their appearance was always eerie. But they were a part of his homeland, where the tall grass whispered stories to him as it swayed in the early morning breeze. If he closed his eyes he could hear the voice of the sparrow that sung to him as he sat beneath the branches of the msasa tree. Every blade of grass had a soul – it was alive, or so his teacher, a much-travelled foreign man, had told him in his lessons at the missionary school. They had made such an impact on him as a young boy, opening doors to lands beyond his humble dreams, whose people practised different religions that strangely, he found, were not unlike his own tribal culture. And it was these stories that gave him his affinity for the wild and his love for the mountains.

Then Nyati was speaking again. 'I have buried many comrades over the years but some, like the *madala*, I have had to leave on the battlefield. He was a good man. But today it was *you* who impressed me; I tell you, *kijana*, I have fought in the bush with both FRELIMO and ZANLA but I have never seen anyone track these hills like you do – it is no wonder they call you *mlima mtu!* So, where did you learn this skill, mountain man?'

It was some time before the tracker spoke. He thought of his family's thatched *rondavel*, one of many in a village that was home to labourers working on the *wazungus'* tobacco farm. The Africans' huts were almost two miles from the homestead, a journey that took the workers across bush teeming with animals.

'Every day I had to walk from my *kraal* across the *veld* to the missionary school near Headlands. And so I learnt from an early age to read the signs that the predators left for me. When you live in the bush like a wild animal, you begin to think like one.' The tracker shook his head before continuing, bitterness seeping into his voice. 'It was acceptable for us to do the *wazungus'* work, *nkozi* – to harvest their tobacco, to clean their house, to wash their clothes and even cook their food. But to live alongside them? Oh no! To them we were *shit;* dirty and uncivilised and no better than the scrawny chickens in our dusty yard. I would often look out over their vast fields of corn and imagine a day when my plot of parched earth would produce such crops. But it was a dream, *nkozi;* just like the fairy tales our fathers told us.' The tracker sighed.

Suddenly there was a strange scuffling sound in the bush. In the blink of an eye Nyati's AK-47 was in his hand and he'd released the safety catch just as the cook boy stepped into the firelight. 'Hey, *pika*, what the hell are you doing? You need to make yourself known when you creep out of the bush or we might lose you!'

'Sorry *nkozi!*' the cook boy gasped, startled by the Kalashnikov pointing at his chest. 'It was the mug, I . . . I dropped it and was looking for it . . . sorry, so sorry *nkozi.*'

Nyati's face softened. 'It's OK son.' He leaned the weapon back against the tree stump and took the plates of food, handing one to Sengamo. 'Go now *pika*, but be careful next time you walk in from the dark.' When he had finished eating, Nyati held his plate to his lips and licked it clean. 'Ah! That is much better,' he said, as he filled the enamel mugs from the earthenware jug. 'Now, what are these fairy tales you speak of *kijana?*'

'You must have heard of them,' Sengamo said, before pausing to take a gulp of the home-brewed beer. 'They are the *madalas'* tales, passed down from one generation to the next, "the history of our people", my father called them.'

Nyati picked up a blade of grass and ran it through his teeth. 'You mean the tribal stories, from the days before the *wazungus* came to Africa?'

Sengamo nodded. 'Have you heard of the white settler, a British explorer who arrived in our country more than a hundred years ago? Baba called him Mister Rose, or maybe it was Rhodes—'

'You mean Cecil Rhodes,' Nyati said, scratching his head. 'Now there was an evil man. He tricked our chiefs into handing over our land in return for beads. *Beads!* What the hell is that all about? Then he divided it up, drawing random lines on a map with no thought for the long-held traditions of our tribal hierarchies.'

'Did our ancestors not fight, as we do now?'

'Of course! But the *impis'* spears and raw-hide shields were no match for the white mans' guns. Our men were slaughtered,' Nyati seethed.

'And I heard that those who survived were made to pay the hut tax?'

Nyati nodded his head slowly. 'That came later. An extra ten shillings every year for each *rondavel*. My father was forced to find work in the gold mines in South Africa to pay the tax. The toxic dust from the years spent down in that hole eventually killed him.'

The sombre mood was shattered by a shout from afar. '*Molo* Nyati!'

'Haraka! Where have you been? Come – join us for *chibuku!*'

'*Nkozi*, you cannot believe how thirsty I am after today's operation.' Haraka accepted the chipped enamel mug and immediately drained it. Letting out a long satisfied sigh, he turned to the young tracker. '*Hujambo, mlima mtu;* you impressed me tonight with your skill in the dark.'

'I tell you, Haraka, the battle is much easier with the mountain man. This young *nganga* throws his magic bones and we are invisible!' Laughing at his little joke, Nyati pulled the blanket around his shoulders to deflect the cold air from his back. 'What is your tribe Sengamo?'

'I am of the Ndebele, *nkozi.*'

'And how old are you?'

'Nineteen, *nkozi.*'

'Ah, so you have been through the circumcision ceremony?'

'*Yebo;* when I turned fourteen the elders shaved my head and I went into the bush with the other boys. After the ceremony we drank the blood from a cow and there was much dancing. We had become warriors.'

'They tell me if you are a Masai or a Wakamba you must prove your worth by confronting an elephant or killing a lion with just your spear,' Haraka added.

'It is also true for the Ndebele – the elders said that the closer you were to the lion, the braver you were.'

'And how close did you get?'

'I could pull its tail!'

Nyati laughed, his bellowing profile highlighted by the flames of the campfire. 'The *kijana* is having a joke with you Haraka!'

'It is no joke, *nkozi* . . . you must understand that I know these hills as I know my own hands. First they were my playground, then my hunting ground. Now they are my battleground.' He paused to drink from the enamel mug. 'In fact it was me who taught the *bwana's* son the ways of the bush. We became good friends. But still the *wazungus* never allowed me to forget where I came from; I was an Ndebele warrior, but to them I was nothing more than a servant.'

'We have always been their bloody slaves.' Haraka defiantly spat a large ball of phlegm into the fire and watched the spittle evaporate on the burning coals. 'It's worse since that hyena's turd, Smith, and his bloody white Rhodesian Front party declared their UDI. We were men without a country, without any rights, not that we had many before that bastard came along. They told us where to build our homes, what bus to take, what job to do . . . we could not even go for a *shit* in a white man's toilet. And then, because we were black, we were destined to spend eternity in a cemetery at the arse end of town well away from the *wazungus*. It was a bloody joke!'

Nyati shook his head. 'You would have been too young to remember all of this Sengamo. We were trying to change the country, to bring democracy to our people. But the *wazungus* wouldn't have it. Can you believe that I was arrested for handing out leaflets – for *our* party?' The guerrilla leader closed his eyes. 'The police rounded up the demonstrators and beat us with *shamboks*. They cuffed me, put leg irons around my ankles and threw me into the back of a prison van. Then they dragged me into the police station and held my face right up to a sign that read "UDI" in big black letters. "Do you know what the Unilateral Declaration of Independence means, *kaffir*?" this fat policeman screamed. "It means no other political parties! How can we let you black bastards vote, hey? You have only just come down from the bloody trees!" Then they locked me up in Chikurubi jail for thirty days, with two broken ribs. This is how I came to be in Mozambique – Rhodesia was no place for an African in those days.'

'But what happened to ZANLA?'

'It was impossible for the party to operate in Rhodesia; they moved the operations to the guerrilla camps over the border, and here, *kijana*, is where we fight from – for now at least.'

Haraka reached over for the *chibuku*. He half filled his mug and then passed the remnants in the jug back to Nyati. 'It was around that time that the Chinese arrived at the Tete camp, on the border of Mozambique,' he said, gesturing towards the peaks in the distance. 'They didn't speak Swahili or Shona but they brought guns – guns like we'd never seen before, that fired hundreds of bullets when you touched the trigger.'

Sengamo looked up from the fire. 'So what were they doing in the camps?'

'They came to teach us their Maoist guerrilla tactics, employed in the many wars they have fought in their own country: methods for infiltrating our combatants into Rhodesia, politicising the people and hitting the isolated white-owned farms. This was the way, they told us, we would drive the *wazungus* off our land forever.'

'You know, Nyati, at the time, I saw the Chinese as comrades because they gave us what we needed: weapons to fight the white man on equal terms, to help us win back our freedom,' Haraka said.

'But what did they want in return?' Sengamo asked.

'Our land – like the *wazungus* who came before them!' Nyati said, letting out a bitter laugh. He stood up and passed the empty jug to Haraka before sauntering off to a small bush to relieve himself.

When Haraka had set off into the darkness in search of more *chibuku*, Sengamo's thoughts returned to his childhood. The African's story had reminded him of the racism he had encountered at Gazelle Farm, when neighbouring farmers would come to eat *boerewors* and let off steam about the '*kaffirs*' and their fight for freedom. He shuddered at the memory.

'Ah, that is better,' the guerrilla leader announced, when he'd returned to the fire. He rubbed his hands together, soaking up the warmth of the orange flames. 'It is a cold night and soon my bed will be calling me. Still, there are no more operations this week and training does not start until tomorrow afternoon – so tell me, Sengamo, what made *you* leave Rhodesia?'

The young tracker was silent for a moment as he collected his thoughts. '*Nkozi*, you remember me telling you of my friendship with the *bwana's* son?'

'Ah yes; you were naïve to put yourself in such a dangerous position,' Nyati said in a stern voice. 'The *wazungus* will never accept us as their equals!'

'Nyati is right,' Haraka said, reappearing with the beer. 'They are not to be trusted. Like the cobra, you never know when they might strike.'

'Tom wasn't like that!' Sengamo protested. 'I taught him to track the bush and in return he gave me food; he didn't care about the colour of my skin.' He removed a stick from the flames and watched as the end glowed in the dark. Then he closed his eyes and for a moment he could see again that first light of morning, when he arose to start his chores. The mountains were golden, basking in the sunshine. In the heat of the day they would turn from green to brown and then back to yellow in the sunset. And before the black of night engulfed them they would fade to a haunting blue and be as one with the empty sky. 'They were good days, *nkozi* – we were like blood brothers.'

'Ah, but you were young then and knew no better,' Nyati said.

'That is so, *nkozi*. But we were not too young to realise that we had to keep our friendship a secret. Then one day a neighbour saw us playing together in the fields and told the *bwana*. He had words with his son, but he didn't punish me. I have always wondered why. Perhaps Tom spoke up for me? But, that wasn't the end of it.'

'Tell us more, *kijana*.'

'Tom had a sister. Her name was Andrea. It was she who despised our friendship more than anyone. When she saw us returning from the mountains, laughing and happy, there was hatred in her eyes.'

'We have all lived with the white man's hatred, Sengamo.'

'Ah, but not like this girl. For a *msichana* she was cruel, but also very clever.' He paused and looked cautiously at the guerrilla fighters. Their faces, alive with concentration, implored him to continue.

'One day she just . . . changed. She would seek me out,

sit close to me and tell me how sorry she was for how she had treated me.'

'Ha!' Haraka said knowingly, scooping strands of tobacco from his pouch and rolling them into a cigarette. Picking up a stick from the fire, he held it to the paper and drew the blue smoke deep into his lungs. 'The problem is you are black, *kijana*, and relationships between natives and white girls were forbidden in the old Rhodesia.'

'That is right,' Nyati said, 'I have seen men shot for such a thing.'

Sengamo accepted the slight. 'In hindsight, yes, I was ignorant. But you must understand that when she called me I had to obey.' His gaze shifted prudently between the two men, finally coming to rest on Nyati. Images flashed through his mind, of idyllic days walking the bush with his friend, pretending they were comrades in arms, tracking wild animals in their beloved mountains. The deception happened on a day when there were no clouds in the sky, when the heat made even the scorpions seek solace in their dark homes beneath the rocks. 'It was three summers ago,' he ventured. 'Tom and his mother were away in Rusape at the doctors. My orders were to sweep the yard and weed the garden. I was digging the soil when I heard Andrea shout my name.'

'What did she want?' Haraka asked.

Sengamo's mouth was dry and he paused to take a sip of the *chibuku*. 'She wanted the milk churns moving from the barn to the dairy. It is something I had done many times before, but when I stepped out of the sunshine and into the barn, there she was, standing beside the brick wall, waiting. All of a sudden I had this terrible feeling that the walls were my prison and the girl my captor.' He looked down at his feet. 'When Andrea put her arms around my shoulders and told me to relax I could not believe this was happening to me. Why would she want a black boy? She was a very pretty girl, you see.'

'It was not you she wanted,' Haraka said, opening the pouch for more tobacco.

'You are right, Haraka. When she saw the *bwana* coming from the farmhouse, she grabbed the front of her blouse and tore it open. Then she began to scream.' He licked his lips, which had dried again at the thought. 'Ah *nkozi*, she was making too much noise! I was so scared – I did not know what to do.'

'Eiee, this is truly a white woman's trick,' Nyati said.

'The *bwana* was a violent man! I had seen him threaten a farm worker with his shotgun over a small incident. And the thought of me supposedly raping their daughter – I would have no chance! I tell you, *nkozi*, they would have hung me from the nearest tree if they had caught me. All I could think of was to run.'

'I can understand your fear *kijana*,' Nyati said, 'the *wazungus* accused my friend John of a similar crime back in Rhodesia. They shot him, but he was still alive when they roped him by his feet to the back of a Land Rover and dragged him through the bush until he was unrecognisable. Then they stripped off his tattered clothes and left him to the mercy of the predators. The vultures finally finished him off, leaving only his bleached bones beside the water hole. I was a boy then, but I remember thinking it odd that we black men also have white bones.'

'So *you* got away, Sengamo,' Haraka said, intrigued by the story.

'I have never been so frightened, *nkozi* – but first I had to see my brother.'

'*Your brother.* You are crazy *kijana!*'

Sengamo nodded. 'I couldn't leave without saying goodbye! Gorho was out working in the fields. I didn't tell him where I was going – how could I? *I* did not even know! I simply said I had to disappear for a while and that I would return one day when we are no longer judged by the colour of our skins – when we are free.'

'Wise words,' Nyati said, 'from one so young.'

'And so this is how you come to fight with us here in Mozambique.' Haraka held his head back and drained the last of the *chibuku*.

The tracker nodded. There was no point telling them about the silver charm that Tom had given him for his thirteenth birthday, the one he had placed around his brother's neck before putting his arms around him for the last time. Merging into the denser bush above the compound, he had looked back and had seen Gorho slumped on the ground in the *mealie* field, his head in his hands, wracked with sobs. This was the image he would carry across the border to the battlegrounds of Mozambique.

It had marked the end of the summer and the end of his childhood.

3

Sengamo was seventeen years old when he left the Highlands of Rhodesia, a wanted man on the run. Since Smith had declared UDI, the minority government had gained a stranglehold on his country and the indigenous Africans had all but lost their independence, once again second-class citizens in their own lands. If Sengamo was ever to return to Rhodesia, he would need to join the guerrilla army and fight for his country's freedom. And he wasn't the only outcast plotting his revenge. Nkomo, Sithole and Mugabe – these were the names whispered around rebel campfires, emblazoned on underground propaganda pamphlets. These men, each of them recently released from jail, had one thing in common: they were leaders of opposition political groups active in the struggle to overthrow the white-dominated regime. Now, with the support of China, Cold War politics was playing its own part in the conflict.

Sengamo's status as a fugitive endeared him to ZANLA, the military wing of ZANU-PF, the Zimbabwe African National Union. He spent his first two years in the hills of Mozambique with them, training for the conflict that became known as the Bush War or, as the Africans called it, the Second Chimurenga.

The Ndebele spiritual leader, Mlimo, led the first revolutionary struggle, nearly a hundred years earlier.

He believed that drought, locust plagues and cattle diseases were a white man's curse and convinced the two largest indigenous tribes, the Shona and his own Ndebele, to unite and fight the British colonialists. It was months before the British army managed to overthrow the rebel leader, and he was eventually assassinated in the Matobo Hills. Cecil Rhodes himself finally ended the war when he persuaded the *impi* to lay down their arms.

The Africans' limited successes in the First Chimurenga were attributed to their knowledge of the land and the tracking skills of the *impi*. It was this expertise, passed down from one generation to the next, which Sengamo employed to lead the guerrillas back to their base in the mountains after blowing up bridges or attacking convoys. Now in possession of Russian-made Kalashnikov AK-47s, explosives and rocket launchers, the freedom fighters were slowly managing to turn the battle for independence in their favour.

After each operation the guerrilla soldiers attended debriefing sessions, in essence a thin disguise for ZANLA's indoctrination lectures. But the political propaganda did not interest Sengamo – his simple goal was to return to his country and live like the white people and he couldn't care less about how he achieved this objective. Over time he came to distance himself from the core of ZANLA's army, preferring instead to fight with Nyati, Haraka and their small band of guerrillas. These highly skilled teams worked undercover, often miles behind the enemy lines, attacking installations as far afield as Harare and Bulawayo.

'When you hear this filth enough times, you almost come

to believe it,' Haraka whispered to the tracker, as they sat beside the campfire watching the smoke lingering in the air like a mist. It was early evening after another debriefing session and the sun had already descended below the treetops. Filtering through the branches, it cast golden shadows over the deserted compound.

'Sorry *nkozi*, but this is nonsense,' Sengamo said vehemently, reaching down to ease the webbing on his boots. 'I can understand killing the soldiers and the *mtengesi*, the traitors that support the *wazungus'* regime – but the innocent tribesmen? No! I cannot do this.'

'Keep your voice down Sengamo,' Haraka said, looking around nervously. Rebellious talk like this was punishable by public hanging. He had seen the bush trials and the naked men left dangling from ropes in the trees, their hands tied behind their backs and their genitals stuffed into their mouths.

'There is no choice,' Lwazi said, joining the conversation. 'We do what we are told. But it is not always easy. I was in a village near the border, before you arrived in the mountains. The officer ordered us to pick out thirty farmers. At random. He demanded to know which of them was responsible for talking to the enemy. I tell you, they were so frightened they were shitting themselves. Each neighbour blamed the other for a crime that did not exist.'

'They kill farmers to keep the villagers in line,' Haraka said.

'But it is the *way* they do it. After the interrogation the *tsotsis* handed a ten-year-old boy a machete and ordered him to execute the men. But first they made them dig their own graves . . . his father's head was the last on the wooden block.'

'It's how they rule the people,' Haraka said contemptuously. 'When the villagers hear the screams of their wives and children burning to death in their *rondavels*, they no longer have the appetite for opposition.' He cleared his throat and spat a ball of phlegm into the bush, in disgust rather than out of necessity. 'I have seen many terrible things but I will tell you something that turned my stomach over. Have you heard of Makonda?'

Sengamo shook his head.

'It's a village near Gorongosa – I was there last summer. The *tsotsis* singled out a *madala* and his family and charged them with "aiding the security forces." Ha! It was an excuse for their filth. Two of these bastards held the old man's granddaughter on the ground – she must have been no more than twelve. Then they stripped her and gang-raped her in front of her grandfather. She cried the whole time, pleading for mercy. And all I could do was stand and watch.'

'And these are the animals that we fight with,' Sengamo sneered. The senseless carnage sickened him. A whole generation of his people were suffering; mother's raped… kids with mutilated limbs . . . their father's heads hanging on stakes . . . homes lying in fields of anti-personnel mines where children could no longer play. The villagers were starving, their gardens having been repeatedly destroyed, first by Rhodesian soldiers accusing them of feeding the terrorists, and then by the revolutionaries in retaliation for their supposed collaboration with the security forces. Yet all they were trying to do was to keep their families alive. 'The death cries of the children will forever remind me of the innocent people who have suffered throughout this terrible war.'

'But do you understand why this violence saddens you so, *kijana?*'

Sengamo shook his head.

'It is because you come from a village just like those you have seen destroyed.'

'We have all been guilty,' Lwazi said, averting his eyes from Haraka's face.

'You think so?' the tracker fiercely objected, thinking of Nyati, who refused to be involved in such atrocities. 'There are some of us who do not go there.'

It was a cold night in the mountains. Haraka fastened the buttons on his coat before looking at the tracker and nodding slowly. 'You are fortunate, *mlima mtu;* it is your skill in tracking that keeps you alive.'

Haraka's appraisal was valid. But this was only a small part of the truth; it was primarily Sengamo's proficiency with explosives that had allowed the small band of guerrillas this operating freedom. Were it not for this, he would have become yet another statistic of the lonely war, hanging like a pod from the branch of a kigali tree.

Then Sengamo spotted a young girl coming from a *rondavel* and crossing the yard. Her body swayed in the simple cotton dress and his hungry eyes followed her every move.

The tracker's appetite for women was insatiable, legendary some would say. While the soldiers were gathered for ZANU lectures, he would often slip quietly away to the company of a girl. They were in awe of him and gave him the name *ngombe*, the bull. The *umfazis* knew of his many lovers, yet they were not jealous lest they miss their chance to lie with him.

'The fighting is hard but at least there is some compensation,' he said, smiling softly, his eyes still on the girl before she disappeared into the darkness.

And his thoughts were no longer of the violence.

***

As the war developed and cross-border activities increased, Nyati's small band of renegade guerrillas gave the ZANLA commanders cause for concern. In particular, it was Sengamo's cavalier behaviour that incensed the hierarchy and rumours of his conduct, circulated by rivals who were jealous of the group's operational freedom, eventually reached his superiors. It was largely ignored because the guerrilla commander, Sithole, thought his skills irreplaceable. Yet, for all the malicious gossip, it took an isolated incident in a small remote village to provoke the burgeoning confrontation.

It happened late one spring day. The troop had returned from fighting Selous Scout soldiers across the border in the mountains above Catandica. The smell of blossom hung in the air, its scent refreshing after the stench of the battlefield cordite, and the last of the sunshine was in Sengamo's eyes. He could see the faint outline of a man standing in the shade of a tree, a Kalashnikov cradled casually in his arms. Then the sun fell beneath the mountain and the guard was plainly visible.

'*Molo* Nyati!' the sentry shouted, upon recognising the guerrilla leader returning with Sengamo and his small band of soldiers.

'My men are thirsty for *chibuku*, Kipenzi.'

Haraka moved forward to join his leader. 'You think only of the beer, Nyati. What about the grilled chicken?'

He turned to the guard. 'The location of your kitchen fire is foolish Kipenzi. If the Rhodesian soldiers smell the *braai*, they have found us.'

The sentry looked uneasy.

'Hey Kipenzi, don't look so worried – it's a joke!' Haraka laughed, patting the man on the back.

'*Nkozi*, it's not that – we have other trouble.'

'What is the problem?' Two of Nyati's men had been killed in the battle at Catandica and he was tired and impatient.

'It is the Chinese, *nkozi*. They wish to see the mountain man immediately.'

As if in response to the statement there was a rustle in the bush and twelve heavily armed soldiers appeared out of the darkness, their Kalashnikovs held menacingly at the ready. The sergeant stepped forward. 'Sengamo, your rifle.'

'What is this nonsense?' Nyati's contempt was plain to see. 'Is this the way you treat the freedom fighters? You, who sit round a fire all day, drinking *chibuku*.'

The sergeant ignored the outburst.

'Answer me, you son of a *fisi!*'

Sengamo calmly removed the magazine from his assault rifle before handing it over. He knew all too well why they had come for him. The previous day he had stumbled across a gang of soldiers pinning a young girl to the ground. At the time he was reminded of Haraka's story in the village near Gorongosa and he was determined he would not tolerate the girl being raped. The officer had been standing over the *msichana*, hunger written plainly across his face as he unbuttoned his fatigue trousers. Then he'd heard the shout from Sengamo and had seen the Kalashnikov pointing in his direction. Reluctantly, he had stepped back while the soldiers released the girl, but his angry retort had carried clearly across the compound.

Now they had come for him.

Nyati turned to his tracker. 'Why are they arresting you Sengamo?'

'Yesterday I argued with the officer at the Catandica village.'

'When you were with the Manica forces? What happened?'

'I stopped him raping a girl.'

'And for this they want to punish you?' Nyati said with contempt. 'We will come with you.'

Sengamo straightened up and smiled. '*Hapana*, Nyati – this is my problem.' Although encouraged by the support, he knew that Nyati's small troop was helpless against three platoons of soldiers barracked in the camp.

The sergeant's indignation read on his face as he turned to confront the guerrilla leader. He was not accustomed to being called the son of a hyena. 'Nyati, you and your men will report to the rehabilitation officer at HQ immediately. And you Sengamo, come with me.'

Nyati watched them leave, not realising that this was the last time he'd ever see Sengamo in a ZANLA uniform. There was anger in his eyes.

As the soldiers escorted the tracker down the mountain path, he searched the dull green walls of the heavy bush for any means of escape, but there was none.

The guerrilla camp was situated in a large clearing, but the over-hanging trees made it difficult to see from the air.

In the centre of the dusty parade ground stood a contingent of African soldiers and a group of Chinese men in ill-fitting brown oriental uniforms. An African lieutenant squatted on a small rustic chair, which was seemingly near collapse under his enormous bulk. Beside him sat a plain-clothed Chinese official, who appeared to find a fascination in fingering the Norinco pistol on his wide leather belt.

'Attention soldier!' the sergeant barked.

The young tracker's worst fears were realised; perhaps at last this was his day of judgement and the bland-faced Chinese, far from being his comrades, were his jury.

The lieutenant looked up from the document he'd been studying. 'Stand easy comrade Sengamo,' he said, reverting to the common African dialect of Swahili.

'*Yebo nkozi.*'

'First, let me compliment you on last month's operation. The bridge you destroyed at Mukuzi is giving the Rhodesians a big headache – our troops have regained the edge over the *wazungus* in the mountains.' He paused to consider what he was about to say next. 'But there is something you must understand, comrade Sengamo. The white people live in brick houses that we build. They drive expensive cars. Yet our people still suffer in poverty. We stand all day on barren land where our oxen pull ploughs through rocks. To add to this humiliation, they call us their "servants". But in reality *we* are their slaves. This *must* change. And the way we will do it is to take up the guns and bring fear to the night.'

The tracker remained silent. Did they think they were telling him something he did not already know? If not, it was scant justification for their terror tactics. He was one of the boys who had joined the ranks of the *gandangas*, one of those who had heard the cries of the freedom songs. Many had come and now many were a part of the earth they called Mama Africa. It did not deter those who followed and they waited for the call north of the Zambezi. But at the end of the day the only winners were the *fisi* and the *makhote*, for they were the ones who cleaned the land.

'You have heard the stories of the martyrs who are dying in battle to liberate our people?' the lieutenant continued. 'Their sacrifices will not go unrecognised.' He raised his voice so that the delegation heard every word. 'They are tomorrow's heroes and we will carve their names with pride on every stone monument in our capital city.'

The tracker smirked; you have no idea *nkozi*, he said to himself – we need to heal our people before we can sing the victory songs. And he really couldn't care less whether they immortalised his name in Harare. *His* simple dream was to return to his home and his family, perhaps even try to explain things to Tom and rekindle their friendship.

The Chinese official stared at Sengamo in contempt and noticed his disinterested look yet, against his better judgement, he allowed the officer to continue.

The star emblazoned across the lieutenant's brown peaked cap indicated that he had recently returned from an indoctrination course in the outer Mongolian deserts north of Beijing. 'Comrades' he began, 'I would like to share with you the thoughts of our hero, Chairman Mao Zedong,' he said proudly as he opened a copy of the Maoist red book.

How can they read this nonsense, Sengamo thought – does this book tell them to plant landmines where they should plant crops? And how can they still believe in it when all around them there are children who will never walk again? He shuffled uneasily from one leg to the other and looked over the lieutenant's shoulder to the mountains beyond the makeshift village.

Suddenly the Chinese official jumped up from his seat, no longer able to contain his anger at this apparent insolence. 'Comrade Sengamo, your insubordination is intolerable!' he said, interrupting the lieutenant. 'You stand here in front of us with a tiresome look on your face. Are we boring you?'

'*Hapana nkozi.*'

'Your behaviour yesterday at Catandica was tantamount to anarchy. It will not be tolerated. You–'

'Is the prevention of rape considered to be anarchy?' Sengamo asked softly.

The official's face turned scarlet. 'You have no regard for orders!' he spluttered. 'Who do you think you are?'

Suddenly it was all too clear to Sengamo that his young life hung delicately in the balance. Then he recalled the *madala* with the sickness, the old man who had sacrificed himself in the ambush below the mountains. He had died in battle, an honourable death for a guerrilla warrior. And acknowledging this, the tracker reasoned that he would sooner take a bullet from a Kalashnikov than hang from a tree. Yet he remained silent.

'Have you nothing else to say?'

'*Hapana ofisa,*' Sengamo replied in Swahili, tempering his voice.

The official turned away to compose himself before continuing. 'We are impressed with your war record, Sengamo,' he said in a restrained voice, 'but not with your insubordination. You need to be educated in our ways . . . disciplined.' He paused to allow the words the impact they deserved. 'Our leaders have decided to give you an opportunity to mend your ways. You will be sent to China for specialist training.'

Sengamo was shocked. He had come to Mozambique to fight the Rhodesian soldiers and he had no desire to join ZANLA's terrorist organisation in the Far East.

'Do you appreciate what we are telling you?'

The tracker set his jaw in grim determination. 'I am more useful here in the mountains,' he replied in Swahili.

'What are you saying? You think you are indispensable?' the official screamed in frustration, his face dampening with perspiration. '*We* tell you where you are useful. *We* give the orders and *you* obey them. Do you understand?'

'I came here to fight for my country, *nkozi*,' Sengamo countered, his eyes never once leaving the officer's face.

For just a moment the impenetrable mask on the cruel face slipped and Sengamo saw clearly the loathsome hate in his superior's features. And then a command was issued in an unfamiliar language, which was hastily translated into Shona for the sergeant standing near the heavily guarded *rondavel*. '*Niletee mfungwa*, bring me the prisoner!'

A young African soldier, dressed only in a pair of ragged trousers, was dragged out of the hut. The bloody flesh on his bare back was a single mass of welts where he had been beaten with a *shambok* and he was blindfolded with what appeared to be the remnants of his own dirty shirt. 'Mercy please *inkozi*, please sir,' the captive begged.

Having finally regained his composure, the Chinese official ignored the plea and looked at Sengamo. He spoke

29

harshly in a cold, monotonous voice. 'You are about to witness what happens to those who disobey our orders.'

The prisoner, struggling desperately against his bindings, was forced onto his knees, his head positioned over a block of wood. Next to him stood a black-hooded man, a machete in his hand. There was a faint smile on the face of the Chinese official as he nodded to the executioner. Then the steel blade flashed once in the bright sunlight and the severed head fell to the ground.

Sengamo glanced briefly at the headless torso, contorted in the dust like a broken rag doll, blood soaking the earth at his feet. The smell of death thickened the air. Then he looked at the official, holding his steely gaze. He felt no fear, nor would he surrender to their regime.

Finally the Chinese man lowered his eyes and turned away to confer once again with his comrades. Was this how it all ended? Sengamo wondered.

Then just when it appeared they would take no more of his insolence, a tall general appeared. The officer was from the Mashona tribe in the eastern district of Rhodesia – Robert Mugabe was their commander-in-chief. This was indeed an important man. But when Sengamo eventually caught his eye, he saw through the disguised detachment; it was Manjaro. How long had it been since he had last seen him? Definitely not since the early days of the war, Sengamo decided, before the second wave of Chinese advisors had infiltrated their camps. Yes, that was it. They had raided Hauna, a small town in the Honde Valley.

It had been a disaster.

Sengamo was the tracker guiding the thirty-man patrol across the border and Manjaro a young lieutenant. The plan was to attack the security forces base below the Nyanga escarpment, the range of mountains that separate Rhodesia from Mozambique. But Rhodesian intelligence had blown the operation wide open and the patrol was on the run, hotly pursued by soldiers from the Light Infantry. Although the tracker was familiar with the remote paths in the mountains, he was unprepared for the killer cars – Alouette helicopters carrying 20mm canons. Whirly-birds, the Africans initially called them. Flying low over the bush, it was easy for the gunship pilots to spot the terrorists from the skies and they would simply drop troops in forward positions to cut off the fleeing rebels. In time the African fighters would master the art of camouflage and go to ground when they heard the sound of rotor blades. But in those early days they were inexperienced and lost many men.

Sandwiched between the infantry and the Selous Scouts, the guerrillas were ambushed in a remote valley and their patrol near decimated. It was dusk and under extensive gunfire from the helicopters, the captain was panicking and making all the wrong decisions. In the confusion Sengamo and Manjaro melted into the darkness. Disguised in the stolen uniforms of Rhodesian African soldiers, they escaped through a remote pass back to Mozambique, the only survivors of the original thirty-man troop.

The general owed his life to the man standing before him and he was not one to forget. After quietly conferring with the Chinese official he stood back and allowed him to deliver the message in Swahili.

'Your actions do nothing for the cause of ZANLA. However, some people,' the official hesitated and nodded

31

at Manjaro, 'speak highly of you and feel you deserve a second chance. You will go to China as planned – do *not* squander this opportunity.' Pausing to adjust his suit in the fierce heat, he concluded with an ultimatum. 'If you do not conform to our orders, this will be your fate,' he said, pointing the leathery tail of the *shambok* at the headless corpse.

It was a thin lifeline.

Sengamo bowed his head and spoke to the ground. '*Asante*, comrade *nkozi*. If it is General Manjaro's wish, it will be an honour to go to your country and learn the ways of the revolutionary.'

'Count yourself lucky, comrade; the general has saved your life. Tomorrow morning you will leave for Maputo. From there we have a direct flight to Beijing.'

'I will not let you down, *nkozi*.' Sengamo lifted his head and glanced across at Manjaro. He had no intention of meeting the flight and the general knew it.

But by maintaining his silence Manjaro had at last repaid his debt.

There was little time to waste. That evening, when the sky was without a moon and the blackness enveloped the bush beyond the camp, Sengamo disappeared. It was the last that either the Chinese or the ZANLA guerrillas would ever see of him.

As the years rolled by, his exploits became legendary. Not even the Selous Scouts, the pride of Rhodesia's Special Forces and the most effective killing machine in Africa, could find him. He became a thorn in the side of both the security forces and his own people. The Chinese foreign advisors were furious at the way they had been double-crossed and the party hierarchy tried in vain to locate him, but he was like a shadow, appearing briefly and just as quickly disappearing again. This enigmatic image gained him the nick-name 'the Black Shadow', and his capture carried a $10,000 price tag, a reward that tempted many an African bounty hunter.

Yet still he eluded them all.

Rumours abounded of his whereabouts. One such story, pieced together by insurgents operating out of Zambia, cast him in the role of a hired gun in charge of a syndicate running diamonds out of Botswana. When that whisper floundered, another, passed on by the refugees fleeing the Congo's war zone, followed. This portrayed him as a feared commander leading a group of mercenaries in the mineral-rich province of Katanga on the southern border with Zambia.

But the myths were far from the truth.

The tracker simply spent the remainder of the war away from the conflict, high up in the Chimanimani Mountains.

4

The war was coming to an end and soon it would be forgotten.

Sitting alone in his cave in the evenings, Sengamo's thoughts would often stray to Nyati and the experiences he had shared with the freedom fighters. The time had come to find them again. Word had recently reached him that the guerrilla leader was holed up somewhere in the mountains above Nyanga, in a small cave known only to a few people.

The four-day trek back to the Tangwena sector was a slow and tortuous journey. Nyati's hideout was somewhere up in these hills and for the next six days Sengamo patiently searched the remote bush for any sign of activity. But his former comrades were experts in the art of concealment. And then, early on the morning of the seventh day, his persistence was rewarded. Crossing a small stream below a rocky outlet, he stopped to drink from the cool clear water and it was here he noticed the faint print of a canvas shoe sole, which from its depth and freshness, the tracker calculated was made less than two hours previous. He removed the Kalashnikov from across his back and checked the bolt action of the rifle before resetting the magazine. Then, moving quickly off the path, he disappeared into the thick bush and made his way up the mountain where he knew the cave must lay hidden.

Sengamo saw Nyati before the guerrilla leader was

even aware of his presence. '*Molo nkozi*,' he whispered, stepping forward from the shadow of a rock. Nyati swung around, recognising the voice, his heavy-set eyes searching for the intruder. He looked so much older now. But then the war had taken its toll on all of them.

'Ah, Sengamo! *Molo, molo!*' The guerrilla leader held out his hand, delighted to see his old friend again. 'You gave me such a fright! I didn't think anybody would find us, or perhaps I am just getting old and careless.'

'It has been a long time, *nkozi*.'

'Too long, *kijana*. Haraka will be pleased to see you.'

'Where is the Quick One?'

'He is out hunting,' Nyati said, a toothless grin on his flat face. 'Did you not see Lwazi when you came in?'

'I saw him, but he didn't see me.'

Nyati laughed. 'Still the elusive Shadow, hey? Nobody sees you!'

Sengamo laughed.

'Come, come. We have *chibuku*. What are your plans?' Nyati said, gesturing the tracker into the cave.

'In the mountains; there are people looking for me.'

'*Yebo* Sengamo, this we have heard.'

'I became weary of all the killings and seeing our people suffer. I had to disappear.'

Nyati nodded slowly. 'We have all grown tired and frustrated with the struggle.'

'What we need is a place where we can hunt and live in peace!' a voice from the back of the cave shouted.

The tracker's eyes searched the darkness. 'I know of such a place,' he said to the faceless voice. 'There is a–' Suddenly a cry from behind interrupted him.

'Ha! Who is this?' Haraka's large frame filled the cave's

entrance and there was a smile on his face that ran from ear to ear. He dropped the brace of mountain hares on the ground and threw his arms around the tracker. '*Hujambo*, Sengamo! Where have you been?'

'Ah, Haraka! It is good to see you! I was just telling Nyati, I have been living in the mountains.'

'Like the leopards, hey? I told you, Nyati. The *nganga* has cast a spell on this man and turned him into a shadow. Nobody can see him!'

The guerrilla leader nodded to his second in command. 'Sengamo was telling me of a place where we can live in peace, away from the war.'

'Ah ha! This one, he knows everything. Where is this place?'

Sengamo looked at the men he had fought with before going on the run, men closer to him than his own family. 'I have found a remote cave, that only the eagles know, in the Chimanimani Mountains.'

'I've never been to that area.' Haraka glanced across at Nyati. 'Do you know of these mountains, *nkozi?*'

'*Hapana.*'

'It is south of the Honde Valley – on the border between Rhodesia and Mozambique.'

'The cave, is it as big as this one?' Nyati indicated the interior of the cavern with a sweep of his arm.

Sengamo's eyes searched the darkness. 'How many men do you have now?'

Haraka hesitated. 'It has been a difficult time without you, *kijana*.' He looked at Nyati for reassurance. 'They keep sending us replacements but we are down to six men again.'

'For a group of this size, the cave is perfect.'

'How do you know of it?' Nyati enquired suspiciously, rubbing his coarse hand across the stubble of his beard while he looked intently at the tracker, 'and how do I know my men will be safe there?'

Sengamo straightened up and adjusted the bandolier that sat easily across his shoulder. 'I have lived there these last two years – like the leopard,' he ventured cautiously, glancing at Haraka. 'The cave is well hidden, high up in the mountains, and neither the *wazungus* nor the Chinese know this area.'

It was an easy decision. The Tangwena sector that Nyati operated in had become extremely volatile. South of the Honde Valley lay the Monomotapa sector. This saw far less activity due to its location in the mountainous terrain of the Chimanimani. It was here that the guerrillas decided to set up a new base. But it was a resolution that would prove to be their downfall.

5

Intelligence had informed the Rhodesian security forces that
Sengamo had fallen foul of the ZANU-PF leaders. Here was
a man who was intimately acquainted with ZANLA's
forward-operating bases, who held sensitive information that
might turn the war in their favour. As such, they were
desperate to get to him first and assembled a small unit of
SAS trackers from F troop who were parachuted directly
into the remote mountains of the Tangwena sector.

The team, led by a tall Irish lieutenant, patiently
combed the area. But it appeared that the man they were
searching for had disappeared and rumours abounded
amongst local tribesmen that he had fled to Beijing.

After two fruitless weeks scouring the mountains the
SAS were close to terminating the operation when a tip-
off rewarded their perseverance. Their captive, a ZANLA
guerrilla and a tough veteran, was initially unwilling to talk.
But once the Special Forces had staked him naked to a
Matabele ant hill, his resistance had cracked. Soldier ants
are notoriously aggressive to intruders and in less than two
hours the reluctant guerrilla, tormented and driven mad
by the scavenging insects, could not divulge the
information quick enough.

'*Nkozi, nkozi*, I tell you – I tell you!'

Chris, the interrogator, looked down at his captive. 'Ah
ha! At last my friends are starting to work their magic.'

'*Tafadhali, nkozi*. They are killing me!' the guerrilla cried, blowing harshly through his mouth to dislodge an ant that had sunk its pincers firmly onto his bottom lip.

'Then talk *muntu!* Or I will cut your skin into shreds to make it easier for the ants to eat you alive.'

'*Nkozi*, I have heard,' he paused to clear his throat, 'I have heard from a fellow soldier – a guerrilla called Lwazi – that there is a small group of soldiers holed up somewhere in caves north of the Chimanimani.'

'You are full of shit! These men do not divulge information.'

'He talked when he was drunk on the s*kokiaan, nkozi.*'

'So, where is their cave?'

'I am trying to think, *nkozi.*'

'Don't mess with me you terrorist bastard. Speak!'

'This is not an area I know, *nkozi* – I promise!'

'You are lying, you black bastard!' Removing the broad blade hunting knife from the sheaf on his belt, the SAS sergeant cut two broad incisions into the terrorist's chest and the ants immediately congregated in a frenzy around the blood oozing from the open wounds.

Screaming, the African twisted his body in an attempt to dislodge the insects. 'I only know the cave is somewhere near Mount Dombe and that they are using the Skeleton Pass to cross back into Mozambique. *Tafadhali nkozi*, it is all I know. Please trust me *nkozi!* Please sir!'

'Maybe you have it right at last, *muntu,*' Chris said, replacing the wet gag in his captive's mouth and walking away.

It was time to go. They had only one decision to make before embarking on their journey to the Chimanimani Mountains.

'What shall we do with the *kaffir* sir?' Chris asked, after passing on the information he had gleaned to his commanding officer. 'Do we take him with us? I doubt he's lying but you know what these bastards are like.'

'Get rid of him Chris,' the lieutenant replied. 'It is too much of a risk to take him and he'll only slow us down. Do it quickly and use a silencer. At least it will put an end to his suffering.'

The sergeant walked slowly over to the guerrilla. Three years ago, while he was away fighting, a band of terrorists had raided his remote farm on the Zambian border. They had raped his wife, forcing his children to watch, before shooting them all. His eldest son was barely alive when the security forces arrived and he had managed to relay the horrors before he died.

'Hey, you terrorist bastard – it's time to say goodbye,' Chris said, screwing the silencer onto the Browning 9mm pistol and forcing it into the terrified African's mouth. 'I have a medicine for your pain.'

The whites of the guerrilla's eyes were wide with fright. '*Nkozi* please!' were the only words he could utter with the cold steel of the weapon in his mouth.

'Open wide *kaffir*,' he said, forcing the gun further down the African's throat. 'This one is for my son.'

The following day the Special Forces broke camp and started the long hike towards the Chimanimani Mountains. Their faces greased black and wearing camouflaged jackets, green bandanas and belts of ammunition, they staked out an area of the isolated mountains near Dombe, moving slowly down forgotten paths now traversed only by wild animals and the occasional tribesman. To avoid detection they made no fires and ate only cold rations. Living off the land was a way of life for these men and they were aware that their survival depended on their fortitude.

'Hey boss,' the sergeant said one evening, after another frustrating day combing the mountain paths for clues, 'we've been here for two weeks now and there is no sign of these bastards.'

'I'm aware of this Chris. Perhaps we need to ask ourselves how reliable your guerrilla's information was.'

The words struck the sergeant like a slap across the face. 'I can't believe he was lying, sir,' he said lamely, looking down at the ground.

'If he was, then he has taken the intelligence to his grave.'

Then late one evening, concealed in heavy undergrowth high up in the Chimanimani Mountains, the SAS received a message from command HQ. The lieutenant replaced the receiver on the portable signal set. 'Martin,' he called out to his lance corporal, 'can you get the troop together for a briefing? Leave Doug on guard outside the camp.'

When the group assembled, the lieutenant looked at the men seated in a circle around him, the same men who had followed him throughout the Bush War. 'I've just had a signal from Umtali,' he said, studying the soldier's faces. 'Our forces have negotiated a ceasefire with ZANU and it's imminent. My orders are to return to our units in Rhodesia.'

All the men, with the exception of the sergeant, cheered.

The lieutenant noticed the defiant gesture. 'You don't look too happy with the news Chris?'

The big man shook his head. 'No sir.' He straightened up. Although his eyes were on his superior officer, he addressed the entire group in a calm and deliberate voice. 'This is the closest we have ever been to finding these bastards and this *kaffir* they call "the Black Shadow". You must give us a little more time sir.'

The officer was perturbed. He sympathised with his sergeant, but it had to be a democratic resolution if he was to put his men at further risk. His cautious eyes moved slowly from one man to the next. 'Can I have a show of hands for carrying on please?' Two of the soldiers hesitantly raised their hands, followed by the rest of the troop in quick unison. Although the lieutenant was aware that he was disobeying orders, he knew that high command tended to overlook the tactics of the SAS, allowing them to operate outside normal military guidelines. He hesitated only briefly before asking the next question from which there would be no going back. 'Are you sure this is what you all want?'

The sergeant spoke for F troop. 'It's what we want boss.'

'Thank you gentlemen, that resolves it; we'll ignore the order from HQ and give it one more week.' Then he turned to his signaller. 'Shut down the radio Martin. The last thing we need is frantic messages from Umtali.'

There are times in life when one makes a decision that has far-reaching consequences. The lieutenant's resolution to continue the search was one such occasion. Was it fortuitous, or perhaps disastrous, that five days later they discovered the fresh tracks?

It happened on a morning when the sun was climbing above the Chimanimani and bathing the day in gold, what a photographer would call perfect light.

At last the SAS were close to their prey.

Only two days to go and we can clear out of these godforsaken mountains, the lieutenant thought. Two days, after ten long years of fighting; two days and it would all be over. But what was there to go back to? There was no longer any Emily, no longer even a Rhodesia.

The lieutenant turned to address his troop. 'Right men, we are close to the enemy. Spread out in line. Twenty paces between each person and no talking.' The small group of soldiers silently nodded their heads and continued to move slowly up the mountain, crossing a stream that was so clear they could see their reflections in the isolated pond. Taking turns to replenish their aluminium water bottles, they then obliterated their tracks and retreated back into the thick cover of the bush.

Nothing moved. Only the faint sound of the wind whispering in the trees disturbed the stillness. Removing his field glasses from their canvas holder, the lieutenant focused them on the mountain. In front of him was a sheer rock face where a small steenbok grazed beside a mountain acacia. It was the only sign of life. The Irishman could smell the fragrance of the pines carried on the light breeze and he wondered how anything violent could happen in such beautiful surroundings. Then the scent of the trees and the early morning light were forgotten as he concentrated on the task ahead.

'They must be holed up somewhere in the rocks below that rim,' he said, pointing to the mountain. 'Safety catches off, selector switches to auto – I'll take the lead. Chris, can you bring up the rear? Silence black-out and watch where you walk.' They were orders given randomly and when the lieutenant thought about it, he knew they were unnecessary – the men were well versed in battle conditions.

'OK boss,' Chris whispered.

The lieutenant moved cautiously forward towards the narrow mountain path, the FN assault rifle cradled in his arm, cocked and ready to fire. The dense bush that had provided cover was behind them as they entered the tall grass, scattered across the open ground.

Suddenly an African appeared from behind a rock at the base of the mountain and scrambled down the narrow path. It was Haraka on his way to the stream to fetch water. Caught unawares by the soldiers, there was no time for him to take evasive action. The lieutenant's FN was already in position on his hip and he opened fire just as the guerrilla raised his AK-47. For once in his life Haraka had not been quick enough and he died with astonishment still etched on his face.

'Take cover!' Rob shouted, diving behind a small rock.

What bloody cover? Chris asked himself, running instinctively for an acacia tree, while the rest of the troop flattened themselves in the grass.

The lieutenant looked around to see where his men were. He noticed Doug, lying ten metres to his left in the grass. 'Work your way up the mountain,' he shouted to the trooper, 'it's too exposed here.'

'You've got to be frigging joking!' Doug swore under his breath. Then the lieutenant was moving, sprinting towards the base of the mountain while his men laid down a concentrated fire at the rocks above.

Concealed in his cave, Sengamo heard the gunfire and

approached the entrance, cautiously moving to a vantage point above it. 'Nyati!' he shouted urgently. 'It's a *wazungu* patrol! I cannot see Haraka.'

The old, battle-hardened guerrilla was already beside his tracker. 'That was the gunfire,' he said. There was a melancholy tone to Nyati's voice, the like of which Sengamo had not heard before in his commander. 'I think we may have lost the Quick One.'

Less than a minute later Lwazi appeared beside them, leaving the remaining three African soldiers taking up their positions in the rocks outside the cave. '*Nkozi*, it is a small patrol.'

Nyati nodded silently, his eyes on the thick grass.

'I thought Sengamo said this place was safe!'

The tracker ignored the jibe. He was unaware that it was Lwazi's loose talk in the first place that had brought the SAS to the Chimanimani Mountains. Hesitating for just a moment, he glanced at Nyati before speaking. '*Nkozi*, I can show you a way off the mountain and into the forest. There are caves below Mount Binga where they will never find us.'

The guerrilla leader shook his head. 'I'm tired of running, Sengamo. I've been running all my life. If they want a fight, let's give them one,' he said, thinking of Haraka.

No sooner were the words of retreat spoken then they were forgotten. 'OK, *nkozi*, I'll cover the left flank.'

Sengamo settled his AK-47 on a rock and waited. Somewhere in the long grass there were enemy soldiers who had not yet managed to reach the rocks. Sooner or later they would have to move. It was just a matter of being patient. Then something caught his eye to the left of a small acacia tree . . . there was no wind and yet the grass was swaying. Opening fire, the tracker raked the ground with a long burst from the AK-47 and he heard the scream that signalled he had hit his target. Then the grass was still again.

The deafening sound of returning gunfire followed the rapport of the Kalashnikov and from his cover in the rocks the lieutenant threw the hand grenade. It bounced off a stone ledge and exploded just below the entrance to the cave, killing one of the guerrillas and seriously wounding another.

'Hey Solomon! *Solomon!*' Nyati shouted. 'Are you OK?'

'This is my lucky day, *nkozi* – the rock has saved me! But Chaipa and Thulani are dead. The *wazungus* have pinpointed our positions. Shall I move?'

'*Hapana!* Stay where you are. Some of them are hiding like snakes in the grass. Concentrate on the area to the right of the acacia tree,' Nyati said, firing another burst at the rocks where the grenade had come from. He then ducked behind a ledge and watched as his men laid down an intensive barrage into the long foliage. There was scant cover for the two SAS men below the mountain and by moving their fire in a calculated arc, the guerrillas eventually found their foe.

'Boss, the bastards have got Martin and Doug!' Chris screamed. 'We need to get the bloody hell out of here!'

'*Shit,*' the lieutenant cursed, the gravitas of the situation hitting home. The capture of the infamous 'Shadow' was no longer his priority; now that he and his sergeant's lives were in jeopardy. 'I'll cover you Chris – make a run for the trees to your left. On the count of three I'll throw them a little surprise. One . . . two . . .' the sergeant was already running as the blast of the grenade shut out the lieutenant's count. Diving behind a tree, Chris swung the light machine gun onto the rocks and continued to fire until his commanding officer appeared beside him.

'Are you OK?' the lieutenant asked, noticing blood on his sergeant's shoulder.

'Just a flesh wound, boss.'

'Right. Let's evacuate this hill before the bastards regroup. We'll look for cover down the valley and wait for them.' As much as he despised it, retreat was now their only option. The lieutenant knew the Africans would follow, but what he could not have known was the strength of the opposition. Removing the powerful Zeiss field glasses from their case, he scanned the grass, searching for any sign of life. Martin's body was lying less than two metres from the rock that would have saved his life. Beside the body lay the radio set – their only means of communication with HQ. It was ironic, he thought, that he had ordered his signaller to turn the set off and now he feared it was irretrievable.

The Irishman was suddenly overwhelmed by grief. Thoughts raced through his mind. Why hadn't he gone home instead of listening to Chris? They would all be alive now. What the hell was he going to tell Martin's wife? Shit, he'd been at their son's christening only last month. Now he would have to break the news to Marion.

The rattle of gunfire brought the lieutenant back to reality. 'There's no sign of life from any of our guys, Chris,' he shouted to his sergeant, who was crouching behind a granite outcrop. 'I'm not getting my butt shot off for the radio and the rifles.'

'Good call boss.' Words did not come easy to the battle-hardened sergeant and he briefly hesitated before speaking again. 'Hey look Rob; I'm sorry it turned out this way. I would not . . . '

The lieutenant regarded the man he had fought with on so many campaigns, the last soldier still alive in F troop. This was no time for recrimination. 'It's not your fault, Chris – the decision was unanimous. Come on; let's get out of here.' He eased himself up from the ground. 'Do you remember passing through that rocky gorge on our way up the mountain?'

'Yeah! It was the last decent cover before this fokken open ground.'

'OK. Then that's where we'll set up an ambush.'

From his vantage point on the mountain Sengamo looked through the scratched binoculars at the enemy below. 'I think there's only two still alive,' he said. 'They're moving down the tree line. Can you see them?'

'I can see one of them.' Nyati picked up the Draginov sniper rifle and focused the telescopic sight on the distant figure. Releasing a shot from the curved ten-round magazine, he watched the bullet ricochet off a rock beside the *mzungu*.

'Ha!' Sengamo laughed, his eyes still glued to the glasses. 'That was close! Now they run like rabbits!'

Nyati knew that if he let the soldiers escape, they would return with reinforcements. 'If we want to continue to live here in the mountains,' he said softly, 'we have to kill the *wazungus*. They have lost their signal set so they will not be able to call the helicopters.'

Sengamo nodded. 'We have the advantage, *nkozi*.'

Nyati looked at the tracker and Lwazi standing beside

him, the heat shimmering off their AK-47s, empty cartridges scattered around their feet. 'OK, let's go,' he said, slinging the Draginov over his shoulder and indicating to Solomon, the only other surviving member of the troop, to follow him.

It was slow work moving between the rocks and trees across the open ground, Sengamo searching for any sign that would show him which way the *wazungus* had gone.

'We need to move faster,' Nyati said, 'or we'll lose them.'

'I'm worried they'll have set up an ambush, *nkozi*.'

'Ambush? What are you thinking of Sengamo? Did you not see them running? They want to get off the mountain while it is still light.'

The tracker shaded his eyes from the bright sunlight and studied the ground. 'From the way this grass is bent, I can tell they're moving quickly,' he agreed. 'Nevertheless, I think we should be careful.'

Nyati was exasperated. '*Careful?* I think you have lived the safe life in the mountains for too long, *kijana!* The signs tell you they are in a hurry; we need to move the same way if we are to catch them.'

'I do not like it *nkozi* – it does not feel right.'

For a moment the guerrilla leader regretted raising his voice. 'Trust me *shamari* – I know what I am doing.'

But the Africans were not to know that the SAS lieutenant was the tracker's equal when it came to bush craft. At a point where the mountain path narrowed between two rocky outlets, he buried an anti-personnel mine and disguised it with leaves before wiping out their tracks. Then he and Chris positioned themselves on either side of the gorge and waited. The guerrillas would have to come this way if they wanted to avoid a long walk around the gorge. At least that's what he hoped would be the case. But amongst the guerrillas was a man who was no ordinary African. And, because of this, the lieutenant remained vigilant.

In retrospect he need not have worried. In spite of the tracker's trepidation, the Africans were moving with speed down the rough track and the ambush caught them totally by surprise. The first soldier in the patrol, Lwazi, missed the anti-personnel mine, but the second stepped right onto it. The blast killed Solomon instantly and seriously wounded Lwazi. Nyati, following at a safe distance, covering the rear, witnessed the explosion as he entered the gorge. And then he saw the rocky outlet a mere ten feet from where the injured Lwazi lay and his only thought was for his fallen comrade.

It was the flash of a watch-face catching the sunlight that alerted the tracker. 'Nyati!' he screamed in desperation. 'On your left! Take cover! *Harakisha*, hurry!'

But the warning came too late.

The clatter of the light machine gun raked the gorge and sent Nyati to the land of his ancestors just as the bullets from Sengamo's AK-47 smashed into the sergeant's chest.

Crouching low, the tracker spread his feet apart and frantically turned to face the one remaining enemy soldier. But he caught only a brief glimpse of the lieutenant before a bullet ricocheted off the stock of his Kalashnikov. It ripped the automatic from his hands and sent him sprawling to the ground as shells splattered the rock face behind him.

Stunned and winded, it was some minutes before Sengamo regained consciousness. When he opened his eyes, the first thing he saw was the soldier, face greased black – and the rifle, pointing directly at his chest. 'You caught us *nkozi*,' he whispered breathlessly.

The lieutenant remained silent.

'What is happening to Nyati?'

'They are all dead,' the Irishman said, without emotion.

Sengamo clenched his eyes shut. He awaited his death, not for the first time in his young life. In spite of this, he was not scared of his old adversary. His only regret was that he would never see his family again. There were no pictures of his brother Gorho or his sister Sumudza and the images in his head had diminished with time. As he lay alone on the ground, he tried to remember them as he had last seen them and there was a strange kind of inner peace that at last it was all over.

The time had come to face his executioner. He waited, but still nothing happened. Then, opening his eyes, he saw that the soldier had lowered the barrel of the FN and he read the reluctance to kill on the *mzungu's* face.

The SAS lieutenant looked down at the African lying on the ground, the dirt on his face smudged by his tears, and he recognised him, from an old poster, as 'the Black Shadow'. The mountain man's clothes were torn and filthy, a testament to his life on the run, and he looked more like an emaciated tribesman than the infamous fugitive. The lieutenant had always held a grudging admiration for the illusive tracker, a man who had caused his own people as many problems as he had the Rhodesians, a man reluctant to kill innocents. His orders had been to capture or kill the African and a bullet to the head would finish off the operation, but for some reason, which seemed strange after the long hunt and the loss of his men, the lieutenant was unable to pull the trigger. He had never before shot an unarmed man in cold blood. The war was lost and he had walked beside the angel of death for too long. Restoration and forgiveness must start somewhere, he thought, and where better than here, on the side of this beautiful mountain? It was only a couple of days' hike through the Chimanimani Mountains to the small town of Charleswood where he could rejoin his unit, and the lieutenant was keen to return home.

He looked at the African lying in the blazing sun. The man appeared to confront death without fear. The tranquillity on his face, like that of a patina upon an ancient god, only seemed to enhance his nobility and the Irishman accepted he could not bring himself to kill the guerrilla. 'The war is over *mwanajeshi*,' he said, in a controlled voice, tinged with sadness. 'They have called a ceasefire; go home to your *kraal*.'

Not for a moment did Sengamo's eyes leave the soldier's face as he rose stiffly to his feet, blood from a hip wound staining his combat trousers. He would never understand white men, never be able to comprehend their emotions. Or perhaps it was just this *mzungu*.

'*Kwa heri, nkozi* – till we meet again in other times, when men will no longer kill strangers.'

The two men stood looking at each other for some minutes. Then the tracker turned and disappeared into the bush, limping like a wounded leopard, his skin and ragged clothes at once blending with their surroundings, the perfect camouflage in this harsh and unforgiving landscape.

ZANLA's victory in the revolutionary war gave the country a newfound independence and the months that followed were wild with celebration. Rhodesia became known as Zimbabwe and Robert Mugabe staked his claim as the country's leader. But the years that followed brought only disillusionment and the tired freedom fighter, not knowing what awaited him in the mountains of Nyanga, was not yet ready to return to his *kraal* and his family. There were still questions to be answered and sometimes, staring into the embers of a dying campfire, Sengamo tried to remember how it had once been, his reverence for all forms of life and the words of the missionary teacher at the little school in the bush.

Where had it all gone wrong?

It had started with a young girl's betrayal, a *msichana* jealous of a relationship between friends and filled with hate. Where was Andrea now? And would she reflect on what she had done and atone for her lies?

For two summers Sengamo drifted through Mozambique from village to village, sleeping in mud huts on foul-smelling thread-bare mattresses covering corners of cow dung floors – two years of *wara* and women while he tried to avoid the sickness.

But at last the freedom fighter was tired of the wandering.

It was time to go home.

6

One evening a young man from the Matabele tribe of central Zimbabwe came to the remote Mozambique village where Sengamo was staying. The night was without a moon or stars, the only light a candle burning dimly on the simple wooden table inside the *rondavel*.

'*Hujambo mapal*, how are you friends?' the stranger greeted the two Africans in Swahili.

Sengamo returned the greeting. '*Sijambo*, I am fine. Where are you from?'

'I have come from Mutare.'

'Mutare?' Sengamo enquired, passing the newcomer a mug of black tea.

'It was known as Umtali in the old Rhodesia.'

'Ah,' said the tired fugitive, 'so in the new Zimbabwe we have different names for our towns?'

'Much is changed,' the stranger said, spooning sugar into the tin mug. 'Now war veterans rule the country.'

'What about the farms?'

'The *tsotsis* are reclaiming the land – with the help of Mugabe's soldiers. They are called the *vanamukoma*.'

'Ah! This is good,' said the second African, moving back into the shadows of the hut.

'It is *not* good,' the stranger said, taking a sip of the hot tea. 'They know nothing of farming and are decimating the land and our people.'

'I see, so you are not a Mashona like Mugabe then, are

you?' asked the voice from the dark corner of the *rondavel*.

'*Hapana*. I am from the Matabele tribe. I have no time for Mr Mugabe and his ZANU-PF party. But all over the land they are saying that the party that won the war must rule the country.' The Matabele man did not recognise the weary soldiers and he talked freely of the ethnic destruction of Zimbabwe.

Sengamo listened carefully to the traveller. The evening cool was blowing off the mountains right through the open doorway of the *rondavel* and it sent a shiver down his back. He pulled the tattered old coat tighter around his shoulders and moved across to the little fire in the corner of the hut. The odour of the damp thatch mixed easily with that of the wood smoke while the blackened cast iron pot of water simmered gently on the hot stones that edged the flames. The smell reminded him of his *kraal* and his family: his mother Betty, Ntimba, his father, brother Gorho and his little sister Sumudza, who had been a young girl when he'd left. She'd be a woman now, perhaps even married.

This was to be his last night at the little village in Mozambique. The only sound to disturb the incessant chirping of the cicadas was an old man playing his *mbira*, the thumb piano's haunting tune reverberating across the empty night sky. Yet sleep did not come easily after that final chapter of the lonely war. Untold thoughts crossed Sengamo's mind and he wondered, after all these years on the run, whether he would ever be able to reintegrate into farm life. And after hearing what the Matabele had to say he knew it was only for his family that he would return to the land of his childhood. He asked himself many questions that night, lying there under the blanket of darkness that framed the Mozambique sky.

And the answers, Sengamo knew, lay on the other side of the mountains.

Early the next morning the tracker set off on an antiquated Volvo bus, squeezed tightly into the upright pseudo-leather seat. Although the fare was cheap, it took almost all of what was left of his small army pay packet. His knees were up against his chest and passengers, crowded into the aisle, fell over him each time the bus negotiated a corner on the rutted road. Tied down on the roof rack, alongside the brown cardboard boxes, furniture, straw baskets, bicycles and chickens, was his small canvas rucksack, which contained everything he owned.

The bus stopped only at little villages with the Indian cheap-goods shops and refreshment stalls. Here the passengers were able to sit in the shade of a dusty acacia bush and take temporary relief from the black diesel fumes that continually penetrated the interior of the bus and irritated their eyes. Although the journey was rough, it was preferable to walking and the following day the Volvo dropped him off on the outskirts of Rusape, some thirty miles from his village.

The main street was deserted. Slinging the canvas rucksack onto his back, Sengamo started to walk east out of the town. The red brick buildings from the old colonial days were still recognisable and the fugitive was happy with his own company, travelling along a road he knew well from a past life, to his destination which lay beyond the hills near the little town of Headlands.

On the edge of the tarmac stood red triangular signs warning motorists of impending disasters, their enamel faces covered in bullet holes like targets on a firing range; landmarks from another time. Now very little traffic used the road, allowing Sengamo to gather his thoughts while he walked alone on the grass verge.

The tranquillity was temporarily obliterated by the intermittent peep of a horn. A dilapidated *bakkie* pulled up next to him and a friendly voice shouted a greeting in Shona through the broken side window. '*Mangwanani*, good morning! Can we give you the lift?'

Sengamo appeared no different from the majority of war veterans returning from the bush. Dressed in ragged clothes, remnants of the long conflict, he looked like any other poor African in need of help. But it was his demeanour and the way he moved with insidious grace, like that of a cat, which set him apart and made people stand up and take notice. '*Tatenda*,' he said, removing his small backpack from his shoulder.

'Where do you go?'

'To Gazelle Farm, near Headlands.'

'This is not a farm I have heard of,' the driver said. 'I am going to Marondera. Headlands is on the way. Just to let me know when you want to get off, please.'

Sengamo threw his rucksack into the *bakkie* before climbing aboard and finding himself a seat amongst the boxes of pineapples. In front of his weary eyes, the countryside of his childhood unfolded like the pages of a book. The trees and the wild flowers were the same as he remembered, but the fields of maize had disappeared, replaced by scrub and bush.

This was a land that had once promised so much but now, two years after the war, Mugabe's Zimbabwe had turned the dream of Smith's Rhodesia disastrously sour.

Eventually the ancient purple baobab tree, which dominated the southern boundary of Tom's farm, appeared on the horizon and Sengamo banged on the roof of the cab, signalling for the driver to stop. He wished to walk the last few miles alone, to gather his thoughts before suddenly reappearing into the lives of people who would have given up all hope of ever seeing him again, and he wondered whether, after all these years, the *wazungu* family had forgotten the incident with their daughter. Surely by now Andrea would have confessed to her lies? Whatever the situation, much time had passed and the tired fugitive knew the answers lay just a few miles away, up the dusty farm track. 'Thank you for the lift,' he said, bending down to talk to the couple in the cab.

'You are most welcome, *induna*. There are not many *bakkies* or buses on the roads now. The petrol is very hard to find in the new Zimbabwe.'

'Ah! Many things have changed since I was last here.'

The woman in the passenger seat nodded her head sadly. 'You must be careful *kijana;* there is too much nonsense, especially on the farms.'

Sengamo gazed at the thin black line of tarmac stretching out across the landscape. 'I have been away from Zimbabwe for many years – all I long for is to see the places of my past,' he said, this time in Swahili.

'Well, go safely my friend – it is not how it used to be,' the driver said, selecting first gear and slowly moving off down the road.

Sengamo watched the *bakkie* disappear in a cloud of dust. The heat from the tarmac shimmered like a mirage, forming imaginative lakes on the distant horizon and through the haze an old woman and a flea-bitten donkey advanced along the road, pulling an overloaded cart piled high with what looked like a family's entire life possessions. The woman, her face lined with the hardships of a cruel life, shouted a greeting and Sengamo nonchalantly raised his hand to return the salutation. But his eyes were on the land beyond her and he could not believe what he was seeing.

The farm he had once known as a child had disappeared. Everywhere he looked the land was devastated and the once beautiful fields of golden corn, which he had envied in his youth, were burnt and dry. All that remained was a brittle stubble overgrown with parched weeds.

At the entrance to the farm drive the old white enamel sign displaying 'Gazelle Farm' hung limply from the wooden post by a single nail, ominously daubed with blood-red war slogans. Sengamo ignored it and walked slowly up the rutted track towards the farmhouse.

It was a naked landscape. The magnificent flame trees that had once lined the approach to the house were now conspicuous by their absence, having been felled to keep the revolutionaries' campfires burning.

The homestead was still standing, albeit a sad reminder of its former self. Bullet holes blemished the brickwork and the white paint, like the years, had been peeled away by countless summers. Old newspapers patched up broken windows in what appeared to be the inhabitant's vain attempt to keep out the draughts. From the state of the land, Sengamo guessed that squatters had already reclaimed the farm.

But where were the *wazungus?* And where was his friend Tom?

Then he spotted the Massey Ferguson tractor he and Tom used to ride standing next to a burnt-out barn, its engine vandalised and its body given over to rust. So, this was what they had been fighting for these ten long years: the new Zimbabwe – a land of senseless destruction.

In the distance an old man ploughed a field with a mule. The only other sign of life was the faint sound of an out-of-tune radio coming from the house. Concealed in the bushes behind the yard, the tracker confronted his demons. It was from here he had run for the mountains all those years ago. There was the barn, now dilapidated, from which Andrea had rushed, her thin cotton blouse ripped open to her jeans. The hatred on her father's face was still vivid in his mind.

But now an even more desolate picture faced him. The squatters had obliterated any evidence that white farmers had ever lived there, returning the land to a decay not seen since the time of their predecessors. Perhaps that had been their aim – to eradicate everything that the *wazungus* had once owned. It sickened him and he kept asking himself why, but there was no answer, only the faint rustle of the breeze in the msasa trees that made the hairs on his arm tingle. Pushing the superstitions from his mind, Sengamo thought of his family and the *kraal* below the barren *kopje*, which was a two mile walk to the west. Without further hesitation, he set off across the arid fields.

When he was still some distance from the village he caught a glimpse of the *rondavels* nestling peacefully in the valley. It was too far away to smell the wood smoke from the open fires. Nevertheless, his memory flashed back to the time when he would sit beside his mother's cooking pot bubbling away on the open fire, with Gorho next to him, listening attentively to his tales about the white man's farm. Quickening his step to avoid the small mopane flies that danced drunkenly around his head, Sengamo climbed the rocky path up the hill. At the top of the *kopje* was a large, over-hanging flat rock, suspended like a fat finger pointing towards his *kraal*. This was his old observation point from where he would look down on the compound far below after tracking the bush with Tom. But his footprints on the orange-streaked rocks had long ago been washed away by the winds and rains that sweep down these desolate valleys in the wet season.

Fourteen long years had passed since the tracker had last seen his family. There was so much to talk about and in spite of his apprehension Sengamo could hardly contain his excitement at the prospect of their reunion. But why did he recognise only half of the village? Even more frightening, where was the old family hut? Perhaps they had moved, he thought. After all, *rondavels* have only a limited life. That was it; with Gorho now working they would be able to afford something bigger to accommodate a growing family. But he knew he was clutching at straws – where was the work in this war-torn land?

Standing there on the bare rock, Sengamo was again touched by the same chill he had felt amongst the msasa trees. And then he saw the remnants of his past life; a group of old men sitting outside a grass hut playing *tsoro*, an African board game, while women pounded maize on flat polished stones, their pestles moving in rhythm to some ancient obscure tune. They were peaceful scenes, in many ways unchanged from the days of Mzilikazi, the first chief of the Matabele and founder of the ancient kingdom. Reluctantly the tracker moved off the *kopje*, striding slowly along the well-trodden dirt path that wound its way down towards the compound like a snake slithering off the mountain.

The first person to see him was Grace, his mother's sister – fourteen years older but little changed. Although time was the master of metamorphosis and its wand was the years, the two recognised each other instantly and the old woman rushed out to greet the fugitive. But there was no mistaking the fear on her face and Sengamo wondered if Grace had been born with an extrasensory perception that enabled her to read the past like an old newspaper. 'Oh Sengamo, Sengamo!' she sobbed, throwing her arms around his bony shoulders.

What terrible things had happened in his absence? Sengamo was too frightened to ask and stood glued to the spot, his face buried in Grace's chest. Eventually he let himself be led like a child to a small three-legged stool outside his aunt's hut. And there, in the stillness of the early afternoon, Grace's story slowly emerged. Her voice was choked with sadness. 'It was the *tsotsis*, with another group of soldiers – they seized the land.'

'Why Grace – we are the same people, no?'

'Not anymore,' she said adamantly, blowing her nose on a dirty rag. 'They are filth from the city. They know nothing about farming – they have destroyed the land.'

'Where is Baba?'

'There was no work on the farm. Your father went to the city but he came back because he could not find work there either. Many of the people from our village now live in the slums of Harare where there is much sickness and poverty.'

'Ah, so Baba is back at the *kraal?*'

Grace looked cautiously at her nephew and chose to ignore the question. 'When the ZANU party members came here they accused us of helping the *wazungus.*' The old woman paused to take a breath.

'We have all at one time or another worked for the white man.'

'What, I ask you, were we supposed to do?' Grace cried, throwing her arms into the air in despair. 'We were only doing our jobs on the farm and we needed the work. How else can we feed our children? If this is the reason for murdering our people, they will have to kill half of Zimbabwe!'

Sengamo fixed his eyes on the woman before speaking. 'What happened *shangazi?*'

Grace dropped her head. 'Ah, it was so terrible, so terrible. You cannot believe the cruelty of these savages. They beat us with bicycle chains and . . . raped our young girls,' Grace cried, wringing her hands together in her lap. 'They kept asking us the same questions over and over: "Who is helping the *wazungus?* Where are the *mtengesi?*" When we had no answers for them, they put a black necklace on a girl and burnt her to death.'

The necklace was a tyre soaked in petrol, which the *tsotsis* hung around their victims' necks. Sengamo had seen such crimes in the war-torn villages of Mozambique and the old Rhodesia; innocent people killed for no other reason than belonging to a different tribe. And now here it was, happening in this compound. There were tears in his eyes when he remembered Haraka's words from long ago: 'You come from a village just like this one, *kijana.*' Slowly he regained his composure. 'Where is my family, Aunty?'

Grace hesitated, struggling to frame the words. 'Some of the jealous ones pointed the finger at them. They said that Betty's child, meaning *you*, used to play with the *wazungus'* children.' This was all too much for the old woman and she started to cry again.

Sengamo put his arm around Grace's wide shoulders. He needed to hear it all and to taste the bitterness of hatred because each word that came from the old woman's lips fuelled the fire inside him. Although he had already guessed the outcome, he nevertheless asked the question. '*Tafadhali shangazi*, please Aunty – tell me what happened to my family.'

The African woman looked cautiously at her young nephew. 'The *tsotsis* rounded them up at gunpoint and forced them into their hut. Sumudza had no idea what was happening. "What are they doing, Mama; why are they doing this thing?" she kept shouting.'

'Baba knew this was the end?'

'Eiee, yes, he knew. But he could not divert the children's attention. Gorho was angry. He tried to reason with the soldiers and they hit him across the face with a rifle, driving him into the *rondavel* like a dog.' Grace was unable to finish the story. She did not have to.

Sengamo was familiar with the *vanamukoma's* methods. When they set fire to the hut it would be like dying twice. His family would have smelt the petrol before they felt the heat and a straw hut is an easy meal for a fire. 'They died in the *rondavel, shangazi?*' Sengamo whispered in a broken voice.

Grace nodded. 'We could hear the screams all over the village.' She sobbed, her hands over her face. 'I will never be able to forget their cries. Eiee Mother . . . Mother . . .

it was so terrible. Oh, Sengamo, I am very frightened!'

The tracker could not speak. The grief was overwhelming. He put his head into his hands and wept as he pictured the flames and imagined their faces – Ntimba, his father, covering Gorho with a blanket to protect him from the acrid smoke which, had it suffocated them before the fire touched their skin, would have been a blessing. And Betty, his mama, holding Sumudza, the beloved sister he had left as a child and now would never see as a woman. There was nothing left. So annihilating were the thoughts, his legs lost their strength and his body collapsed to the ground. 'If only I had come home earlier, maybe I could have saved them!'

Grace knelt beside him. There were no more words. She put her arms around his shoulders and pulled him close. The familiar smell of an African woman's body and the comfort of her hold reminded him of his mother.

It was time to say goodbye. Whatever hope he'd had of coming home had been destroyed forever. His vision of an Africa of brick houses and green fields remained what it had always been, a dream. But then he was not a farmer, a tiller of the soil – his tools were his gun and knife. In this lawless country both were more useful than the spade and he knew his rage would not diminish until those responsible were made *late* in the same way as his family.

The sun cast its lingering shadows over the young man and the old woman and entwined them as one, bathing them in a golden light. When Sengamo opened his swollen eyes he saw only shadows fleeing the day, disappearing out of the village down the same well-trodden path he was about to walk. Releasing himself from Grace's arms, he rose to his feet and looked down at her. How resilient my people are, he thought. How used to tragedy. And then he gently took his aunt's hand and kissed the palm, holding it for a minute against his face, like the comfort rag he held as a child whenever he'd been afraid.

'I'm sorry Grace. I cannot return to the past but I will search out the thugs responsible for this. One day, when Mugabe's animals have been eliminated, we will have a better future.' But deep down he knew this would never happen because the tribal divisions that had always entrenched Zimbabwe were slowly killing the country, helped by the *wovets*, so-called war veterans who were nothing more than legalised thugs. They were the ones who had destroyed everything he and his fellow freedom fighters had fought for.

Grace lifted herself off the little stool and flattened out her billowing dress. She looked at the tall man standing beside her, proud like an *induna*. He was different from the boy who had run away so long ago. It was not just time that had changed him, but something more; there was toughness, honed through war, and his former youthful exuberance had been replaced with rage. His brown eyes reminded her of the muddy waters down by the creek, which reflected the trees when the evening sun transposed the images onto the still water. But unlike the murky waters, which were peaceful, his eyes were haunted with memories of unspeakable violence and the natural warmth on Grace's face could not conceal her sorrow for a youth lost. 'Let your children make the future,' she said at last. 'Go safely *mtoto*.'

Their cheeks touched briefly. '*Kwa heri shangazi*. I will

only return when the *tsotsis* responsible for these atrocities are in their graves.' Although the words were as empty as the dams before the rains, he needed to say them.

'Be careful my child.'

Sengamo took one last look over the old woman's shoulder at the little village that had once been his life. Not one of the villagers looked his way and he was reminded of the three monkeys that sat on the shelf above the large wooden table in the missionary school and the words of his teacher when referring to them: 'Hear no evil – see no evil – speak no evil'. By adopting this mantra the survivors in the barren *kraal* were at least able to face their uncertain future.

The tracker turned and slowly walked away from the remnants of his childhood.

Grace stood transfixed to the little square of dirt, her bare feet a part of the unforgiving earth, as she watched his exodus from the compound. There was a stoop to his shoulder, a symptom of the pain he suffered.

Sengamo did not turn around, because in his heart he knew there was no going back.

***

The little graveyard stood on the outskirts of the village below the *kopje*. Sengamo squatted next to the four simple wooden crosses, the last resting place of his family. He read the names that someone had cut into the faded wood with a blunt penknife – Betty – Ntimba – Gorho – Sumudza. No other inscriptions or dates, just their names. There was a solitary tear on his cheek and in his hand a sunflower that he'd picked from the field. Looking at the raised mounds of earth, he wondered if life, like the yellow flower, would ever be bright again. His eyes swept the cemetery and then followed the hills up to the peak of Inyangani, standing dominant below the darkened skies. Stretching his arms to the heavens, he yelled to the gods that the lives of his family would be avenged. It was the war cry of the *impi*, the ancient ancestral Zulu warriors, and its echo reverberated across the valley, down his childhood paths and across his adolescent battleground. And the sound of one man became one thousand as the *mhondoro*, the spirit, entered his sinewy body and possessed him. He drew the machete from his belt and touched the four crosses with its tip. A fierce retribution replaced the sorrow when he thought of the broken promises and of all the years in the bush fighting for a cause that was no longer valid. 'There was a time when we had a dream,' he shouted to the empty sky, 'when we first started down the long road to freedom!'

The fight was no longer for the future of his country. It was for justice and for his family.

The sun kissed the last of the little wooden crosses before the grey evening descended and shut the door on the desolate burial ground. The tracker stood tall beside the grave, alone with his thoughts in this place of the dead. Then the moon came out from her hiding place behind the eerie clouds, catching his profile briefly and throwing his shadow across the grassless mound. And for just a moment he saw himself beneath the earth with his family. Eventually a low cloud drifted overhead, turning out the light, and the shadow disappeared, leaving him alone in the darkness. It was then he recalled the simple poem that the nuns had recited at the Ntembe mission station after one of Mugabe's terror units had destroyed it.

How long ago was it? He remembered standing alone on the edge of the missionary compound in the little border village and watching, powerless as the terrorists marched the children into the wooden church before locking the doors and setting the building alight. The screams, which he imagined were the cries of his own family in the flames of their straw hut, still played aloud in his head. A young nun, a woman of God from another country, had stood beside the mass grave in the burnt-out churchyard, the hood of her long grey habit hiding her light blonde curls. And when she spoke to the African children, lying in the newly dug hole, it was through tears.

None of my prayers will ever bring you back, children.
I know, because each night I've tried.
Nor will the questions I have asked my God,
Or the tears that I have cried.

Sengamo turned and walked out of the cemetery. The dampness on his cheeks felt like the dew on the early morning flame lily. It was a long trek back across the moonlit scrub towards the farmhouse in which he'd not set foot since the day the *msichana* had framed him, condemning him to fourteen wasted years on the run. Andrea could not, even in her wildest dreams, have known what would come of her plan. She was, in some obscure way, not only responsible for ending a childhood friendship but also for the deaths of his family.

But where was Tom now?

Then, as if in answer to his question, another solitary cloud passed briefly over the moon's shining face and covered the ground again in an inky blackness.

And in this darkness the tracker felt a presence. *Someone was following him.* He stopped and the hairs on his arms stood erect but he heard only a rustle in the grass. In the gloom he could make out the shape of a termite mound and, squatting down next to it, he paused to listen while his keen eyes searched for whatever it was lurking in the bush. The rustling sound came again. Careful not to let his eyes rest on any one object for any length of time, the tracker concentrated all his senses on trying to find the noise. And then he froze.

Standing beside the slender branch of a lone msasa tree was a figure. Sengamo recognised his friend immediately. It was Tom. There was a smile on his face and he raised his arm in a greeting. A shiver passed through Sengamo's body. He was about to return the salutation when the cloud ventured away from the moon and the land was once again bathed in light.

But the figure was no longer there.

The tracker was not superstitious about the dark or the *nganga*, the witch doctor. Yet what he had seen had been real and he knew in that moment that Tom was dead.

The apparition could only be a warning. 'Ah, eiee!' he screamed, as the *guti* touched his body, the thin mist bringing a chill to his skin.

It was time to return to the killing fields.

Turning his back on the shadows and the ghosts of his past, the tracker continued on his way across the redundant moonlit pastures. As he walked he began to formulate a plan, which he kept running in his head until he'd satisfied himself that it would work.

He needed to find whoever was responsible for these atrocities, and he believed the answers lay with the squatters occupying the farmhouse.

7

Sengamo stood in the dark shadows that framed the farmhouse yard. There was no longer electricity in the building, the mains cables having been ripped down and the copper sold for scrap. The only visible light came from the dull glow of a candle in the kitchen, which threw flickering images across the fragmented windows, like effigies produced from a poor signal on a television screen. The silhouettes of two people manifested in the dim light.

Positioning himself below the sill of the broken kitchen window, the tracker could make out the voice of a man speaking in Shona. A smouldering cigarette highlighted his dark face and in his bibulous state, he was boasting to his woman. 'The fight was not easy,' he said, emptying another bottle of beer. 'They shot eight of my men. Eight!' he slurred. 'Can you imagine?'

'Oh Nyoka, you are so brave!' the girl said.

Or maybe you are like the snake, Sengamo thought, hearing the man's name and understanding the translation.

'We were so angry,' Nyoka said. 'We shot the farmer and then the *nkozikazi* and her daughter surrendered. Hey, I tell you – we made them pay for killing my men.'

'Ah! What did you do?' the girl asked excitedly.

'We dragged them out of the house and then we took turns to have our fun with them.'

'Are the *wazungu* women good?' The girl absentmindedly flicked the top off another beer and handed it to her companion.

'No, they are rubbish,' Nyoka said, shaking his head. 'They were screaming so much – I had to take off my socks and stuff them into their mouths. When we'd finished with them, which took much time because all my men wanted the sex, especially with the young *umfazi*, we chased them off the farm.' Nyoka drew deeply on his handmade cigarette and contemplated the glowing tip before blowing smoke rings at the faded ceiling. 'The mama was complaining that she could not walk and the *msichana* was crying so we told them to crawl, like the dogs they were.'

From his hiding place under the windowsill, Sengamo's stomach turned.

'Ah Nyoka, it must have been good to see *wazungus* on their hands and knees with the sorrow on their shoulders.'

'It is the way we have had to live for too many years, Precious.' Nyoka paused to swallow his beer and then banged the table with his clenched fist. 'Now we are the new rulers, the ones in charge. You are looking at a man of much importance in Mr Mugabe's government, my little one, and I intend to keep it that way.'

In spite of his assurances the girl looked worried. 'This is a good farm, Nyoka. Will the *umfazis* try to reclaim it?'

Nyoka shook his head. 'One thing is for sure, Precious – the *umfazis* will not be back. Let me tell you why – I think you will like this my girl!' He paused to take a drink from the bottle of beer and then burped. 'We followed them down the drive, hitting them with our *shamboks* – we drove them like our cattle!' Just the thought of the white women crawling on bleeding knees started the inebriated official laughing again. 'When they reached the road they smelled very badly of the *wazungus'* sweat, which, as you know, is not like ours.'

'Ah, I know of this smell – it is not sweat to the *wazungus;* I have heard my madam call it perspiration and they disguise it with perfume.'

'Ha!' Nyoka laughed. 'No perfume could hide this smell – it was the smell of fear! And you see, Precious, we had to get rid of it . . . so we gave them a bath.'

'A bath?'

'In petrol! Then old Kibaka asked them if they would like a cigarette,' Nyoka spluttered, hardly able to restrain his laughter. 'The *wazungus* have taught him very good manners! He placed the cigarette in the mama's mouth and he threw her a light. The trouble is that the petrol does not like the match.'

'Before I came to Headlands, I was at a farm where they burnt an old *wazungu* couple. I tell you Nyoka, the whites, they make so much noise when they are on fire.'

'Noise? You can't believe the noise. It was so funny. The young *umfazi*, she was running around screaming, trying to tear her clothes off. Kibaka was doubled up in laughter. Then we left the bodies in the bush for the hyenas. I hope they like their meat well done,' Nyati leered. 'No, Precious, I don't think they will be back.'

Sengamo stifled a cry. So, they were all dead. He tried to find some compassion for his former employers, but after the way they had treated him, it didn't come easily. It was a rough justice of sorts.

'I am glad about this Nyoka. They got what they deserved. And now we have a good house where we can raise our children.'

'That is for sure. And the *mtengesi*, the traitors in the compound, also had it coming.'

'The workers?'

'*Yebo*, the ones who were friendly with the *wazungus*. We put them to bed in their hut and then we torched the *rondavel*. Hey man, what a *braai!*' Nyoka threw back his head and emptied the bottle of beer, spitting the dregs out of the window.

'That is the way to treat the *Tshombes*,' the girl giggled in agreement.

'Ah, eiee – they were singing well when the flames ate the hut! It is the last time they will work for white farmers.'

A blind rage welled up inside Sengamo as he listened beneath the window. So, this fornicating mother scum was one of those responsible for the death of his family. Somehow he forced himself to stay calm, but it took all his restraint not to rush into the room and put an end to the evil killer and his vile woman. However this would only raise the alarm and disclose his presence – he needed information on the *vanamukomas'* whereabouts, which he could only get by remaining patient.

So he waited, while the hours walked the night.

The more Nyoka drank, the less plausible became the conversation between the man and woman. Precious was only half-listening to the slurred words as she cooked the food over the hot coals.

Somewhere from within the depths of the house Sengamo heard a baby cry and the girl withdrew from the room to investigate. Thoughts now clamoured through his mind. There had been no mention of Tom – had his friend been away that night? No, he could not believe it –

the ethereal figure he had seen briefly in the darkness convinced him that Tom was dead.

Then a bank of clouds sailed slowly across the open sky and once again obliterated the moon. Nyoka moved towards the kitchen window, sucking the dying breaths from a cigarette before tossing the butt into the ebony darkness. Sengamo watched its trajectory, like that of a glow worm, flitting across the path where he crouched in the shadows.

From the candlelit room the booming voice of the swaggering African broke the stillness of the night. 'Hey woman, the drink is finished,' Nyoka shouted, opening the last bottle. 'I am going to Rusape for more beer.'

'What about your dinner?'

'This *is* my dinner, Precious.' Nyoka held up the bottle of Castle lager. 'It's a liquid meal!'

'You are very funny Nyoka.'

'It is still early so I will be in the beer hall – don't wait up for me.'

'Ah, that is a shame *nkozi;* I had an interesting night planned for you.' The girl's carefree laughter filled the room.

'What have you in mind?'

Throwing her arms around her partner's neck, the girl whispered innuendos into Nyoka's ear and Sengamo saw his chance. Moving across the yard to the truck parked next to the derelict maize barn, he melted into the shadows of the building, his hands searching the ground for something to use as a weapon. Eventually he found what he was looking for, a half brick that appeared to have come from the demolished barn wall.

The minutes passed slowly and still nothing happened.

Where was the *tsotsi* and why was he taking so long? Then the front door opened and, in the dim shaft of light, the tracker watched the intoxicated African stagger haphazardly across the yard, each step more difficult than the last. When the drunken man finally reached the vehicle he was overcome by an urge to relieve himself.

This was the opportunity Sengamo had been waiting for. Jumping silently out from behind the cover of the truck, he brought the brick down on the side of the official's head, taking care to exert just sufficient pressure to render him unconscious. There was a dull thud as his beer-stained body crumpled to the ground, landing in the pool of his own urine. Removing the *bakkie* keys from Nyoka's wet trouser pocket, he then lifted the dead weight into the passenger seat.

There was no longer any noise from the farmhouse, nor any sign of the girl. Sengamo doubted that she would even miss her companion. It was a common enough occurrence for African men to stop the night in town after visiting the beer hall, and because women so rarely questioned the actions of their men-folk, it would be a day or more before the girl reported the man missing.

By then he hoped to have his information and be well clear of the area.

The truck moved off slowly down the drive with only the side lights to negotiate the dark. On the cream retro dashboard, illuminated by the speedometer dial, Sengamo caught sight of the chrome St Christopher badge riveted to the fascia. Was this one of Tom's father's vehicles, abandoned when the *vanamukoma* had invaded their home? He could not help wondering if his childhood friend had once sat in this very same seat and a brief reminder of days lost flashed through his mind. But as quickly as the thoughts appeared, he obliterated them and concentrated on the job in hand, tapping the fuel gauge to ensure the reading, which an erratic needle registered half full, was correct. The *wovets* had sole access to black-market fuel stores and Sengamo allowed himself a small grin of satisfaction when he thought of his comatose passenger who held the key to the next chapter.

However, first he had to find the track that would lead him to his old hunting ground. The dim headlight beams did their best to penetrate the mud-stained glass lenses and obliterate the shadows as Sengamo searched for the gnarled old gum tree where he and Tom used to hunt the guinea fowl. It finally came into view over a small humpback bridge and he slowed the truck to a standstill.

All was quiet. No other vehicles had passed him in either direction on the main road, which was not unusual because of the fuel shortages. Turning off the tarmac road, Sengamo found himself back on familiar territory, except now the track was nothing more than a disused path riddled with dried-out potholes. Low branches hung down over the rutted earth like outstretched fingers on a giant's hand trying to reclaim the ground and return it to virgin bush. Somewhere in the darkness he heard the call of the nightjar, which reminded him briefly of his fallen comrade Nyati, who had perfected the cry to summon his men.

A small herd of impala sprinted across the path. Glancing to his right Sengamo saw in the *bakkie's* headlights the deep red glow of eyes, sparkling like embers in the undergrowth. *Fisi* – hyenas, the ghouls of the bush. It was they who were responsible for spooking the impala.

He smiled and looked down at his passenger, aware that the scavengers may yet prove useful.

When he was a safe distance from the main road, the tracker eased the vehicle off the track and sat patiently in the dark, observing his surroundings. From the dense thicket came the raucous jabber of a francolin followed by the whining howl of a jackal. Minutes later the bush noises abated and Sengamo heard for the first time the faint breathing of his captive and he wondered whether he had struck the *tsotsi* with too much force. Placing his finger across the African's arm, he found the pulse. The man was alive, but it would be a while before he regained consciousness. Enough time to search the truck, Sengamo thought, his eyes growing accustomed to the darkness. Was it by good fortune or fate that he found the torch underneath the dashboard and the heavy-duty rope coiled up behind the spare tyre? Even more surprising, the torch worked. These ancillaries would make the task considerably easier and suddenly the formerly half concocted plan was now clear in his mind.

First he stripped the African naked, using his own shirt to gag his mouth. Then binding his hands and legs with the rope, he threw the loose end over a stout branch high up in a nearby tree. All that was now required were dry twigs and small logs to build a fire. Survival in the war was somewhat dependent on making fires without creating smoke and the tracker was adept at this particular skill. When the kindling caught with a crackle, Sengamo added more fuel and watched the flames rise out of the darkness while he squatted on his heels and softly hummed an old Ndebele tune.

A muffled cry, accompanied by an agitated shuffle, suddenly interrupted Sengamo's song. 'Ah ha, so you are waking up at last!' he said softly, in his mother tongue of Shona, as he knelt beside the prostrate figure. The prisoner continued to struggle against his bindings, shaking his head violently in an attempt to shout through the cloth. The tracker smiled. 'Rest easy my friend, and save your energy. We might be here some time and I have important questions for you.'

A puff of smoke escaped the flames and diverted the tracker's attention. He raked the embers and watched them smoulder in the dark before adding more fuel. Perhaps another ten minutes and the fire would be hot enough for the job he had in mind.

The agitated official doubled his efforts to voice his protestations. Sengamo ignored him, feeding the fire with larger pieces of wood until he'd satisfied himself that it was ready. The heat was now so intense that it forced him to move away and squat beside his victim, trussed like a chicken about to be roasted.

In the dancing light, he studied the man. There was something hanging around the official's neck, something that looked oddly familiar, which he had failed to notice when he'd stripped the *tsotsi* in the dark. Shining his torch onto the African's neck, his worst fears were suddenly realised. There in the dim battery light was the silver charm on the black cord that Tom had given him for his thirteenth birthday, which he in turn had gifted to Gorho before going on the run. 'Something to remember me by; wear it until I return,' he had told his younger brother the day he'd said goodbye.

There were tears in Sengamo's eyes when he recalled the moment. Standing together for the last time in the field outside the compound, they held each other without words. Then he had spotted the plume of dust rising above the acacia bushes. They had only minutes for a brief silent farewell before he broke away and disappeared into the bush.

Sengamo wiped his eyes with the back of his dirty shirt sleeve. What was this repulsive creature doing with his brother's charm? Ripping the cord from the African's neck, he placed it in his pocket and reached for his hunting knife. It was halfway out of the kudu sheaf before he stopped himself – first he needed answers.

Nyoka's face was gesticulating frantically in the half-light of the fire and Sengamo placed a finger across his lips, indicating that he wanted silence. 'I have two very simple questions for you,' he began, holding the torch to the official's face to scrutinise his response. 'Listen very carefully to what I am about to say and don't make any noise.'

Easing the gag out of the African's mouth brought an immediate reaction, a violent scream that penetrated the stillness of the night. 'Hey, you hyena dung! What the hell do you think you are doing? Where are my clothes?'

Sengamo's huge fist smashed into Nyoka's face, breaking the soft flesh of his fat lips and shattering two of his front teeth. 'I told you to be quiet and listen,' he said calmly, ignoring the insult and wiping the blood off his hand down his shirt. 'You will have the chance to speak in a minute.' The vision of his family burning in the grass hut remained vivid in his mind and the tracker felt no remorse for his actions.

The captive's arrogance turned to fear and he nervously licked the blood seeping from his broken lips. What the hell was going on? After all, he was an important man in the Rusape district and men of his stature were not to be treated this way. Clearly robbery was not the motive, although the aggressive imbecile had ripped the charm from his neck. But that was hardly worth all this nonsense.

Sengamo looked at the man with revulsion before asking his next question. 'I would like to know who is in charge of reclaiming the farms between Headlands and Rusape and who was responsible for killing the African workers at the Gazelle *kraal*.'

'What are you saying? I know nothing of this!'

Sengamo ignored the interruption. 'Finally, I wish to know where the *vanamukoma* are now.' His voice was calm and composed. 'You may speak, but think very carefully before you answer because I do not want your lies.'

Perhaps it was the mellifluous tone of Sengamo's voice or the way in which he patiently delivered his questions that led the official to mistakenly interpret a weakness. 'I have had enough of your stupidity!' he shouted. 'Do you not listen? I told you I know nothing about the workers on the farm!' Pausing to spit out flecks of blood, he continued in the same belligerent manner. 'I am the Rusape area representative for the ZANU-PF party and I demand that you release me right away!'

The tracker had anticipated this response. The loose end of the rope was hanging from the branch above and he put his weight behind it and tugged the dazed African up into the air, leaving him swinging like a broken doll, his head hanging over the searing fire. After securing the rope he turned again to his captive. 'You are an obstinate man, my friend. I think that we will need to warm your brains a little to help you remember the answers to my questions.' He hesitated briefly. 'And there is no point in screaming because nobody will hear you. All the noise does is make me very, very angry.'

'*Tafadhali*, please understand – I know nothing!'

The sound of Sengamo's large flat hand smashing into the side of the *tsotsi's* face was like that of a pistol shot. 'Don't you understand Shona? I told you I do not want your lies.'

The heat from the fire singed the African's hair and the whites of his eyes were like china plates, clearly visible in the bright glow of the flames. Unable to contain his bladder, warm urine ran down his bare chest, forming droplets on his head before dripping onto the fire. The hot coals sizzled. 'I was obeying orders!' he cried, in desperation. 'Believe me; I was not involved in any of the killings. I am just the official from Harare, coming here to look after the welfare of our people!'

Sengamo loosened the rope and allowed the dead weight of the body hanging in the tree to drop further towards the flames. The terrified African screamed as the heat burnt his skin. 'OK, OK! I tell you! I tell you! Please do not burn me!'

Sengamo nodded. Reluctantly, he winched the body back up into the air and away from the flames. He was starting to lose patience. Moving his face close to that of the official's, he could smell the stale beer-soaked tremors on his breath. 'This is your last chance – I am growing tired of your lies. Answer the questions or I will burn you alive, like you burned my family. And then I will fetch your woman and *braai* her the same way.'

A brief look of recognition flashed across the official's face. When one is paralysed with fear, one does not lie easily and the traumatised words spewed out faster than his brain could cope with them. 'We had our orders from ZANU headquarters. They told us to kill all the black *Tshombes* and get rid of the farmers. It is the Fifth Brigade who is responsible – they are the ones who did the killing!' Nyoka tried to focus on the figure in front of him, which he found difficult being trussed upside down, and his voice degenerated into a pathetic whine. 'You and I, *rafiki*, we are the same people,' he said, reverting to the common dialect of Swahili in his confusion. 'Please let me go and I will give you money!'

Sengamo ignored the offer. 'Where is your Fifth Brigade now?'

'They told us they were going to reclaim the farms south of Juliasdale,' he stuttered. 'That is all I know, I promise *rafiki*, please, you must believe me.'

The words disappeared over Sengamo's head and into the dark. A flame touched a twig on the fire and it flared up. And in the flames he saw the frightened faces of his family, tearing at their hair and their clothes and trying desperately to beat out the fire before collapsing in the excruciating heat of the burning grass hut. Then he remembered the promise he had made to the gods as he stood alone above his family's graves in the shadow of the ancient granite mountains. There, amongst the simple wooden crosses, he had sworn vengeance. Removing the silver charm from his pocket, Sengamo dangled it in front of the hysterical African. 'If you are not responsible for the deaths of my family,' he asked, in an emotionless voice, 'then where did *this* come from?'

The game was up. Nyoka, paralysed with terror, tried to plea for his life but the cry stuck in his throat. It was too late. Sengamo released just sufficient rope to allow only the African's head to drop into the fire. The searing heat immediately devoured his skin, transforming his face into a grotesque mask, and his body, hanging from the tree, jerked around above the flames like a puppet on a string before death finally stifled any further movement. All that remained was the stench of burning flesh that saturated the clear night air.

When Sengamo was satisfied that his prisoner was dead, he cut the rope and pulled the remnants of the corpse out of the ashes. Although he had seen people burnt to death many times in the war-torn villages he had passed through, the scene still shocked him. But this time it was different, he assured himself. This man deserved to die.

Who was it who said that he who lives by the *assegai* would surely die by it?

Now there was just the body to dispose of, preferably away from the killing field. Then Sengamo remembered the hyenas and for once he was grateful for Africa's ugly scavenging predator. The strange hunchback creatures were the bush cleaners, killing the old and infirm and tidying up after the big cats before the grotesque *makhote* finished the job. Man-handling the charred remnants of the body away from the fire, he lifted them onto the back of the truck. The embers, which still held the faint smell of human remains, were dying. Nevertheless, Sengamo was careful to cover the ashes and his tracks with sand. Only the occasional wisp of smoke now escaped and soon there would be no evidence at all of the horror that had taken place.

The appearance of the full moon made the task of clearing up easier. In the artificial light the bush appeared undisturbed and when Sengamo was satisfied that nothing remained to link him to the killing of the government minister, he set off back down the track.

The giant sandy termite mounds were easily recognisable in the headlights, standing like ancient carved figures in the dry grass. It was here that his lights had first picked up the smouldering eyes of the hyenas. The *fisi* were creatures of habit and they would not have moved far, especially if they were with their cubs. Hoisting Nyoka's body onto his shoulder, as though it were a bag of grain, he then disposed of it in the thick grass. The powerful jaws of the predators would do the rest. 'Clean the plate,' Betty, his mother, used to say to him, when there was still *sadza* left over from his dinner.

Sengamo checked the luminous dial of his watch before turning the vehicle back onto the strip road. By his rough calculation he hoped to be south of Juliasdale before first light for the next phase of the operation.

The truck would attract attention so it needed to be disposed of before daybreak.

And six hours of darkness was all that remained.

8

INGOMBE

Isabella sat on the wooden *stoep* and watched the sun cast its shadows across the dry Zimbabwean bush. Her maid, Shazi, had finished her work for the day and had left to return to the nearby African compound. Now the late afternoon stretched into the evening, a canvas on which the woman could sketch her memories. Soon the sun would start its descent and Isabella reflected that in spite of the danger, her whole world was here.

From out of the bush behind the msasa trees, a shy little klipspringer, an antelope no bigger than a dog, came bounding across the yard. It stopped for just a moment, adopting its curious tip-toe stance before disappearing back into the bush. This was what Isabella loved about the farm – the wild animals, their bodies awash in colours of red and gold, skittering cautiously across the dry earth to catch the last of the sun's rays before the golden ball disappeared behind the far-flung mountains.

A movement in the corner of the *stoep* caught her eye. A gregarious sparrow, no bigger than a bulbul, hopped from the railings to the table and then onto the floor, scavenging the boards for a crumb. The bird was undisturbed by the light breeze touching the msasa trees and the woman imagined the branches were nodding to her in approval. It was then she recalled the distant days when she had sat on this very same *stoep* with Francesca.

Had it really been so long since the malaria had taken her mother away?

Isabella had spent most of her life on the farm, a 300 acre holding in the Nyanga Valley, alongside a little river close to the border of Mozambique. Edward, her father, had christened it Ingombe after the mountain Inyangani that dominates the distant landscape of the Eastern Highlands. The valley is ringed by hazy purple mountains and the faces of the ancient caretakers of this ethereal land appear etched into the rocks, their features seemingly predating time itself. She liked to think of the boulders as monuments to the Stone Age tribesmen, the Saunyama, who once walked these craggy terraces of Zina, their ancient city.

Isabella's father was a dreamer and a storyteller. Many years ago he had spoken of his former life amidst the smoky skyline of an industrial war-torn England where he had met and married Francesca, the Spanish girl from Andalusia, and she had followed him, like the Pied Piper, to this distant land in Africa.

The fluttering wings of the little sparrow diverted the woman's attention from her thoughts. 'Ah! So you *are* hungry,' she said to the speckled bird. 'Here – let me find you some bread.'

The afternoon was moving slowly towards the evening and noise from the squatter camp in the valley below imbued the air. But it was the woman getting up from her rocking chair, and not the campfire songs, which frightened the tiny bird, and it flew off nervously into the cobalt sky.

Isabella returned to the house and selected a guitar concerto – one of her mother's favourites – which she placed onto the turntable. Closing her eyes for a minute, she let the music wash over her like waves caressing a beach. The gentle strings of the Spanish guitar were out of context in the wild landscape, but nevertheless the nostalgic tune seemed to momentarily drown out the noise from the compound.

When Isabella next opened her eyes, the first thing she caught sight of was her reflection in the mirror on the hall wall. Although she was only thirty-six years old, the image in the glass was that of a stranger. Dark brown hair rested gently on her bare shoulders and the face it framed appeared strangely remote. Perhaps the result of living on my own for too long, she thought. Even the dimples beneath her high cheek bones lay hidden, waiting for a smile to resurrect them, although it seemed that laughter had deserted her features long ago. But it was the eyes that struck her most, big, almond-shaped brown eyes that seemed to carry a sadness, a manifestation of the tragedies that had invaded her life.

Then she thought of Danny, her friend and neighbour, and what he had once said to her about not living in the past and she promised that she would make a conscious effort to take more pride in herself. Running her fingers through her hair, she gave the mirror a cautious half-smile, which immediately brought her face to life. 'That feels better,' she said to the reflection in the glass before returning to the *stoep* with the bread.

The bird had not reappeared. Nevertheless the woman broke up the crust and scattered it onto the *stoep* and the dusty ground below. The late afternoon had brought with it a tranquillity, disturbed only by the fervent beat of a drum which, once the guitar record ended, would become more noticeable. Isabella breathed deeply of the honeysuckled air and thought of Joseph, her husband. The noise would not have frightened him. 'They're just having a good time, Issy,' he would have said, with the easy confidence of a man who knew where he was going. But that was in the days before the Bush War, before the terrorists had taken up arms in earnest. 'I do so miss you Joseph,' she whispered to the perpetual shadows stretching out beneath the msasa trees and it was the memory of the good times that made her realise that since Joseph's death, time had coalesced into but one single day.

As such, Isabella could not shake the feeling that her life had become like an empty wine bottle, the cork pulled and the fun already drunk. But to change it she would have to leave Ingombe and move away from Nyanga.

And was what lay beyond the mountains any better?

9

The sound of tiny feet scratching the floorboards alerted the woman. The sparrow had returned for the bread. In fact, there were now three of them pecking wildly at the crumbs, but they seemed oblivious to her presence. Then a martial eagle flew low over the yard before perching at the top of the msasa tree and the sparrows, fluttering their small wings hysterically, scuttled off to a low acacia bush.

Swallows, the epitome of freedom, weaved in and out of the derelict barn, but they were too swift for the eagle, which seemed to nonchalantly observe the activity. "'*Inkonjane*", the Africans call them,' Edward had once told her, 'the restless ones.' Spellbound by their incredible dexterity and seeing them preparing for their long trip north, Isabella was reminded of the same journey that she and Joseph had embarked on after their wedding in Juliasdale.

It was the summer of '71, before the darkest days of the Bush War. They had set off for Europe, which was a long way from the afflictions of Africa, and Isabella's life then was still carefree. Those were the days spent dancing the flamenco in the squares of Seville, visiting the galleries and street cafés of Paris and climbing the hills to the villas and the vineyards of Tuscany. There was a bar in every town and in every bar there was a stranger who became a friend. Like Vladikov; 'Mad Vlad,' Joseph had called him.

They had met in a dim club, lost somewhere down the backstreets of London's Soho. The Russian had introduced them to vodka shots, drunk neat, after which they'd throw the drained glasses into the flames of the fire. The night had ended in a blur and they lost count of the number of smashed glasses and empty bottles lining the table, like Russian men of war, in a battle finally lost to the early hours of the morning.

Isabella had no idea what time it was when she regained consciousness the next day. The first light from a grey sky filtered through the nicotine-stained curtains and she found herself lying sprawled across the settee, with Joseph still out cold. In the shadowy light she focused her bleary eyes on Vlad sitting at the table holding a glass of the frozen liquor, as steady as if it was his first of the evening.

When the Russian saw the woman's eyes blinking in the new day, his booming voice reached out across the room and penetrated her foggy haze. 'Hello my *Ingles*, I am your bodyguard! I look for you,' he declared in his finest pidgin English. His laughter filled the bar and for a moment, the woman's hangover was forgotten in the merriment. 'You come to Russia' the slurred voice said, 'and drink the vodka with me.' Was it a question or an order? Whatever, it sounded like a good plan and the travellers decided to extend their trip into Eastern Europe.

Rhodesia seemed a long way away.

Then, just when they were beginning to feel invincible, fate casually strolled back in and proved otherwise. The shrill ring of a telephone shattered the peace of their bedsit in the East End of London and their newfound world collapsed around them.

'Isabella, hi! It's me – Sally. Can you hear me?' the voice shouted over the faint line from Juliasdale. The call was further hindered by the anguish in her Aunt Sally's voice. Fear embraced the woman and she knew that something terrible had happened at Ingombe.

'Sal, whatever's wrong?'

'It's your father. It's Edward.'

There was a long pause. An icy wind seemed to blow, sending cold shivers down Isabella's back, and in the pregnant silence she was unable to ask anything else.

'I'm sorry Issy, I'm so very sorry.'

'How?' The question was whispered into the receiver. Somewhere in the far off distance she heard the reply.

'FRELIMO guerrillas. From Mozambique. They crossed the border last night and attacked the farm.'

'Where were the servants?' Isabella strained to hear Sally's scarcely audible voice.

'He was alone, Issy. Most of the workforce has deserted Ingombe. Intimidation on the farms is terrible now.'

All alone, Isabella thought, holding the strange Bakelite object and thinking of the staff that had been with them for years. 'We'll come home as soon as we can, Sal,' she said, desperate to rid herself of this purveyor of bad news. 'I'll call you tomorrow.' Then she turned to Joseph and collapsed into his arms. 'Why FRELIMO?' she cried. 'Why on earth are they coming over the border? Surely they are fighting for their independence from Portugal, not Rhodesia?'

'It's the guns Issy – they were after the guns,' Joseph had said, holding his young wife. 'Living alone on that farm, so close to Mozambique – he was an easy target.'

The following morning Isabella and Joseph sat on a park bench overlooking the Thames. Rowing boats drifted by, their oarsmen oblivious to the young couple. Isabella was scouring *The Times* from cover to cover, searching for even the smallest mention of this latest atrocity in her country. There was nothing. Edward was but another statistic on a long list not deemed worthy of report outside Rhodesia. It was a small war, a forgotten war, and as such it was easy to ignore, to think of it as someone else's problem. She hated the fact that nobody cared; her father was British, but because he was living on a farm in Rhodesia, his home country had abandoned him. Jumping up from the bench in fury, she blocked the stream of hurried commuters. 'Why don't you tell the world what's happening to my country?' she screamed. Confused, the strangers merely looked the other way and her question might just as well have blown away on the wind.

Joseph put his arm gently around her shoulder.

It was the end of the honeymoon – and time to return to Africa.

On the day they arrived back in Rhodesia they picked up Edward's body from the mortuary at Mutare and buried him next to Francesca, on the *kopje* behind the farmhouse at Ingombe. As is the tradition in that part of Africa, they built a rocky mound of stones over the grave to protect the body from the wild animals, which Isabella called a *shamba*, the Swahili for "plot" or "small farm". That was how she saw her parents' last resting place.

In the evenings when the sun slowly ambled across the

valley away from the mountains of Nyanga, she and Joseph would return to the burial ground and place another stone on the *shamba*. It was their simple way of remembering her father.

Isabella could barely accept that she would never see Edward again. There would be no more walks in the bush; no more waking up to his cheery voice in the mornings and seeing a mug of hot tea in his enormous hands; no more sitting on the *stoep* talking of the future and their plans for Ingombe. This was probably the most profound loss.

Then she recalled one particular moment on the *stoep*, many years after she had lost her mother. A light breeze had moved through the flame trees and dislodged a leaf. Caught in the wind, its dance on the thermals reminded Isabella of nights spent watching Francesca sway to the flamenco music. Suddenly her father turned to her with tears in his eyes and asked the question that would continue to haunt her throughout her life: 'Why did she die, child?'

Isabella put her arm around Edward's shoulder and held him gently, watching the stars close the door on the day, scared to let go lest their world fall asunder. 'I don't know Dad,' she said softly.

It would be a long time before they would laugh again. But then sadness is like an old coat – sooner or later you grow tired of wearing it.

Since the young couple's return from Europe the country had dissolved into insanity, descending into a maze of no-go areas. When they looked up, the skies above Nyanga were awash with helicopters, their high-pitched screams sending the animals into stampedes. But in spite of the escalating violence, they continued to farm at Ingombe, as Isabella's father would have wanted. However, it had not been easy.

'Joe, what are we going to do?' Isabella asked one evening, while they sat together on the porch, enjoying sundowners before dinner. Joseph did not answer, preferring instead to concentrate on lighting his pipe, which was proving difficult in the northerly wind. 'Joe, don't ignore me!' she had cried in frustration. 'Put that damn pipe down and speak to me!'

'Hey, Issy, calm down. What's the problem?'

'Are you blind Joe? There's mayhem everywhere. Didn't you read in the papers what happened yesterday?'

'Hmm?'

'Mugabe's thugs dropped a tree across the road between Chirundu and Marongora. They stopped a car and set fire to it. The couple managed to escape from the vehicle, only for the murderous bastards to cut them up with machetes.'

'Yes, I read that,' Joseph had solemnly replied.

'Doesn't it bother you?'

'Yes it does. But not enough to make me want to run.'

Isabella lowered her voice. 'What's happening to this country Joe?'

'Issy, we are living in a time of *change.*'

'Oh please, don't give me that crap!' Isabella shouted, frustrated by her inability to make Joseph see sense. '*Change?* Change seems to be the standard excuse for all our problems these days.'

Joseph remained calm in the face of the woman's anger. 'You know what the newspapers are like.

Everything is blown up out of all proportion and most of it is propaganda. Anyway, that episode happened on the Zambian border – the violence hasn't reached the Highlands yet. Let's just deal with it when it comes.'

'Joe, you can be so bloody frustrating. If you won't take notice of the papers then why don't you talk to Bill?'

'Bill?'

'Billy Walker. I was in Juliasdale yesterday and he was telling me that the political guys are on the rampage again, terrorising the local tribesmen. These thugs roam the villages and the beer halls demanding to see party cards. Some of the farm workers on Roy's compound near Rusape were not members of ZANU, so the bastards beat them up with bicycle chains and petrol-bombed their houses.'

'I had no idea,' Joseph said, sitting forward in his chair, his attention finally captured. 'What are the police doing about it? Have they caught them?'

'No. The bastards just slip back into the townships where they all look the same – you would have to arrest the whole bloody shanty.'

Joseph smiled. He knew his wife was concerned, but sometimes he wished she would spend more time in the kitchen and less time on politics.

Isabella caught his bemused look. 'It's not funny Joe,' she said slowly, her anger dissipating in the face of Joseph's repose. 'How long before they start intimidating *our* workers and stopping *their* children from going to school?'

Joseph looked at his wife – she had the same passion for this land as he, the same stubbornness to stay put. 'All right, all right,' he said, leaning forward and clasping both her hands in his. 'Look, let's take one step at a time. When the *munts* start to harass the Highland farms we'll go back to Juliasdale and stay with Sal. OK?'

But Isabella's concern proved worthy; all too inevitably the violence eventually seeped into the mountains of Nyanga. Crossing the border from Mozambique, the rebels decimated remote churches and schools and lawlessness invaded the residents' lives. The terrorists now fought with machine guns and explosives, provided by communist elements from China and the struggle, or Chimurenga, intensified as isolated farms along the border were attacked and burnt to the ground. Many of the white farmers had no other option but to retreat to the towns and cities.

The Highlands became a region where opposition spelt death. To protect Ingombe, Joseph had lined their security fences with razor wire and built bars into the windows. At night he would close the shutters and sleep with a gun by his side, holding the cold metal like a lover in the dark.

By the spring of 1972 the Bush War had gripped Rhodesia in a fervour. Joseph had already been through Special Forces training and he was conscripted into the Selous Scouts as a tracker and sent to the western operational area, between Hwange and Victoria Falls. It was there, in the Zambezi Valley, that small groups of Scouts patrolled the bush along the Zambian border in an attempt to capture the terrorists and turn them, to gain information on guerrilla bases and movements.

And each day the body count increased.

With Joseph away fighting, Isabella felt abandoned and

vulnerable, and as the war escalated and the ruthless cross-border attacks continued, she accepted at last that she could no longer remain alone on the farm. The only option was to move back to Juliasdale and settle into small-town life with Sally in the corrugated tin-roof bungalow on the main street.

The beat of a drum released Isabella momentarily from her memories. She glanced down at the luminous dial of her watch. It was a man's chronograph, a birthday present that Joseph had given to her in Lisbon, the first stop on their European honeymoon, and each time she looked at it she thought of the man she had loved, and lost.

Moving into the house, she watched the dappled sunlight bathe the kitchen in gold before casting shadows across the wall. There was an easiness, a comfort about the room, borne out of the many wonderful moments it had played host to over the years. She removed a bottle of Castle lager from the fridge and flicked off the top. The froth flowed down the glass and onto the kitchen worktop, reminding her briefly of the falls where she and Joseph had once stood on the bridge amidst the spray that the Africans call *mosi-oa-tunya*, "the smoke that thunders".

A second drum started to beat frantically. Although it was the rhythmic sound of Africa, this time it only seemed to spell doom. They must have produced a good batch of *wara* this year, she thought. The home-brewed beer made from maize and rapoka millet lifted the African's psyche, but now they were adding yeast and methylated spirits to create an illegal quick-brew called *skokiaan*, a dangerous mix that increased their aggression.

In the past there had been little hostility at Ingombe

and the Saturday night singing was just a part of their colourful lives. But now the woman felt a change in the air. She had seen the army tents in the compound and, although she was assured that they were there for her protection, there had been rumours that break-away militants from Mugabe's violent Fifth Brigade had infiltrated the camp. It was these Korean-trained soldiers who were notorious for unleashing violence on the white farmers in their attempts to reclaim the land.

Isabella tried to ignore the noise, concentrating instead on the guinea fowl quarrelling over their territory beneath the msasa trees. She knew that she couldn't just up and run every time she heard the beat of a drum – she may as well leave the door to Ingombe open and invite the *tsotsis* in. Turning up the volume on the stereo, she closed her eyes and let the sound of the classical music momentarily take her away from her worries. The memories of her time spent cosseted in Juliasdale during the Bush War were still fresh in her mind. Then she remembered the vow she and her husband had made.

The young couple had been sitting beneath the jacarandas, on a weather-beaten street bench in Juliasdale, when Isabella asked the question. 'Joe, when this war is finally over are we going back to Ingombe?'

It was the day before Joseph was due to return to his unit on the Zambian border.

His eyes, ever apprehensive, rested on the narrow strip of tarmac climbing steadily towards the distant mountains of Nyanga. 'It's all we have Issy.'

Neither realised then that it would be seven long years before they'd be able to return to their farm.

'Do you remember the good times, Joe?' Isabella had continued, confronted with her concern for her husband and his involvement in the fighting along the Zambezi Valley. 'What happened to them?'

'I guess they disappeared along with everything else when Smithy declared UDI.'

'So have you ever considered that all of this might just be a lost cause?'

'No, Issy. I've never, ever believed that.'

10

Isabella opened her eyes. Joseph's words still rang in her head. Many white Rhodesians had refused to accept that Africa was changing. They thought that by winning the Bush War, it would spell victory for the whites in other African countries. But what they had failed to understand was that the outside world would never allow this to happen.

And so the killing continued.

As the conflict escalated, Joseph changed. He was never able to talk about the horrors of the war; the death and destruction of the tribal villages, children seeing their mothers raped and then burned alive . . . the mutilated limbs hacked off with machetes . . . the screams . . . the graves. Yes, the graves: they would always be there as a reminder of the war. Sometimes it was more than he could bear and he would huddle on the floor in a corner of the room with his hands over his head.

The terrible images were a part of his life that he was unable to share with his young wife and as time went by he become more of a stranger. Restless and remote, he had withdrawn like a hermit into a shell that nobody could penetrate. But it was his eyes that worried Isabella. They had grown old from pain rather than age and his shoulders slumped from the burden they carried. There was a time not too long ago when Joseph was the optimistic one.

Now only the whisky bottle brought him comfort.

So, as always it was left to Isabella to try and lift his spirits when he arrived home on leave, and this she did by whispering words of encouragement. 'Joe, please be happy for us,' she would say in her usual buoyant way. 'Things will change for the better after the war.'

'Will they Issy?' Joseph had replied, dubiously.

Sadly, he would never know the answer.

She remembered it as if it were yesterday.

The autumn had just come to the Highlands and the early morning sun was lifting the evening chill. Leaves of red and gold had gathered on the edge of the pavements, waiting to be pushed around by the next breeze or by the kicking shoes of some young child. Sally had left for the village store to buy the weekly groceries when Isabella heard a knock on the door. She must have forgotten something, Isabella thought, it was just so much like her.

She flung open the door, expecting to see Sally's apologetic smile. Instead she was confronted with a young man, immaculate in his infantry officer's uniform.

'Mrs George?' the lieutenant enquired.

A green army vehicle was parked across the road, conspicuous amongst the local cars and *bakkies*, and curious prying eyes peered out of windows from behind thin net curtains – eyes that left a sinking feeling in the pit of her stomach. She already knew why the officer was on her doorstep.

'Yes, I'm Isabella George. Can I help you?'

'Could we go inside please Mrs George?'

Isabella's tongue nervously traced a path across her dry lips. She thought of their neighbours, the Wrights. An officer had visited them only last week and three days later they had buried their father's body. 'I'm sorry, yes, please come in.' She moved aside to allow the young messenger into the house.

Across the street a curtain closed and Isabella realised that it was her turn to be the brunt of the town's gossips. Her life had become like the weekly wash, hung out in full view for everyone to scrutinise, and in her annoyance at being spied upon, she slammed the front door shut with more force than she had intended.

The soldier and the woman stood in silence in the semi-darkness of the hall. A print of an English country scene in a cheap wooden frame hung on the wall above their heads. It depicted a landscape not unlike the Cotswolds paths that she and Joseph had ventured down on their travels. Isabella thought it strange that she had never noticed the picture before. With a tremendous effort she forced herself to tear her eyes away from the imaginary life and back to the soldier's solemn face.

The sadness in his grey-green eyes confirmed the news before the message came tumbling out. 'I am so very sorry Mrs George.' He paused to find the right words. 'It's Joseph.' Two simple words that said everything.

Joseph was not coming home.

'Mrs George, the Scouts want you to know that your husband died a hero. He epitomised everything that we stand for.'

'I don't want a hero,' she shouted. But somehow the words had never reached her lips.

The lieutenant had continued, 'Joseph's Land Rover detonated a landmine, near the Zambian border, south of Livingstone. The explosion killed him. It was very quick.

He would not have . . . known anything about it.'

'Was it really that easy?'

The young officer looked surprised. He'd clearly never encountered such a question before. 'I . . . I don't know Mrs George,' he stammered, lost for words.

She stared blankly into his face, incensed with anger. 'Who is to blame?'

'I'm afraid I don't understand what you mean, Mrs George.'

'Well, is it Smith and his dreams of UDI, or the people who condone the segregation of our country?'

'We are all fighting for Rhodesia, Mrs George.'

Joseph had said the very same thing to her not too many months before. 'I'm Isabella,' she said quietly, exasperated at the sound of her married name.

'I'm sorry, Mrs . . . Isabella.'

'Rhodesia, Zimbabwe: what does it matter?' she said, ignoring the apology. 'Can't we all live together as equals?'

'I'm afraid I can't answer that.'

'So tell me; why is it that each time a new regime or tribe comes to power, the disposed suffer?' Standing there in the darkened hall of Sally's little bungalow she found it difficult to mouth the words she so wanted to say because she knew that the answers were lost somewhere deep in Africa's past.

'Mrs George,' the lieutenant said patiently, allowing for the woman's distress. 'If the war in Rhodesia is lost, South Africa will be next to fall.'

This time the woman ignored the formality; the soldier, well versed in party propaganda, personified all that Ian Smith and his Popular Front's vision of white supremacy stood for and there was no getting through to him. 'What about my Joseph who is lost. Where is he? Is he just another cross in yet another field?'

The soldier hesitated. His face was the colour of pale straw. 'There was no body,' he said gently, having misinterpreted the question. 'What they were able to find they buried beneath a baobab tree on a hill overlooking the Zambezi.'

Isabella felt her legs go weak. Somehow she had managed to stumble across to the armchair. Oh! My God! The Zambezi – like nowhere else, it typified Africa: wild, rugged, remote and savage. Joseph had always loved the valley with its turbulent river, which had so nearly drowned him in a white-water rafting accident some years before. Yes, if there was such a thing as a last resting place, Joseph would have been happy with the Zambezi; in many ways the little acre surrounding the wild falls had been his church, a place he had worshipped.

How many times had they stood together above the seething cataracts, looking out at the river? During the dry season the water had flowed gently, almost serenely towards the chasm where branches, broken by elephants, had temporarily lodged themselves on the rocks that edged the falls. Eventually, the current would ease them around the obstacles, like Pooh sticks, leaving them with no place for escape. Swept over the edge into the precipice, they would drop through the luminous silver cloud of spray, through the multi-coloured rainbows to the narrow gorge below, where they would surface in the turbulent cauldron of water and resume their journey between the sheer granite cliffs towards Mozambique and the distant Indian Ocean. Was this the odyssey Joseph had now begun by himself?

Isabella stood up and looked out of the bungalow

window, down the main street towards the mountains. Poignant tears were followed by uncontrollable sobs and for a moment the lieutenant stood riveted to the spot, his eyes on the young woman's grief-stricken face. Then he walked over to her and hesitantly placed his arm around her shoulder, holding her head gently against his chest. 'I am so very sorry Mrs George, so very sorry.'

Tears stained the soldier's immaculate brown shirt and she felt his heart beat as she tried to wash away the past. Then somewhere deep within her subconscious she heard the front door open.

That was how Sally had found them.

It seemed like there was nothing left of her world; first her mother and father, then the farm and now finally Joseph.

Where would it all end?

11

A week after Joseph's death, Isabella had awoken to the sun shining over Juliasdale. The jacarandas dusted the shabby street with their purple carpet. It was May in the mountains and the air was crisp – a new day, but nothing was going to bring Joseph back. Although it would take many years to obliterate the sadness, she had realised that she must move on because bitter, vengeful thoughts would surely kill her as effectively as any soldier's bullet.

The timing could not have been worse. Sanctions imposed by the United Nations at the behest of Britain had sent Rhodesia's economy into a downward spiral. Restricted to life in a small town away from her beloved farm, Isabella had thought many times of leaving the country, of putting all the tragedy behind her. This she may well have done were it not for her parents lying on the *kopje* at Ingombe and her childhood friend, Danny, helping her through the dark times.

Danny lived at Rigby's Creek, a fruit and cattle farm five miles down the road from Ingombe. He was an only son and walked with a limp, a childhood defect caused by polio, which had made him ineligible for the services. When all the men between the ages of seventeen and fifty had departed for war, Danny had been thrust into the role of Juliasdale's odd-job man. With his hippy-length hair he looked so different to the other boys, most of whom sported army-style shaven heads. It was a look that was more akin to a rock musician than a Rhodesian farmer. Yet on Danny it was somehow appropriate, framing and softening a face that was almost angelic.

As adolescents he and Isabella had been inseparable; the imaginary big game hunters of Ingombe with plans to open their own game reserve one day. Now with her parents and Joseph dead, the dreams were unobtainable, or so it seemed. In spite of this, Isabella had reasoned that maybe when the war was over life would return to normal, just as she had once said to Joseph.

The inspiration for this hope had been Danny. He was the brother she never had and the reason she clung onto her fragile uncertain existence in Juliasdale.

'Issy you cannot just up and leave.'

'So what is there to stay for, Danny?' she responded in exasperation. 'This place has gone to the dogs!'

'Where would you go? We still have our farms, our land and our livelihood.'

'You really believe that if we lose the war the new Zimbabwe will let you keep your land?'

'Yes, I do. We have the expertise the Africans desperately need. Mark my words, Issy,' he had said in no uncertain terms, 'there will come a day when the country will cry out for people like us. We are too much a part of Rhodesia to desert her in her hour of need.'

'I wish I could share your faith, Danny,' Isabella had murmured quietly, 'because you have more reason to go than anybody I know.'

This much was true. As farmers deserted their land in droves, heading for the safety of the towns and the cities, Danny's parents had elected to stay on their farm, maintaining that they would not be intimidated by a bunch of lawless thugs.

It had been a tragic decision.

On the day that changed his life, Danny was twenty-six years old. He'd been up in the mountains trying to find the stray cattle that had wandered off, before nightfall would render them easy prey for the leopards. As he'd crossed the escarpment and come over the low ridge, he'd seen smoke coming from his farm. By the time he had galloped down the hill and into the yard, the old Holland and Holland .375 rifle cocked and ready, it had been too late. All that remained of the house was a charred shell, blackened rafters still smouldering in the heat of the day. Although there was evidence of a struggle against overwhelming odds, his folks had never stood a chance. It was clear from the tracks that the terrorists had surrounded the house, forcing his parents to take cover in the building. They had then stacked straw bales against the wall and set them alight. There was no way out.

When they found the bodies, they were together as one, his mother choosing to die by her husband's side in the inferno rather than leave herself vulnerable to the thugs.

Danny had left the clear-up to the security forces. Retrieving what little he could from the farm, he'd then rented a room at Mrs Jackson's boarding house on the main street in Juliasdale.

For most of the next day, Danny wandered the rapidly expanding graveyard alone, searching for a burial plot. Finally, he found what he was looking for beneath a weeping willow tree and they interned what they could recover of the ashes while the local pastor conducted the simple service to the strains of the hymn 'The Old Rugged Cross'. The paean reverberated across the graveyard, sung from the heart by most of the townsfolk who had come to pay their last respects.

A gentle babbling brook ran beside the cemetery and poppies raised their paper heads in the yellow grass that grew in wild abandon between the fading tombstones. In this distant corner of God's little acre a *madala* tended the plots. Smelling of wood smoke and with a string belt holding up his patched trousers, the old man must have seen much sorrow over the years, but his watery eyes betrayed no emotion. The graves were his children, and he tended them with the same love a mother would bestow upon her child. On the edge of the cemetery, fever trees, echoing with birdsong, stood tall and proud beneath the blue mountains, resembling Roman centurions guarding the tranquil garden. There was a peace in the graveyard that was far removed from the violence of the country. It was there, standing beneath the spindly branches of the old willow tree, that Danny had thrown a lump of earth onto the pine coffin. Not the easiest of ways to say goodbye to his mother and father.

That summer had seen a dramatic increase in the arrival of body bags and it was Danny who helped to dig the graves and carry the coffins, draped in the Rhodesian flag. The long walk from the chapel to the cemetery became an all-too familiar journey with each grave representing the futility of the conflict; the youth of Rhodesia, blown away like autumn leaves. The soldiers lay in neat rows under identical white tombstones, their story of pointless sacrifice told in a simple inscription.

Now, deprived of their families, Isabella and Danny were lost souls, orphans in a lonely border town. Yet it only served to bring them closer together.

At Oom Tanya's tearoom and book shop on Juliasdale's main street, the two young friends would spend every free moment planning how they were going to rebuild their brittle lives after the war. Languishing with cups of coffee and notebooks, they would write endless lists while drawing up elaborate plans for Danny's new farmhouse. In this way it afforded them a degree of sanity during the disturbing times.

***

April 1980 saw the end of the Bush War. The country once known as Rhodesia was now Zimbabwe, its coat of arms displaying a hoe and an automatic rifle, which symbolised the transition from war to peace.

It could not have been further from reality.

Isabella had arrived back at Ingombe to find a farm without livestock. Where terrorists had broken fences, nature had already reclaimed the land and the few farm animals they had not eaten had been driven off into the bush, leaving them at the mercy of predators.

Fortunately the farmhouse was still intact, even though squatters had rendered it uninhabitable. In the final years of the Bush War it had lain abandoned, its heart torn out and left to die. Broken windows and a front door that hung on one hinge had been no resistance to intrusion. But at least the squatters had not burnt it to the ground, a fate many other farms in the area had suffered. Perhaps its reason for survival was that a party leader, with delusions of grandeur, had one day envisaged living in the house when Mugabe's promises of land-share came to fruition.

Pushing open the front door, Isabella had found excrement covering the floors and the roots of bushes doing their best to retrieve what had once been lost. She had been heartbroken. Where would she ever conjure up the enthusiasm to start all over again?

And in that moment, standing there on the overgrown lawn, she wished that she had never come back.

'Issy, come here,' Danny, the eternal optimist, had said, beckoning her over to one of the heavy corner supporting posts. Hugging the timber like a bear, he had tried to dislodge it. When the first attempt was unsuccessful, he had then attacked it with a sledgehammer.

'Have you completely lost your senses Danny? What on earth are you doing?'

Sweat poured off his body as he fought to move the post, but it was as firm as an old oak tree. 'You see Issy – there are foundations here that we cannot destroy.'

It was then she realised that the house her father had built would live again, and there was a light in her eyes that had remained dull for too many years.

Aroused from her daydreams by the harsh voice of a starling, Isabella stretched out her long legs on the wooden floorboards. Beyond the *stoep* lay the front garden, now a field of dust, and she thought of the rainy season when the lawn either side of the path would be green again. The easterly wind had dropped and in the stillness the breath of the bush spoke to her softly, whispering the familiar sounds of her childhood. In front of the house the rows of msasa trees ran along either side of the drive, down the valley towards the corrugated road. Having been spared the axe during the occupation, they stood proudly to attention in appreciation; soldiers, guarding Ingombe.

There was still much work to do at the farm and little money to complete it. Because of this the land lay derelict and unattended, allowing wild animals to graze where once they had farmed dairy cows. In the ten years of war, shrub and bush had spread across much of the ground beside the avenue of msasa trees, leaving the land untamed and no longer productive. And yet in a natural, unsophisticated way, it had retained its beauty.

Isabella had made her choice: she would stay to face life in the new Zimbabwe, even though the 'war veterans' had brought a renewed sense of fear to the area. These *wovets* were a joke. Most of them were *tsotsis*, scoundrels – too young to have ever seen combat, yet still they adopted the name. But to Isabella they were no more than predators, waiting for the right moment to strike. And what had happened just two months earlier reinforced her fears.

Without warning, a group of Mugabe's supporters had ambushed and shot a white farmer and his son at Gazelle Farm near Rusape. The mother and her daughter had been brutally raped and then burnt to death. In spite of the precaution that government ministers had taken to censor the news, the *Mutare Standard* had plastered the story across its front page. But events had been quiet since, with some pro-government newspapers playing the murder down as an unfortunate accident carried out by over-exuberant activists. To reinforce the regime's stance,

Mugabe had himself appeared on television to issue a statement assuring the local farmers that the Highlands were to remain in white hands. But he had issued these proclamations before and in the back of the woman's mind there was still a nagging fear that it would not be long before the *vanamukoma* invaded Ingombe.

Isabella closed her eyes again and thought of the fable Shazi had told her when she was a child; the nocturnal leopard standing tall and proud on the rocks, calling out to the night. Slowly the late afternoon sun started to hide her face behind the mountains and the woman let the last of the warmth linger on her skin.

12

A breath of wind touched Isabella's cheeks and she reluctantly opened her eyes. In the distance the sunset was painting the hills amber behind the faraway trees, where the shadows were longer. Stretching out her body in the bentwood rocking chair, she watched the enormous red ball reach for the horizon. Soon it would disappear and cast reflections over the distant massif that formed the border between Mozambique and Zimbabwe. Francesca, her mother, called these hills the 'mountains of the moon' because they reminded her of the snow-capped Rwenzori in Central Africa. A far-fetched romantic idea, Isabella decided, having seen an image of the Rwandan mountains in a magazine.

Yet, despite her mother's artistic licence, Isabella never grew tired of the panoramic view. Her father had built the house on a high promontory, below the hills he loved. It was away from the road and inaccessible to vehicles coming from any direction except the front drive; 'Fort Ingombe', he had once laughingly called it.

Far below in the lush valley lay the paths of her childhood; little ribbons she had walked with Edward and Francesca, and later Joseph. And in the corner of the dusty yard lay the remains of the hop-scotch pitch her father had drawn many years before. If she closed her eyes tightly she could see herself as a little girl, throwing the smooth, flat pebbles into the squares before hopping across the ground. Long rains and dry summers had obliterated most of the lines, although the large corner stones were still there. Perhaps, had Joseph been with her today, they could have redrawn them for their own child to enjoy. But it was a dream that had disappeared beneath a baobab on the edge of the Zambezi escarpment.

Above the valley a cloudless sky intensified the light and as Isabella's eyes grew accustomed to their surroundings, she suddenly noticed a distant plume of dust tracking the landscape. It followed the lonely corrugated dirt track that linked up with the strip tar road to Juliasdale. Danny apart, there were no longer any neighbours in the area and only the army Land Rovers, returning to the squatter camp with provisions from Rusape, used the road. This intrigued the woman and she stood up and reached across for her father's old Leica field glasses, which hung from a nail on the wall. Adjusting the focus ring onto the dust helix, she noticed a flock of hooded vultures feeding on the remnants of a roadside kill. As the vehicle approached, the birds scattered into the trees and waited for the encumbrance to pass before returning to scavenge the carcass. It finally stopped where the drive to Ingombe intercepted the dirt road. For perhaps five minutes it remained stationary at the crossroads, the driver seemingly undecided on which direction to take. Then it hesitantly moved off the corrugated road and turned onto the farm track, slowly climbing the valley. The dust from its slipstream dispersed a small herd of impala grazing on the nearby lush grass and as the dust disappeared so did the animals, leaving only the green painted Jeep – a model much favoured by the notorious Selous Scouts – framed in the powerful Zeiss lenses.

When the vehicle eventually reached the edge of the farm it passed through the inner security gate and into the yard. This gate was usually locked in the evenings to minimise the risk of a night attack, but in her lethargic state Isabella had forgotten to close it and she silently cursed her carelessness.

The Land Cruiser finally came to rest in the shade of the large msasa tree, barely 30 yards from the farmhouse. African sand roads had caked the bodywork of the vehicle with a fine red dust and the sun had faded the canvas canopy to a pale yellow. Scratched side panels were further evidence of a harsh life in the bush. A heavy duty winch and a long coil of thick nylon rope were fixed to the protruding front crash-bar. Up-rated springs gave the vehicle a high ground clearance and, with a profusion of spare tyres, extra Gerry-cans and sand-tracks on the roof rack, it looked capable of travelling vast distances.

But it was its resemblance to the army Land Rovers, used in tracking operations along the Mozambique border, that made the woman shudder and she moved back towards the front door and reached for Joseph's old .22 rifle. Only when she had eased the heavy wooden door shut did she consider her actions; if there was to be any trouble would she not be better off locked inside the building where she would be able to reach the telephone? But by the time she had thought of this it was too late to turn back.

A tall, slim man stepped out of the vehicle. He wore faded blue jeans which were held up with a wide leather belt and his shirt was khaki, washed out to the same colour as the truck's canvas canopy. His bush hat, like the belt, was stained from years of perspiration and, almost carelessly, a curl of silver hair crept out from under the wide brim. Although they were ordinary clothes, there was a worn splendour about his appearance.

Standing silently next to the Land Cruiser, the stranger observed his surroundings, allowing his eyes to sweep the farm. Hard work had transformed Ingombe since the war, but there was still much to do and – the house aside – the farm was in a pretty sorry state. However, it was coming together slowly; roses splashed the edge of the garden with their vibrant colours and at this time in the afternoon the wild honeysuckle perfumed the air. To complete the picture, an old bougainvillea framed the *stoep* while vlei lilies competed for space beside the dusty lawn.

Moving out of the shadow of his Land Cruiser, the stranger strode purposefully across the yard towards the house, his pale cream desert boots instinctively staying clear of the soft dust on the edge of the path in a subconscious attempt to avoid leaving a spoor.

The woman felt a chill touch her bare skin. Its coolness was strange in the warmth of the late afternoon sunshine, and she found herself gripping the rifle so tightly that her fingers were a bloodless white. Somewhere behind her, the warble of a honey guide, searching for the beehives behind the msasa trees, broke the stillness.

When the stranger reached the edge of the *stoep*, Isabella saw him clearly for the first time. There was a rangy lankiness about him and light stubble covered his tanned face, making him look older and harder than perhaps he was. Yet in spite of his rough appearance, she guessed he must be somewhere in his fifties.

The stranger's pale blue eyes eventually settled on the woman. She had an unusual face, with high cheekbones and a full mouth, but she was apprehensive, which tightened her lips. She would almost be beautiful, he decided, if she relaxed. He made no comment about the farm. Instead a slow, friendly smile swept over his features and deepened the crow's feet around his eyes. 'Hi there. I have a bit of a problem with the Land Cruiser,' he said, in a gentle husky voice. 'It seems to be losing a lot of water. I'd appreciate filling up the Gerry-cans.'

The woman remained speechless and cautiously watched the man, her finger on the trigger of the rifle.

In spite of her apprehension, the stranger was nevertheless puzzled by the reception. 'I'm sorry if I frightened you,' he said patiently, the frown deepening on his forehead. 'That was not my intention. I have quite a way to go and I'm desperately short of water. But I'm also a bit lost and perhaps you can help me. I've come down the old road from Troutbeck and I'm looking for a bush track that should take me across the Ruda River to the Chapungu Falls. There is supposed to be a campsite there. The OS map tells me I need to come off somewhere along the Scenic Road, but I think I've missed the turning.'

There was still no reply.

From the state of the land, it appeared to the man that the woman was alone, which would explain her anxiety. 'I'm sorry to have bothered you,' he finally said when there was still no welcome forthcoming. 'I should have realised that times have changed since the war. I'll be on my way.' He was about to turn away when the woman found her voice.

'It's no bother,' she said, finally convinced that the stranger meant her no harm. 'I should be the one apologising. Of course you are welcome to water – there's a tap around the back.' This she said nervously in a high-pitched voice.

'Ok, thanks, I'll help myself.' The half-smile tucked away at the corner of the stranger's mouth softened his features and further eased the woman's concern. He had already started to walk back to the Land Cruiser when she interjected again.

'By the way, you are only slightly lost – the track you are looking for *is* off the Scenic Road. You must have missed the turning at the T-junction. You can also reach Chapungu from the Nyakupinga Road but the track to the Falls is overgrown and full of potholes. Not many folk come to Nyanga these days.'

'Thanks again,' he said, facing the woman. 'There's enough light left in the day to retrace my steps – shouldn't be too difficult to locate the Nyakupinga Road.'

'Oh, it's not. Just up the road there's a turning on your left. But the track you are looking for is hard to find.'

What happened next turned out to be one of those strange moments in life that perhaps only ever occur instinctively. Over the years the woman would come to ask herself many times why she'd done it, but she would never find an answer. Was it the first hint of youth rekindled? Or perhaps she'd felt an air of the first dance when eyes meet across a room? Whatever the reason, the words seemed to come from afar, almost like someone else had spoken them, and Isabella's invitation was out in the open before she had time to reconsider it. 'It's quite late,' she said cautiously, 'and the campsite you are looking for no longer has any facilities.'

The stranger waited for the woman to finish speaking.

Isabella blinked uneasily. 'It's not very safe around here these days, especially after dark,' she said, blurting out the words. 'Why don't you stay the night?'

The frown deepened on the stranger's brow. 'Thanks for the offer, but I don't want to impose upon you. I– '

'It wouldn't be an imposition,' she interrupted, feeling guilty for the way she had treated him before.

'You are very kind, but I need to make ground before it's dark if I'm going to find this track. I'm not really bothered about the lack of camping facilities.'

The stranger had barely finished speaking when a shout reverberated from the squatter camp. Isabella shivered and stepped back a pace. 'Please stay – you would be doing me a favour. The natives have been drinking heavily today and I'm really worried what might happen.'

The stranger looked away from the woman's face towards the squatter camp. Then his eyes moved to where the last glow of the sun had settled for the night on the distant mountains. 'I guess some things never change,' he whispered, his gaze shifting uneasily across the landscape, taking in the farm and the little garden of roses before climbing slowly towards the *kopje* behind the house where Isabella's parents were buried. He wondered why the woman lived alone in such a remote place, but he decided against asking her. Then the slow, lazy smile returned and the past was behind him. 'Are you sure it's not an inconvenience?'

'It's no bother at all,' the woman replied.

'Well, I have a long journey tomorrow and a bed sure would be a big improvement on the Land Cruiser bunk.'

'Look, I feel terrible about the way I have greeted you,' she said, offering him her hand. 'I'm Isabella. Welcome to Ingombe.'

'My name is Robert. Robert Doyle.' The coarseness of his palm, ingrained over many years from working with the tools of the land, made her skin tingle. Then he took a step back and looked at the rifle, which the woman still held loosely in her left hand. 'You can put the gun down now – you really are quite safe with me,' he teased, trying unsuccessfully to control a wide grin.

Isabella felt her cheeks burn with embarrassment, like a little girl admonished for bad behaviour. 'Sorry,' she said, pointing the barrel towards the floor. 'I guess it's a sign of the times.' It was only when she looked down at the rifle that she realised the safety catch was still on and she hoped Robert Doyle had not noticed her oversight.

'No problem. If I was in your position, I would have acted the same way; you just can't be too careful these days. Nothing has been the same since the war. I've noticed travelling down through Zimbabwe that folks tend to shy away from hospitality nowadays.'

The calmness reassured the woman. How easily the stranger had defused the awkward situation, to the point where she felt like she was holding a broom rather than a rifle.

'Would you like a beer?'

'A beer would be good – it's been a long and dusty day.'

'Please – make yourself at home,' Isabella said, indicating the chair on the *stoep*.

Robert Doyle ignored her offer and instead lowered himself onto the top step of the veranda. The dark green foliage of the msasa trees, disappearing in a line down the drive, shimmered in the late evening sun and there was an unusual orderliness about them that made the stranger feel at home. Settling his back against the wooden post, he watched the woman retreat to the kitchen.

Isabella removed two lagers from the fridge and flicked the tops before examining herself in the little mirror on the work surface. The face that stared back at her was flushed and she found it bizarre that just a short while before she had been lonely and wishing that Danny were here. Now there was an excitement in the air and she felt like a young girl on her first date after the embarrassing introductions were over.

For the first time since Robert Doyle's arrival, the woman realised that the stereo had stopped and the noise from the *kraal* below was clearly audible. In a curious way it no longer bothered her. Neither did she feel the need to play another record. All she yearned for was conversation – anything other than farming talk or 'Juliasdale gossip', as Sally sometimes called the inane chat of the townsfolk.

And then she thought of the stranger on the *stoep* – was he real or a figment of her vivid imagination? Picking up the beers, Isabella rushed back outside, frightened that her fear would be realised and the stranger would have disappeared. She need not have worried – Robert Doyle was slouched against the roof post and the early evening sunlight had settled on his face, casting shadows beneath the worn brim of the African bush hat. As she passed him the beer, her hand brushed his arm and for an instant they touched. She shuddered at the contact.

Robert Doyle smiled gently at her awkwardness and held up the bottle. '*Gracias, por su hospitalidad, salud,* thank you for your hospitality.'

'You speak Spanish?'

'Only when I toast a lady who looks like she would be more at home in Catalonia than Zimbabwe.'

Isabella laughed, amused by his intuition. Suddenly she felt she was on a merry-go-round and the intimacy placed her totally at ease in a way she had never known before, not even with Joseph. '*Salud*, Robert.' She returned the salutation in a bubbly voice before curling her long legs beneath her bottom on the seat of the rocking chair. 'I am intrigued by your use of my mother's native tongue,' she said, her eyes on his face.

'Ah, so I *was* right!' he said, smiling. 'Well, I don't speak much – just a few words here and there. So your mother is Spanish?'

'Was. And you are nearly right. Catalonia is close. She came from a little village near Cordoba. When I was a child I could speak the language fluently. It's lovely to hear it again. Wherever did you learn it?'

'From Carlos, an Argentinean I once knew in Mozambique. Actually, he was my best friend. I wish I could have learnt more, but there never seemed to be enough time to get past the basics. I used to sit in the squares in the little villages, far from the big cities of Beira or Maputo, and listen to the old men talking in Portuguese. It wasn't until Carlos translated the stories that I finally knew what they were saying.'

'My mother often told me about the little stone villages high up in the hills of Andalusia; goats wandering the cobblestone streets on their way down to the olive groves; old men in black hats sitting outside the *cantinas*, rolling cigarettes and drinking glasses of homemade wine; the sounds of a Spanish guitar.' She paused to flick a strand of hair from her face. 'Different villages to those in

Mozambique, but I guess they're the same squares. She was a dancer and could play the classical guitar almost as well as she could dance the flamenco.' For a moment Isabella was somewhere else and her thoughts drifted over to the barren *kopje* where Francesca was buried. 'Do you want me to put a record on – something Spanish?'

Robert Doyle smiled. 'Please,' he said, dumbfounded by the way the woman's demeanour had changed so suddenly, and in a way that left him completely mesmerised.

Flicking through the LPs, Isabella came across a cover displaying a dark-haired, olive-skinned man sitting outside a hacienda with a classical guitar. It was an old rendition of 'Rodrigo'. She removed the record from its sleeve and placed it on the turntable. The sound of the guitar strings filled the room and embraced her before drifting out through the door.

'Ah! Now *this* takes me back to those squares,' Robert Doyle said, his eyes on the woman returning to the *stoep*, 'long ago, in the days before the Bush War when it was still easy to slip across the border.'

Isabella settled back into the rocking chair, pulling her legs up against her chest. 'Music is the earliest memory I have of my mother – it was such a big part of her life. She would sit here on the *stoep* with the volume turned up on the old gramophone and sing along to the classics. You know, I can still hear her voice floating across the yard.'

Robert Doyle was captivated. 'I guess music is like a switch that turns on the memories.'

'Oh, what a lovely way to think of it! You are right – whenever I hear 'Aranjuez' I'm always reminded of the Andalusia hills, where my mother was born.'

Isabella was astonished at how easy it was to talk to Robert Doyle. It was as though she'd known him all her life. A moment ago he was a stranger and now… well … just watching him, she felt again the exhilaration in the pit of her stomach, and she wondered how the evening would unfold.

***

In all of the excitement the woman had failed to notice the dog, a huge, brown, grotesque animal. It jumped down from the back of the Land Cruiser and paused to urinate on the vehicle tyre before settling in the shade of the msasa tree. In the fading light, Isabella studied the animal, hoping to learn more about the man. Both looked such a part of the land.

'I've never seen a dog quite like that!' she said.

Robert Doyle glanced at the animal. Its ears were erect as if waiting for a command from its master. 'Her name is Shamari, "friend" in Shona. She's a real mixed breed – ridgeback, rottweiler, bullmastiff and great dane. I rescued her from a *kraal* when she was just a puppy. She was the ugliest and most aggressive dog I have ever seen. Her body was covered in wounds – she looked to have been beaten half to death. Somehow she had managed to escape her tormentors and was taking refuge under a mopane bush – had I not found her, it wouldn't have been long before she died.'

'That's terrible! Aren't some Africans just so cruel?'

'They don't see it that way. To them, animals are expendable.'

'So, just because she was ugly she was an outcast?'

'It happens in all forms of society.'

'Yes, I guess you are right,' Isabella said, slowly nodding her head and thinking of her school friend who had been bullied because of her harelip. 'So, what did you do – adopt her?'

Robert Doyle smiled to himself. 'I guess that's one way of putting it. I took her home, cleaned her wounds and fed her – and now I can't get rid of her!'

The animal raised her head instinctively, as though she knew they were talking about her, yet she remained indifferent to her surroundings.

There was an obvious affinity between the man and his dog, a bond no doubt forged over many years that Isabella understood well from her own experiences. It was a devotion that had been hard earned. When she was five, she had walked off alone into the bush. Her father had been frantic and searched everywhere for her, but it was their border collie, Rufus, who had found her, wandering aimlessly up the mountain, perilously close to falling onto the rocks in the gorge below. Isabella had been devastated when some time later they came across the remains of Rufus' bones, a nocturnal leopard having taken his life.

Although her thoughts were with Rufus, her eyes were fixed on Shamari. The dog's long tongue was coated with saliva and hanging almost to the ground. It caught Robert Doyle's attention and he placed his half empty bottle of beer on the floor and came to his feet in one easy movement, before striding across the yard.

When he reached the Land Cruiser, Shamari nuzzled up to him, letting him run his fingers through the wiry fur around her ears. She then waited patiently while he reached into the back of the jeep and brought out an old tin bowl which he filled with water from a Gerry-can. The dog was thirsty and drank quickly, her tongue showering the ground with minuscule droplets of water.

All of a sudden Robert Doyle's attention wavered for a moment from the animal. Something was bothering him. He felt like he was being watched, and not just by the woman. Glancing up into the dark shadows where the branches blotted out the last of the sun's rays, a movement caught his eye. He thought he could distinguish a silhouette in the trees, a strange outline where there should only have been leaves. He looked away briefly to clear his vision and then searched the shadows again. Whatever he had seen was no longer there. Perhaps it had been a monkey, or simply a figment of his imagination? Whatever it was, it had not alerted Shamari, but then the light wind was blowing towards the trees and the dog would not necessarily have picked up the scent.

Before he could work out what was troubling him, Isabella was shouting from the *stoep*. 'Does Shamari want feeding? I have some cold sausages left over from yesterday.'

Robert Doyle looked away from the trees to see the woman leaning against the banister rail. 'No thanks,' he replied, walking slowly back to the *stoep*. 'We have food.'

'It's no trouble!'

The trees and the incumbent shadows were temporarily forgotten as the man eased his lanky frame back down onto the step. 'Thanks for the offer but it's not necessary.' He picked up the beer and adjusted his bush hat. 'Shamari does her own hunting.'

'Really? What does she hunt?'

'Pretty well anything, although I've discouraged her from tackling the big cats.'

Isabella laughed. 'What an amazing dog!'

Robert Doyle nodded briefly but said nothing. His eyes were focused again on the shadows deepening in the undergrowth, searching the bush for anything unusual.

Nothing moved.

13

In Africa the day changes quickly to night. The Ndebele say that it is the gods turning out the lights. And this was how it was when the sun finally settled behind the mountains and cast its dying reflection across the yard.

In the half-light Isabella followed Robert Doyle's gaze across the river to where she could just make out the silhouette of Inyangani. As the night descended the bush chorus broke into song – first with the cicadas, then the dikkops, followed by the occasional snort from the wallowing hippos in the river. Waiting for him to continue his story, she basked for a moment in the music of the African bush. The serenity of the evening was disturbed only by the sound of a distant drum beat – a pugnacious noise that was unsettling the dog. The animal raised her head from the bowl of water and sniffed the breeze, her yellow teeth drawn back in a grimace.

'Stay Shamari!' Robert Doyle's voice carried easily across the yard. The dog lowered her head churlishly and moved back to where she had been lying beneath the msasa tree. 'If you treat a puppy cruelly it will take on that aggression. Shamari thinks all Africans are the same – she has an inbred hatred of them. I have never been able to change that, which I guess was no bad thing during the war.'

The outline of the moon appeared in the cloudless sky. Soon the darkness would cloak the landscape, but Isabella was too engrossed in the story to notice. Not even the tiny orange and black ladybird that landed on her arm could divert her focus. 'Was she with you throughout the war?' she asked, gently blowing the insect from her skin.

'For most of it. Saved my life on more than one occasion.' Robert Doyle faltered slightly. 'I guess we are both a breed that has outgrown our time. You know, sometimes I feel that we are from a different era, out of place in the new Zimbabwe.'

'Perhaps you are. I have certainly never met anyone quite like either of you.'

In the evenings, when the sun goes down, low winds sweep across the Eastern Highlands from the faraway mountains. Isabella felt the chill. Was it the weather, the noise from the *kraal*, or perhaps a raw nerve that the stranger had inadvertently touched? They were only feet apart and, noticing her shiver, Robert Doyle stood up and reached for the jumper lying over the back of the woman's chair, placing it gently around her shoulders. Isabella had an overwhelming desire to reach out to him. Somehow though, it wasn't right. After all, she had only known the stranger for a few hours. So she changed the subject with a frivolous smile. 'You must be starved. Come and tell me all about yourself while I rustle up something to eat.'

Robert Doyle looked at her tenderly. It had been a long time since he had looked at a woman in this way. There was something about her that he could not explain. Was it the way the light reflected on her hair or the way that she smiled at him? Or maybe it was the way she stared into his eyes, almost as if she was reading his very thoughts. 'I'm not really sure there is much to tell,' he said frankly, in reply to her request. 'But I do talk much easier with a drink – it kind of loosens my tongue.'

'Oh, I'm sorry! Would you like another beer?'

'Well, I was going to offer you a glass of wine.'

'Wine? Wherever did you manage to find wine?'

'I happened to drive past the bottle store in Troutbeck today. They were off-loading a consignment from South Africa, so I stopped and picked up a case of Robertson. Why don't I grab a couple of bottles?' He paused. 'Or would you prefer a beer?'

'No, I'd *love* a glass of wine!' How easily the gaiety crossed her lips when she laughed. It was a puerile laughter, the kind that Robert Doyle had not heard for many years. 'This *is* a treat! It must be the first delivery they've had in months – wine is reserved for special occasions only these days because of the sanctions.'

Robert Doyle held her gaze. Frivolity lingered in the corner of his eyes and replicated her giggle. What could be more special, he thought. To come here looking for water and instead to have found a beautiful woman and a bed for the night. 'Well,' he said, 'this is definitely an occasion that deserves a good Merlot.'

A flush of colour appeared on Isabella's cheeks and she subconsciously flicked a delicate strand of hair from her face. The action of doing this allowed her light fragrance to touch the air. It was this freshness that captivated Robert Doyle and yet the woman was not even aware of her allure. He watched her walk away. There was an indiscreet abandonment in the way she moved and it was all the more provocative for being unpremeditated. She seemed to flow like a river ambling off a mountain, washing over sandy banks and rocks, touching branches on her journey to the sea. Perhaps, like the river, she touches everyone this way, Robert Doyle thought, and she does not even realise that she is doing it. The reflection was still on his mind when he followed her into the kitchen. 'Do you have anything to open the bottle?'

Isabella reached into the drawer and pulled out her father's old wooden-handled corkscrew. 'Will this do?' she asked, placing two wine glasses on the table. There was something familiar about the situation – it was comfortable, like an old leather settee. And the woman felt a part of the room; now there was a purpose, a reason for preparing the food, and she wasn't about to take this moment for granted.

The cork came out with a loud pop. Robert Doyle held the bottle over the glass. 'Are you all right with red?' he asked, before pouring the wine. 'It's a Cape Merlot.'

'You bet – it's my favourite!'

He put the bottle down. Smiles were exchanged across the table and, holding her eyes, he picked up his glass and touched hers. '*Salud*, Isabella.'

The wine was on Robert Doyle's lips and in the cool, clean African air he contemplated the last two hours. Having always shied away from superstition, he firmly believed that a man made his own luck. Yet the moment he'd chosen his path at the crossroads, he'd no idea that the woman existed. Now he had an urgency to be with her. Did she feel the same way? Then he admonished himself; it would be just one night, and there had never been a suggestion of anything other than a bed in a spare room.

But somehow he knew deep down it was not going to be that easy.

14

The lights of Rusape glowed pale, barely illuminating the edge of the main street. Fifty miles to Juliasdale, Sengamo thought, glancing down at the dashboard. It was 12.20 a.m. and the only sound to be heard was the occasional bark from an emaciated dog.

Dark figures covered in thin dirty blankets lay huddled on cardboard sheets in the deeper shadows of a store doorway – they were outcasts, the war veterans having driven them off their own farms like stray dogs. Some folk would call them the lucky ones because they had survived being shot, hanged, burnt or mutilated.

Sengamo shuddered and asked himself again what the war had achieved. Who were the real victims and would anything ever change? Sure, there was now a black government in power, but corruption was rife and it brought huge benefits to the black elite, leaving the ordinary African people with nothing. Then he thought of Nyoka.

The government official from Gazelle Farm had told him that the *vanamukoma* were camped south of Juliasdale. He had no cause to doubt the man. After all, one does not lie easily when one's head is hanging over a fire, and even if the *tsotsi* was not telling the truth, he would still find those responsible for the death of his parents.

There would be no hiding place.

An hour and a half later Sengamo was on the road south

out of Juliasdale, climbing towards the mountains where the undergrowth was impenetrable. Moonlight softly radiated the dark bush and the tracker could occasionally make out the profile of a small herd of eland and the odd water hog, their knobbled grey heads alert for predators of the night. Although they were repugnant to look at, he admired their ferocious strength; many were the tales of these ugly tusked pigs ripping open a leopard's side, which was by no means an easy task.

Tiredness was just starting to creep in when the old truck rumbled across a small concrete bridge. Its headlights swept the flat grassland towards a bend in the river where a gap in the thick bush would adequately hide the vehicle. Only the cicadas with their relentless hum disturbed the night, and when Sengamo was satisfied that he was alone, he locked the doors and closed his eyes.

The tracker was awake with the dawn. For a moment he lay still with his eyes shut, listening to the birdsong that resurrected the day. The sounds of the bush were familiar to him but there was a strange shuffling noise that alerted his attention. Something was moving in the undergrowth, something he could not see. Sitting motionless, Sengamo looked out beyond the dusty windscreen. Thirty feet away, almost totally hidden in the thick bush, a young waterbuck nibbled at the new shoots growing close to the river, its brown eyes oblivious to the vehicle's presence. The tracker smiled. Although the distraction was fascinating, there were more pressing matters on his mind and he dismissed the waterbuck and studied the distant landscape for any sign of activity.

In the first light of morning he saw the terrain he'd

crossed from the road and he nodded, satisfied with the hiding place he had randomly chosen in the night.

Now that the curtain of dark had lifted, it was time to move. Conscious that the catch on the door of the *bakkie* was noisy, Sengamo carefully eased the handle down before stepping out of the vehicle. But in doing so his scent touched the breeze and immediately alerted the waterbuck, sending the animal scampering off through the trees. Having lived long enough in the bush to know that the first rule of the wild was to always let the wind favour you, he reprimanded himself for his error.

The plan was to abandon the *bakkie* and walk. There was no immediate intention to retrieve the vehicle because when the official failed to return to the farm the truck would be reported missing and become a liability.

The tree line along the river was about 40 yards from the old road and the vehicle tracks were clearly visible in the red sand. They had to be obliterated. Removing the machete from his belt, Sengamo hacked off a dry broken branch from a msasa bush and walked to the edge of the road. Working from the strip-tar back to where the truck was concealed, he brushed the soft earth. Then, dismantling the rotor arm from the distributor of the vehicle, he slowly retraced his steps across the scrubland back to the road, removing any sign of his footprints. The ground now appeared harmonious with the surrounding *veld*. Finally, to pinpoint the vehicle's location, he built a small unobtrusive stone cairn on the grass verge. Standing next to the pile of stones was an antiquated red tin sign, a hangover from the old colonial days when motorists would be warned of impending potholes in the dilapidated road. Now, because of the state of the road, or perhaps the country, the sign was of little use.

The first sun of the day was low on the horizon when the tracker set off from his hiding place near the bend in the river. Walking on the red baked earth along the edge of the road where the yellow daisies grew, he inhaled the faint scent of the wild flowers that lingered in the air.

The countryside was devoid of traffic or people. Although it was still reasonably early in the morning, the heat was already shimmering off the tarmac and the tracker was aware of the folly of walking aimlessly in the intense sun. His eyes constantly scanned the bush for a place in which he could rest and watch the road. An hour later he found what he was looking for – a low acacia tree growing beside a river, which would offer him a modicum of shade. The only other problem was fresh water. The trickle of the slow-running river could not be trusted and, acutely aware of the need to conserve his meagre supply, Sengamo adopted an old bush trick of sucking on a small pebble. This allowed the tiny amount of saliva it produced to trickle down his throat and alleviate his thirst.

Below the acacia tree a column of black ants were busily moving the dissected limbs of a locust to their nest in the rocks. Their ability to communicate briefly with each other while carrying their enormous burdens fascinated the tracker and he wondered what messages they passed on when their bodies touched. Picking up a large rock, he placed it gently in the path of the column. The industrious little insects hesitated only briefly before continuing around the obstacle, almost as if it had always been there. They employed a strict work ethic and a discipline that the tracker admired, an ethos that he himself had adopted.

This was his land – a land that had once been the young Sengamo's classroom – and it was here that he had mastered the art of patience during the long hours spent tracking dainty steenbok with his uncle Hodari. And it was not long before his fortitude was rewarded. In the distance an African approached the *kopje* on a rusty bicycle. The muffled sound of the narrow tyres on the loose gravel resonated in perfect harmony with the noisy chrome pedals. The tracker leapt to his feet and frantically waived his arms. '*Molo kigali!*' he shouted, at the top of his voice.

The African pulled over and jumped off his bicycle. There was a look of apprehension on his face when he noticed Sengamo's worn combat outfit. '*Molo nkozi,*' he replied hesitantly. The old man wore patched clothes, threadbare hand-me-downs, and his feet were bare and scaled from the many years spent walking on dirt roads. But it was the pain in his eyes and the lines on his parched skin that told the story of a hard life.

The *madala* stood in silence. Behind him a martial eagle hovered above the sun-burnt plain, its sharp eyes searching the scrub for rodents or rabbits while its wide wings held it almost motionless in the sky.

Sengamo recognised the wariness in the old man's reaction. Nevertheless, he needed to take the *madala* into his confidence. Quickly clasping his hands together, he bowed in respect. '*Tafadhali kigali,*' he said humbly, 'can you help me? I am coming from Rusape to find work so I can feed my family. The *tsotsis* have destroyed the *bwana's* tobacco crop and driven all the workers off the farm.'

'I am sorry for you, *kijana*,' the *madala* said, with a mixture of relief and empathy. 'We live in bad times.'

'They told me in Juliasdale that there is work on the land around here,' Sengamo said. 'Do you know of this?'

The old man looked into the tracker's eyes, searching his face for the truth. 'There is much suffering on these farms,' he said at last, in a despondent voice. 'I am coming this morning from Missy Isabella's farm at Ingombe, but I think it will not be long before the *nkozikazi* loses her land. Already the aggressive ones from Harare make a camp by the road that runs alongside her farm.' He paused to wipe the mucous from his nose with the back of his sleeve. 'They sit around the compound all day, drinking. Then they amuse themselves by taking whatever woman they want. It is a very bad business. Only yesterday my niece Liana was raped by one of those dogs.' His watery eyes blinked away the tears. 'She is only fourteen years old. Ah, I tell you *kijana*, this is a terrible place!'

Sengamo flinched at the thought of the scum who ruled through intimidation, violating young girls who often bore their bastard children, contaminating them with HIV. Witchdoctors compounded the problem further by declaring that sex with a young virgin cured these men of the sickness. But the worst of it was that the girls were now outcasts, sometimes even from their own families. Only the orphanages sheltered them. What had the country come to? Anger raged within him but to betray his fury would be to reveal his mission, so he forced himself to remain calm. 'Where are these farms, *madala*? I need the work, please – to feed my family. I have no money.'

Although it was against his better judgement, the old man hesitated only briefly. 'There are only two farms in this area,' he said, adopting a more kindly manner. 'About four miles up this road there is a turning on your left.' Squatting down on the edge of the corrugated track, he flattened the soft sand on the edge of the road and picked up a stick, which he used to draw a crude map on the sandy canvas. 'The first farm you will come to on the right of the old gravel road is Rigby's Creek.' His frail hand marked the location. 'It is another three miles to Ingombe, which is on the other side of the road.' He again marked its position. 'You must stay away from this place. The "boys of the soil", as the *vanamukoma* like to call themselves, have made a large camp at the farm entrance. Five days ago many soldiers from the Fifth Brigade arrived in a big truck.' The *madala* looked away for a minute, his eyes misty with thoughts of his young niece. There was no hurry and he sat silently on his haunches, trying to compose himself. 'I think it is better if you look for work at Rigby's Creek,' he said finally, his voice trembling. 'There are not many *tsotsis* on this farm yet.'

But it wasn't work the tracker was after. He stood up and helped the old man retrieve his battered bicycle. '*Tatenda kigali*, you have been much help.'

'*Hamma*, it is nothing, *kijana*.' Words were no longer of any importance. The *madala* glanced one last time at the tracker and, with an almost imperceptible gesture on his weathered face, he climbed onto his bicycle and rode off towards Juliasdale. Wild poppies, struggling in the dry earth at the side of the road, nodded their paper heads in the breeze as the wheels of the bicycle passed by. The *madala* did not see them. His watery eyes were fixed on a horizon that did not exist, a vista that was only in his mind.

The tracker stood glued to the spot, as if made of

stone, and he watched the figure fade away until he eventually disappeared into the distance. Only when the sky had swallowed up both man and bicycle did he once again squat in the road. After studying the sketch, he decided on a route that would cut off the corner and take him directly across the bush to Ingombe. If the *madala's* drawing was accurate – and he had no reason to doubt its authenticity – it would be an easy walk.

When the map was rigidly embedded in his mind, Sengamo eradicated all evidence of it from the ground and set off due east through the parched grassland.

It was one of those early afternoons when the gods were surely happy with their creation. The vista stretched from the desiccated grassland through the acacia bushes to the distant mountains. As he rested for a moment in the shade of a sickle bush, a light wind touched Sengamo's skin and then parted the branches in front of him to reveal the land beyond. The intense heat of the midday sun had forced the animals to seek shade wherever they could find it and apart from the irritating sand flies, which fed frenziedly on his skin, all was quiet. The bites were annoying the tracker. Waiting patiently for one of the insects to settle on his body, his huge hand moved like lightning, squashing the exasperating sand fly against his flesh. Where one died another appeared and, tiring of the little game, the tracker moved off through the bush.

Half an hour later he crossed an open area of *veld* and spotted a small herd of impala in the distance, just visible in the brown thicket. The sentries stood to attention away from the main group, their delicate almond eyes scanning the thick undergrowth for predators while the rest of the herd gorged on the dry grass, their snow-white fluffy tails swinging in rhythm to their feeding. The slightest sign of danger would send them leaping off into the bush with their trampoline legs springing over the low shrub. And like the impala, the tracker scrutinised the foreground for signs of danger lurking in the long yellow grass.

There was none.

Neither was there any sign of the vultures. The *makhote* rode the thermals searching for the dead and Sengamo knew they would show him the carcasses if there was a kill. And where there was a corpse, there were predators. The safe option, he finally decided, was to avoid the thick grassland in favour of a less direct route across the open shrub.

Eventually he came to a shallow waterhole, more mud than water, and stood cautiously for some minutes beneath a nyala tree, studying the landscape like a scholar would read a book. The leaves of this unusual tree had not yet been stripped by the tiny green caterpillars that inhabit its branches. These insects were capable of destroying the tree in a matter of weeks before they descended to the ground on silk threads, transforming themselves into grey moths.

Marabou storks stood on spindly legs in the thick mud. Beside the storks a heron waited patiently on a sand bank while a fish eagle hovered overhead, her eerie cry penetrating the African stillness. Beneath the msasa trees a family of guinea fowl issued mournful cries from their roosts and when Sengamo looked at the speckled birds, he was reminded of the hunting days he had once shared with Tom. But it was the two young eland, drinking calmly from the bracken water on the edge of the waterhole, which finally assured him that there were no predators in the immediate vicinity.

Then, checking his position against the sun to ensure he was still walking east, Sengamo continued on his way. Occasionally he would stop and take a sip from the battered water bottle hanging from his webbing belt, only allowing himself sufficient liquid to wet the pebble in his mouth and quench his thirst.

By mid afternoon he had stumbled onto the wire security fence, the original boundary to the holding, which would once have enclosed the entire farm. Judging by its dilapidated state it appeared to have been erected many years before, with little or no maintenance since. The barbed strands of wire ran towards the road and it was not long before he came to the first break where a large section of the fence was missing, confirming his suspicions that the land no longer operated productively.

Animal tracks littered the sand. Dropping to his knees, the tracker studied the spoor. It was predominantly impala and waterbuck, which was no cause for concern. Satisfied that there were no human footprints, he slipped carefully through the fissure and resumed his path along the fence to the corrugated road.

It was the wood smoke, filtering through the trees 400 yards ahead, that pin-pointed the squatter camp. Edging his way cautiously through the bush towards the encampment, he eventually found what he was looking for: a tall sycamore fig tree, which with its thick low branches and dense canopy would not only conceal him, but would also provide him with a sweeping view of life in the compound.

The surrounding landscape was synonymous with the new Zimbabwe. Many of the indigenous trees had been felled and used to construct a group of plastered huts, their walls covered in *daga*, the muddy cow dung mix. Grass roofs, yellow against the indigo sky, were shrouded with the thin blue smoke from continuous wood fires that cast a low haze over the shabby community.

A large woman in a colourful print dress came out of a *rondavel* and for just a moment Sengamo thought he recognised his mother. He closed his eyes and when he reopened them a minute later they were misty and the woman had disappeared.

Randomly scattered to one side of the mud huts were the tents; olive-green canvas blobs that somehow looked incongruous. They were home to the soldiers from the infamous Fifth Brigade, Mugabe's notorious terror unit – the very same men he'd been looking for. A Bedford truck and a camouflaged Land Rover were parked to one side of the tented city, bestowing a military presence upon the camp. They were the only vehicles in evidence.

Behind the rondavels was a large clearing where once the community would have gathered. Now only young men, dressed indiscriminately in army uniforms, occupied the space. They sat in a circle, drinking *skokiaan* and smoking *mbanje*, their AK-47 rifles carelessly propped against a pole on which a ragged flag of the new Zimbabwe fluttered limply in the light breeze. When not engaged in fetching beer for the soldiers, the women went about their work. Some collected wood to keep the fires burning while others walked back from the river with baskets of washing or clay pots of water balanced precariously on their heads. Four young girls digging wearily in a pumpkin field were oblivious to the soldiers, their infants sleeping peacefully on their backs, tightly wrapped in colourful blankets. When he closed his eyes to the soldier's tents, the scene of rural domesticity reminded him of his *kraal* at Gazelle Farm. But the *kraal*, like his childhood, had irrevocably changed.

Stretching his limbs to avoid cramp, Sengamo breathed deeply on the eucalyptus scented air, his attention on the soldier's movements. What he now needed was a rifle and, if possible, explosives, but he knew he would have to wait until there was sufficient cover of darkness to steal the weapons. For the moment, there was no urgency.

It was when he turned around to look at the purple mountain dominating the skyline, that he noticed the *wazungu's* homestead lying in the shadow of the distant *kopje*, almost hidden by the rows of msasa trees running up the valley. How different it was from the only home he had ever known, a dirt-floored *rondavel* on the small corner of a parched field.

But it was the swallows that held his attention, diving in and out of the trees in their search for food. 'The messengers', Baba used to call them. Each year as the summer disappeared, the tiny birds would leave on their long journey, crossing great deserts and endless seas to faraway lands he had only read about in the white man's books – beyond Zimbabwe, beyond even Africa. And his eyes were wet when he thought about his father.

Apart from the birds, few creatures ventured out into the heat of the day. Even the soldiers, sleeping on the hard earth in the shade of the *rondavels*, were oblivious to their surroundings, unperturbed by the mangy dogs that yapped at the irritating flies. Occasionally one of the men would wake up and signal for the woman to serve *chibuku* from the wooden gourds before falling asleep again.

How did we ever win the war with men such as these? Sengamo thought, shaking his head in disgust. But then, he reminded himself, these undisciplined youths in the squatter camp were hardly comparable to the mountain guerrillas from ZANLA.

He had seen all he wished to see for the moment.

It was time to acquaint himself with the farm.

15

The track up to the farmhouse was lined with msasa trees and on either side thick virgin bush had reclaimed the land. Sengamo read the tragedy in what he saw, understanding that the land would have once supported cattle and irrigated fields.

There was no activity. In fact the farm appeared almost deserted. Nevertheless Sengamo avoided the main drive as he made his way up the valley towards the homestead.

When the house came into view, he bent down and picked up a long blade of grass, which he held up to the wind. A light breeze, in his favour, was blowing directly across the land from the mountains. It was the time of day when the evening sunset stained the trees gold and changed the colour of the leaves like a chameleon walking across a brightly painted canvas.

To the side of the homestead, growing amongst the woodland of msasa, sycamore and mango trees stood a tall marula, its fig-like fruit a favourite with the elephants. But the mountains were now deserted of these great mammals; those that had not been poached for their ivory during the war had fled to the plains. However, the marula, with its thick tall stem and broad canopy, would make a perfect vantage point from which to observe the house.

In the surrounding woodland there was a cacophony of birdsong. Noisy Cape glossy starlings and weaver birds flew from their nests, seemingly unperturbed by the

African's presence in the broad green leaves. When the starlings settled, sounds of the African night replaced their calls. Frogs, their legs playing an evening song reminiscent of a percussion instrument, competed with the chirping of the crickets that in turn drowned out the faint drumbeat from the squatter camp.

Sengamo focused the old scratched field glasses onto the house and saw what he thought were the servants jovially bidding their missus goodbye before they walked down the hill towards the compound. Their departure reminded him that he had not eaten all day and he reached into the side pocket of his combat trousers and pulled out a stick of *biltong*, the spicy meat that was the only food he carried in the bush. He cut off a piece and chewed it slowly. Although the flavour was irresistible, the tracker was reluctant to eat too much of the dried meat because the salt made him thirsty. Removing the battered aluminium water bottle from his webbing belt, he drank cautiously. It was still a quarter full, which was sufficient to last him well into the evening when he could replenish his supplies under the cover of darkness.

Then he noticed a wide wedge towards the top of the marula tree, formed by the stout branches in the midst of the canopy. The tapered trunk would not only provide a comfortable place to sleep, but also give him a commanding view of anyone approaching the house.

It was the incessant beat of the drums, an intimidating sound floating through the valley from the compound, that reminded him why he was here and his attention returned to the woman sitting in the rocking chair on the farmhouse *stoep*. She was dozing in the diluted sunshine, listening to the strange music coming from the house, a bottle of beer beside her on the small rattan table.

Sengamo smiled to himself. The *wazungus* were so clever in many ways, but why did they fill their heads with these curious sounds? Then he remembered what the *madala* had said about the violence at the farm and he understood why the *umfazi* would want to disguise the noise from the camp.

From beyond the pale blue mountains, a gust of wind touched Sengamo's arm and he picked up the scent of rain. It was followed by the roll of distant thunder that broke like the soft growl of a prowling lioness. The solitude was infectious and he closed his eyes to the remoteness. And in the stillness of the late afternoon, sleep came easily.

Minutes later, the scrape of a chair, its resonance carrying clearly across the yard, woke the African. The woman was on her feet, watching a sparrow hopping about in the dust searching for food. Then she raised her arms up high into the air and, standing on tip-toe, tried to reach for the sky, a posture she held for a few minutes before returning to her seat.

Sengamo would never really understand the *wazungus'* strange rituals. Nevertheless, he could see that this was a proud woman. She walked like a Zulu, the ancestors of his forbears the Ndebele, moving like the wind, softly and silently. Only a strong woman, or perhaps a stupid one, would live alone in this wilderness with uncertainty on her doorstep. What a shame she was not black, he thought – she would make a good partner.

Her eyes were closed as if in a state of reverie.

She's daydreaming, Sengamo thought to himself. This was not an extravagance he could indulge in. The comforting images of his childhood had been blotted out by traumatic scenes of war. Now when he closed his eyes all he could hear were the screams; of the old men crying in agony as flames engulfed their fragile bodies; of young girls being raped and contaminated with the sickness, their lives destroyed; of children who had not eaten for weeks, their bellies bloated from the malnutrition. Did this woman know of the pain his people had suffered? Had she heard the cries of girls brutally torn apart and pleading for their mothers? Or their muttered prayers, when the last of a stream of soldiers had finally broken the youngsters' resolve? What was the use of prayers anyway – where was God in all of this? Could this *umfazi* know the torment of a mother helplessly watching as her child is devoured alive by starving dogs? If she had witnessed anything like this, she surely would not remain alone on this farm with the *vanamukoma* as neighbours.

Sengamo tried in vain to wrench his thoughts away from the nightmare images that repeated themselves over and over again, in the same way an annoyingly repetitive tune would sometimes run through his mind. But the only way he found he could dispel the incubus was to concentrate on what was happening below.

Looking at the woman sleeping on the *stoep*, he tried to appease himself with the thought that peace and contentment might one day be within his grasp. And perhaps it would also be so for the millions of other Africans like him.

Holding the thought, he closed his eyes.

The sound of a vehicle approaching the house awakened him. There is an interval between slumber and consciousness, a no man's land where one is vulnerable, but this did not apply to the African. The years of living and fighting in the bush had sharpened his senses to a razor's edge and the instant he was awake, he was in full control of his faculties.

The Land Cruiser, parked beneath the shade of the msasa tree inside the security fence, evoked in him memories of the war. Then a tall man, wearing a faded leather bush hat, stepped out of the vehicle.

And Sengamo froze.

Although the man's back was to him and he was unable to see his face, he recognised the unusual ribbon fluttering from the back of the bush hat and the way the tall stranger held himself, like an *induna*. The shock registered for barely a minute. Breathing deeply and desperately, the tracker shook his head. It was not possible – how could it be? He must be imagining what he was seeing.

But he knew he was not mistaken.

Before him stood the soldier who had set up the ambush on the mountain back in Mozambique, the *mzungu* who had spared his life on that day in the remote Chimanimani. Although it was some years before, Sengamo would never forget him. Then he thought of the security forces – the soldiers he had once fought. Most of them were racists and they took no prisoners. Brought up on African soil, under a white umbrella, they had an assumed superiority that their God had made them special and that He had neglected the African people because they were black and stupid. It was partly this egotism that had spurred the hatred on the killing fields.

But this man was different. This soldier had spared his life; perhaps in vain – a bullet to the head in the mountains would have relieved him of the pain of finding his family murdered. However, these were now irrelevant thoughts because the *mzungu* was moving across the yard to the farmhouse *stoep*. Although the tracker was unable to hear the conversation, he could see a familiarity starting to develop between the *wazungus*, which he found strange, since the woman had initially threatened the man with a rifle.

Then just as he was starting to relax, a movement caught his eye to the side of the Land Cruiser. It was the dog. The animal was the size of a hyena, but even uglier. And he shuddered when he thought of the consequences of the *imbwa* detecting his scent. Lying down in the shadow of the msasa tree, ears cocked to the noise coming from the camp, it was as alert as any wild animal. And then the soldier gave it a drink with the same tenderness he had shown the tracker on the mountain in Mozambique.

Suddenly the *mzungu* turned around. Something had caught his eye and he looked up. His eyelids narrowed as he squinted intensely towards the marula tree, and for just a moment Sengamo thought the reflection of his binoculars had betrayed his hiding place.

But it was not to be.

However, it was only when the woman's voice drifted across the yard, calling the *mzungu,* that Sengamo was finally able to relax.

Back on the *stoep* the conversation now flowed easily between the man and the woman, as it does between people who have formed an immediate kinship. And as the light faded and the evening sky shrouded the farm in darkness, the *wazungus* disappeared into the house.

Occasionally Sengamo caught faint glimpses of their silhouettes through the dusty window pane, effigies projected in the pale glow of the 60 watt lamp hanging from the ceiling.

Another hour and the day would vanish into oblivion.

How alike he and the *mzungu* were, the tracker thought to himself – both seemingly drifting through a life that no longer held much meaning. Only the colour of their skin differentiated them and, in a peculiar way, the African felt an affinity towards the silver-haired stranger.

One thing he knew for sure – he would rather be with him than against him.

16

Robert Doyle moved across to the kitchen table and instinctively sat down in the old beech chair with his back to the wall. The position afforded him a clear view of the room, the front door and the corridor. The war had taught him to keep people where he could see them and old habits died hard.

Although it was Isabella's favourite seat, she said nothing, choosing instead to hum softly to herself while she prepared the meal. The haunting Spanish tune floated across the room against a backdrop of clattering cooking utensils on steel pans.

Robert Doyle recognised the 'Recuerdos de la Alhambra' and his thoughts drifted back along the road to the little squares with the faded colonial architecture where jacaranda trees grew along deserted streets. And he was reluctant to break the spell which bound him to this moment.

Framed in the front door, the darkness hid the mountains that formed the border to Mozambique, the area he had once patrolled in the search for ZANLA guerrillas. The manoeuvres took the Special Forces to remote parts of the country where the solitude only served to sharpen their hunger for female company. After eight weeks they returned to civilisation for three days, with only one thing on their minds: girls. And the hunger had been reciprocal.

Robert Doyle looked at the woman standing at the

kitchen sink and he was reminded of those days. She stood tall and proud, her skin a tone paler than the deep brown, weather-beaten tan worn by most Rhodesian farm girls. Her light cotton skirt and blouse enhanced her figure and when she moved the fabric moved with her, emphasising her curves and leaving little to the imagination. Her brown hair was tied in a bun and held in place by a colourful clip, which left the flawless skin of her neck exposed. A thin gossamer gold chain fell loosely from her neck towards her breasts and Robert Doyle found himself wondering where it had come from. He looked at her legs, long and smooth beneath the hem of her skirt, and for a moment he was captivated. Then, apprehensive that the woman would notice his stare, he tore his eyes away from her body and returned to the shadows in the open doorway.

'A penny for your thoughts Robert,' Isabella said, turning to face him.

The question caught him by surprise. 'I was thinking that I am glad I stayed,' he lied, having not known the woman long enough to lay bare his feelings.

'I'm happy too.' She moved away from the stove and reached on tip-toe into the high-level cupboard for a plate. And as she stretched for the crockery, her blouse fell off her shoulder and exposed the thin black strap of her bra. He shuddered briefly.

On her left hand was a ring. Yet the woman appeared to live alone. Or maybe he was mistaken? So he asked the question; it was direct, but then he knew of no other way to ask it. 'Is there a man in your life Isabella?'

For a moment she said nothing and he thought he had offended her. Then she spoke softly. 'There was once.

Joseph. He was killed in the war.'

'I'm sorry,' Robert Doyle said, feeling guilty for bringing up the subject.

'Don't be. It was a long time ago,' she said, reluctant to talk about it further.

Robert Doyle respected her privacy. When he had first seen her standing on the *stoep*, with the rifle held nervously in her shaking hands, he had felt a surprising urge to protect her. At the time she'd been as reticent as a young girl on her first date, but with each passing moment she seemed to grow in confidence. There was a complexity about the woman that was at odds with her aura. This worried Robert Doyle. Not for many years had he met anyone quite like her and he reached for his wine glass to steady himself. 'So, what's all this about the track down to the Chapungu Falls?'

'Oh it really is quite dangerous at night.'

'Well, I sure am glad I didn't take the chance!'

'You're teasing me!' the woman laughed, colour washing over her cheeks. 'So, where were you going after the Falls?'

'To South Africa.'

'Aren't the Highlands a little out of the way if you're headed to the border?'

'I wanted to divert through the Chimanimani.'

'Why?'

'Nostalgia, I guess – it was to be a last trip to visit friends in the war graves at Chipinge.' There was an air of despondency in his voice.

'I was there last year. It's a very sad place.'

'I reckon. Though time has a way of making it all just seem a part of the past.'

Isabella removed the olives and pimentos from the

packaging and spooned them into the stew. The odour of the cooked meat mixed easily with that of the garlic rice and saffron and escaped into the air, hanging like a mist in the room. The woman didn't want to talk about the war, so she changed the subject. 'And then you came to my crossroads,' she said. 'I watched you for a while through the binoculars, making your decision. Perhaps I shouldn't be telling you this but I was hoping you would come to Ingombe; not many folk pass by here these days.'

This was at odds, Robert Doyle thought, with the reception he had received at the end of a rifle. Nevertheless he smiled. 'So it's all your fault that I am here!' His light-heartedness dispelled the uneasiness and the war graves were forgotten. 'Actually, it was either your farm or Juliasdale. I noticed a problem with the Land Cruiser at Tucker Gap and then the old girl started to lose water at quite a rate. Before I reached Pungwe Drift, I had to stop every few miles to refill the radiator. So I guess it had to be your farm.' He paused to look at the woman. 'I reckon it may have turned out to be a real good decision.'

A teasing half-smile appeared on Isabella's face. 'I'll let you know later.' Then her attention was diverted by the sound of the stew bubbling over onto the stove. 'Now look what you've made me do!'

'I'm sorry.'

The woman laughed. 'Don't be silly, Robert – I'm not being serious!' From the reflection in the glass cupboard, she could see him looking at her. And it pleased her.

The atmosphere in the room was easy. Robert Doyle felt the woman drawing him into her little world and he welcomed the invitation. Yet he reminded himself to be careful; it had been a long time since he'd felt affection for another woman, a long time since Emily. Most of his subsequent liaisons he had paid for – women in bars whispering the right words and making all the right noises for the right money; just faces, seen through the bottom of a whisky glass and disappearing with the dawn. He was a drifter, a man of the road – what could someone like him possibly offer a woman like Isabella?

Her voice brought him back into the room. 'Where are you going to in South Africa?'

'I have a little farm in the Drakensberg.'

With her back to the room, Robert Doyle failed to notice Isabella wrestling with her next question. 'Can I show you something of my farm before you go?'

He was taken back by the forwardness of her offer, but was nevertheless happy that she'd asked. 'I would like that very much,' he said softly, conscious that perhaps the urgency to leave had all but disappeared.

Robert Doyle continued to watch the woman going about her work, spooning the herbs into the stew. She seemed reluctant to want to talk about her past and he once again pondered the ring on her finger, contemplating the man who had placed it there. It reminded him of his fellow soldiers in the lonely frontier towns. Some of them, like Harry, the seventeen-year-old boy from Chegutu who was caught in crossfire, were just kids. They had left their sweethearts weeping by the side of the road to return to the fighting. At the time he had tried to distance himself from them, these transients, arriving to replace those who had been lost. They had been a distraction to the fighting and yet in hindsight his heart ached for this lost generation – especially Harry, who had been like a son to him.

The past was a blanket over Robert Doyle's face and

it suffocated him. Without uttering a word, he stood up and walked down the corridor and out of the open front door to the *stoep*. The night was clear and stars blanketed the sky. He breathed deeply of the mountain air, which carried the faint smell of wild honeysuckle. A light dew was beginning to form on the grass and soon it would touch the upper branches of the msasa trees. His back was to the door when he heard the woman's footsteps on the wooden floorboards.

'Robert, whatever is the matter?'

He turned to face her, embarrassed at being caught with his past. 'I'm sorry. For a moment I was somewhere else. Back in the mountains.'

'I don't understand,' Isabella said, moving up close to him.

Robert Doyle looked out into the inky darkness. Shamari lay still with her head on her paws in the far corner of the *stoep*. The woman's perfume dusted the air next to him. 'I was thinking of the little towns we came to for R&R during the war. Towns not unlike Juliasdale, I guess – I was there briefly before the war.'

'We didn't have any soldiers staying here – I know there was a camp at Rusape.'

'I'm sorry – sometimes the past catches up with me. I've never… '

'Oh, don't be!' Isabella said, brushing over his awkwardness. There was a new self-assurance about the woman. Then, taking him gently by the hand, she led him like a child, back to the kitchen. 'Dinner is nearly ready. If you really want to make yourself useful you can pour the wine.' It was not open to argument. She held out her glass, which was still half full, and watched Robert Doyle pour the dark red Merlot. The leather bracelet on his wrist reminded her of Joseph, who used to wear a similar band and as the alcohol began to slowly take its effect, it gave her a false sense of confidence. But she didn't resist it. 'Thanks Robert,' she said in a beguiling voice. 'I'm starting to feel a little tipsy. You wouldn't be trying to get a girl to lose her inhibitions now, would you?'

Robert Doyle laughed, the embarrassment of a moment ago forgotten. 'Would I do that Isabella?'

The woman looked at him without replying and smiled. She had a hankering to know more about this unusual man. 'If you want, you can speak to me about your past. I would love to know more about you. And start at the beginning.'

Robert Doyle's eyes were on Shamari out on the *stoep*. A glint of moonlight had captured her standing in the shadows, her ears alert to the African voices in the distant compound. But the noise was too far away to concern the dog. Robert Doyle listened for a moment to the sounds of the night and then he drew in a deep breath before speaking. 'Well, let's see now, where do I start. You asked for the beginning. Well, I was born in Bulawayo, but raised in the Eastern Cape of South Africa. My father was Irish, hence the name, but that was all he gave me before he disappeared. I guess my mother tried her best but she worked full time as a nurse, so it wasn't easy. I left boarding school when I was fifteen and returned to Rhodesia – to Salisbury, where she lived. But I had no qualifications and no real options, so I became a bit of a drifter.'

He watched the woman set the table and then he picked up the glass of Merlot and drank slowly. It tasted of long ago times. 'You have to remember that these were the days before I joined the army – we seemed to spend most of our time drinking in bars like Chico's in the old Salisbury, watching life pass us by.'

'I've never heard of that place.'

'You wouldn't have – it was long before your time; they closed it down in '69. Anyway, it was not a place for respectable girls.'

'Is that how you see me?' Isabella asked wistfully.

Robert Doyle shifted uneasily on his chair. 'I don't know you well enough to make that sort of judgement.'

The food was simmering on the range and Isabella smiled to herself when she thought of Vlad, her friend from the Russian bar in Soho. What would Robert Doyle have made of him? 'So where did it all end?'

'With the war,' he said quietly. 'Nothing was ever the same again after Smith declared UDI. It changed everything and put an end to the simplest of dreams.'

Robert Doyle stopped speaking when the woman put the food on the table. The aroma was captivating and he could not remember the last time he had smelled anything quite as good. The spoon was barely out of his mouth before he was showering her with compliments.

'It's the herbs that bring out the flavour,' Isabella said, smiling in appreciation. 'One of Mother's old Spanish recipes.'

'You certainly seem to have inherited her culinary skills!'

'Well she was very passionate about everything: food, music, dancing.'

'Tell me about her.'

'That's the problem – I don't really know that much about her life. Dad once told me her father had been a fiercely independent Republican soldier. Maybe that is why she was so intense. Then Franco and his fascists swept

162

through Spain and she was forced to flee the country. Apparently she had a group of friends who managed to smuggle her across the channel to England and she lived there with an aunt, in the countryside. After the Second World War she returned to London and went back to her career as a dancer in a nightclub. That was where she met my father – the man she called "my Eduardo".'

'So you have her Spanish passion?'

The woman laughed the frivolous laugh that Robert Doyle found so appealing. 'I guess so!' She held out her empty glass and addressed him in a soft, teasing voice. 'Is there more wine?' When the glass was half full, Isabella put her finger over the rim and indicated for him to stop pouring. 'I think I'm going to have to slow down.' Then, reaching over, she placed her hand gently on his arm. 'Thank you for coming here and sharing your story with me.'

'No, it's me who must thank you for your hospitality.' Although the woman had moved away, the touch of her hand on his arm was still warm.

Isabella ignored the compliment and reminded herself to keep a hold of her faculties. But the wine and the man's husky voice were making it difficult. She needed to change the subject. 'So what were you doing before the war?'

'Well, I left Salisbury to work on a project called Operation Noah. They had just finished constructing the concrete wall across Kariba, which transformed the whole valley into an enormous lake. It was my job to relocate the animals from the islands.' He paused briefly and wondered whether to mention Emily, but decided against it. He had never been able to talk about her, and there was still too much pain to contemplate it now. 'That was the year before the Bush War. There was a drought – you might just remember it. By October there had been no rain for months. I can still remember the heat; a relentless sun beating down on a land already parched and turned to dust. The water had disappeared from the small dams around Kariba and most of the fish were dead. The Batonka told me that this was Nyaminyami's vengeance on the *wazungus* who stopped the flow of the Zambezi.'

'Who is Nyaminyami?'

'The serpent river god. The warning was there but we ignored it.'

Isabella remembered the year all too well; that was the summer her father had died and the summer Joseph had gone off to war. 'It was a terrible time,' she whispered.

'The worst in living memory; the water holes dried up so the animals drifted back towards the lake, easy pickings for the predators that lay in wait by the water's edge. The corn didn't grow so the grain ran out. I used to drive past the reservations on the road from Mutare to Marandellas and see the skeletal cows seeking refuge under the acacia bushes, awaiting their death in the relentless heat.'

'It's particularly hard on the African tribesman, Robert, because the animals are their wealth.'

'That's right. With their cattle dead, they came in their droves to the towns, desperate for work. There was very little employment so many of them ended up walking the streets, begging for food and sleeping in doorways at night.'

'We had just moved back to Juliasdale,' Isabella said. 'Shazi and her family came to work for us at Sally's house, but the rest of the staff had to be laid off. God, that all seems so long ago now. What have we done to this beautiful country, Robert?' She was thinking of Kariba, the flooding of the Zambezi Valley and the displacement of so many families.

'Screwed it up I guess. It was late November before the rain finally broke the drought. I was working at the Hwange Game Reserve. At long last the waters rose and the tiger fish once again leapt the rapids, their silver coats shimmering in the sunshine. We would stand on the banks of the Zambezi River and try to catch them, which was almost sacrilege because they were so beautiful.' For a moment he stopped talking, his eyes on the rectangle of darkness that was the open front door. 'The long hot summer was over,' he said at last, 'and I left Hwange to join the army.'

'Robert, I have never heard anyone describe Africa quite like you do.' There was a mist in her eyes.

'Hey, enough of the serious talk,' he said spooning the last mouthful of food into his mouth before wiping his plate clean with a crust of bread. 'That was a great meal.'

Isabella glanced down at his empty plate. It was so good to feed this man. She felt a sense of satisfaction that had been absent for too long – since the times she and Joseph had spent together, sat at this very same table. 'Can I offer you more of the *caldereta*?'

'How could I possibly say no? Matter of fact, I don't know how I am ever going to face cooking for myself again.' Without looking up, Robert Doyle mouthed his thanks and tucked into the stew for the second time. And for the moment there was only the sound of him eating. When the plate was as clean as a new whistle, he pushed his chair back from the table. 'That was the best *caldereta* I have ever tackled! If there is any left I think I'll go for a third helping when this lot has settled.'

'There is a little left,' Isabella replied happily, 'or I can warm up the apple pie?'

Robert Doyle smiled his appreciation. 'I'd love some pie,' he said, patting his stomach, 'if I can handle it. Don't know when I last ate like this!'

'Well you are going to have to earn it – I would like to hear more of your story first.'

Robert Doyle ran his fingers through his silver hair. 'If that's all you want, it will be the easiest pie I've ever earned.' The smile was still warm on his gratified face when he tried to recall where he had left off. 'Let's see now; well, with the war coming there was only one thing I really wanted to do.'

'What was that?' Isabella asked, as she walked over to the sink with the casserole dish in her hand.

'Join the Special Forces.'

The words hit her like a sledgehammer. She put the dish on the draining board and held on to the worktop to steady herself. 'My Joseph was with the Selous Scouts,' she whispered softly.

'What was his name?' Robert Doyle asked, unaware of the effect the conversation was having on the woman.

'George. Joseph George,' Isabella said, after taking a minute to compose herself.

For a moment there was silence. 'Joseph George . . . no, I haven't heard of him. Where was he stationed?'

'In the Zambezi Valley and on the Zambian border. Where were you?'

'We operated from the Tete province right up to the Tangwena sector.'

'That's not far from here.'

Robert Doyle nodded. 'Just over the border in Mozambique.'

'You know, I used to wonder how Rhodesia could ever

lose the war with men like you and Joseph.'

'You are putting me into some pretty fancy company; there are better men than me in the graves at Chipinge.'

'You're being modest,' she said, smiling before looking into his eyes. 'So, where did you do your training?'

Robert Doyle had kept the past hidden, but it was somehow easy to talk to the woman. 'Well, it started with selection for the SAS in the Matopas Hills,' he began.

'The Matopas . . . yes, I went there once to see Rhodes' grave. Dad called it the land of Monomotapa.'

'It was once a part of the ancient kingdom of Great Zimbabwe.'

'From what I remember the land is very desolate – it must have been difficult.'

'Not really. I was young and working as a ranger – I knew the bush.' He recalled the trucks dropping them off individually with just an OS map and a rucksack filled with bricks. Then, walking through the tall grass, listening to it whisper to him in the wind, he followed a compass bearing across the dry yellow hills to a designated point he had to reach each day. 'After two weeks in the Matopas I could see the end of the road. The selection course had cut the original sixty recruits down to just the three of us.'

'What happened to the others?'

'They fell by the wayside. On the last day Whitaker, Mallon and I sat at a bar on Rhodes Avenue in Bulawayo, drinking Lion lager and reflecting on where our lives were going. Little did we know . . . '

Isabella looked at the table with its empty plates and clutter and decided to ignore the mess. 'Nobody knew in those days what was going to happen,' she said poignantly.

Robert Doyle reached over for the second bottle of

wine. 'Anyway, that's enough about me for now.' He removed a hunting knife from a sheaf on his belt and cut around the aluminium foil on the neck of the bottle.

The woman noticed him doing this and laughed. 'How are we ever going to domesticate you when you open wine bottles this way?'

'I still need a corkscrew.'

'Don't you guys just break the neck over a rock?'

Robert Doyle laughed. 'Only when we don't have a corkscrew and,' he paused to look at the woman, 'when we're not in the presence of a lady.'

Isabella slid the tool across the table. 'So you are on your best behaviour are you?'

He laughed again. It was so effortless being in the woman's company. He held the bottle over her glass and looked up with an enquiring glance.

She nodded and smiled, stopping him again when the glass was half full. The story fascinated her, but it was not just that – it was also the storyteller. He seemed to be constantly alert; whenever Shamari pricked up her ears, Robert Doyle stopped speaking and would listen. Only when the dog put her head back down onto her paws would he continue. Having survived the Bush War, the experience had obviously solidified within him but one objective: to stay alive. He and the dog were the same beings, predators – much like the gunmen in the old Westerns she loved reading as a child.

But there was a gentle side to him – one that greatly appealed to the woman.

The room was harsh in the glow of the electric light, which mesmerised the hawk moths thrashing themselves against the naked lamp. Isabella walked over to the dresser and picked up a candle in a terracotta holder. She placed it on the kitchen table and struck a match, holding it to the wick. When the candle was ablaze, she switched off the overhead light and sat down opposite the man. The warmth from the tiny flame cast flickering shadows across the wooden table, bathing the woman in its soft light.

Robert Doyle was unable to pry his eyes away from her. She raised the glass to her lips, watching him over the rim, and he noticed that her face was flushed. He had to remind himself again that he had come to the farm for water and directions only, and yet . . . yet there was an aching for something more, especially when she looked at him in this way. The wanting was so tangible there seemed to be nothing but the woman sitting across the table, hanging onto his every word; a woman as fresh as the first daisies that scattered the hills with colour in the early spring.

Singing and shouting, carried on the wind from the squatter camp, broke the spell. Isabella glanced towards the open door. 'Robert, you fought the Africans. How do you feel about them now they have taken the country?'

'Well,' he said, settling back into his chair, 'it is *their* country after all. Ever since I was a child I was brainwashed into believing that they were our servants. And during the war I couldn't care less about the colour of their skin – they were the enemy, and I hated them each time one of my men died. But it took an incident towards the end of the war to show me the futility of it all.'

'Really? What happened?'

'We were on an operation near Chigamane in Mozambique, trying to prevent the terrorists from crossing Gaza Province into Rhodesia. The K-cars had just decimated a village suspected of harbouring the guerrillas.'

'K-cars?'

'Killer cars. Helicopter gunships. After the attack I was walking down a track towards a *kraal* when I came across an old African sitting outside his burnt-out *rondavel*. His skin was as wrinkled as a crocodile's and there was such sadness in his eyes. The gunships had wiped out his entire family, all except for one boy who stood by his side. The *piccanin's* bloated stomach stuck out in front of him and flies were crawling all over his face.'

'That's so terrible,' Isabella grimaced. 'Why is it that the children suffer most?'

'Old men and children – it was not their war. I can never forget the way the *madala* struggled to his feet and removed his dusty old hat; he had no teeth and when he greeted me I could see that he was in terrible pain. But it was his humility that was the hardest thing to stomach. For the first time in my life I felt ashamed to be wearing the uniform of a Rhodesian soldier.'

'How on earth did you carry on after seeing such atrocities?'

'Well, you obey orders and convince yourself that you are fighting for your country – we didn't know how it would turn out. The aggression destroyed what friendship there had ever been between us.' Robert Doyle picked up the water glass and then, realising it was empty, put it back down on the table. 'You know, before the war I loved Rhodesia – the people, the animals the mountains and the sunsets – it was my Africa. Now I fear what is to come.'

Isabella returned from the kitchen sink with a fresh

jug of water. Filling the glasses, Robert Doyle noticed again the ring on her finger. 'Look, I'm sorry to be forward – but please tell me about Joseph?'

'He was killed while fighting in the Zambezi Valley – there's really not much more to tell. You must have seen it all so many times yourself.'

'Yes, but you never quite get used to it. I still sometimes ask myself what it's all about. In the last operation alone, I lost my whole troop – five men I had served with throughout the war. In fact, that's what I was thinking of when you caught me on the *stoep*.'

Isabella reached over and placed her hand on his arm. 'You know the answer Robert.'

'Yes, maybe you are right. I'm sorry to have brought up the subject.'

'Please don't be. It's easier to talk about it now. I do sometimes wonder why I still wear the ring – I guess it's my way of remembering Joseph. We were teenage sweethearts.' She smiled shyly, her eyes on a photograph perched on the dresser shelf. 'I met him at the local rugby dance,' she said, trying to lighten the mood. 'My best friend Lindsey persuaded me to come along and swap my jeans for a dress. As a teenager I was a stick insect, tall and thin.' She leaned back in her chair and put her knees against the kitchen table. 'I can't believe now how short my hair was – I must have looked like one of the boys! And I could out-run and out-fight most of them, too. But the best part of every day was when I threw off the stuffy school uniform and got into my baggy shorts and khaki shirt – my "freedom rags", I used to call them.'

'Somehow I can't imagine you as a tomboy.'

'Nor could my mother! She dreamed her daughter

would be a proper girl in flowing colourful skirts and was horrified that Africa was making me so wild.' Isabella reached forward, picked up her wine glass and recalled those magical days, running barefoot through the bush with the innocence of a child. 'When I was not marking time at school, I was out riding my horse across Ingombe. The only downside of this "reckless abandonment" was that I scared all the boys away; none of them would come anywhere near me. Until Joseph.'

'Your first love?'

'It was eighteen years ago. Many things happened that night. Perhaps though, most significantly, it was the night that I finally said goodbye to my childhood. I guess you never forget your first boyfriend.'

Robert Doyle continued to watch the woman, fascinated by the way she ran her fingers through her hair when she searched for the words from her past. 'Where was Joe from?'

'He came down from northern Rhodesia after the federation broke up; to work as a manager on a tobacco farm near Rusape. Like many Rhodesian men, he saw romance through a beer glass, preferably one full of Lion lager. Even his proposition, when it came, was on a Rusape pub terrace – let's just say it wasn't how I'd imagined it would be.' Isabella stood up and walked over to the kitchen window. In the distance the twinkling candles lit up the native compound and she was reminded of the lights on that long ago dance floor.

'We were all like Joe once,' Robert Doyle said, interpreting her thoughts. 'It was a case of what you see is what you get. I was—'

'I know,' Isabella said. 'Maybe it's the books I read but

I do ask myself whether there is more to life. Perhaps I'm just too fussy.'

'That's not always a bad thing.' There was the suggestion of a teasing smile in Robert Doyle's deep-set eyes. 'And I bet your father was happy to see you tamed.'

'He was ecstatic,' Isabella said, replicating the grin, 'although to this day I'm still not sure whether he was pleased to see me sorted, or just delighted to have another pair of hands and some male company on the farm.'

'What about your mother?'

The question, asked inadvertently, killed the conversation. It was as if a switch had been flicked and the easy-going laughter had been replaced with confusion. Isabella turned towards the sink, her eyes fixed on the darkness beyond the kitchen window. She recalled the day the fever came and took Francesca away. It had been as if someone had closed a door that had remained locked forever. Even after all these years she sometimes found it difficult to face the beginning of a new day without her mother. To her father it had been devastating.

'She died three years before I met Joseph.'

Robert Doyle's face registered surprise. 'I'm sorry. I . . . I seem to be asking all the wrong questions tonight.'

Isabella shook her head. 'There was a time when I could not talk about my mother, but it's getting better. The only downside is, living out here at Ingombe . . . the memories are always with me.'

'I know what you mean; but wherever you go, pain is a companion you carry.'

Isabella's intuition told her that Robert Doyle's own anguish also involved a woman. Picking up her glass from the kitchen table, she swallowed the last of the wine and was about to ask him the question that was on her lips when a hostile cry from outside the house shattered the quiet atmosphere of the kitchen and the security light illuminated the yard.

'*Hondo umfazi!*'

Isabella dropped the glass in alarm and turned to the window, searching the shadows beyond the trees. But there was nothing to be seen, only the eerie silence of an African night.

Robert Doyle was on his feet. 'Lock the doors and windows and dim the lights! I'll take a look around.' Although his voice was gentle, there was a sense of urgency and his reaction frightened the woman.

'I don't understand,' she said, her eyes continuing to search the yard.

There was no reply. It was only when Isabella turned around that she realised she was talking to an empty room. Robert Doyle, like the dog, had disappeared into the darkness.

She locked both doors before finally closing the shutters on the windows. It was then, while securing the last of them, that she caught a brief glimpse of Robert Doyle standing beside the Land Cruiser. He was holding something in his hand and it was a few seconds before she realised it was an automatic rifle.

And when she looked again he was gone.

17

The aggressive scream in Shona brought a renewed fear to the little homestead. Robert Doyle understood the language, but why this shout of war? He paused for a moment in the deep shadow of the roof post before stepping out into the glare of the tungsten security light and pulling the heavy door shut behind him. There was no sign of the assailant, only his calling card – an *assegai* embedded in the ground below the wooden steps. Tied to its shaft were the feathers of the hooded vulture, which to the Africans is a symbol of death, and he knew that this would seriously frighten the woman were she to find it. With that thought in mind, Robert Doyle pulled the spear out of the earth and disposed of it in the bushes below the *stoep*. Then walking over to the Land Cruiser, he retrieved his rifle, torch and night vision glasses.

The cicadas had at last resumed their singing. Listening quietly to the noises of the night, the man pursed his lips and emanated a low pitched whistle. Minutes later the dog responded, emerging from the shadows of the bush. With the animal at his side he rubbed his hand over the bristled fur and then whispered softly, 'Track Shamari.' The dog immediately understood the command and disappeared silently into the velvet undergrowth.

Robert Doyle continued to wait patiently in the protective shade of a low branch, the selector switch of his FN set to single shot. This was the rifle he'd acquired on the black market after the war, an automatic identical to the weapon he'd carried in the conflict, except for the serial numbers, which had been surreptitiously erased.

When his eyes had eventually grown accustomed to the darkness, he followed the dog down the valley through the thicker bush, taking an almost direct line towards the squatter camp. He knew all too well what the spear meant. Last year, when driving through the Zambezi Valley, a similar incident had taken place on a farm outside the Hwange Game Reserve. This was an area that had seen some of the bloodiest fighting of the Bush War and it was land that the boys of the soil wanted back. Zimbabwe had recently gained her independence and ZANU had been determined to clear the area of all white inhabitants. The smallholding on the edge of the reserve had received an eviction notice that ordered the *wazungus* to vacate immediately. It had been nailed to the door of the homestead with an *assegai*, similar to the one that had been thrown here. The owners refused to leave and summoned lawyers to fight their case in the Harare courts. But days later a hundred-strong mob, high on *mbanje*, had attacked the farm, killing the farmer, his brother and their three sons. They then raped the women and the two young daughters, one of whom was only eight years old, before burning the bodies. It was a clear warning to the white man that ZANU would not tolerate opposition and the land would be returned to the Africans.

Now it would appear that the same crowd had arrived at Ingombe. It was not his fight, yet Robert Doyle was unable to stand by and let these thugs intimidate an innocent woman. But why had only one soldier attacked the house? In all probability the *tsotsi* had either been high on *mbanje* or drunk on *skokiaan* and perhaps assumed the woman was living alone. Certainly, when he had first arrived at Ingombe there had been no visible sign of either soldiers or villagers but then the African compound was set well back from the drive and hidden by a wall of evergreens, a common enough practice in the days of segregation – and this was their Africa, Robert Doyle thought churlishly.

His thoughts were interrupted by a blood-curdling scream that split the night, followed by the faint, far-off sound of a dog growling. An image flashed through Robert Doyle's mind as he ran, of a long-ago incident, an ambush near the border of Mozambique. Shamari had attacked a terrorist – bringing him down like a lion – and the four other guerrillas had scattered for their lives. And before he reached the clearing, he realised he was too late.

Shamari was standing over the prostrate figure, the brown hackles erect on her body. A wooden *knobkerrie* lay abandoned on the floor and a machete was still in its sheath on the soldier's belt. There was no rifle, which led Robert Doyle to believe that this had been an act purely of intimidation.

'Stay,' he whispered softly to the dog.

The animal backed away from its quarry. From the smell of *skokiaan*, it was now obvious that the young pretender had indeed been trying to make a name for himself. But was he from Mugabe's Fifth Brigade? And had he announced his intentions to his fellow soldiers? If so, his comrades would surely come looking for him. Like despotic animals, these bullies rode the winds of change while they held the reins of power. But often they were not paid and would simply desert their units and return to their *kraals*.

But this soldier, lying in a pool of blood, was going nowhere. There was an enormous gash in his throat and chest where the dog had ripped open the flesh. If by some remote chance the *vanamukoma* did find the body, hopefully they would assume a leopard had killed their comrade, Robert Doyle thought. But he was a cautious man and he needed to know what was happening at the squatter camp. This was his opportunity.

He called the dog and the animal moved affectionately to his side, tense and alert. For perhaps ten minutes they waited silently in the dark. At one point during the quiet vigil the dog's ears pricked up and Robert Doyle thought he heard a twig snap. When there was no further noise he put the faint sound down to his imagination, which these days tended to play tricks in the dark. It was time to go.

Slowly, he edged his way towards the *kraal*. The cloud cover, which was low over the valley, resembled a crocheted table cloth, its many holes allowing the moon to occasionally reveal her face and dispel the inky blackness. And when the light again fell on the land, Robert Doyle saw what he was looking for: a tall fever tree, which would give him a commanding view of the makeshift village. He smiled to himself when he thought of how the tree was given its name: early settlers camped beneath them where they grew prolifically in swampy ground and weeks later they would be overcome with a fever and die. It was many years before they discovered that in fact the tree was not the cause of their deaths; they had been bitten by mosquitoes and malaria was their killer. By that time, however, the name had stuck. And, as if to reinforce the substance of the fable, Robert Doyle heard the drone of the tiny insects' wings. He hated them with a vengeance and would rather confront any of Africa's predators over her deadliest killer – at least he could see the animals and snakes. When the mosquitoes' noise abated, the feeding would begin and he waited for one of the insects to settle on his wrist before swatting it. A tiny red blot of blood appeared on his skin and, realising that it was only a matter of time before he'd be plagued by the virulent insects, he clamoured up the stem of the tree, careful to avoid the thorns, and settled into a stout branch.

Using the night vision scope, he noticed a large section of the bush had recently been cleared and trees had been replaced by straw-roofed mud *rondavels*. The little settlement was expanding and eventually, like a cancer, it would cover all of Ingombe and kill it. In the centre of the compound was the *shebeen*, the drinking area where a large group of about forty soldiers sat around a fire, smoking *mbanje* and singing their war songs. Occasionally one of them would signal to the women for more *chibuku*. Many were the times that Robert Doyle had drunk with them around their campfires and in their beer halls, in the days of the old Rhodesia, when the SAS mixed freely with the African regiments. He knew they could not hold their liquor. That was when the fighting started.

And to the young men, it was a way of life.

On the edge of the square a *madala* was playing his *mbira* while in front of him a young girl danced provocatively to the beat of a drum, watched by an appreciative crowd of drunken youths. They were spellbound by the sight of the slender naked body, her skin shining with perspiration, reflecting the light from the dancing flames. Oblivious to the audience and drugged on *mbanje*, she moved rhythmically, in a world of her own.

Robert Doyle was mesmerised. The ebony-skinned girl reminded him of Nubuco. Now there was a woman with an insatiable appetite for both men and raw whisky; a woman who could dance as well as she could fight. Before she had joined the freedom fighters, she had fought alongside Robert Doyle. But all of that was a long time ago. Nubuco had died in the early days of the Bush War – destined to never grow old, she'd lived her life as though there was no tomorrow. He smiled when he remembered the girl with the bright red bandana and how they would drink *chibuku* before going out to hunt terrorists. But it was Nuboco's *toyi-toyi*, war dances, which were the stuff of legend. By performing them she was able to incite the guerillas to acts of almost foolhardy courage. But she had a predicament, in that her loyalties lay with the dollar rather than the cause, and it was this that led to her downfall.

However, the dancing at the camp below was not a war dance and, as such, Robert Doyle accepted that the solitary soldier's appearance at Ingombe had not been orchestrated. Nevertheless, the *vanamukoma* were here in strength and it was clear from their numbers that they were on a mission to reclaim the land.

Subconsciously he reminded himself to talk to the woman about what he had seen.

The music intensified and the young topless girl, dressed only in a loin cloth, reacted instinctively to the beat, moving faster and faster, her bare feet tracing circles in the dust while she gyrated in the light of the flames. Eventually she collapsed to the ground through sheer exhaustion and another girl entered the square to take her place.

The drums continued to roll but Robert Doyle was

satisfied with what he had seen and, slinging the FN across his back, he descended the fever tree.

From out of the dark bush the dog materialised, sniffing the light breeze blowing towards the compound. It carried a scent that was making Shamari nervous.

Unbeknownst to the man, he was being watched and the danger was coming from the bush. At any other time he would have picked up on Shamari's signs, but there were other things on his mind and he was eager to get back to the farmhouse.

It was an oversight that he would come to regret.

Robert Doyle was a man without complications in his life – no wife, no family, or at least not any that he was aware of. He travelled light, with his jeep, his rifle and his dog and it seemed like he'd spent his entire life either fighting or drifting. And he was tired of it all. But there was also the farm in the Drakensberg, a smallholding in a grassy escarpment, which would benefit from the gentle touch of a woman. Could it be Isabella? But when he thought of this he was again troubled with uncertainty. Did she reciprocate his feelings or was his presence merely a welcome diversion from the danger so close to her farm? Whatever the reason, thinking of her resurrected a desire in him that he did not recognise.

In the distance the first clap of thunder hammered the air. The animal sensed the rain but was reluctant to abandon the scent of an intruder that she was keen to investigate.

Again Robert Doyle failed to recognise her anxiety.

'OK Shamari,' he whispered, patting the dog in a reassuring manner, 'let's go.'

Hesitantly turning her head away from the bush, the dog slavishly followed her master along the narrow path that led up the valley towards the house, where there was a woman, a bottle of unfinished wine and a night that was still relatively young awaiting them.

The tranquillity that precedes an African storm hung solemnly in the air. Suddenly the thunder struck again, smashing into the night and drowning out the sound of the distant drums. It was followed by a blinding flash of forked lightning, momentarily turning the night into day. And then the rains fell, as only rain can fall in Africa – a sheer blanket of water cascading down out of the black sky. The bushes offered little protection and within minutes both Robert Doyle and the dog were soaked to the skin.

Through the curtain of water, the homestead emerged, silhouetted against the backdrop of the black mountains. Lights glowed in every room and radiated a warmth that welcomed both man and dog.

On seeing the house Shamari broke into a run through the puddles and across the muddy yard to the front porch, where she jettisoned the excess water off her coat with an almighty shake. Then, sniffing the old worn blanket that lay discarded in the corner of the *stoep*, she settled herself down with a disgruntled look on her whiskered face.

Robert Doyle's only thoughts were of a warm kitchen and the woman. And for once in his life he was grateful that he had lost his way, for by doing so he had found her.

18

Sengamo stretched his limbs in the marula tree – the land was covered in a blanket of darkness with only the odd star, twinkling like a glow worm, scattered randomly amongst the clouds. It was time to return to the army camp. There were *umfazis* there and it had been a long time since he had last touched soft skin. He thought of the Shona women. They knew how to seduce their men. First they talked with their eyes and their desire was like a web from which there was no escape. Then they watered their victim with *chibuku* so he would become ripe. And finally they took the seed deep within their bodies. To Sengamo, all women were beautiful and would it not be extremely bad manners to reject their advances?

Excited by the thought of his next liaison, Sengamo descended the tree slowly, conscious of the *imbwa*. Like most Africans, he had an inbred fear of large dogs and not for one moment did he allow his attention to be distracted from the animal. Once he had reached the base of the marula tree, he melted into the shadows and waited patiently.

Sengamo saw the *tsotsi* before he heard his shout.

The night sensor had switched on the tungsten security lights and illuminated the aggressor's figure as he entered the yard. He saw the man lift the *assegai* above his shoulder. Then he saw his back arch before he hurled the weapon towards the house where the shaft embedded itself in the grass to the side of the *stoep*. The tracker knew well the threatening scream of '*hondo*', for war had been shouted many times across this land.

In the nebulous bush, the dog paced around, anxiously sniffing for any sign of the *tsotsi's* scent, undecided on whether to wait for the *mzungu* or chase the prowler. Then the front door opened and the light from the hall cast a shadow of the soldier's profile across the *stoep*. Closing the heavy door behind him, he retrieved his rifle and whistled softly. Minutes later the *imbwa* disappeared into the bush.

But where was the woman?

Sengamo glanced up towards the house. The lights had been dimmed and there was only the faint glow from a crack in the kitchen shutter.

Suddenly a piercing shriek split the night.

It was the chord of death, an intimidating sound that the tracker had heard all too often. Ensuring his scent was up-wind from the dog, he followed the *mzungu* down the valley. In spite of the low humidity, perspiration dampened his shirt with its pungent odour as he cautiously edged his way through the bush. There was little to concern him because, in his hurry, the soldier was leaving an easy trail to follow in the bright moonlight. Eventually Sengamo came to a small clearing and it was there he saw the carnage.

Through the small window in the canopy of dark leaves, he watched the *mzungu* drag the corpse into the thick bush. Then a cloud covered the moon and pitched the night once again into darkness, shrouding both man and dog. Minutes went by and still there was no movement. This disturbed the tracker and he moved forward. In doing so he stepped on a twig and froze at the sharp retort. Although noises at night always seem louder to the perpetrator, the African was taking no chances and he remained perfectly still.

Only when Sengamo was sure that the danger was over did he retreat to his original position, from where he watched the soldier climb the tree. Having witnessed what the dog was capable of, he forced himself to remain vigilant.

After some twenty minutes the *mzungu* descended the tree and called to the *imbwa*. Without looking back, they started the long walk back up the valley towards the farmhouse.

One thing was for sure, the tracker was not sorry to see them go.

The smell of rain was stronger now and it reminded Sengamo of his planned excursion to the army camp and his desire for three things: a rifle, food and, if he was lucky, shelter with a young woman from the impending storm. When he was sure it was safe, he rose quietly to his feet, stretched his cramped muscles and proceeded towards the sound of the drums.

The layout of the squatter camp was still embedded in his mind. Taking care to avoid the army tents, he moved silently towards the *rondavels* where he was able to blend into the shadows. Embers from the huge fire in the centre of the compound whirled their way skywards, casting reflections onto the brown walls of the mud huts. Here, in the veil of shade, his position gave him a commanding view of the youths drinking in the yard, their automatic rifles propped casually up against the wooden ceremonial pole. It was plain to see, from the euphoric state of both the soldiers and the dancers that the *skokiaan* was flowing freely.

Young girls, their ebony bodies gleaming with animal fat, danced on the soft sand in rhythm to the animal skin drums, their naked brown breasts bobbing provocatively while their arms flailed in a state of frenzy. Lustful eyes ravaged the bodies and each time the *msichanas* threw themselves into the air their colourful loin cloths parted and evoked drunken laughter from the inebriated crowd. When one girl would collapse through sheer exhaustion another would leap to her feet to take her place, sustaining the hypnotic performance of ancient tribal war scenes for the *mudzimu*, the African's ancestral spirit.

And all the while the drummers beat their drums, the girls danced.

The eurhythmics excited Sengamo, who saw the women only as ripe cherries, waiting to be picked. However his attention was fleetingly diverted by the low growl of thunder manifesting itself over the distant mountains. Although it was too far away to register with the soldiers around the campfire, Sengamo knew that once the imminent storm burst, they would pick up their Kalashnikovs and take shelter, which would make his task that much more difficult.

Then the beat of the drums intensified almost as if they were anticipating the thunder and lightning. There was no time to be lost. Checking his surroundings, the tracker was about to move forward when a sentry strutted down the baked earth path, searching for a spot to relieve himself. The three stripes on his arm indicated he was a sergeant. Momentarily taken by surprise, Sengamo pressed himself against the dark corner of the mud hut, his body taut as a violin string and ready for action.

It never came. The sentry was too engrossed in his bodily functions to notice anything untoward. His Kalashnikov was slung over his shoulder and an ammunition bandolier straddled his chest above the grenades hanging from his webbing belt. A walking armoury, Sengamo thought, as he watched the sergeant pass close by. Then a smile flirted across his face as it dawned on him that this had been the second time in twenty-four hours that he'd made contact with the enemy. And both times the men had had their hands full.

The sergeant belched loudly, fascinated by the urine spray splashing the mud wall of the *rondavel*, scenting the evening with the grainy smell of *chibuku*. Clearly not anticipating any problems, his self-assurance betrayed his careless attitude towards surveillance.

Tonight this would all change.

Sengamo pulled the homemade steel knife from the buckskin sheath hanging on his belt. As the sentry returned to the deep shadows between the mud huts, the tracker struck. Clasping the intoxicated soldier's mouth with his left hand and repelling the shout that was already in his throat, he plunged the ten-inch metal blade deep into the sentry's chest. The body collapsed without a sound. Then, supporting the dead weight, Sengamo dragged the corpse into what appeared to be a deserted *rondavel*, the scarcely audible noise of boots scraping on the ground absorbed by the revelry around the fire.

There was no time to waste. Working swiftly in unfamiliar surroundings, Sengamo removed the soldier's AK-47, ammunition belt and grenades before stripping him of his camouflaged jacket and beret. A small candle burning dimly on a battered tin plate threw a feeble light on the dark interior of the hut, revealing a mat and blankets covering the earth floor. These he used to hide the body.

It was then he noticed the small table on top of which stood a wooden gourd, which emitted a faint smell. *Muti*, herbs – he was in the *nganga's* hut. 'Ah ha, this is good,' he said to himself. Witchdoctor's huts were only ever used for ceremonial occasions and as such the corpse ought to remain undetected for some time. Unlike most Africans, Sengamo didn't set much store by the superstitions surrounding the *mudzimu* and he nodded in satisfaction at the place he had randomly chosen to dispose of the body.

Removing the magazine from the AK-47, he was surprised to find it filled with ammunition. Just as astonishing was the action of the Kalashnikov, which not only worked well, but, from the smell of the gun oil, it had been recently maintained. Finally he checked the grenades to ensure the firing pins were secure. Then, dressed in the uniform of the *vanamukoma* sergeant – a disguise that would allow him to pass through the camp undetected – the tracker cautiously exited the deserted hut.

It was the smell of a cooking fire that attracted him to a distant *rondavel*, set away from the army tents. Through the open doorway he could see a woman's profile, highlighted by the dancing flames that licked the cast iron pot and, although she erred slightly on the large side, she was young. This was how the tracker preferred his women and he could not believe his luck.

Then, remembering the story the *madala* had told him of the girl who had been raped in this same compound, Sengamo wondered whether his sudden appearance might alarm the woman, which would cause her to alert the soldiers over by the campfire. Hesitating for just a moment, he decided it was a risk worth taking and he entered the *rondavel*.

The girl glanced up from her cooking pot. 'Eeeeh, who are you?' she gasped in mock outrage, secretly admiring the tall soldier.

'I am the one sent by our esteemed president to look after the people,' Sengamo answered. 'And you look like you are a *msichana* in need of protection.'

'Is this what you think?'

'*Yebo*. Are you on your own?'

The girl laughed at the cheeky question. 'My father is away in Mutare,' she said, a coy look on her face. 'So it is good that you offer this protection! Can I pour you a *chibuku?*' There was a teasing tone in the Shona woman's voice – she was making him ripe because she wanted his seed, the tracker thought, relieved that he had found a willing conquest.

The girl reached for a plastic mug and filled it with the cloudy liquid. 'Please,' she said, offering it to Sengamo. 'I have meat in the pot and *muputabayi* – there is enough unleavened bread for both of us.'

Sengamo feigned reticence. 'It is only my duty to protect you.'

The girl smiled and lowered her head while she continued to stir the stew. The braids of her hair fell towards the fire. Occasionally another dry twig caught and a flame would reach up and embrace the pot, painting shadows on the circular walls of the mud hut. Then, looking up, she noticed the medal on Sengamo's chest. 'My father would be very pleased to know I am taking good care of one of our country's war heroes.'

'The pleasure is all mine!' Sengamo smiled again. And

in the faint light of the little fire his brilliant white teeth flashed.

This was going to be a good night.

The crack of thunder killed the sound of the drums. It was followed by an enormous flash of lightning, like the forked tongue of an adder. Briefly lighting up the interior of the hut, it disappeared as quickly as it had come, allowing the damp darkness to return.

Then the rain began to fall in sheets on the thatched roof of the *rondavel*.

The young girl moved towards the protection of Sengamo's arms; the smell of wood smoke and her naked breasts appealed to the young warrior.

Yes, it was going to be a good night, the guerrilla said to himself, a very good night indeed.

19

The storm swept down the valley with a vengeance. Isabella was sitting in the kitchen staring at the shuttered window when the first clap of thunder reverberated across the distant hills and a bolt of lightning wrenched the darkness apart, illuminating the faraway mountains and bringing light to the depth of the night. African storms usually filled her with excitement; 'the Ingombe fireworks', her father used to call them. But that was a long time ago and with this storm, and the threat that had preceded it, came a sense of foreboding.

Another bolt of lightning struck the *kopje* just above the house and the lights flickered. In the top drawer of the dresser was a box of candles. Isabella placed one into each of the four terracotta holders before distributing them around the room. She felt for the box of matches in the pocket of her skirt but decided against using them until it was absolutely necessary.

Where was Robert? Looking through the crack in the wooden shutter on the hall window, she searched the perennial darkness for any sign of the man and his dog, but only the msasa trees, their naked branches flinging around in the wild, were visible.

Beneath them, in the spectral shadows, stood the Land Cruiser, strong against the tempest. It comforted her because it was the only tangible proof that Robert Doyle was still at Ingombe. In the kitchen the half full bottle of

Merlot lay unattended on the old scrubbed-pine kitchen table. It no longer held any appeal for the woman. But the biggest regret was that Robert Doyle had been torn away before finishing his story. It was like reading a novel and finding that the last ten pages were missing out of the book. And she yearned to hear more from this strange man who sat with his back to the wall and told her tales from another era.

The only sound to break the silence was the loud tick-tock of the wall clock. For a moment the simple timepiece mesmerised Isabella as the hands circumnavigated the face, moving slowly from one digit to another, like a weary old man walking with heavy steps.

She was in this other world when the shrill ring of the phone made her jump. Living in isolation on this wild frontier, Isabella had soon learned to always keep the phone within easy reach – it was her only means of communication with the outside world and to lose it could spell the difference between life and death. And yet she still expected the worst every time it rang at night. With trepidation, she lifted the receiver from its cradle.

'Issy! Is everything all right?'

The woman breathed a sigh of relief, her fears temporarily dispelled by the sound of the voice coming down the crackling line. 'Hi Danny!'

'There's a real bad storm on the way. Is your electricity still working?'

'It flickered a few times but it's OK. I have the candles ready if the lights go out.'

'Do you want me to come over?'

Isabella's eyes settled on the bottle of wine. If she let on to Danny that she was frightened, he would drive straight over. But a stranger had walked into her life that night, and there was so much more she wanted from him. For a moment the memories stirred her body; the sound of his voice, the way he laughed and, perhaps even, loved. But, oh God, what was she thinking!

'Issy are you there?'

'I'm fine Danny,' she lied. 'You know me and storms; I'm going to open a bottle of wine and watch the rain sweep the valley. Call you if there's a problem – promise!'

She had never before lied to Danny and in doing so she now felt a tinge of guilt.

'I have to go to Mutare tomorrow. Just for a few days – is there anything you want from town?'

'No, I don't think so, ah, unless Vicky has wine?'

'OK, I'll look in on her. I'm staying with Doug – give you a call when I'm back.' Nothing in his voice indicated that he was aware of her duplicity.

'Give my love to Doug and Maggie.'

There was a short pause as Danny searched for words to prolong the conversation but in the end all he said was 'Take care and ring me if you need me.'

She thought she detected disappointment in his voice. Perhaps her friend was more intuitive than she gave him credit for. 'See you in a couple of days Danny.'

After half filling the wine glass from the bottle of Merlot, Isabella took a small gulp, trying to maintain the equilibrium between sobriety and recklessness. A clap of thunder overhead was followed by a bolt of lightning which again devoured the night, heralding the rains. When the squall eventually came, the torrent hammered on the corrugated iron roof and the lights flickered before plunging the room into darkness. Isabella fumbled for the matches in her pocket and was about to strike one when the power returned, bringing with it a sense of relief.

This was ridiculous: at any other time she would have weathered such a storm on her own – although she lived alone, she rarely felt lonely. How had the presence of a stranger brought about such a sudden change in her?

But she knew it was not just down to Robert Doyle – the drums and the intimidating shout in the dark were what had frightened her.

The storm was short lived. As quickly as the rains had started, they receded, leaving behind a state of tranquillity in the valley. Switching on the radio, Isabella was greeted by a newscast. 'More killings in Matabeleland, more farm reclaims and more political brainwashing.' It was all too depressing. The weather forecast was slightly more encouraging: 'Storms over Nyanga are moving south towards Swaziland. The next two hours will see bursts of prolonged heavy rain. This should clear before dawn leaving a–' That was enough. She turned the knob on the tuning band and stopped when she came to a violin concerto that she recognised; it was Mendelssohn and it reminded her of her mother.

And, for a brief moment, Robert Doyle was forgotten.

20

Minutes later the rain returned. Although still wild, it lacked quite the same intensity and, with the volume turned down on the radio, Isabella was able to listen to the sound of the wind bending the branches on the msasa trees as it howled its way through the valley.

From the hall came the faint sound of a knock. Was it the wind rattling the front door? There it was again – a bang that could be heard above the inclement weather. She walked cautiously into the room and listened. This time the loud knock rattled the front door.

'Who is it?' she shouted out.

'It's OK Isabella.'

Recognising the deep husky voice, the woman slammed back the bolts on the heavy wooden door. It flew open in the wind and Robert Doyle stood sheepishly in front of her, drenched to the skin. 'Oh Robert – look at you, come in – quickly!'

He removed his hat and ran his fingers through his hair, pushing it away from his forehead. 'I'm sorry. It's been quite a storm,' he said, stepping onto the quarry-tiled floor in the hall and leaning his rifle against the wall. The wind was driving the rain into the house and it took much of his strength to force the door shut.

Aware of the woman standing close to him, Robert Doyle turned around.

Then she was in his arms.

In later, quieter times, Isabella would ask herself what had driven her into Robert Doyle's embrace that night. Had it been the intimidation of the war cry or the sheer relief of his safe return? Whatever it had been, in the comfort of his strong arms she felt a shameless emotion surge through her body.

Her head was under his chin and her sobbing muffled against his chest. She was conscious of the dampness on her blouse. And yet none of this mattered, not the storm or the aggressive shout – nothing, except that he was back, driving away the fear.

Robert Doyle did not know how long he'd been standing in the little puddle of water holding the woman. The ache in his body cried out for her and his only wish was that he could stay there forever. And then he felt the woman stir and her head move away from his body. She lifted up her face to look at him. There was a question in her eyes that did not need to be answered with words. Her lips parted and her hand moved to the back of his head.

And then it happened.

Robert Doyle was aware of his clothes, rough and wet, and his hands, callused and hard, but where their lips touched it was soft and warm, and he could taste the wine on her tongue. Her back was arched and her fingers were in his hair, gripping it and forcing his head down. And then he was floating like a fish eagle on a thermal and he kissed the tears in her eyes, tasting the saltiness.

She held him in her arms, her thin blouse almost as wet as his shirt. Through the fabric he could feel her small breasts against his chest and the hunger was more than he could bear. And then he felt her shiver. 'I'm sorry,' he apologised, 'my shirt is soaking you.'

'It doesn't matter.' The woman put her arms back around his waist. 'I don't want you to go Robert.'

Her body trembled and he put his head down to the place where her neck curved and kissed the soft skin. The tightness in his throat was restricting his breath.

'Oh God, Isabella! I have not felt like this in such a long time.'

'Nor I, Robert.'

'It was when I saw you for the first time, standing on the *stoep* that I . . . '

She lifted her head off his chest and laughed, clearing the air of its solemnity. 'What, when I was holding the rifle and threatening you?'

'It wasn't much of a threat with the safety catch on,' he said with a grin.

Isabella laughed. The relentless rain continued to hammer on the door and droplets of water fell around their feet, making tiny puddles on the clay tiles. Then she stepped back and, gently holding his hand, led him down the corridor to the bathroom. 'Robert we need to get these wet clothes off,' her voice was both warm and controlling, 'and then into a bath.'

He smiled shyly before turning to face her. 'There really is no need,' he protested mildly, 'I have a change of clothes in the Land Cruiser.'

'It's no bother,' she insisted, in a voice that left no room for argument. 'And anyway, it's my fault that you were out there in the storm. I'm not having you catch your death of cold.'

Robert Doyle smiled to himself. How many times had he walked through the rain and then merely sat in the jeep to dry off? But there was no denying this woman. He noticed how she had again taken control of the situation; this was one argument he wasn't going to win. And, he admitted, it felt good to be fussed over. Standing back, he looked at the woman, her hair shining in the light of the low wattage lamp and her little snub nose scattered with tiny freckles and then onto the soft mouth that he had just kissed. Finally, he looked into her warm brown eyes, which still carried a hint of concern. 'Isabella, I'm sorry I had to leave you but there is nothing to worry about now.'

'I missed you Robert. I have never been so frightened, not since the war.'

'It's all right now,' he repeated, moving cautiously towards the woman.

She smiled, putting an end to the discussion – she didn't want to face it yet. All of that was for later. For now there were other things on her mind, not least the man standing awkwardly in front of her. She opened the hot water tap and watched the steam fill the room with condensation. 'Go and fetch your clothes. We have the rest of the night to get to know each other.'

There was a rascally glint in his eyes. 'Will it really take that long?'

Isabella smiled to herself. 'Not if you do as you are told,' she said, pushing him towards the door. 'Now go!'

The fierce rain of a moment ago was now just a fine drizzle and, moving his rifle out of sight, Robert Doyle opened the front door and walked out across the yard to the jeep. Shouldering the small carpet bag, he locked the Land Cruiser and made his way back towards the house. When he reached the top of the steps, Shamari raised her head and whimpered. Robert Doyle paused in his stride and walked over to the dog. 'What's happening to us old girl?' There was only the blink of her eyes for an answer as he stroked the dog's head and waited for her to settle back down on her blanket. Only when she was comfortable did he return to the house.

The woman was still sitting on the edge of the bath running her hands through the water, testing the temperature. Then, satisfied it was warm enough, she closed the taps.

Robert Doyle stood uncomfortably in the bathroom doorway and smiled reticently. '*Hola* Isabella,' he said, as if saying it for the first time. And perhaps he was.

She took his hand and brushed his lips with a kiss. The invitation to respond to her flirtation was in his eyes but she pushed him gently away. 'Come into the kitchen when you are ready and I'll pour you a glass of wine.' The words were said with the confidence of a woman who knew what she wanted.

Robert Doyle closed the door and undressed. Hanging his wet clothes over the edge of the toilet, he stepped into the tepid water. The delicate fragrance of the bath salts hung lightly in the steamy air. It was a scent he was unfamiliar with, yet he enjoyed it. As he lay in the water he thought briefly of the events of the night. There was no need to talk about the incident until the next day, he decided. After all, a little information can be a dangerous thing and it would only frighten the woman.

The thought was still on his mind when he pulled the plug on the bath. The warm brown water spiralled down the drain, taking with it the dust of the road. Removing the razor from his carpet bag, he then contemplated the face that stared back at him through the misty glass of the bathroom mirror. The crow's feet were evidence that there had once been laughter on his face. But it was to the eyes he spoke. Could he stay the night with this woman and then walk away from her as if nothing had happened? No, he couldn't. He knew very little about her, and yet he wanted to know so much more.

But did not confessions bring complications?

And then he thought of the story an old man had once told him, many years before. It was a strange tale, about a waterfall that was fed by a little river, and it had taken him some time to figure it out.

During the summer, when the river was just a stream, a waterfall trickled gently over a granite outcrop, cascading to a pool far below. The waterfall flirted with the stone but the granite was strong and she resisted her charms. Then the rains came and the river intensified. The water rushed to the pool, battering the granite with an urgency that was difficult to resist. But still she was defiant.

Finally, one day there was a big storm in the mountains and the river became very angry. She sent down a torrent of water, which covered the granite in a shroud of spray and blinded it with a colourful rainbow, like a bracelet of diamonds hanging over the black stone. It was then the granite succumbed to the waterfall and in doing so she became nothing more than a pebble lying in the pool.

Robert Doyle mulled the fable over and over in his head. Why had it come back to haunt him now? These had been the words of a melancholy *madala* and somehow he could not associate them with the woman Isabella. Or was there a hidden agenda? Was Isabella the waterfall?

And when he asked these questions he found it difficult to shake off his anxiety.

The internal walls of the farmhouse were thin plywood partitions through which the faint sounds of a familiar song played on the radio. Robert Doyle opened the bathroom door and stepped into the corridor where the music was louder. His thoughts were again with the woman in the kitchen and there was the first sign of a flush on his face when he saw her standing beside the range, staring out of the open window. In her hand was a glass of wine. But somehow she seemed far away. A restless wind was playing with her hair, blowing it across her face and taking with it her fragrance. At that moment in time she was still a stranger and he wondered then if he would ever really cross the divide.

Outside the rain had died away completely and a faded moon was trying to show her body through the broken clouds. Light trembled in the window, reflecting itself in the wine glass, and Robert Doyle was reluctant to destroy the magic. '*Hola* Isabella,' he said again gently, so as not to frighten her.

She was in a world of her own and had not heard him enter the room. When she did see him, she reached over and picked up the wine from the table and then, with just the slightest hint of embarrassment, handed him the glass. They were very close. Strands of her hair fell towards her neck and were lost in the shadows of her profile.

She was not of this room.

'You are so very beautiful,' he said.

Her frivolous laugh enchanted him. 'Not really. But if I am to you, that is all that matters,' she whispered in an audacious voice. '*Salud* Robert.' Their glasses touched and at last there was no longer any awkwardness. '*Salud mi extranola*, my stranger.'

Isabella's glass was still half full when she put it down on the table and moved slowly towards him, impetuous and light-headed with the wine, holding him with her dark Spanish eyes. Then her arms were around him and there was no escape as she hunted for his lips.

The sensation was one of falling from a great height; off a barren mountain that had been Robert Doyle's refuge from the outside world, a mountain so different from the one he was now sharing with the woman. Here there were flowers that carried a scent on the breeze, gentle paths that ran haphazardly across the landscape. Here there was no tomorrow, only the present where he could wander, lost in her loveliness, drugged on her fragrance. He tried to capture her breath as if it would propel him to the skies and beyond. In his preoccupation with the woman, none of what went before mattered now, not the thoughts and questions he had asked himself standing in front of the bathroom mirror, not the recriminations or the *madala's* stories . . . none of it. Because with her body pressed tight against him, there was only this room and only now.

Isabella held his hand and led him down the narrow corridor to the bedroom. There was no longer any laughter on her lips. When she stepped into the room and unbuttoned her blouse, the contrasting paleness of her breasts against her tanned body was too much for Robert Doyle and with unrestrained hunger he walked towards her.

She smiled, that tease of a smile again, and held out her arm, whispering in a soft voice: 'Wait Robert,' while she continued to hold him with her dark eyes. Then, releasing the wide belt holding up her skirt, she let it slip down her body to the floor.

There was suddenly an urgency to Robert Doyle that had long lain dormant. He picked the woman up and carried her to the bed and where once they were lost, now they were together as if their very lives depended upon this moment.

***

Isabella had given herself completely to the stranger. She turned on her side to face him, the thin cotton sheet barely covering her breasts. 'Are you happy Robert?'

'Happier than you could ever know Isabella.' He let his finger trace a line down her face towards her shoulders. Then he reached forward and kissed the long curve of her throat while her hand held the back of his head. 'What has happened here will never be lost,' he whispered into the softness of her skin, 'because here I have died.'

Isabella shuddered when she heard the words. They sounded like remnants of a long-forgotten poem. Letting her fingers run softly through his hair, she held his head against her neck. The dim table lamp cast a pale glow around the simple room and in that moment in time she did not identify with anything other than the man beside her – not even with the black and white photographs in their dark wooden frames. They belonged to another time and another place.

Robert Doyle closed his eyes and in the warmth of the woman's arms, sleep came easily. Isabella felt his body relax against hers. There was no tiredness within her. Tomorrow was a long way away and she wanted only to perpetuate this night. She could hear the soft breathing of her man as he slept. Her man. Her Robert.

How easily the words formed in her mind.

The moonlight crept through the transparent curtains and the faded cloth danced in the breeze, billowing gently through the crack in the window frame. 'I feel a part of you now Robert,' she whispered to the wind, 'and no matter where you drift across our Africa, I will always be with you.' In her fantasy a puff of air had captured the lyrics and carried them away, to a place where they could only be murmured on still nights, a place where the easterly winds caress the mountain peaks.

A place of her dreams.

Any relationship with this man would not be easy. She knew that. He was like the wind, and the wind cannot be tamed. Just when you think you have caught it, it changes direction and is gone again; down across some valley or over some distant mountain, roaming free.

***

Robert Doyle woke with the first light of dawn. It took him a few minutes to realise where he was and then the sleepiness, like the darkness, rapidly dissipated. The woman was lying on her side, the profile of her body transparent beneath the thin, white cotton sheet, and he felt again the desire he had first known last night when he came out of the storm. He put his arm around her waist and buried his face in the scent on the nape of her neck, holding her as if by this very action he could keep her. Then somewhere out of the dark the old man's story returned and he silently cursed the words away. After all, what did any of this have to do with waterfalls and rocks?

Isabella opened her eyes and rolled over to face him,

unashamedly allowing the sheet to fall away from her body. A lazy smile crossed her lips. '*Buenos dias* Robert,' she whispered, letting a solitary finger trace a path across his face. Then, opening his lips with the top of her nail, she touched his tongue with her finger and rekindled the lust. And by the look on her face, he could see she knew what she was doing.

Lost within her body, there was only the sound of her scream piercing the stillness of the morning. 'Robert! Oh, Robert!' she cried, lying motionless on top of him. 'What is happening to us?' Then, closing her eyes, she held him within herself, trying desperately to prolong the moment.

To Robert Doyle, it was like coming out of the darkness and into the daylight. Her body was over him and he hardly dared move because to do so would be to lose her. All he could see was her pale skin, flesh that was normally hidden to anyone else, and he was briefly reminded of an illusion that had once come to him a long time ago.

Driving along a narrow strip of black tarmac, which ran straight as a die through the desert, he saw a mirage shimmering on the horizon. Yet no matter how far or how fast he drove, he never reached the water. It always stayed tantalisingly close, tempting him, and yet, frustratingly, it was always out of his reach. And when the sun disappeared and the heat of the day dispersed, the image vanished. Was this woman, with her dark brown hair fanning the pillow, a mirage? There was a mist in his eyes as he gently caressed the hair that flowed across her shoulder and he held her with hands that were big and strong, rough from a life of toil.

And yet the woman felt only a softness, her eyes on the defining line across his body where his shirt had marked a border below his neck. Above this line his skin was bronzed from the sun, while beneath it the translucent white melted into the sheets. 'Robert, I cannot remember there ever being a time quite like this. I am so happy.' She moved her eyes from his body to his face. 'Was it good for you too?' she asked, in a voice of youthful innocence.

A ray of sunlight broke into the room. Filtering through the curtains, it cast shadows on her skin. He pretended not to have heard the question. She was so very beautiful that for a moment he could not speak. 'For me, Isabella, it was as never before.'

'This is a good happiness then, because it is shared. But has there ever been anything like this for you before Robert?'

He knew he could tell the woman anything she wanted to hear but this was not a time for untruths. 'Only once, and that was a long time ago.'

She moved close to him and let her head rest against his chest. 'There has only ever been one person for me too,' she whispered languidly, 'and that was also a long time ago.'

Robert Doyle let his fingers run down her bronzed shoulders to the pale skin below her waistline. He remembered a time some years ago when he had travelled across the Namid, to a place where the desert winds blow through the barren mountains, where they whisper in the tall grass on the edge of the plains. He looked down to where the sheet lay above the perfect symmetry of her body. 'There is a place I know in the desert where the winds talk to you. It is a place that is both peaceful and beautiful. When I lie here next to you, listening to the echo of your voice, I am reminded of this place because I know that only I will ever be able to hear the words.'

There were tears in her eyes. 'We have only been together for half a day, but I feel like I have known you all my life. You have released something inside me that has been lying dormant for too long. And it is engulfing my whole being.' She repeated one sentence after the other with such urgency, almost as if time itself was a dying commodity. 'Is it possible after such a short time together that I should feel no shame?' She seemed desperate to be understood. 'Does this make sense?'

Robert Doyle brushed her cheeks with his lips. 'It makes much sense, Isabella. There is no shame in love and time has nothing to do with feelings. All we have done . . . is find each other.'

It was Sunday morning. Robert Doyle's original plan had been to get back on the road. In six hours he could cross the South African border and reach the Drakensberg before nightfall. But lying next to this woman, in a homestead on the edge of Nyanga, he felt no incentive to go. However, there were practicalities to consider.

'Come on lazy bones, let's go and see what the night has left us after the storm. I'll feed Shamari and take a look around while you rustle up something to ease the hunger pains.'

Isabella laughed as she watched him pull on his old blue jeans. His stomach was flat and muscular but the tiny blond hairs on his chest were now more white than yellow. Why, oh why does time destroy everything? she asked herself.

He finished dressing and looked down at the woman lying languidly on the bed sheets. She reminded him of a painting of an anonymous nude he'd once seen hanging in a gallery. At the time he could not understand why the artist had obscured her face. 'If I fill in the detail, what is left to the imagination? Now she can be whoever you want her to be,' had been the artist's explanation. And looking at the woman, he realised how much truth there was in that simple statement.

Moving over to the bed, he placed a kiss on her stomach and slowly let his lips move up her body to her face, where his mouth lingered on hers. '*Adios* Isabella,' he said. And then he was gone, a fleeting figure disappearing down the corridor. She heard the front door open and Shamari's greeting. And then it closed and all was quiet.

The imprint of his body was still faintly visible on the sheet. Isabella traced her fingers over the shadow and then reluctantly she climbed out of bed and walked to the bathroom. Her image appeared briefly in the mirror before the steam from the shower finally obliterated it. The warm water made her body tingle as it ran in tiny rivulets across her skin, washing away the redolence of last night's passion. There was just the first hint of a tummy above her long thin legs and, smiling in satisfaction, she let the soap follow the contours across her stomach, filling the pores with its scent.

The morning was relaxed and Isabella dressed slowly, exercising care over what she picked to wear. Tight jeans that emphasised the curves of her figure were perfect. To complement them she chose a pale silk blouse which lay revealingly across her small breasts. They were not only garments that she was comfortable in – they made her feel attractive.

The bed was in a mess and the room had a stuffiness about it. All of this could wait until later, she decided, as she opened the faded curtains to let the sunlight into the room. Another perfect day.

There was no sign of either Robert Doyle or the dog. The drumming of the cicadas had disappeared with the night, as had the singing from the squatter camp. Suddenly Isabella remembered the disturbing events of the previous night and she made a mental note to ask Robert Doyle about them when he returned.

But it was not upmost in her mind; her attention was on the lourie birds dancing across the branches of the msasa trees before diving into the corn fields in search of the first meal of the day. Their action prompted the woman to return to the kitchen. Humming to herself, she set about preparing breakfast, wondering how she was going to explain Robert Doyle's presence to Shazi the following day. Or was it presumptuous of her to assume that he would still be at Ingombe by then? Then she smiled when she thought of her middle-aged maid who was rather old fashioned when it came to relationships.

The steam from the kettle cast a mist over the kitchen window and Isabella once again felt satisfaction in preparing a meal for the man. When the switch on the kettle turned itself off, she spooned coffee into a jug and poured the boiling water over the granules, letting the aroma from the African beans percolate throughout the room.

Reaching up for the bowl of sugar, a birthday card on the plate rack above the range caught her eye. It was from

Danny and already the edges were frayed from the heat. For a moment she reflected on her friend. Never mind about Shazi; how was she going to tell Danny about Robert Doyle?

But then, she assured herself, Danny was only a good friend . . . wasn't he?

21

The sun of the new day was starting to raise its head above the mountains of Mozambique. In the distance Isabella could just make out the tall figure of Robert Doyle below the dam, wrapped up in his bush jacket against the morning chill. His rifle was across his shoulder and he had one arm on the stock and the other on the barrel. Shamari loped alongside him and neither one looked like they had a care in the world.

Then they disappeared from view into the heavy bush.

She thought again of the night. Their lives had been changed irrevocably. And when she thought how easy it would have been for him to have missed her place yesterday, she shuddered. Coming down from Nyanga, he would have passed other farms around Tucker Gap and could have stopped at any one of them. But then, like her mother, who perhaps had a touch of gypsy blood, she believed in fate.

Her only concern now was how it would all end.

When she next caught sight of him, he was walking at a pace through the short grass at the upper end of the valley. Caught in the early morning sun, filtering through the canopy of the msasa trees, he appeared to almost shimmer over the *veld*. It was from this very same spot that Isabella used to watch her father coming back from the African compound before breakfast. Both men walked with a purpose and she realised then how alike they were.

The valley was magical in the morning light. The grass verges to the side of the track, now unattended, ran in wild abandon into the darker bush. Small white clouds wandered aimlessly above and it seemed that everything the sun touched turned to gold, transforming the landscape into a kaleidoscope of colours, almost as if an artist in the sky was painting the scene. In the distance a flock of wild geese left the dam. The snow-white squadrons, their large flapping wings reflecting shades of flamboyant orange, skimmed the river on their journey towards the far-flung mountains and the tranquillity seduced the woman. This was what made it so difficult to contemplate living anywhere else. Perhaps, she conceded, there was life outside the valley, but she had never, not even on her travels to Europe, seen anywhere as beautiful. And then there were the ghosts of her family. They were not malevolent spirits, but rather voices that spoke softly to her and, like the animals and birds, they held her at Ingombe.

The whir of tiny wings caught her attention. It was a phosphorescent blue butterfly hovering beneath the canopy of the swing seat, trapped in the canvas. Surely the insect deserved her freedom on such a serene day Isabella thought, cupping her hands and catching it gently before releasing it back into the wild.

Preoccupied with the butterfly, she failed to notice Robert Doyle's presence. It was Shamari's deep-throated bark that alerted her to him as he approached the crest of the hill, the bush hat pulled down low over his face, as it had been when she had first set eyes on him.

'Breakfast is ready!' she shouted as she waved.

'Sounds good – I'm starved!' There was a boyish grin on his face. 'Just give me five while I feed Shamari.'

The smell of sizzling bacon, sausages and mushrooms filtered through the farmhouse kitchen. When the woman heard the light tread of footsteps on the porch floorboards, she cracked the eggs and dropped them into the frying pan.

The breakfast would rein in any appetite. To Robert Doyle, coming in after a long walk, it was irresistible. 'Hey, Isabella, what are you doing to me?' The humour was back in his voice. 'I could taste the *boerewors* from the bottom of the valley.'

The woman smiled. 'It's one way to bring you back.'

'Are there other ways?' His eyes captured the setting. Like the lens of an intrusive camera, they missed no detail. And the scene filled him with a long forgotten warmth, one that he'd last shared with a girl called Emily somewhere deep in the Zambezi Valley.

But all of that was a long time ago.

Isabella sensed his presence beside her before she felt him. Then his arms were around her waist, one hand mischievously tracing the seam of her Levi's while the other rested softly on her stomach, exploring the tender space above her belt. She turned to face him, meeting his lips. 'Food first,' she said, realising that if she succumbed the breakfast would be ruined.

Robert Doyle laughed and moved back to the table. 'It was bath first last night.'

'I thought you said you were starved?' Pouring the steaming coffee into a large white mug, she walked over to the pine table and placed it in front of him. 'Perhaps this will satisfy you until the food comes.'

Robert Doyle put the mug to his lips. 'You know, your coffee is to die for.'

'I wouldn't go as far as that.'

'Trust me! I'm a connoisseur, having drunk everything from African chicory to Brazilian beans.'

'Wow, I didn't realise I was entertaining an expert! I'll have to up the standards.'

'You couldn't do that Isabella.' It was said in a way that suggested he was referring to more than just the coffee. And his eyes were on her.

She turned back to the stove, her cheeks flushed from the barely hidden innuendo. 'Where did you walk to this morning?' The question carried an underlying agenda: to change the subject and distract his attention.

'Oh, just down to the bottom of the valley.' His voice was level and calm. 'It's my early morning time with Shamari.'

'Did you get as far as the compound?'

'No.' He was reluctant to take the conversation any further.

Isabella put the meal on the table and refilled the coffee cups. The loud scrape of the kitchen chair told Robert Doyle there was something bothering the woman, but he remained silent and concentrated instead on the *boerewors*. In the prevailing stillness there was an atmosphere. He looked up from the table. 'Something on your mind, Isabella?'

The woman hesitated only briefly. 'What was all the noise about last night?'

After his earlier assurances he had hoped the subject would be forgotten. The fork was halfway to his mouth, suspended in mid-air, and he found himself acting indecisively. When he replied it was quick – almost as if he was trying to evade the question or perhaps hide the truth. 'Everything's fine,' he responded at last. 'I guess the *tsotsi* just got a little over excited. Too much *chibuku* – you know how it is.'

'Robert, please don't treat me like a child. I've lived here a long time on my own amongst these people and I would rather know if there is a problem.'

Right, so here it was – the opportunity to tell the woman she was no longer safe at Ingombe; his chance to persuade her to leave behind the instability of the new Zimbabwe. And yet, even as he thought this, Robert Doyle deliberated whether it was really his place to make these suggestions. After all, he was only passing through this valley – or was he?

Take it slowly, he reminded himself, looking deep into Isabella's trusting eyes, which held on to his every word. And then he wondered why he had ever contemplated concealing the facts – this was a woman who could handle the truth. So he told it as he saw it: plain and straight. 'The guys down at the squatter camp are getting restless. They want your farm. Not just your farm, but every bit of white man's land they can lay their thieving hands on. What happened last night was just the start. I figure it won't be long before they make their next move – I've seen it all happen before.' He stopped talking and looked out of the window. 'I hope I'm wrong this time.'

For just a moment Isabella was shocked. 'I think you are, Robert. We have an assurance from Mugabe.'

'What sort of a guarantee is that?'

'I guess it's the best we can hope for – it's all anybody has these days.'

Robert Doyle nodded and picked up his mug, trying to come to terms with the glazed inscription painted into the clay which read 'Rhodesia is forever'. Even that was a joke. Rhodesia was history, dispatched to the waste bin. Then he looked at the woman he had made love to the previous night, in the bedroom with the framed pictures of her past. Something had happened there. Yes, that was it; there the past had died. Now there was a glimmer of a future and the woman sitting across the table from him was perhaps a part of that expectation.

It came down to a simple choice – ignore the danger or leave for the Drakensberg as soon as possible. All of this he thought of before speaking, before framing the question from which he knew there would be no going back. 'Do you want me to stay on at Ingombe for a few more days, just to ensure nothing gets out of hand?'

A few more days! Isabella's face almost betrayed her emotions. After all that had happened, she had assumed that leaving would be the furthest thing from his mind. How fragile the situation was, she thought. With Danny, she didn't even have to try – he was always there for her, which was a comforting thought. However Robert Doyle was different and, in spite of what had happened the previous night, she nevertheless wondered where it was all going to end. But then what was more important, Ingombe or Robert Doyle?

It was a question she would come to ask herself again and again – many times over.

What she did know, though, was that after just one day she was falling for this man. But she tempered her feelings because something was still holding her back. 'Robert . . . although I'm worried about Zimbabwe, I can't leave the farm.' She stood up and walked over to the window, pointing her arm towards the mountains where her gesture was meant to encompass not just the immediate land, but everything that lay beyond it. 'Dad built all this from nothing, from dust,' she said softly, her eyes as damp as her voice. 'Sometimes, while he was working on the house, I would join him in the evenings and we would sit around the campfire listening to the roar of the lions or the distant sound of a child screaming in a faraway *kraal*.'

Robert Doyle walked across to the percolator to refill his mug. 'More coffee?'

Isabella shook her head. 'When we finally moved in here I made friends with the local children. Oh, we'd have such fun together – while all the other kids at school were into Enid Blyton, stories of *The Famous Five*, we were brave warriors in leopard-skin battle dress. And our king was Lobengula. I can still hear our war cries reverberating across the valley.' She laughed at the memory.

'You are fortunate to have lived here in the good times, when the country was still raw.'

'I know I'm lucky Robert, but what I *really* love about Ingombe are the yellow sunsets over our little dam at the bottom of the valley. I remember one time when a pair of hippos took up residence and mated there. They would keep us awake at night, wallowing and grunting like submerged submarines.'

'You still have *hippos* in the dam?'

'No. They were all shot during the war. So were most of the elephants! I will never forget them and their babies – the way they hold on to their mother's tails with their little trunks. It was only the bull elephants that really worried us when they stood their ground in the middle of the road, guarding the herd, their ears all erect above their wrinkled heads, almost daring us to advance.' Her voice trailed off as her eyes crossed the valley and settled on the distant squatter camp at the crossroads. 'Yes, the elephants have all gone now,' she said, in an accusative tone, 'replaced by squatters and soldiers. But you know, Robert, there was a time when the natives would dance for fun. Now they only dance with hate.'

She tore her eyes away from the camp below and looked at him. 'Don't *you* want to stay Robert?' she asked, in the capricious voice of a child, echoing the moment in which she'd first asked him to stay the night.

Cleverly, she'd managed to turn the situation around once again. And by doing so, she had put him in a position where he was now reliant upon her.

But it did not matter to Robert Doyle. His whole world had shrunk down to this farm and the woman and he did not want to lose her. There had been too many nights alone. Pushing the chair back from the table, he stood up and walked over to the window. 'I told myself, last night that I could not love you and then leave.' There was a worried look in his eyes and his next words were soft, barely a whisper. 'I meant that Isabella.'

She went to him and he held her in his arms. Shafts of sunlight bounced through the prisms of the handmade glass in the kitchen window, their refracted beams throwing gentle colours across her back. She knew youth was on her side and she held him with an irreproachable look. Her smile said it all. 'There is nothing I want more than to be with you, Robert. And because of this, I need to understand that it is also what you truly want.'

Robert Doyle recognised what she was saying. He saw the scene unfolding before his eyes. Words now spoken would be redeemed later and so he chose them carefully.

'It *is* what I want Isabella,' he said, looking down at the woman. Her eyes were closed and he touched the strands of hair that fell gently across her face.

And he knew that once he took this path, there was no going back.

22

The darkness inside the *rondavel* embraced the tracker. He had accomplished everything he'd hoped for – a weapon, a good meal and a woman. The previous night had resurrected the old days, his moving between villages, a different girl in a different hut every night and he could not remember when he had last enjoyed himself quite so much, even if this girl was from the Mashona tribe, who he considered inferior to his ancestors, the Ndebele. But she was young and buxom, and when he had told her he was a soldier from the Fifth Brigade on a special mission to return tribal land to its rightful owners, she had been most impressed. The medal on his camouflage jacket had also excited her and in her ignorance she assumed her lover to be a man of special importance.

In spite of her infatuation, the girl would not have made a habit of sleeping with strange men; to the Mashona the act of taking the body constitutes a betrothal. However, the tracker had no desire to make the situation permanent. Because of this, his only option was to leave the compound while it was still dark and the girl slept. If she talked to the *vanamukoma* then they would be out looking for him, which would make the situation that much more difficult.

An intimidating darkness covered the village as Sengamo dressed by the dim light of the single candle. The sergeant's clothes were a good fit, albeit a little on the large side, but he found it strange being back in a uniform after all these years. Strapping the bandolier on over the camouflage jacket, he then fastened the dark green webbing belt that carried the grenades around his waist, adjusting the band until it felt comfortable.

Soon the first hint of dawn would penetrate the darkness of the hut. He picked up the AK-47 and glanced down one last time at the figure huddled beneath the thread-bare blanket. She lay in front of the dying embers of the previous night's fire, sleep having transported her to another world, which was just where he intended to leave her.

After blowing out the candle, Sengamo whispered his farewells and crept quietly through the bamboo curtain and out into the dark alley that separated the rows of mud huts. The early dawn carried a fresh dampness that was invigorating after the stuffiness of the *rondavel*. Drawing in a deep breath, he filled his lungs with the cool air. 'Ah! Almost as good as *tshwala*,' he said to himself.

He was about to move off when he felt something prick his flesh. It was the pin of the medal. The clasp must have come undone when he'd removed his clothes in haste the previous night. He had no desire to keep the Zimbabwean decoration so, in his frustration, he tore it off the tunic and threw it into the open doorway of a compound hut, figuring that it would make some young child very happy to wake up and find it.

The only other sound to disturb the early morning stillness was a scrawny, emaciated cat that dashed across the path with a shriek. Moving undetected across the short distance of open ground, Sengamo melted into the bush, searching for a vantage point that would allow him to observe the army camp.

As the first rays of sunshine struggled over the distant peaks and bathed the *veld* in a soft pink, they highlighted a small rocky *kopje* to his left. Perfect, he thought, clambering up the stone path to the summit of the hill from where the compound square was clearly visible.

The narrow column of blue smoke spiralling into the still air was the only indication of life in the drab, olive-green tented city. Most of the soldiers were still asleep after the celebrations of the night before, suffering from their overindulgences.

Fashioning a makeshift bed in the elevated rocks, the tracker then allowed himself the luxury of a cold *mealie* stalk. The fruit brought a buoyant laughter to his lips when he remembered how keen the girl had been for her 'soldier' to be well fed. If only she knew the truth.

The years on the run in the Bush War had taught the mountain man to grab sleep when and where the opportunity presented itself and after the activity of the previous night he needed the rest. Before long the girl was again dominating his dreams.

It had been a good night for the young *umfazi*. She had been most obliging; happy to be playing her part in accommodating a warrior of the new Zimbabwe. The soldier came with the dusk and brought with him such strength, the likes of which she had never seen before. And it was proper, she told herself, that she was able in her small way to repay a war veteran of her country. After all the years of struggling there was now a new future and a part of her expectations lay with this warrior. How fortuitous that her parents were away visiting her aunt in Mutare. She did, however, consider that it might be prudent to keep the encounter a secret, since she was sure her father would not approve of her rewarding soldiers in this manner.

The first strains of the new dawn appeared through the cracks in the bamboo curtain. Rolling over on the lumpy mattress, the girl pulled the blanket closer to her body, shutting out the early morning chill. Her first job of the day was to feed the chickens but after the frantic lovemaking of the previous night she needed her rest. The soldier had disappeared but the side of the bed, on which he had lain a short while before, was still warm. Where was he? Perhaps outside relieving himself, she thought. And, thinking about him, she eased the blanket down to look at her body. It was much bruised, but she felt only warmth and a deep contentment. 'Eeeh,' she said to herself, 'what a man this was.' He would make good strong children. But she did not even know his name. Perhaps she should ask the commander about him. But then she remembered his words before she fell asleep: 'This must be our little secret, *zuri*. It will make much trouble for me if my superiors know that I am taking liberties with the local girls.' It was the first time anyone had ever called her beautiful. But then what if there was a child? Her father would be furious and they would have to marry. And first he would have to pay the *lobola*, the bride payment. The girl lay on the mattress, confused. Her father wasn't due back until the following afternoon so she still had sufficient time to decide what to do.

In the meantime she would keep her promise to the warrior.

23

Robert Doyle splashed his face with cold water. The bathroom mirror reflected an image he found difficult to reconcile, a softness that had replaced his usually gaunt look. Isabella's clothes hung on a hook behind the door. There was just a faint hint of fading perfume that still impregnated her blouse and he wondered if the smell would always remind him of the woman, or would the memory of it eventually fade away, as it would soon do on the cotton? Then he thought about the conversation they'd had after breakfast. Isabella had a passion for this land and deep down he realised it was not going to be easy to persuade her to move on. But then in reality, what would it take – another *assegai* or a drunken mob?

Although he had made a commitment, the *vanamukoma* worried him. However he decided to bide his time and wait for the right opportunity to talk to her again.

Crossing the kitchen floor, Robert Doyle noticed steam from the percolator hovering in the air. But Isabella was nowhere to be seen. It was only when he walked out of the front door that he saw her on the *stoep* with a cup in her hand, seemingly in a world of her own, much like he had found her the previous night by the kitchen window. Beyond the security fence the morning sunshine filtered through the msasa trees and only the splash of a white cloud, which resembled a sail in the sky, disturbed what was an endless sea of blue stretching from horizon to horizon.

'A Zim dollar for your thoughts?' he said, putting his arms around her waist.

She turned to face him, a light-hearted laugh on her lips. 'Is that all they are worth?'

He smiled. 'You tell me.' He took the empty cup from her hand and set it down on the work surface before kissing her on the cheek.

'Coffee?'

'I'd love a cup,' he said, taking a seat in the bentwood chair. The weaver birds were attacking the fruit trees and beyond the river a swarm of lappit-faced vultures, high on the thermals, forged out circular patterns in the sky. Another kill, Robert Doyle said quietly to himself. Then his thoughts were interrupted by the sound of the woman's footsteps on the wooden floorboards. She placed the mug on the table and moved over to where he sat.

The waistband of her jeans was close to his face and she held his head against her body. 'Look at this Robert,' she said, pointing to the farm. 'It's where I sit every morning with my coffee watching the mist hanging over the valley. It lingers in the trees until the sun breaks it up.'

Robert Doyle relaxed his face against the denim fabric of her jeans.

'Then I come back here with my tea in the late afternoons to watch the acacias throw shadows across the bush. This is also the time of day that the guinea fowl will venture down to our murky dam for a drink. On the odd occasion I walk to Shazi's *kraal*, I'll chase them and always end up laughing when they scatter into the undergrowth before I can get to them.'

He closed his eyes and tried to picture the tranquil scene the woman painted.

'I love that walk – it's so primeval. Those people are living in a time warp; nothing has really changed since their ancestors lived there.' And thinking of the natives, she remembered the *kraal* and the open fires and the wood smoke that curled its way up into the endless blue sky, and the naked *piccanins'* faces that would light up when they recognised her. They would shout their greetings in Shona while she listened to the faint harmony of their mothers' singing in the fields.

'But it's the evenings I love best,' she said softly, watching the lourie birds dancing in the fig trees, 'sitting here with a beer, reminiscing. In fact, that's what I was doing when you arrived yesterday – watching the sun set and thinking of the old days before the war.'

Robert Doyle said nothing. A gust of wind picked up a small brown leaf and blew it across the yard. It rode the currents in the sky and as the breeze subsided, the leaf fell to earth where it waited patiently for the next flurry to move it along. What a simple existence to be totally subservient to the wind, he thought, as he stood up to face the woman.

She pulled him towards her body. Strands of her soft brown hair obscured his face, buried in the nape of her neck. Her fingers were in his hair, running through the silver curls, and his hands moved instinctively to her hips. There was no resistance. Then, lifting his face, she kissed him long and hard. Eventually she pulled away and looked at him intensely. 'I was planning on walking to the river today.'

Over her shoulder, Robert Doyle saw Shamari lying under the shade of a small tree fuchsia, her head on her paws, and he knew the invitation did not include the dog. Picking up the cup of coffee, his eyes crossed the valley and he could see the thin green line where he knew the river must be, just beyond the distant trees. 'Do you know what the Mashona call the river?' he whispered, putting the cup back down on the table.

Isabella shook her head.

'*Mupfuri*. Roughly translated, it means "one who passes by".' A moment of sadness touched his eyes. 'Like the river,' he said pensively, 'we all pass by.'

'How long have we known each other Robert?'

'Just over half a day, I guess.'

'That's a lifetime to a dragonfly.'

Robert Doyle understood the implication of the statement immediately and he no longer saw the road out of Ingombe. He only saw the woman.

Suddenly afraid that time was of the essence, Isabella spoke softly into his chest. 'Everything is so fragile in Zimbabwe. We have to live for today.' There was a sense of urgency in her voice. 'Robert, the river is where I used to swim as a child! Will you come with me?' Her eyes were soft and warm. 'Tell you what, why don't we have a *braai*?'

'Sure,' he nodded. 'Shamari can stay here and look after the house.'

The dog was still sitting patiently in the same spot, but at the sight of her master she came swiftly to her feet and nuzzled up to the harsh fabric of his denims. Robert Doyle stroked the wiry fur on her forehead and the dog lifted her head, a warning in her melancholic eyes. For perhaps just a minute he tuned into the animal's perception and together, in the dusty yard of Ingombe, they were once again man and beast, in perfect harmony.

But the moment was short lived.

24

When they set off for the river, Robert Doyle adopted the lead. The valley was changing from green to gold and a gentle breeze swayed the branches of the msasa trees, rustling the leaves and forcing them to fall to the ground. They ran lightly over the grass and eventually settled in heaps beneath the acacia bushes. Only the local tribesmen now used the earth path down the valley and in places it had totally disintegrated, reverting back to the way it had been long before the white man came to the Eastern Highlands.

Silken webs, home to the infamous tiger spiders, sporadically spanned the narrow overgrown section, catching their unsuspecting prey and holding it captive in the intricate smooth strands. Robert Doyle had once walked into one such web in the Zambezi Valley. He and Emily had been patrolling the river high above the gorges when it happened and it was an experience he did not wish to repeat, having had to remove half his kit to find the spider. 'Robert, how come spiders can get you to take off your clothes quicker than I can?' Emily had asked when she had finally managed to stop laughing.

The memory brought a smile to his face.

Isabella was not privy to the amusement. Her thoughts were on the river and the little pool that held so many memories.

The last time she had been there was with Joseph, long

before the Bush War, yet it seemed like only yesterday. She could still see herself jumping over the stepping stones that formed the path across the river, trampling over the cool heather and lying in the yellow grass with the smell of the earth in her nostrils. In the evenings she and Joseph would sit in front of the log fire at the old Rhodes Hotel, drinking Amarulas and telling the tourists tales about the wild fruit that the liquor comes from, and the elephants that eat it.

The tall man walking in front of her reminded her of the elephants. His *veldskoens* softly padded the ground and in a strange way he seemed to subconsciously avoid the loose twigs, much like a wild animal. He was a part of the earth, the sky, the rivers and the mountains that are Africa, and his cautious eyes were everywhere, constantly alert and anticipating danger. But there was also something strangely intoxicating about his remoteness. Apart from the brief glimpses into his life during the Bush War, she knew little else about him. Perhaps this was the day they could lay bare their ghosts and form a relationship without restraints.

Robert Doyle felt her eyes on his back. He stopped and turned around.

'Am I on the right path?'

'Sure, this is the only way down to the river. There's an old bushman's cave at the bottom of the *kopje*. The path splits there – we take the left fork.'

'How far to the river?'

'Maybe half a mile from the cave?' Isabella was hot and there was a smudge on her forehead where she had wiped away the perspiration with the sleeve of her shirt.

'Do you want a break yet?' Robert Doyle asked, noticing her discomfort.

She pushed the hair away from her face. 'No, let's spend the time at the river.'

'Good call,' he shouted over his shoulder, moving off cautiously down the hill. On his belt, in a worn leather sheath, was the hunting knife, and from his right hand hung the automatic rifle, barrel down, an extension of his arm and ready for use.

Isabella's thoughts were still with the river when suddenly the illusion that all was well was shattered. Robert Doyle stopped dead in his tracks. Raising the rifle up into the firing position, he beckoned to the woman to be quiet.

'What's wrong Robert?' she whispered, in a frightened voice, all the while moving closer to his body.

'A black mamba,' he murmured without looking at her, 'there, below the overhanging rock, just to the side of the cave.'

'Oh my God!' she screeched, when she caught sight of the enormous snake. It was lying in the sunshine, its small, sinister eyes following their every movement. Having picked up their vibrations from the path, the reptile would have been aware of their presence long before Robert Doyle had spotted it. The erect head, high above the coil of its body, resembled the shape of a coffin – ironic, Isabella thought, since most of its victims end up in one. She huddled behind the man's back.

'Just stand still,' he urged. The FN rifle, like his eyes, never left the snake and, eventually sensing that there was no threat, the mamba put its head down and slithered off into the undergrowth.

'Phew, that was close,' Isabella said, clinging to his side. 'Why didn't you shoot it?'

'It wasn't doing us any harm,' he said as he lowered the rifle and eased the safety catch back on.

'It could have killed us!'

He shook his head and looked back to where the reptile had disappeared into the bush. 'Most snakes will only attack when they are threatened – mambas are fast but puff adders are probably the most dangerous. They lie in the sunshine on paths like this and they look like sticks, making them difficult to see. The Africans walk in the bush barefoot and step on them – that's when they strike. But they are not naturally aggressive.'

'You know, I've lived on a farm all my life and yet I'm still terrified of snakes.'

'Don't worry, it's gone now. Shall we go?'

She nodded. However, her eyes remained intensely fixed on the grass to the side of the path until she'd safely passed the spot where the snake had been lying.

When they reached the bottom of the hill, Robert Doyle took the left-hand fork past the cave as the woman had instructed, and continued down the narrow overgrown trail to the floor of the valley.

The brook, a tributary feeding the shaded river, was a slow-moving torrent. The water resembled a dark mirror and it reflected the overhanging branches that tickled its surface. 'Follow the stream up towards the mountain,' Isabella said, when she eventually caught up.

The path ahead was indistinguishable from the surrounding bush, but in spite of this it was an easy walk and before long they arrived at a deep pool where the grass ran down to the river. Water gently licked the shoreline and its mesmerising tranquillity cast a spell. For a minute Robert Doyle was speechless. 'This reminds me of the mountain pools where we used to swim – up in the Chimanimani,' he whispered, putting the rifle and the rucksack on the ground, 'in the days before the war.'

On the edge of the river, a pied kingfisher dived into the water with its head down and its wings folded back, only to emerge seconds later with a small fish struggling in its beak. The bird was a reminder that this little corner of Nyanga was still unspoilt and yet Isabella wondered how much longer it would stay like this. 'The only way to reach these deep pools is to use the path. I guess its isolation is what protects it. But they are relics from the past,' she lamented, 'from a time when the river was my playground.'

Brightly coloured dragonflies hovered above the water lilies in the clear still water of the pool. Everywhere was a confusion of colours; the yellows and pinks of the wild flowers mixed comfortably with the deep green of the msasa leaves against the backdrop of a cloudless blue sky. Neither of them spoke. There were no words capable of doing justice to this remarkable picture.

Then Isabella moved into Robert Doyle's arms and reached up for his lips. Her skin was hot from the walk and it radiated a hint of the lilies of the valley and when she kissed him, it was as if it was for the first time.

'Robert,' she said softly, 'we are alone here – no inhibitions.'

He lay on his side on the grass and watched her slowly peel off her jeans followed by her small lace pants. There is an art to removing clothing, and she managed it in a way that was all the more seductive for being uninhibited.

She was looking down at him and she felt no shame, only a deep satisfaction in knowing that he enjoyed watching her. Then, unbuttoning her blouse, she discarded it onto the little pile of clothing on the ground.

'You are so very beautiful,' he whispered, staring at her naked body.

'And you talk too much.' Standing over him with her arms by her side, she watched him remove his shirt and jeans. Then a lazy provocative smile crept over her lips and she lowered herself onto his body.

They loved like neither of them had ever loved before. And it took their breath away, as though for each of them it was their last time.

And perhaps it was.

The minutes seemed like hours when they finally closed their eyes. They felt each second die and thought not of the twilight that was still some time away, but rather of where they had just been.

Lying there under the outstretched arms of the mountain acacias, Robert Doyle wondered again how long this could really last. He was about to say something when she placed a finger on his lips. 'Remember Robert – no inhibitions.'

He watched, fascinated, as she jumped into the water. Ripples ran across the surface to where he lay, hypnotised by the scene unfolding before his eyes. And then he was with her in the cool darkness of the pool, where the water was touched by the chill of the mountains. Birdsong echoed above in the eucalyptus gums and the haunting cry of a fish eagle somewhere in the distance was the only sound to shatter the harmony.

'Robert, it's freezing!'

Treading water, Robert Doyle held the woman and felt

the softness of her naked skin. He kissed her and she laughed in that carefree way. And when he felt her shiver, he carried her, wet from the pool, to where the sunlight touched the soft grass.

In spite of the warmth, he shuddered and he knew it was not from the coldness of the water. Perhaps all of this really was just a dream, like the illusion of the girl he had once imagined across the room in the café. Her hair was as black as a raven. When she had taken his hand and led him out into the night, he had not known where he was going. But she had told him she loved him and nothing else mattered. There were many girls in many cafés but they were all in his mind. For a moment he was afraid to touch the woman lying next to him, apprehensive that she would disappear like all the others.

Her eyes were shut and her hair, brown with flecks of gold, framed her face and cascaded towards the ground. Reaching over, his hand traced a contour across her body and he felt her skin, perfect under his fingertips.

Unaware of Robert Doyle's fears, the woman opened her eyes and smiled at him.

And then he knew it was not a dream.

'Robert, can you open the wine, please?'

He unfastened the strap on the rucksack and removed the bottle and the corkscrew. When he pulled the cork, it sounded like a gunshot in the still air and a pair of kingfishers, sitting on a branch of a msasa bush beside the river, scattered for the safety of the trees. Was it the wine that was intoxicating or the way she moved in the light which so enchanted him? He was seeing her as if it was for the first time; seeing her like he had never seen her before. And in that moment he felt something he had not felt for so long. The woman was talking and yet he did not hear the conversation, only the music of her voice. And there were tears in her eyes. He reached over and she slid into his arms. Nothing seemed to matter now – not the squatter camp or even the state of the country.

Then she closed her eyes again and he knew she was someplace else, a place he could not go to. And all of a sudden he felt a yearning to have her back. 'Don't leave me Isabella. I can't follow your dreams.'

She looked up at him as she wiped her hand across her face to dry the tears. 'You don't have to – you know you will always be a part of them.'

He did not look at her again. It was too painful. He saw only the grass and the places where the wild flowers grew and beyond that the water where they had just swum. Then the moment was broken by the woman's voice and the practicalities of everyday life.

'We should start the *braai*.'

There she goes again, Robert Doyle thought, moving from one frame to another like a cine film, each clip cherished for just a moment. 'How can you think of food at a time like this?'

'You make me hungry!'

He laughed and laid large flat stones on a bare patch of grass beneath the high ground. Dry twigs formed a triangle on top of the paper, and when he lit the kindling, the flames licked the wood and the pale blue smoke rose up towards the trees. The woman lay naked, watching him with a coquettish look on her face.

'Are you warm enough?' he asked.

She nodded. 'Just a little underdressed . . . and my glass is empty!'

He laughed. 'You are an easy lady to please,' he said, retrieving her clothes and handing them to her.

'I like to think so too.'

While they waited for the wood to burn down to charcoal, they sat together with the wine and watched the sun start its slow descent towards the mountains. Isabella spoke more about her childhood; her mother and her father and the days growing up at Ingombe. She told him about Joseph, their travels to Europe and of happier times so long ago.

He listened without interrupting, occasionally fanning the flames of the fire.

Then she spoke of the war, the loss of her parents, Joseph, and finally the farm. Behind them the smoke from the fire fabricated a light mist over the river as it meandered slowly across the pebbles at the water's edge, washing them smooth.

Robert Doyle's eyes were not on the woman. They were on the distant mountains climbing above them towards the shadow of the moon and he knew that after today the rest of their life would feel normal in comparison.

Then Isabella mentioned Danny and he felt a small pang of jealousy, which he immediately regretted. Why should he feel threatened? He had no right to walk into this woman's life and stake a claim. Danny was her rock, the one who always picked up the pieces, and she needed a friend like him.

The leaves from the overhanging branches cast dappled shadows on the still waters, leaving Isabella too infatuated with her immediate surroundings to notice his covetous moment. 'OK Robert, now it's your turn – your story.' The smile that he had come to love appeared in the corner of her mouth. 'Tell me about Emily.'

25

A canopy of evergreens cloaked the sandbanks of the river where the dikkops played. It was some time before Robert Doyle answered. Sitting beside the *braai*, he looked over the woman's shoulder into the bush on the far side of the river. 'Emily,' he paused, the memories bringing with them a pain. 'Emily was my wife.'

The words caught the woman by surprise.

'We met at Kariba, you know, where I was employed as a ranger, relocating the wild animals from the islands on the lake to the mainland game reserves.' Robert Doyle chose his words carefully while he occasionally prodded the embers of the fire with a sharp stick, as if the flames were the total object of his attention. 'Her home was in England – she was in Rhodesia on a two-week safari holiday at the Hwange Game Reserve. As part of her itinerary, she spent a day sailing on Lake Kariba and the night camping on one of the larger islands. That evening the group left the camp on a walking safari and somewhere along the trail three of them foolishly decided to do their own thing and wandered off from the main party. Emily went with them – she had been led to believe that she was with an official tour guide. It transpired that the so-called "guide" worked in the bar at the camp and this little jaunt was his way of trying to impress her.'

'Whatever happened?'

'They ran into difficulties. Without a compass and

unfamiliar with the land, they lost their bearings. It wasn't until the early hours of the morning, when the main party was on their way back to camp, that someone realised they were missing and raised the alarm. I was called in to organise the search and I found them just after dawn, taking refuge in a tree. They were cold and petrified, which was not surprising as there were lions and hippos in the area – but at least they had the sense to get off the ground. Being as there weren't any leopards on the island, the tree was probably their best option, not that they would have known this because the "guide" panicked and ran off as soon as he realised they were lost.'

'Just left them? They could have been killed.'

'That's right. But I guess when you are in Africa on safari for the first time you think every *mzungu* you meet in a bar is a big white hunter. All they need is the gift of the gab to convince the tourists.'

'Did they catch him?'

'Nope. We found one of the dinghies missing the next morning. He must have taken off into the bush and that was the last anybody ever saw of him. Hwange is not far from the border so he probably crossed the river into Zambia. He did me a favour, though, because he brought Emily into my life. And, luckily, the incident didn't put her off Africa; in fact, quite the opposite. A week later she tore up her return ticket and joined the staff at the game reserve. From that day on we were inseparable.'

'Did she never go back to England?'

'We both did eventually. To meet her folks. They're extremely wealthy and live in an old country pile in Dorset. But I was never happy.'

'It sounds like utopia.'

'Not my scene. England is too cold and crowded.'

'So you came back to Africa. To the war, the violence, the poverty, the mess – why?'

'Zimbabwe is my country,' Robert Doyle said simply.

'And what about Emily?'

'She became my assistant at Hwange.'

Isabella turned to look at him. 'Was she very beautiful Robert?'

The question was unexpected, but he did not shy away from it. 'She was like the wild flowers that embrace the mountain paths in the early spring. Africa was her life and the people, her love.'

The woman was aware from the hurt in his voice that there was something more. 'You say "was", Robert; what happened?'

He looked to the water's edge where the dragonflies hovered above the reeds. They momentarily reminded him of the ear-piercing screams of the helicopter gunships and the horrors of the war. 'I was away in Bulawayo. Terrorists crossed the border from Zambia and hit the reserve.' His voice was barely more than a whisper. 'When she died a part of me died too. But they didn't just kill her . . . they killed my unborn son.'

'Oh God, I'm so sorry! I would not have asked the question if–'

'You were not to know. What they did to Emily turned my world to hatred. It was this rage that carried me through the war.'

'And yet you are not bitter?'

'Like an incurable cancer, it was slowly killing me. It took many years and countless deaths before I realised you can't live that way forever.'

'So what changed? What took away the animosity?'

'I spared the life of an African terrorist.'

The impact of the words hit her like a sledgehammer – and yet, yet she wondered why she was taken aback by the revelation – after all, wasn't this the sensitive side of him she loved? 'It was much the same for me after Joseph died,' Isabella said quietly. 'Although it is a great sadness, you have to move on. Where is Emily buried?'

Robert Doyle's eyes were still on the river. 'You know, it's crazy but we often talked about that when we walked the bush. She didn't want a grave; instead her ashes floated away on a breeze over Kariba while an old man played a *mbira*. I stood alone on the sand bank, listening to the music and throwing pebbles into the water . . . watching the waves run to the shore.'

'My God Robert, that is so beautiful.'

'It was. A *madala* had once told me the lake was home to Nyaminyami and the ripples were the river god's way of sending back her reincarnated spirit to me. I can't believe that fate has brought us together and given me another chance.'

'Given us *both* another chance,' Isabella quietly corrected him.

Although it was still the middle of the afternoon, the sun was slowly beginning her walk out of the valley towards the hills where she would finally rest. All of a sudden a trout jumped out of the pool and for a brief second its scales shimmered in the sunshine before the water once again devoured it. The movement caught the woman's attention. She smiled in contentment and eased herself into Robert Doyle's arms, watching the dragonflies playing in the mirrored reflections of the placid pool.

Hovering above the water, their delicate wings supporting colourful bodies, they were unaware that time was fading away and diminishing what was left of the day.

A light breeze moved through the trees and the shadow of a branch touched Isabella's shoulder, leaving tiny goose pimples on her skin. 'We must eat and then go,' she said, looking at the place where the shade darkened the pool beneath the trees.

'All this talk and I've forgotten about the food. I'm sorry – it won't take long.' He reached over for the packet of *boerewors* and laid each sausage neatly on the griddle above the hot coals. They ate in silence, the embers from the fire dusting them with the light smell of wood smoke. Across the water they could make out the elongated shapes of a pair of hadedas searching for lizards and snails with their long curved beaks. And, as if to announce their presence, the birds issued their loud, strident cry – ha-ha-ha-ha-haa – which made the woman jump. 'Come on Robert,' she said, finishing the last of her food, 'I'm ready for a sundowner.'

Robert Doyle was on his feet. Packing the rucksack with what was left of the food and the empty wine bottle, he then covered the remnants of the fire with sand. Although they were jobs most folk did in the bush, somehow Robert Doyle managed them with an efficiency that Isabella found absorbing. The rucksack was on his back and the rifle at his side, hanging down in that easy manner, when he turned to the woman. 'Right, that's the lot. Let's go.'

Isabella fell in behind him on the mountain path. Before they reached the bend in the river, Robert Doyle stopped to look back. Although the twilight was still some time away, the colours were now chasing each other and running with the sunset. This would be the last they would ever see of the dragonflies and the only words that were spoken were done so subconsciously, as though each knew what the other was thinking.

26

It was late afternoon by the time the first strains of dusk touched the bush. They transformed the deeper shadows beneath the trees to a murky darkness on the narrow path that wound its way back up the valley to Ingombe.

Isabella thought of the day. And what a day it had been – waking up next to Robert Doyle in the bed with the crumpled sheets and then lying next to him by the river. And then she imagined the night ahead. She wanted to look her best for him and so she thought of the dress she had bought in Paris, but had never worn outside the house. The previous night she had looked closely at herself in the mirror for the first time, and she had seen a different face, one she wanted to make beautiful. Digging deep into the bedroom chest, she found lipstick and make-up that had long been forgotten and she felt again like a girl on her first date.

When the homestead came into view, the first sound they heard was Shamari's high-pitched bark. The dog was apprehensive when she eventually caught sight of the woman trailing behind. Isabella was hot and tired but nevertheless she tried to be friendly. 'Hello Shamari!' she shouted affectionately. The dog backed off and emanated a low growl, to which the woman shrugged her indifference.

Robert Doyle laughed uneasily. 'Don't take offence Isabella,' he said. 'Shamari's a mean old bitch. If it's any consolation, you'll probably get more affection from a jackal.' There was a barely noticeable wag from the animal's tail when she nuzzled up to her master and his hand gently stroked her ears. In the distance were the mountains that marked out the border with Mozambique, where he had been involved in some of the bloodiest fighting of the war. And for a moment his eyes were misty with memories of the time he had shared with the dog. Then he turned to face Isabella. She was watching him. 'I'll give Shamari the leftovers from the *braai*. How about that drink on the *stoep* afterwards?'

'Great – give me a few minutes to change and grab the glasses.' The words were thrown casually over the woman's shoulder as she disappeared into the house.

Walking down the corridor, Isabella was staggered at how Ingombe had taken on a different character – somehow lighter . . . safer? When she reached the bedroom, she unbuttoned her blouse and dropped it to the floor. Opening the wardrobe door, she was greeted by an array of dresses, all seemingly vying for her attention. Life on a remote farm was a world away from city living so the dresses were her companions and, like all good friends, she had never been able to discard them. Sometimes, when life became repetitive or when a sense of isolation crept in, she would spend a lazy afternoon trying them on. Although some were from her younger days and no longer fitted her, she would nevertheless hang them around the room while she lay on the bed trying to remember where she had last worn them. The clothes were the story of her life, her one luxury in the bush, and they conjured up memories, some happy, some sad, much like turning the pages of a book.

Idly flicking through the rack, Isabella rejected them one after another until she came to the one she had in mind – the little black Balenciaga dress, still draped on its original wooden hanger and exquisite in its simplicity. It was perfect. She and Joseph had been travelling through Paris in the summer of '71 when they had found it hanging in the shop window of a little Parisian boutique in the Latin Quarter. Joseph had died before she had the chance to wear it and with his death, its appeal had diminished. As such it had remained hidden in the wardrobe. If there ever was a good time to show it off, Isabella thought, this was it. Removing the dress carefully from the rail, she slid it over her body. Then, studying herself in the mirror, she touched her eyelashes lightly with mascara before applying her lipstick and perfume.

The room was quiet, almost eerily so. On the dressing table, partially obscured behind a bottle of perfume, a dusty old monochrome picture of her mother with a guitar caught her eye. That's it – yes, that's what we need to go with the wine, she thought – music! Selecting a record from the shelf in the kitchen, Isabella placed the vinyl on the turntable. The scratch of the needle preceded the strings of the Spanish guitar, bringing the room to life. It was the music of her mother's country, a haunting song played by a gypsy, and it transported her back to her childhood. And when she closed her eyes she could see the flamenco dancer swaying onto the floor and the castanets rattling in harmony with the fervent strumming.

Robert Doyle was on the *stoep* when he saw the woman, her figure framed in the open door, the music floating behind her. It rendered him speechless and it was some seconds before he regained his composure. 'My

God, Isabella . . . you look just . . . amazing.'

She smiled, frivolously dancing over his words and ignoring the compliment. 'Robert, what does a girl have to do around here for a drink?'

He reached for the bottle on the table and half filled the glasses. Just when he thought he knew her intimately, she walked back into his little world looking even more beautiful, if that was at all possible. The gramophone record filled in the background and he raised his glass to the woman in the little black dress.

'You know, I wore this dress for the first time in years, just three weeks ago.'

'What was the occasion?'

'Oh, nothing special – I was alone, with a bottle of wine, the valley, the cicadas and my memories.'

'Alone? I don't like to think of you lonely.'

'But I wasn't.'

Robert Doyle nodded in recognition. He touched her glass and the last of the sunshine caught Joseph's simple ring on her wedding finger, the gold band contrasting vividly against the dry red Merlot.

'This is what I have always imagined,' she breathed, 'on all the nights I have sat here alone on this *stoep*. And then fate brings you to my farm. How strange is that?'

'I guess it's all down to the damaged water pump. Shall we drink to the Toyota as well as the little black dress?'

Isabella sank down into the cushions on the old swinging seat. The wistful smile, when it materialised, came from a long way away. It came from a past which Robert Doyle knew nothing about, a place he would never be able to go to. Yet how he wished he could capture this moment and keep it. Would he ever again see her looking as lovely as she did that evening, caught in an African sunset, her childlike feet swinging idly over the settee? He silently cursed time because of what it would eventually do to the woman. Even if one could take a photograph of her, print it on celluloid and put her in a frame, like a butterfly pinned to a board, it would never be the same.

With this sudden sombre mood he was reminded again of the anxiety he had felt when he'd left the squatter camp the previous night. Although his intentions were good, he charged in like a bull at a gate without thinking of the repercussions. 'Isabella, you know what we were talking about earlier – about me staying with you? Well,' he stuttered trying to find the right words, 'having thought about it, I'm still really worried about you living here next door to the *vanamukoma*.' No sooner were the words spoken, than he regretted them.

'What do you mean *me* living next door to the *vanamukoma?*' she said guardedly, misinterpreting his concern. 'I thought you said this morning that you could not love me then leave me?'

This was not going to plan. Did he detect scepticism in her voice or was it his imagination? He had made a commitment because she'd been frightened. And then last night it had transformed into something more. Or so she had told him in the room with the faded curtains. And when he thought of the night and the woman, he remembered the Namib Desert.

The dream had first occurred shortly after Emily had died. In it, he was walking up a steep sand dune with an aggressive wind blowing the shifting sand into his face. And as the wind blew, it whistled a tune, a melancholy song that called him. Rubbing the grains of sand from his blood-shot eyes he looked up to see the figure of a young girl standing on top of the dune, framed against a vivid blue sky. He tried to walk quicker but was unable to cover any more ground because the sand was moving down the dune faster than he could climb. In desperation he fell onto his hands and knees and tried to crawl, but it made no difference. He remained in the same spot. Then the wind intensified, covering him with a fine yellow cloak. The girl on top of the dune still sang her haunting song. But no matter how hard he tried, he was unable to reach her. She was unobtainable.

The dream seemed so real that each time it had happened he'd woken up in a cold sweat. Who was the girl in the desert? Was she, like the girl in the café, a figment of his imagination? He realised then that by asking such questions of its meaning, so long after Emily, he'd once again lost his independence.

But wasn't that what he wanted? He was tired of travelling, of the endless road. And yet there was still this fear of responsibility. Was that why he insisted on continually analysing the future instead of simply accepting it in whatever form it came to pass? You have found something special here, he told himself. Don't change it. Because if you do, you will lose it.

The evening sun had set the *stoep* alight and Robert Doyle looked at the woman again. Her eyes were closed and tresses of brown hair fell across her neck onto the thin shoulder strap of the black dress. And when he looked at the hem, which lay midway between her waist and her knees, he was unable to keep his gaze from her long legs. She opened her eyes. 'So where would you like me to live then, Robert?'

The question took him by surprise and it was a minute or two before he found an answer. 'Anywhere other than Zimbabwe,' was all he could finally say.

The swing seat came slowly to a rest and Isabella studied Robert Doyle's face. There were thoughts between them that were now out in the open. She knew what she wanted and, with a woman's intuition, she knew how to go about getting it. 'Robert, there is something I want to show you,' she said softly. 'And then perhaps you will understand my affinity with Ingombe.'

'I never questioned it.'

She ignored his interjection. 'Will you come with me to my parents' grave?'

He nodded cautiously, knowing it would not be easy.

And with that, she was on her feet. Picking up her camera from the table inside the front door, she then took his hand and guided him around the back of the house and up the narrow stone-lined path. Halfway up the *kopje*, it was only possible to walk in single file and Isabella moved ahead to show him the way.

Robert Doyle felt uncomfortable. Everything had changed since they'd returned to Ingombe from the river and he could not comprehend how it had all gone wrong.

The heat from the midday sun was still in the air and the woman in her little black dress seemed somewhat out of place when they reached the summit. It was only when he read the names carved into the simple wooden crosses that he at last understood why her mood had altered. She was making her last stand – digging her heels in. She had no intention of leaving Ingombe and perhaps she resented this stranger for trying to change her mind.

He quietly cursed himself; he'd known of her obligations to the farm, so why had he impetuously revealed his fears? But he didn't stay angry for long; this game of second guessing would have to come to an end sooner rather than later – the danger was imminent and the woman would have to face up to that reality. And, as if to reinforce his concern, the foreboding sound of a distant drum drifted over the *kopje*.

'Robert, can I have a picture?'

He pulled himself out of his thoughts. 'Sure! Do you want me to take it?'

'I want us together. I'll set up the timer.'

Isabella placed the camera on a flat rock and when she peered through the viewfinder she saw Robert Doyle gazing out across the valley – her valley – squinting into the sunset beneath the wide brim of the bush hat, worry etched onto his face.

'Smile Robert!' Pressing the release button, she then ran the short distance into his arms and waited for the shutter to click.

She'd never forget that moment; she would put the photo by her bedside and look at it as soon as she opened her eyes each morning.

Under a clear blue sky, the *kopje* was picturesque, but the graveyard would not have been Robert Doyle's first choice of a setting for the photo. Yet he said nothing, just continued to hold her. Then he noticed the stone in her hand.

Moving out of his arms, she placed it next to the wooden cross. 'This is something Joseph and I would do each time we came here. It was our way of remembering. Will you put a stone on the *shamba* please Robert?'

As strange as the bizarre ceremony was, if it made the woman happy, then why not? By his feet lay a large granite pebble, washed smooth over time by the wind and rain. He was about to place it on the *shamba* when a ray of sunlight crept out from behind a darkened cloud and touched the upright of the wooden cross, throwing its shadow across the grave. The silhouette seemed to symbolise the crossroads at which the woman now stood. Soon she would have to make the choice between her freedom outside this mountain prison and the memories that kept her locked within it.

They walked slowly back down to the house. His arm cradled her body and their shadows blended into one. The last of the evening sun was disappearing behind the violet *kopje* and bleaching the *veld*. It was unbelievably beautiful. Isabella leaned back into Robert Doyle's arms. 'How can I leave this?' she whispered again in a perturbed voice, looking out over the multicoloured canvas.

Robert Doyle said nothing, just gently squeezed her shoulder. Time was not on their side; soon events would dictate their destiny and he did not want to end his life in this valley.

But the die was cast and there was no going back.

When they reached the steps to the house, Isabella took his hand and led him on to the *stoep*. Was it really only yesterday that the stranger had appeared? So much had happened and yet the woman knew that there were issues to resolve before they could move on. And treading carefully was not in her nature. 'You want me to leave the farm, don't you Robert? Yet you said you would stay here with me; you said it was what you wanted. So why have you changed your mind? What's happened?'

So many questions. Robert Doyle paused and then began slowly, choosing his words carefully. 'You know how much I love being with you Isabella. But it's the farm I'm worried about. Can't we just–'

'You really don't understand, do you?' she interrupted, before looking into his eyes for reassurance. 'This is all I've ever known – it's all I have.'

Well, here it comes, Robert Doyle thought. The woman was driving him into a corner and searching for assurances he could not give her. He turned around to face her. 'You asked me at breakfast what happened last night and my first thought was to brush over it. But you insisted on the truth and I started to tell you. Then you spoke of all the reasons why you loved Ingombe and I didn't have the guts to contradict you. But when I hear the drums, I am reminded of what those guys are doing down at the squatter camp.' His voice had taken on a more significant tone than he intended. 'And it will not be long before it turns ugly. The soldiers at the crossroads are not your local native; they are Mugabe's Fifth Brigade. If you stand in their way they will not hesitate to kill you,' he said, the vision of Shamari's quarry clouding his mind. He paused to allow the words the effect they deserved. 'I'm sorry to be the one to have to tell you this, but in their eyes this is *not* your land. You *must* understand that. Whether you like it or not, someday you *will* have to go.'

'Someday could be a long time away, Robert, and Mugabe did promise that the Highland farms would stay in our hands,' she repeated defiantly.

253

'Is that what you really think? Then why are the *vanamukoma* camped on your doorstep?'

'They are *tsotsis* and they are there illegally!'

Robert Doyle's pale blue eyes were filled with concern. He had feared all along the woman would ignore his advice so he tried a different approach. 'Look Isabella, it does not really make any difference if they are here legally or not; they are still dangerous. You said a moment ago that Ingombe is all you have. How about this for a suggestion? I have a little farm in the Drakensberg. It is not unlike Nyanga.'

The woman turned away and sat down wearily on the settee; it was her way of ignoring what she did not want to hear. 'Robert, is there wine left in the bottle?' The request was whispered in a voice that had the haziness of an early morning mist. 'I think I need a drink if we are going to discuss whether or not I stay at Ingombe.'

'You don't need that.' But in spite of his conviction he poured the wine and leaned back against the wooden post. The day had disappeared and a ghostly moon appeared through tattered clouds and cast an eerie light across the yard. The growl of a distant hyena was the only sound to penetrate the rhythm of the cicadas. There was no other noise. No revelry or singing. Even the everyday sounds of the squatter camp had died away.

'OK Robert,' she said reluctantly, 'tell me about the Drakensberg.'

He looked up, grateful for the chance to explain further. 'It's as beautiful a spot as I guess you'd find anywhere. The farm lies in a natural amphitheatre, like a small version of the Ngorongoro Crater, but with a river, waterfalls and lush grazing land. We are only ten miles from the small town of Winterton and a few hours' drive from the east coast beaches.'

Isabella closed her eyes and listened.

'My idea,' he continued, 'is to set up a hiking and riding centre and run white water rafting and fishing on the Tugela River.'

'You make it sound so idyllic,' she said, opening her drowsy eyes.

'It is.' Robert Doyle watched Shamari wander up onto the *stoep*. She sniffed her blanket and then settled down with a dejected air. The dog craved affection, but he had other things on his mind and this was not the time.

'There is one problem though,' the woman said, looking straight at the man.

'What's that?'

'My mother and father. What do I do about them?'

Why bring this up? They are dead. She is clutching at straws. 'I guess it's going to be pretty difficult for us to take them to South Africa,' he said, misinterpreting the question.

Isabella glared at him with a stony face and he immediately realised his mistake.

'You don't really understand, do you Robert? I took you to the grave in the hope that you would appreciate that I have roots here – why it is that I can't leave!' There was an undertone of hostility in her voice that Robert Doyle unintentionally replicated.

'Have you thought that you might have to leave them or you could be joining them?' No sooner had he spoken the words than he regretted them. But what would it take to make her see sense? It felt as though he was banging his head against a brick wall.

Isabella sat up sharply, unable to believe he could make

such an insensitive remark. Retreating further into a corner of the settee, she wrapped her arms around her knees and stared silently out across the valley. When she was finally able to control her voice, it still held a hint of anger. 'It's not just the dead that keep me at Ingombe. Zimbabwe is my Africa, my land and my people.'

'But it is all changing Isabella: greed and starvation now dictate the future.'

'Change – that's all anybody talks about these days. You don't need to tell me this – the bloody war veterans killed all my cattle before I came back to the farm and now they are killing all the wild animals in the bush for their meat or their ivory. Some of the parks across the country no longer have any game. This is *change!* Have you not seen it happening?'

It was an irrelevant question which did not warrant a reply; from the look on the woman's face there was more to come and he wasn't sure he really wanted to hear it. However, these were the memories that bound her to this valley, and so he remained silent.

'Robert,' she said, a plea in her voice to be understood, 'the Highlands are like nowhere else I've ever seen. In spite of the storm clouds hanging over Ingombe, I am linked to the ordinary Africans here; I feel a great responsibility and a genuine love for the staff that work for me. They are the only family I have now. It is me who puts flowers on the graves of their ancestors,' she said vehemently. 'Can you not understand this?'

The words were like a cancer that was eating away at her very being.

'I'm only telling you to leave because I'm concerned by what may happen to you,' he said weakly, the wind taken out of his sails.

'I know Robert, but where does it all end? I resented the Bush War because of what it did to me. It took my entire family and ruined my farm. It made me a prisoner in my own home. And yet I love this country for all the reasons I've shown you today. I'll probably be known as a "good old Rhodesian" for staying.' She paused to take a breath. 'And I'm not even a Rhodesian now. I'm a Zimbabwean.'

Africa talk, Africa politics. Robert Doyle had heard all this before, around the campfires and in the bars and the cafés across Zimbabwe; bitter talk about a lost dream, an inability to accept the winds of change blowing through Africa. Most Rhodesians could not leave anyway. Nobody would buy their farms and many of them were too old to start again. 'The things that you love about this country you will also find in South Africa,' he said stubbornly, trying to placate her.

'How can you say that? I've been to South Africa – I've seen the shanty towns where the Africans live in sheds made from plywood packing cases. The walls are still plastered in Marlboro cigarette adverts. And they're raising their children amongst drug dealers! It's a terrible environment, a perpetual state of poverty.'

'You are talking about the Africans. I know the conditions in the townships are bad, but they go south Isabella because the alternative is to starve or be persecuted by that scum down at your squatter camp, whose sole objective is to rid this country of the Matabele and the whites and keep it just for *their tribe.*'

Isabella took a sip from the wine glass. She'd heard enough of this talk and her shoulders were rounded from exhaustion. She tried to catch her breath and then looked directly into Robert Doyle's eyes. 'OK, so tell me this,' she said indignantly, 'who won the bloody war? What was the purpose of all the killing?' Without realising it, the intensity reverberated through her voice and she spat the words out virulently. 'You fought in the bush, but do you really know . . . or do you even care?' The questions were asked in the heat of the moment before the woman had a chance to think about them. And by asking them she had crossed the line, gone beyond the point of no return. But then, what right did a stranger have coming here and insisting she leave her home?

Robert Doyle rose slowly to his feet. Walking over to the railing on the *stoep*, he looked deep into the unknown darkness. The weight of the question rested heavily on his shoulders. He did not turn around or look at the woman. Instead he uttered his answer to the night, to people who would never hear him, because they were the ghosts from his past. When he spoke, the words were simple, delivered in a voice devoid of all feeling. 'I don't know who the winners are,' he said slowly. 'I guess I don't see the picture like you do any more, nor do I have your passion. Once I was young and enthusiastic and I shared your ideals. But too many deaths have killed my emotion and put out the fire. Men I've loved, brothers in arms, are no longer here. Maybe they are the winners because they have found their peace – most of the guys I know who survived have either hit the bottle or, if they're lucky, they have found God. But they never forget, because they are the ones who have to live with what they have seen.'

'I'm so sorry Robert,' the woman said, realising too late the implication of her question and the pain it caused.

He ignored the interjection. 'Isabella, for just a short while you have helped me forget the past. But I have just been kidding myself. There is really no going back – right or wrong, the killing will always be with me. It's the burden I will carry to my grave.' He turned and, with a vain attempt to resurrect a smile, he walked over to the woman who just a short while ago he had desired so much. The woman in the black dress. Suddenly he was overwhelmed by the events that had transpired and a future without her. 'Perhaps Mugabe and his henchmen are the winners,' he said quietly, putting his hand gently on her shoulder. 'I'm sorry Isabella – I know how you feel about this place. I guess I read it wrong; I just didn't realise the extent of your commitment. I've travelled across most of this country since independence and I've seen the way it's going. It's never going to get any better. This idyllic valley will always be just that – a wonderful paragon. And maybe going south is only delaying what Africa will eventually do to all of us . . . I don't know.'

She could feel the pain in his words and placed her hand on his arm. Too many truths had been laid bare, too many questions asked. Robert Doyle needed time alone to come to terms with the answers. Withdrawing her hand, the look in his eyes told the woman far more than words ever would: nothing seemed to matter anymore. He had tried so hard to point out the dangers but she had blindly rejected the warnings and thrown them back in his face.

Stopping briefly in mid stride, Robert Doyle turned to face her. 'There's only one thing more I can do for you now, Isabella . . . I'll move on in the morning.'

Then he was gone, a ghostly figure drifting across the yard in the light of the moon, leaving the woman alone with her anger and regret.

27

Isabella gazed out into the empty darkness. Bats swept down low over the *stoep* in their nightly search for insects. In the face of this simple existence her anger dissipated like raindrops on the parched earth. She cursed her Spanish temperament and outspokenness. Robert Doyle was right; the Drakensberg was the sensible option. They would be free there and perhaps they could even run a little game reserve in conjunction with the riding and hiking, just like she and Danny had dreamed about when they were teenagers.

But could she just walk away from everything? From her father, her mother and Joseph, and *their* dreams and aspirations? And what about Shazi, Thomas and the rest of the staff who were dependent upon her? Should she also abandon them in favour of the Drakensberg? It was easy for Robert Doyle. He had nothing to tie him to Zimbabwe. She acknowledged that events had become a little agitated down at the compound with Mugabe's *tsotsis* but the country was in a period of transition and, as Danny often reminded her, they would one day need the white farmer's expertise. But deep down Isabella knew this was unlikely to happen. At least not until the opposition, the MDC party, gained power.

The wine held little appeal to the woman now and she put her glass down on the little wicker table and walked through to the bedroom. The black dress, which a moment ago had been an icon of expectation, also seemed to have lost its attraction. She let it fall to the floor. In its place she pulled on an old cotton T-shirt over her faded blue jeans. The slogan on the front, '*Tot siens Suid Afrika*', goodbye South Africa, was a reminder of the moment in the war when Rhodesia's one and only friend had pulled her support, leaving the country high and dry. Worldwide pressure had caused a rift between the neighbours and brought the Bush War to a quick and bloody end.

Stepping over the dress, Isabella returned to the kitchen to prepare dinner, a simple tomato pasta. As she sliced the onions, she gazed out of the window, half expecting to see the tall figure of Robert Doyle emerging from the shadows, but there was no sign of him – only his final words that lingered in her mind: 'I'll move on in the morning.'

Surely he had not meant it.

Suddenly the shrill ring of the farm phone interrupted her thoughts.

'Danny! You're back early?' Hearing his exuberant voice reminded her how much she had missed him and his sound advice.

'Doug's had to go to Harare. OK if I drop by?'

The question immediately put her in a predicament. But perhaps talking things over with her friend was the answer; he would understand. 'Danny, I've something to tell you.'

'Nothing serious is it?'

'Oh Danny!' Isabella laughed, hoping her voice sounded relaxed. 'Have you ever known me to be serious? How about getting together tomorrow at your place?'

'Make it late afternoon and I'll chill a couple of bottles of Sauvignon Blanc – Vicky's bottle store was full of the stuff so I've stocked up.'

Vicky was certainly doing well. But then in the new Zimbabwe demand always exceeded supply because of currency restrictions. There was a pause on the line and she thought for a minute that Danny had hung up without saying goodbye. Then his bubbly voice was back, softer this time.

'Issy, I've missed you.'

'Hey now, don't go getting all maudlin – it's only been a day or so.'

He laughed at the way she shrugged off his concern. That was more like the Isabella he knew, cutting out the starry-eyed nonsense and getting on with life.

Isabella dropped the Bakelite mouth-piece back into its cradle and stared at the telephone hanging on the wall. Danny was the only one who really understood why Ingombe held her in its mountain fortress. But despite this, she was confused. The time was drawing ever nearer when she would have to make a choice: stay on at Ingombe or leave Zimbabwe with the man who had walked into her life just two days ago?

The pasta was almost ready. After letting it simmer for a while longer, Isabella turned the heat off on the hot plate and put the food in the oven. Minutes ago the *stoep* had been the scene of a battlefield of words. Now it was deserted and a spectral silence hung, like an empty picture, over the shadows on the wooden floorboards. And in that moment the woman recognised what Robert Doyle had meant when he said there was fear in the air.

'Robert!' she shouted from the edge of the *stoep*. Her apprehensive voice was swallowed up by the sounds of the bush and there was no reply from the emerging darkness. Neither was there any sign of the dog. The only evidence that they were still on the farm was the Land Cruiser, standing abandoned beneath the msasa tree.

***

Isabella saw him before she heard him. His lanky figure filled the open frame of the front door and there was an easy smile playing around the corners of his mouth. She ran into his arms. 'Oh, Robert, I was so worried you might have gone!'

He held her in his gentle way and whispered softly into her hair. 'Would I go without saying goodbye?'

'I'm so sorry for my outburst; I didn't mean it to come out that way.'

Robert Doyle shrugged off the apology as if he were obliterating an unwanted chapter. 'It doesn't matter Isabella,' he said nonchalantly.

'Robert, please don't let's fight. I don't want our words to become spears which we thrust at each other and afterwards wish we could take them back. Because by then it's too late.' She held his hand and led him through the hall.

He did not pull away but neither did he surrender. When they reached the kitchen he stopped and released his grip. 'Isabella, I've had time to think about Ingombe. I figure I know where you are coming from.'

'You don't have to say this.'

He hesitated. They were standing beside the kitchen table and he looked out of the window and down the valley, watching the shadows playing in the rows of msasa trees that lined the track. 'I said before that I would stay with you till you showed me the door. I meant that. I'm just sorry I had to frighten you with my concerns.'

The woman put her arms around his waist. Her voice was almost a whisper. 'I will never show you the door. That has to be your decision.'

He could feel the softness of her body and smell the fragrance on her neck. 'What have these last two days been about – have they not meant anything?'

'You know what they mean, Robert.' A gust of cold air blew through the open front door like an unwelcome stranger and yet she felt only his warmth. 'Nobody can take that away – what we have shared will always be ours.' She paused, conscious that the words and her presence were holding him where she wanted him. 'And another thing; what you are offering to do for me is more than I could ask of anybody.'

His gaze encompassed not only the woman but the room and her entire little world. 'I am doing it—'

Isabella placed a finger gently across his lips and carried on talking. 'Please, Robert – as you yourself said, can't we just take one day at a time? At the first sign of danger I will come with you to the Drakensberg.' A teasing smile flirted across her lips and she held up three fingers to the side of her head. 'I promise.'

Then she kissed him, little realising the implication of her pledge.

28

'*Wapi ni etu mwanajeshi?* Where is our soldier?'

The frantic shout woke Sengamo. He had been asleep less than ten minutes. Instinctively, he checked his rifle and picked up the high-resolution field glasses. The *vanamukoma*, in black balaclavas, were searching every hut in the compound, presumably on the hunt for their missing comrade.

The girl was on Sengamo's mind. Would she be sensible – or frightened – enough to keep their liaison a secret? He guessed the latter. They would rape and kill her if they suspected she had been sleeping with the enemy. He tried pinpointing the location of her home but all of the huts looked identical.

On the edge of the compound a *madala* gesticulated wildly towards the *vanamukoma*, who were dragging a pregnant woman out of a *rondavel*.

An argument erupted and the old man never saw the heavy fists that connected with the side of his head. Nor did he feel the hobnail boots that tore open his face. When they became bored with kicking his motionless body, they dragged him over to where a cow was tethered to a wooden pole and sat him upright, slapping his face and throwing buckets of cold water over his head until he regained consciousness. The first thing the *madala* saw when he opened his eyes was the *tsotsis* hacking off the cow's rear legs with a machete. Blood covered the dirt yard and the animal's bellowing death throes could be heard across the camp. Children screamed, further provoking the aggressors, and in their frustration they beat them with *shamboks*. Everywhere panic-stricken mothers were running to and fro, trying desperately to stifle their childrens cries.

When the soldiers moved on, a villager untied the cow and the animal attempted to crawl the short distance across the yard to the shade of a scrawny acacia bush before it lost consciousness. There it lay on the hard earth and awaited its slow death. Sengamo had seen this despicable act of cruelty many times before; the soldiers would justify their actions by saying it kept the meat fresh. But this was different – this time the savagery was designed purely to intimidate the villagers and it was these so-called war veterans who were resurrecting the nightmares. Would the horrors inflicted on the innocent people of this country never end?

Sengamo picked up his AK-47 and focused the barrel sights on the officer in charge of the search party. Although his finger was on the trigger and a voice in his mind instinctively told him to fire, he forced himself to remain calm. The target was out of range and to take action now would only expose his position.

His time would come soon enough.

In the space of a few minutes the *vanamukomas'* brutal methods had cleared the village; the inhabitants having fled in fear to the refuge of their *rondavels*, making it easier for the soldiers to continue the search. Occasionally a worried face would peer out of a darkened doorway and then just as quickly disappear when a soldier arrived.

Suddenly a piercing scream split the now still air. On the far side of the camp two soldiers dragged a young boy by his feet down the alley between the huts, ignoring his howls of pain as he tried desperately to protect his lacerated head.

When the soldiers eventually reached the centre of the compound, they threw the child unceremoniously onto the ground. An officer, wearing a camouflaged jacket and a brown Chinese peak cap, sauntered over and dangled something in front of the boy's face. Sengamo focused the field glasses on the object. But not even in his most vivid imagination was he prepared for what he saw. In the officer's hand was a medal; the very same one he'd thrown away before leaving the compound.

Then the interrogation started – animated questions followed by protestations of innocence. When there was nothing forthcoming, the agitated officer nodded to his soldiers and the beating began; slowly and systematically at first, the dull thud of steel toe caps and *knobkerries* resonating each time they connected with the boy's body. The child curled up into a ball, desperate to protect himself from the fighting sticks that eventually knocked him unconscious. Frustrated that their captive could no longer feel the assault, the soldiers intensified the beating. But it was getting them nowhere, and in his fury, the officer shouted an order in Shona.

A young *tsotsi* wearing a dirty bandana emerged from the crowd and walked over to where the youth was lying senseless on the ground. He gazed at him with contempt. Then a sadistic smile crossed his face as he emptied the contents of a petrol can over the boy. Encouraged by the soldier's shouting their party slogans, the *tsotsi* struck a match and, with a blasphemous shriek, he threw the paper torch at the emaciated figure. The explosion was instantaneous. Flames engulfed the boy's limp body and for an instant it came alive, contorting in grotesque agony.

In a matter of minutes there were no longer any recognisable remains of the burning corpse. The officer, bored with the proceedings, then turned to the soldiers and pointed in the direction of the *rondavels*. They immediately dispersed and returned to searching the huts on the edge of the square. But Sengamo was confident it would be some time before they found the body of the missing soldier; it was bad *bahati* to violate an *nganga's* hut.

In the distance beyond the compound – and out of sight of the soldiers – a large woman ran hysterically along the road towards the farmhouse. It was the *wazungu's* maid; the same woman he'd seen leaving the farm the previous night. Was she scared she would be the *vanamukoma's* next victim? After all, she worked for the white woman, which in their eyes made her a *mtengesi*. But how long would it be before they traced her movements?

Ah ha! This was a new twist to the unfolding saga, the tracker thought.

By discarding the medal, Sengamo was responsible for the tremor that would eventually engulf them all. But the guilt he felt at having unwittingly signed the boy's death warrant was not on his mind, for what troubled him now was the farmhouse and the danger that drew ever nearer to its door.

29

Isabella's mind was blanketed in confusion. For much of the night she had lain awake thinking of the man in the spare room at the end of the corridor and yet, in spite of her concern, she had not gone to him. There were still issues to resolve, unanswered questions, and her stubbornness was a barrier between them. Then the first light of morning had come and she had heard the click of the latch as Robert Doyle closed the front door.

That had been over an hour ago.

Suddenly her thoughts were interrupted by a knock on the kitchen door. She flung it open, expecting to see Robert Doyle. Instead she found herself facing Shazi. The African had been an intrinsic part of Isabella's life, from the early days after her father's death when she and Joseph had continued farming at Ingombe, to the dark days during the war. Her large frame had provided a refuge for the family over the years; without her, the daily toils of the farm would have been prodigious, which was something Isabella would never forget.

When Shazi first came to work at Ingombe, Joseph had built a small brick building with a bedroom and a toilet for her family, but they had been forced to abandon it during the war when the terrorists invaded the farm. Angry at seeing their people employed as servants, the guerrillas had destroyed the building and moved Shazi and her children back to the native compound down by the crossroads. In spite of this, she had remained loyal to Isabella, continuing to work for her.

Now, standing outside the kitchen door, breathing heavily from the sheer exhaustion of climbing the hill in a panic, she cut a pathetic figure.

'Oh God Shazi! Whatever is the matter?'

The maid was unable to speak for some minutes. Her buxom physique would normally hold up a house but now, clinging to the doorframe, it was the wooden post that was supporting her.

Isabella gently led her into the kitchen. 'Sit down Shazi,' she said, indicating a chair at the big pine table, 'and tell me what on earth has happened.'

Shazi's eyes were blank and without hope. They darted around the room as if infected with the *nganga's* curse. And still there were no words.

The kettle was bubbling away on the stove, its steam curling languidly towards the ceiling. Isabella picked up a huge, white enamel mug from the plate rack and filled it with the sweet, white tea that the Africans love. It was then that she heard Robert Doyle walk into the kitchen. Unsure what the circumstances were after their talk the night before, she was nevertheless relieved that he had returned and she greeted him without looking up.

'Shazi, this is Robert, a good friend of mine – whatever you say to me you can say to him. We are both here to help you.'

The maid continued to stare into space without even so much as acknowledging Robert Doyle. Indeed, he might not have even been in the room. He did not sit down, nor did Isabella ask him to. Instead, he leant against the wall, facing the open door, alert and wound like a coiled spring. He had a good idea what this was all about.

Strange, Isabella thought, how his presence injected her with such strength and confidence. Just knowing he was there was a comfort. Holding the mug up to Shazi's lips, she waited patiently while the maid slowly drank the hot tea.

And, in between the sips, her brutal story emerged.

'*Nkozikazi*, it was early this morning. The soldiers come to the compound to search huts. We know there is trouble because they are wearing black masks, hiding their faces. Eiee! There was too much shouting and abuse,' she said, putting the mug of hot tea on the table. 'They look for missing soldier and are very angry because they cannot find him. So they are beating everyone with *shamboks*, always asking question, "Where is soldier?" She stopped speaking for a moment and looked down at her mug as if it was the sole object of her attention in the room. 'Old Samson – he was not afraid to face them. He told them strongly that they should not treat us this way.'

Isabella had known Samson since she was a child; he'd been the foreman at Ingombe when her father was alive and he was also the village elder. As headman, he stood no nonsense, which made her even less prepared for what Shazi was about to reveal.

'The soldiers do not like Samson interfering – they knock him to the ground and beat him and kick him. Ah missy, I tell you, it is horrible – there is blood everywhere! I thought Samson is dead.'

The shock registered on Isabella's face and her hands were shaking when she picked up the enamel mug from the table and passed it to the maid. 'Drink the tea Shazi.'

There was a moment's silence while Shazi finished

what was left of the sweet drink. Then she looked up at her mistress with terrified eyes. 'I am so frightened I run into my hut with the children.' Her voice was quivering. 'I am looking through crack in the door and I see them cut the hind legs off Daisy . . . you know, missy?'

Oh God, Isabella did know – she herself had named the cow when it was a calf.

'They are laughing at Daisy. She is trying to drag herself across the yard.' For a moment Shazi stopped speaking and stared straight into the woman's eyes.

Isabella wondered how she would ever forget that haunted look. It was as if she was glimpsing into the very depths of despair, looking into a place where there was no hope or a future, an Africa vilified through yet another grotesque act.

'Then they see Lumbu. He is wearing a medal; they say it belong to the missing soldier. There is much screaming and they ask him where it comes from. He told them he found it on the floor by his hut. But they did not believe him so they drag him by his feet to the square and kick him and beat him with sticks. All the time they are shouting questions, "Where is the soldier? Where is the soldier?" Lumbu cannot answer because he is on the ground with his hands over his head. How could he know where missing soldier is? Then he becomes unconscious.' Shazi paused for a breath. 'Ah, missy, I thought . . . he is only a child. Why are they doing this bad thing to him?'

Isabella put her arm around the maid's shoulders. 'Please don't be frightened, Shazi,' she whispered, 'you are with us now. We will protect you.'

The African maid dug deep for the courage to

continue. 'They just keep on hitting him and hitting him and calling him liar even though he cannot hear them. Nobody could do a thing. There were too many soldiers.' Shazi stopped to take a gulp of air. 'Lumbu is proud to find medal and wear it. He did not know what he has done.' She paused again and looked up from the kitchen table. 'I saw many bad things in the war, *nkozikazi*, but not like what is happening here.'

Shazi's telling of her story was like climbing a mountain, one step at a time. But if Isabella thought she had heard the worst of it, she was wrong. The maid breathed deeply, her body rocking backwards and forwards as she spoke. Despair hung heavy in the room. 'Lumbu is lying on the ground. We think he is dead. Then they pour petrol on him and set him on fire. Eiee, *shem, shem*, missy! It was so terrible. They are savages!'

Isabella's mouth dropped open in shock. How could the bastards do this? She had seen so much cruelty and suffering in Africa but this was just totally barbaric. Having known Lumbu and given the boy reading lessons at the farm, she needed all her strength to prevent herself from sinking into the chasm where the African had fallen. Lumbu was Shazi's nephew – if the soldiers made the connection, how long would it be before they imprisoned her family in the *rondavel* and set the hut alight?

Just the thought of this sent a shiver through her body.

Throughout the maid's story, Robert Doyle stood quietly in the corner, neither moving nor uttering a word. Isabella looked up at him. There was a slow burning anger in his eyes. Then he turned and, without uttering so much as a word, he left the room.

Shazi did not see him go. Her head was buried in her podgy arms on the pine table.

Isabella felt her world collapsing around her. After the arguments of the previous day, it had taken one tragic incident to make her finally see the light. At last she understood what Robert Doyle had been trying so fervently to tell her: it was time to move on. Tomorrow they could be out of here. If the Africans could start again after losing everything, why couldn't *she?* She turned to the maid. 'Shazi, you must go and fetch your children and bring them back to the farm. It's too dangerous now for you to stay at the compound.'

The maid raised her head from her arms. 'They will know we go,' she protested. 'They will come to this house to look for us!'

'We will take you to Juliasdale. You and the children can stay with Sally,' Isabella said firmly. 'You will be safe there until we sort this out.'

'But missy—'

'No buts Shazi; nobody will know where you are. Go and fetch the children and I will call Sally and explain everything.'

'Ah *nkozikazi*, it is too much you are doing for me!'

'It's nothing Shazi, you are one of the family. Bring only what you can safely carry. And whatever you do, don't let them see you leaving the compound.'

The maid picked herself up from the table and, flattening her worn cotton dress, she stumbled towards her mistress. Isabella noticed for the first time the abundant stitching covering the fabric, which reflected the care shown towards it throughout its long life. 'Robert or I would come with you but it is too dangerous for us to be seen at the camp. We will be ready when you come back. But please, please be quick.'

Shazi wrapped her arms around the woman and held her, like she had all those years ago when Isabella was a child. '*Nkozikazi*, I am very frightened.'

Isabella pushed the maid away. 'Go Shazi – hurry, before anything else happens!'

When Shazi had disappeared, Isabella left the house to look for Robert Doyle. He was nowhere to be seen. The gate to the yard was open and she retraced her steps back past the old ramshackle barn. And then, in the distance beyond the wooden building, she caught sight of him, leaning casually on the ranch fence with Shamari by his side. He was gazing towards the horizon with such an intensity he appeared to neither see nor hear her approach. Even the dog, usually so aggressive, was unperturbed by her presence. The woman felt an indescribable sadness over the burden she was placing on his shoulders.

'Robert!' she called out.

The sunlight was dancing lightly in the msasa trees when the man turned, his body swinging around in one easy movement.

'What is going to happen to us Robert?'

The anxiety that just a moment ago had engulfed his features was replaced by a smile and the easy banter in his voice was reminiscent of how he'd been the very first day she'd met him in the yard. 'I have a plan,' he said, putting his arm around her shoulders and walking with her back down to the house. 'Now where are the eggs, bacon and *boerewors* that everybody is talking about down the road?'

Isabella laughed and squeezed his arm. Oh, how she loved the way he made everything seem so inconsequential; he knew what needed to be done and he would do it. She had only to be with him. And if the plan was to move on, then she would go.

This was her last chance.

The previous night had been a time for each of them to retreat to their own space. It had not been easy for Robert Doyle, lying there alone in the spare room, but he had reluctantly accepted Isabella's decision, having been too long out of a relationship to argue otherwise.

Then Shazi had appeared at the door and nothing would ever be the same again.

When the breakfast was ready he put his thoughts to one side and they sat and ate in silence. It was a good meal but because their minds were elsewhere, the action of putting the food into their mouths was purely mechanical. He waited for the woman to finish eating and then pushed his chair back against the wall.

'Isabella,' he started cautiously, 'you said yesterday you would leave when it was no longer safe here.' The smell of the bacon still lingered around the stove but, in the face of the question, the breakfast was forgotten.

The woman looked up from her empty plate to respond.

'Please, just hear me out. You can't stay here any longer and I think you know it. You are in too much danger now.'

She nodded quietly and allowed him to continue.

'You and I both know it won't be long before the *vanamukoma* return. If they attack the farm we could try and defend ourselves, but it won't be easy. I know the house is shuttered but the bastards will smash the wood and lob a petrol bomb through the window. All you will hear is the sound of breaking glass and then the whole place will be on fire.'

The woman sat in silence, shivering when she remembered what had happened to Danny's parents at Rigby's Creek.

There was a solemn note in Robert Doyle's voice when he continued. 'Don't think for a minute that because you are a woman they will be any less brutal – look how they treat their own kind. And don't even contemplate phoning the police, because even if the bastards haven't cut the lines, you won't get any support from the law. Mugabe condones these thugs – you cannot win.'

Isabella's debilitated eyes held on to his every word. And seeing her like this, Robert Doyle was tempted to close the conversation. After all, the last thing in the world he wanted to do was to scare the woman. But then he contemplated the alternatives. And he knew there was no going back – he had to lay the truth on the line. It was time to face up to reality.

'Even if you leave the farm and go to somewhere like Harare, it is only a matter of time before you'll be forced to move on again, because the way Mugabe is going he will ruin this entire country. There is nothing more certain than that. Petrol and food prices are already out of control, but either way it won't matter because your money will be worthless; an entire suitcase full of Zimbabwe dollars won't even buy you a loaf of bread.'

The woman sat clutching her hands, staring nervously out of the open door.

'Isabella, I'm real sorry this is so harsh,' he said,

genuine concern clouding his eyes, 'but I have seen it all happen before up at Hwange.'

Isabella picked up her mug. The chicory taste in the cold coffee was unappealing. She knew he was right. 'Robert, I appreciate all of this but what are we going to do?' Then she thought about the time they had wasted. 'What I said yesterday . . . was it all in vain?'

He ignored the question. 'I can try and take care of you but it won't be easy here,' he said in a quiet voice. 'Those guys at the camp have the law on their side, which gives them the freedom to do whatever they want. And what they want is your land.'

'I know that now,' she said despondently. 'I guess I've just been doing the old ostrich thing and burying my head in the sand.'

He nodded. 'Look Isabella, this is just another part of Africa that is dying – we will never see it again. But you don't need *me* to tell you this.' He stood up and walked over to the window. For a while he just stared down the valley and the room was in silence. Then, pulling his eyes away from the landscape, he looked directly at the woman. 'You asked the question were your words in vain.' He shook his head. 'No, I don't think they were. You understand this country. You know how the Africans toil in the heat and the dust; you have seen the droughts come and their livestock die. This was an innocent land before we came along and soaked it in blood.' Exasperated, he walked out into the yard and returned with a handful of sand. Standing in front of the woman, he let the deep red soil spill slowly from between his fingers and onto the table. There was an ache in his voice when he looked down at the little heap of grains scattered on the pine. 'Do you know why the sand is red?'

The woman shook her head.

'The Matabele say it is the colour of the blood that has been spilled in our country.' Moving back to the window, Robert Doyle was suddenly afraid that his words would be lost if they remained unspoken. 'What Shazi has told you is only a small part of the atrocities Zimbabwe has suffered, atrocities committed by *both* sides during the war. UDI gave the Africans a common enemy: the white man, *us*. Now we have lost the battle, the violence is an issue between the tribes.'

Isabella wanted to go to him, to hold and comfort him, and yet she did none of these things because she was struck speechless by his fervour and she needed to know the outcome.

It was not long in coming.

'I will never forget what I have been through in the Bush War and what I have done, and this is the way I want it to be. Because at the end of the day we are all guilty, whether or not we fired the guns.' Then his eyes were back on the valley. 'I've travelled over most of this continent but Zimbabwe is like no other African country. And it's the reason I came back to fight in the war. You were right in what you said yesterday – South Africa is beautiful, but it's not Zimbabwe.'

'And yet you chose to live in the Drakensberg?'

'Yes.' His eyes were on the valley. 'But whenever I cross the Limpopo and return to the Eastern Highlands, it's like returning to a lover, one I cannot live without.' His speech slowed right down. 'What we have done – right or wrong – will stay with us. But Zimbabwe is dead. This is why I keep telling you there is no future here and you have to leave.' He paused, turned away from the window and looked into the woman's eyes. 'My only regret is that I am the one who has to tell you this.' Then, walking over to the table, he picked up the neglected cup of coffee. Standing there, with what remained of the cold dregs, he delivered the words that would help the woman finally make up her mind.

'Don't let it all end here, Isabella.'

The woman sat riveted to her seat. She had no idea of the depth of his passion for Zimbabwe and of the pain he was suffering in having to leave it. And she could only feel shame for her outburst the previous day. She had acted like a spoilt, selfish child, and now she went to him and put her arms around his neck, burying her face into his shoulder. 'Robert – why are you doing this for me?'

'I am doing this for *us*, Isabella, and I am doing it because I cannot bear to see you die a violent death at the hands of the *vanamukoma*. You know, before I drove into this valley I was resigned to a life alone. You have changed all of that.'

There were tears in Isabella's eyes. Only the day before, Ingombe had been so important and now it did not matter at all. This latest terrible atrocity had finally shown her how fragile Zimbabwe had become. 'Take me away from here Robert,' she said. 'I don't care where we go, as long as I am by your side.'

30

The sun was climbing a ladder in the morning sky, touching the valley with its delicate pink brush, as they ventured out to the *stoep* to wait for Shazi. There is a brief interval during which the colours are magical, before the sun leaves the horizon and transforms itself into a ball of fire. The only sound sweeping the landscape was the wind whistling amongst the msasa trees and just for a moment it reminded Isabella of a fiddler she had heard long ago in a smoky pub outside the little Irish village of Kildare.

Robert Doyle turned the bentwood chair to face the woman and sat on it with his arms over the backrest. 'Look, when Shazi returns I'll drive them to Juliasdale and you can pack. Take only what is essential because we do not have much time.'

He was about to turn her world upside down and yet he made it sound as though he was going in to town to do the daily grocery shop. 'Do you want another coffee while we wait for Shazi?' Isabella asked, moving towards the front door.

'Why not – can I take it black, please?' His eyes were on the path that wound its way out of the compound, searching for the maid through the Zeiss glasses, but when he heard the woman's footsteps, he put the binoculars down and turned to face her.

'Here we are. Black and sweet,' she said, handing him the cup.

'I realise now what all this means to you Isabella.'

'Do you?'

'Yes. And I'm sorry you'll have only the memories to keep.'

'Some good, some bad, I guess,' she said , her thoughts with the maid. 'It's not going to be easy.'

'You will miss Shazi, won't you?'

'Yes, tremendously. What she's done for me over the years . . . and with her life, so difficult . . . she and her children are all squirrelled away in that little mud hut, the same one she grew up in – primitive conditions! But she is resilient and strong, both physically and emotionally. And thank God for that, because her husband is a nasty drunk who sometimes beats her up and steals her money. Joseph wouldn't stand for it – he'd often chase him off the farm and once threatened to shoot him if he ever came back. It worked for a while at least.'

'Sadly for some, this shameful behaviour is commonplace.'

Isabella nodded, still unable to comprehend the morning's events. 'And now even Daisy is dead – the cow was the only possession the family had left, apart from their dwindling stock of maize. You know, I often wonder what the Africans make of us white people, living in "luxury" in our brick houses, a different meal on the table every night, fresh water as soon as we open a tap . . . and poor Shazi has to walk all that way to the river, morning and evening, lugging those heavy clay pots! I don't know how she does it. But she's not at all envious of us, you know – she once told me how an old spirit man had said that greed would one day kill the country. Ha! And now that prophecy is turning out to be true.'

'I guess you are right. I know AIDS is killing half of Africa, but inflation is the new enemy here and Zimbabwe dollars are the biggest joke of all.' Suddenly Robert Doyle spotted the African family exiting the bushes at the bottom of the valley. 'Here they are now. One last coffee before I go?'

'I'll make it. Come on into the kitchen.'

Isabella was standing by the window when Robert Doyle entered the room. There was a nostalgic look on her face and when he looked again the sun had wandered past a tree that was shadowing it. Suddenly released, its beam swept through the glass and caught the woman. For just a moment he was struck dumb by the way the refracted light played games with her profile. He kissed her and her breath was that of the mountains.

'I love you Isabella.'

'Oh Robert, how I hunger for those words. It is because of your love that I have the strength to leave all this behind.' She was looking at the land beyond the window where the paths on which she used to ride her horse ran down to the river. She saw again clearly – perhaps for the last time – the dusty yard in front of the house that was once her playground. And there was a mist in her eyes when she thought of this precious valley that held the footprints of her childhood.

Was this how it all ended?

Robert Doyle put his arm around her shoulder and she rested her head against his faded khaki shirt. Beyond the trees was the distant river where they had made love on a grassy bank beside a pool where dragonflies played, before this one moment of madness with Shazi. All of that was yesterday, the past. The future was the

Drakensberg. Yes, that was where she would go with the stranger who had come into her world just two days ago. And when she thought of this, the words came easily: 'I love you so much, Robert Doyle.'

Then she closed her eyes and let him hold her.

'I'm sorry Isabella,' he said for the umpteenth time, knowing the pain she was experiencing in having to leave her home, 'but I can't think how else to do this. If I could make it work any other way, you know I wouldn't be taking this option. The tragedy is that they will not stop here. It's only a matter of time before they destroy this entire valley. I reckon your friend Danny's farm could be next. In fact, thinking about it, perhaps he should come with us.'

31

Shazi's knock put an end to the intimate moment. Isabella disentangled herself from Robert Doyle's arms and opened the kitchen door to a sombre-faced African maid. Her three youngest children stood beside her, *piccanins* in ragged clothes, standing barefoot in the yard. Africa's next generation, she thought. Suddenly she realised how much she wanted to help them; to be a part of their lives. 'Did you manage to leave the compound without anyone seeing you?'

'*Yebo nkozikazi*,' the maid whispered in a breathless voice. 'The *tsotsis* are still looking for the soldier. They are very angry.'

'Good, it will give us time to get you safely to Juliasdale before they realise what is happening. Can you wait by Robert's truck please? He won't be a minute.'

The maid ushered her children across the yard to the Land Cruiser and Robert Doyle looked at his watch. Ten o'clock. 'I'd better make tracks.'

'Ok, Shazi knows the way. I'll write a note for Sally – the old farm phone sometimes plays up, but I'll try her anyway.' Suddenly a thought occurred to Isabella as she started to write. She put down the pen and looked up at Robert Doyle. 'The squatter camp.' There was concern in her eyes. 'It's hidden from the drive, but I've sometimes seen soldiers near the farm entrance – maybe you should avoid going that way.'

'Is there another way?'

Isabella finished off the note and handed him the paper. 'Come – I'll show you.'

To the rear of the house was an overgrown path that was barely recognisable. 'Here we are. This is the original track Dad used before he constructed the new drive.'

'You call that a track?'

Isabella smiled. 'Well nobody has driven over it for years, but in a four-wheel drive you should be fine. I've walked it fairly recently; it'll be tricky in places but there's been no rain and the ground is firm enough for you to improvise. It'll bring you out on the main road about a mile down from the farm entrance. When you come back, use the same route.' She reached over and kissed him lightly on the cheek. 'And don't be long.'

Suddenly Robert Doyle was struck by an intuition that told him to take Isabella to Juliasdale, but no sooner had the thought occurred to him than he dismissed it as unrealistic; there were jobs that needed doing at the farm and being seen together in Juliasdale would only cause tongues to wag. They returned to the kitchen, respectably apart for the sake of Shazi. 'Bring the Isuzu to the back door when you load up. I'll leave Shamari with you, but if you see anyone approaching up the valley, call Sally straight away and ask her to find me. I won't be far away.'

'I'm sure everything will be fine. There's no reason for them to come here.'

'Let's hope so. Oh, and can you call the garage? This is what you need to tell them,' he said, handing her a short note he had scrawled out earlier.

'I'll ring Wayne when you go. He should be able to repair the vehicle this morning while you wait.'

'Good; then I'll be back just after lunch.' The FN was where he had left it by the front door. He checked the gas regulator and then turned to the woman. 'If you need a rifle to threaten anyone, use this – it's a lot more effective than your old .22. Just slip the safety.'

Isabella eyed the weapon with suspicion; what on earth did he think was going to happen? Keeping her composure, she walked over to where he was standing and kissed him gently on the lips. 'I don't want your rifle. Now get going; I'll come and say goodbye to Shazi.'

'OK, I'll be as quick as I can.'

'Don't be silly – it will probably take me most of the morning to pack. We won't make the border before it closes, so why don't we leave early afternoon and stay the night at Masvingo? It's about halfway to Beitbridge. Then tomorrow we will be in South Africa.'

'Hey, what a good idea! Have you seen the ruins at Great Zimbabwe?'

'A long time ago.'

'They're worth another look.'

Outside, the African family waited patiently in the shade of the derelict barn. Isabella put her arms around her maid's shoulders and hugged her. 'Goodbye Shazi. I am sorry for the way everything has turned out, but when we're settled I will come back and fetch you and your family. That's if you would like to come and live with us in South Africa?'

'South Africa? Ah, *yebo nkozikazi!*' the maid cried, holding onto her mistress. 'This I would like very much.'

Isabella smiled and gave her a last hug before turning her attention to the children. Their shyness was so reminiscent of all her African workers, and it almost broke her heart when she realised that it might be some time before she would see them again. Then she walked over to where Robert Doyle was sitting in the driver's seat of the Land Cruiser. 'Off you go,' she said softly, trying not to show too much emotion in front of the youngsters.

He wanted so much to kiss her and to hold her and to reassure her everything was going to be all right. But all of that was for later. 'I'll be back before you are even packed. Don't forget to call Danny.'

The face she loved seemed to show its age that morning. 'I'll phone him as soon as I've spoken to the garage. I'm not sure he'll come with us, but I'll do my best.'

Robert Doyle shrugged. 'That's his call – just remind him that there's plenty of land in the Drakensberg.' Then the Land Cruiser engine burst into life and before she could utter another word, the vehicle had disappeared down the old bush track.

The woman stood in the yard watching the pale dust cloud track its way down the valley. It was then she realised that, for the first time since Saturday, she was once again alone.

32

The road to Juliasdale stretched down across the mountain and into the distance. Over the low rise, Robert Doyle could see the squatter camp lying deep in the valley. Stopping momentarily to allow the dust to settle, he searched the compound with his field glasses. It seemed somewhat subdued, almost shrouded with an air of abandonment, but he realised that this was merely the lull before the storm. The violence at the camp this morning decreed the next chapter in the saga and the passengers in the vehicle were testament to that.

Shazi hadn't uttered a single word since leaving the farm. Her hands were clasped tightly together and when she caught sight of her home far below at the crossroads, she shuddered. The only other sign of life in the vehicle was the odd sniffle from the girls sitting in the back, but a reprimand from the boy, issued harshly in Shona, brought total silence.

In front of them was a steep rocky section. Robert Doyle eased the gear lever into low ratio before releasing the clutch. The Land Cruiser jumped forward, slowly descending the escarpment, picking its way over the rocky terrain. Twenty minutes later they exited the bush onto the gravel road.

There was no sign of life.

Turning right, he was about to drive off when he noticed his tyre imprints on the sandy verge. If the *vanamukoma* saw them they would discover the track to the farm and he felt tiny goose pimples tingling on his arm at the thought of them going up to the house. Only after obliterating any evidence of the Land Cruiser, did he continue on his way.

The scenery changed little on the journey. Occasionally, an impala grazing harmoniously by the roadside would relieve the monotony of the bush. In the rear-view mirror the faces of the frightened children were cast against a curtain of brown dust suspended behind the Land Cruiser. Passively emotionless and conditioned to Africa's violence, their perpetual blank stares painted a picture of promises that had not been kept – tomorrow's generation, sleepwalking through life.

Robert Doyle glanced across at his companion in the passenger seat. Her anxious eyes were fixed intently on the road ahead and he wondered what future Zimbabwe would offer her. 'Shazi, don't be frightened,' he reassured her, 'you are safe now.'

The African said nothing. She, like him, was the product of an ongoing hostility from which there seemed no respite; a period of savagery that Robert Doyle found difficult to reconcile within himself. These were the ghosts of war, a belligerent time that was best forgotten. Yet it was not that easy. His mind still conjured up memories of the security forces poisoning village drinking wells or forcing suspected terrorists to walk in front of convoys to detonate potential landmines. It had been a lawless frontier and now, facing the *vanamukoma* again, he felt he had returned to the battlefield. Was there no escape from the past, he wondered, or was this the price he had to pay for staying with the woman? He looked across at the

African maid. 'Shazi, tell me about your compound – how many soldiers are camped there?'

The African remained silent. Perhaps she was apprehensive about divulging information or maybe just plain frightened that her ancestral spirits collaborated with the *vanamukoma*.

Her silence started Robert Doyle thinking. He was aware that on occasions home-help had been 'turned', either through intimidation or their own sheer greed. This had been particularly true during the Mau-Mau Rebellion in Kenya in the 1950s when the motives of the terrorist movement had been ingrained into the workers. Some had even murdered their employers in terrible acts of atrocity every bit as violent as those for which the *vanamukoma* were notorious. But he could not believe Shazi was capable of such actions.

When she finally spoke, it was in a flat voice, devoid of any emotion. 'I'm not sure how many there are, *bwana* – maybe forty or fifty? They come and go and only bother us for *chibuku*. Or when they want us to go to the indoctrination *pungwes* to sing their war songs.'

Revolutionary songs, such as 'A Luta Continua', or 'The Struggle Continues', were infamous. Robert Doyle had heard them sung many times during marches in the tribal villages. They told the story of Mama Africa and of a land where one day the ground would open and the dead would walk again on the path to freedom and independence. Ian Smith had attempted to ban them because of their tendency to incite violence. But you cannot suppress a whole people on the road to freedom.

'What are they saying at the meetings, Shazi?'

This time there was no hesitation. 'They say the white

man has no place in new Zimbabwe, that it is time he goes. They also say land belongs to our people and it will come back to us and that the rivers will run red with blood.' She glanced uneasily at Robert Doyle before continuing. 'They say pretend to be loyal to the *bwanas*. But when the time is right we must rise up.' She turned to her children sitting quietly behind her, reluctant to continue. But she knew, for Miss Issy's sake, that she must help this *mzungu*. 'The farmers will have chance to go but if they do not go then we must kill them when they are sleeping.' There were tears in her big brown eyes as she watched the countryside flee past the vehicle and disappear into the dust. 'How could I kill the missy? We are like sisters, *nkozi*.'

'Shazi, it will be all right.' Robert Doyle's serious voice carried a hint of compassion. 'You do understand that Miss Isabella must leave before the *tsotsis* come for the farm?'

'This I have told her many times, *nkosi*, but she does not want to go.'

The deserted road dropped down a small hill through a series of bends before the faded sign outside Juliasdale announced their arrival at the settlement. It was a small place, no larger than a hamlet, with a main street flanked by a scattering of clapboard holiday cottages and brick houses. Each building was separated by an unkempt yellow lawn where occasionally bougainvillea hedges splashed the shabby houses with a hint of colour, disguising their starkness. Low white picket fences, their paint peeled in the sun, enclosed the gardens. The only building out of place in the street was the Kwik-Save supermarket, where several Africans loitered aimlessly on the ground, waiting for the odd hand-out.

Robert Doyle noticed the garage set back from the road. An array of dilapidated vehicles stood on its forecourt. 'Where is Sally's house Shazi?'

The maid pointed out the little bungalow with the red corrugated iron roof beyond the post office. It was diagonally opposite the ramshackle old hostelry that bore the sign 'Juliasdale Hotel – Your Retreat in the Highlands', perhaps rather pretentious as the worn exterior of the faded building had long since shown any sign of warmth to its clientele.

Robert Doyle parked the Land Cruiser outside the house and gazed westward across the intermittent forests to the granite domes on the horizon. It was difficult to believe that this was where Isabella had lived during the war, where she had made so many plans which now lay scattered in the dust. He tried to imagine her waiting for Joseph to come home on leave, but all he could see was the soldier standing on the steps, bringing the news of her husband's death, and he determined there and then that nothing like that would ever happen to her again.

'OK Shazi. Let's go and see Sally.' By the time Robert Doyle had reached the sidewalk, the maid and her children were already out of the vehicle and standing together patiently, waiting for their next instructions. 'Here, let me help you with your luggage,' he said, opening the tailgate of the Land Cruiser and passing the bundles of clothing to the children. He swung the old cardboard suitcase onto his shoulder and was halfway to the gate when the front door of the bungalow opened and a plump middle-aged woman with a rosy complexion and bleached blonde hair going to grey rushed down the narrow herringbone brick path to greet them.

'*Kunjani* Shazi?' There was no opportunity for the maid to reply to the greeting before Sally was speaking again. 'Isabella telephoned to say you were coming. I'm so glad to see you. It's all worked out well because Mary – you know Mary, our maid? Well, she went back to Harare yesterday. Her mother is very ill.'

'I am sorry *nkozikazi.*'

'At least you'll be safe here,' Sally said. 'Although I don't know what Isabella is going to do without you.' Hardly a breath was drawn between sentences. Then she turned to Robert Doyle and introduced herself in her bubbly voice. 'You must be Robert – Isabella has told me so much about you, and your place in South Africa. In fact, I just got off the phone with her. We have so much to thank you for.'

Robert Doyle immediately saw why Isabella was so fond of this exuberant woman with her kindly face and infectious attitude. He dropped the case to the ground and took her extended hand, placing a light kiss on her rubicund cheek. 'Really, there is no need.'

'Isabella did warn me to watch out for your charm,' she stuttered.

'I think perhaps you are the one to watch.'

Sally laughed to cover her embarrassment and noticed the little group of children standing patiently on the path. 'Come on in out of the heat and let's get you settled. Do you want tea or something a bit stronger?' This last question was directed at Robert Doyle.

'I need to see Wayne about the water pump. Perhaps I can take you up on your kind offer later?' He handed her Isabella's note and the suitcase.

'Of course, Issy said she'd let him know you were on

your way. Come and join us for something to eat when you are ready, and then you can tell me all about your plans. It sounds so exciting!'

He stepped to one side to allow the children to fall in behind their mother, and the family followed Sally, as a line of chicks would, up the garden path and into the bungalow.

33

The ballad on the radio reminded Isabella of the sixties, with its remorseful lyrics about a boy who loved his girl and was unable to live without her.

It bathed the room in an erroneous tranquillity.

Focusing the binoculars onto the valley below the escarpment, Isabella saw the Land Cruiser disappear into the tree line before it reached the corrugated road. Then something caught her eye below the steps. If it was not for the hooded vultures' feathers on top of the shaft, faintly distinguishable between the leaves of a sickle bush, she would not have seen the *assegai*. So this was what all the commotion had been about on Saturday night. Why had Robert Doyle told her about the *tsotsi* and the war cry but failed to mention the spear? Furthermore, it looked like he had tried to hide it. And what had happened to the *tsotsi?* He'd brushed over that too.

The house was the safest place for the *assegai* until she could dispose of it. If anyone found it she would be in serious trouble, especially if one of the soldiers was dead. Shaking with fear, she removed it from the bushes and leant it against the gun-cupboard door. Then she remembered Sally and how much there was still to do and for a moment the spear was forgotten.

First she called Juliasdale Motors to explain the situation. It was an easy conversation; Wayne was a straightforward guy and he would be the last person to indulge in small talk or inquisitive gossip.

Next she called Sally, which had been more difficult, since she loved a drama. Isabella had kept the conversation brief and, despite her curiosity, Sally had lived up to her kind nature by promising to help.

Her call to Danny would be the most delicate. She dialled the number. Halfway through the process she replaced the receiver to allow herself more time to reconstruct her thoughts. Perhaps it would be easier after a cup of tea. Then she recalled Robert Doyle's advice: 'Tell him the truth Isabella; you owe him that much.'

The stranger's presence was in the room and her hands were still shaking when she tried the number again. This time she let the call go through trying, without much success, to hide her anxiety.

'Everything all right Issy?'

'Danny, I'm frightened.'

'What's happened?'

'It's Lumbu.'

'Yes?'

'He was murdered . . . at the compound.'

'What?'

'They accused him of killing a soldier and they burnt him alive.'

'You're joking – Lumbu wouldn't hurt a fly!'

'It's terrible Danny. Shazi is in such a state . . . she thinks her family will be next.'

'Oh God. Do you want me to come over?'

She had to tell him about Robert, but where did she start? The situation would have been easier to explain face to face but events had overtaken them and they'd run out of time. 'Danny, so much has happened.' She paused, trying to think of what to say next. 'A friend called while you were in Mutare and, well, he's—'

'A friend?' Before Danny had the opportunity to question her further, Isabella was talking again, filling him in on the horrific events of that morning.

'Robert has taken all of them to Sally's house. He's in Juliasdale at the moment having his vehicle repaired.' The line fell silent. 'Danny? Are you still there?'

'Yes Issy, I'm here . . . I just don't understand. Why didn't you call?'

'I don't know. I'm all confused.' She paused briefly. 'Do you remember our agreement when the killings first started? You know, after the violence at Headlands?'

'Yes of course – we said we'd go at the first sign of trouble.'

'Well, there *is* trouble now Danny. If they take my farm then yours could be next.'

Danny's reply was controlled, without the slightest trace of jealousy or vindictiveness, and yet there was a sadness. 'Hey Issy, hold on! When did all this happen?'

'This morning. Will you come with us Danny . . . please?

'Issy, you know I would go anywhere with you or help you in any way I can if your life is in danger. You know that. But isn't this all a bit sudden? When do you want to go and *where* will we go?' There was a brief pause, and then: 'I always thought we would see this out together, perhaps even plan it together, like we've done in the past.'

'There isn't time – Robert thinks we should go to South Africa, and as soon as possible. If he manages to repair his truck, we hope to be on our way sometime this afternoon.

Danny, that's why I'm ringing you, I thought we–'

'South Africa? Bloody hell Issy – why South Africa?' Danny asked, exasperated. 'How can I pack my life into a Land Rover in a couple of hours? You could have rung me yesterday, given me some warning! And who is this "Robert" who has persuaded you to go against everything we agreed?' His voice deteriorated into a whine. He thought he knew all of her friends – after all, Juliasdale was a small place. 'This is very confusing.'

'Danny, *please* try to understand.' Isabella's voice was now composed. 'I've had the *vanamukoma* camped on my doorstep for a while now. In spite of this, I was still not prepared to leave Ingombe. You of all people should know that. But after what happened at the squatter camp this morning . . . everything has changed.'

'But Issy, let's be sensible. Let's–'

'No Danny,' she said, interrupting him again, 'it's my life that is in danger. I'm sorry if it's short notice, but it's just the same for me – I'm really terrified of what they'll do next.' She knew she was repeating herself and the last thing she wanted was to finish the conversation on a sour note, but she was getting impatient. 'Look, I realise what you have put into your farm and I will understand if you want to stay, but I really must start packing. I'll speak to you before we go.' There was nothing left to say and she hung up quickly without mentioning Robert Doyle's name again. For a minute she stared at the receiver hanging in its cradle and the simple length of wire that could convey so many emotions.

The keys to the Isuzu were on the hall table. She was halfway out of the kitchen door when the shrill ring of the telephone called her back.

299

'Hey Issy, look – I'm sorry.'

'Danny, I appreciate how you feel. Please don't apologise – it's me who should be sorry. I just have a feeling they are going to take Ingombe at any moment, and after what happened at Gazelle Farm I don't want to be here when they come.'

'That's why I should know better. I was totally out of order – I knew the *vanamukoma* were at Ingombe but I didn't realise the extent of their harassment. Mugabe keeps coming on the TV and telling us they are there for our protection. But you're right; we cannot live in fear. Just let me know where to meet you. I'll be ready.'

'Are you sure this is what you want Danny?' It was the same question she had asked Robert Doyle the previous night. 'I know what Rigby's Creek means to you.'

'Not as much as you mean to me,' he said quietly. 'If you can leave it all behind then so can I. Anyway, you don't think I'm going to let you go gallivanting off with some strange fella that I've not even met, do you? A pretty girl like you? Never know what might happen.'

Isabella laughed, still a little out of breath from running for the phone. 'Oh Danny! I feel so much better now. We should be ready to leave early afternoon. We'll probably break the journey and stay overnight at Masvingo and then cross the border tomorrow. Oh, and don't forget the money from the safe. I'll call you later with the details.'

As she walked across the yard to the roofless barn, she reflected on what Danny had just said: 'Not as much as you mean to me.'

Why had he never said that to her before?

34

In the east the wind was blowing off the purple-headed mountains and with each gust it took the oppressive edge off the morning heat. Just before the woman reached the Isuzu a movement on the ground caught her eye. Coming out from behind the rocks, a long-tailed scorpion scurried across the path in front of the vehicle. Its massive tail was poised menacingly above its grey and black body. Isabella knew that its excruciating sting was a deterrent to most predators. She stopped in her stride and then remembered the mamba they had stumbled onto the previous day and Robert Doyle's advice: 'Just give it room to escape.' Like the snake, the scorpion sensed no danger and eventually strutted off. But because it had diverted her attention, the woman failed to see Shamari pacing the fence behind the wooden barn, anxious for her master's return.

She opened the door of the Isuzu and jumped into the driver's seat. Although the vehicle was old, its reconditioned petrol engine started on the first turn of the key. Reversing the *bakkie* to the house, as Robert Doyle had instructed, Isabella sat for a moment staring at the view from the front windscreen. Suddenly the years fell away and she saw Francesca and her father standing beside the water well. And there was Joseph, the first time he knocked reluctantly on the kitchen door to ask her out for a date. His hair was slicked down with Brylcreem and the jacket, a size too small, sat uncomfortably on his large frame. All of this just to impress her. And when she saw the images she found it difficult to accept that the house with all its memories would soon be annihilated. The thought overwhelmed her and she stepped out of the vehicle and away from her torment.

After the Bush War, life on Zimbabwe's farms had become somewhat transient. Canvas suitcases were already partially packed should the need to flee arise and despite Isabella's reluctance to leave, she was no different. Joseph's letters and special mementoes filled one of her cases, but other personal possessions were still left scattered around the house. Isabella didn't feel sentimental about them. After all, material objects come to mean nothing when your life is in danger.

It was then that she noticed the photograph, a black and white picture of her parents in a faded wooden frame – she'd accidentally pushed it to the back of the bookshelf where it had remained hidden behind an ornament. Picking up the picture, she wiped away the film of dust on the glass. Eduardo looked like a film star, very Gary Cooper in a rugged way. But it was Francesca's beauty that encapsulated her. Long, straight, black hair framed an oval face and her ethereal eyes appeared to be beguiled by someone standing behind the photographer. Who or what was it that was amusing her? It was a question that grieved Isabella because she would never know the answer.

It's uncanny how our brains are conditioned to hear only what we want to hear. In the background the sounds of Maputo radio were floating on the air, playing a selection of old blues numbers. The disc jockey had just introduced the song 'Cotton Fields' and Isabella's mind filtered out all extraneous sounds as she hummed along to the song. Because of this, she missed the distant hum of a vehicle struggling up the hill. It continued to draw nearer. When she eventually tuned in, the memories associated with the song were banished from her mind and she thought of Robert Doyle. She looked at her watch; less than two hours – goodness me, that was quick. The Land Cruiser must have been easier to repair than he'd anticipated. But why had he come up the front drive? Perhaps there'd been problems with the old track?

In her excitement, Isabella rushed out onto the *stoep*.

But it was not Robert Doyle.

Shamari was lying in the shade near the corner of the house. When she saw the approaching vehicle, she rose silently to her feet and moved out of sight.

No one noticed her go.

The dog was the last thing on Isabella's mind as she squinted in the sunlight to get a better look at the vehicle. And what she saw shocked her: it was a white police Land Rover – the CIO. She had heard all about the Criminal Intelligence Organisation, Mugabe's henchmen. His secret police were a law unto themselves; notorious for their brutality at Harare's central prison, they were the thugs who carried out the *vanamukoma's* dirty work.

But what were they doing here?

Isabella felt only revulsion for these bullies. A friend of hers had spent six months in solitary confinement at one of their military prisons near Harare. His crime? To have questioned the validity of Mugabe's land reclaim. When he was eventually released he was a shadow of his former self. These scum were the last people in the world she would welcome.

The sergeant – in fact, a boy barely out of his teens – approached the house. In his right hand was an AK-47, his badge of authority. But it was the aggression in his voice that startled the woman. 'Where is the maid that works for you?'

Clenching her fists by her side, Isabella returned the pugnacious stare. 'She has not been well lately,' she lied, in a brave attempt to keep the fear out of her voice. 'I gave her pills yesterday and told her to take the day off. Perhaps she is in bed.'

'Don't try and be clever with us lady! This is no longer colonial Rhodesia where you arrogant white people think you can treat us like monkeys.'

Shocked at this sudden turn of events, Isabella nevertheless maintained her composure. How often had she heard friends warn her not to be cowed by these bastards, that they'd take advantage of any sign of weakness.

'I refuse to be spoken to in this tone of voice,' she said, squaring up to the youth.

The sergeant ignored the woman. 'We know you are lying – the maid and her children were seen walking to your house this morning. Perhaps we will find them when we search the place,' he continued belligerently.

Across the yard the senior officer leaned nonchalantly against the side of the Land Rover, chewing a blade of grass. He was satisfied that his sergeant had the situation under control and was happy to let him handle the questioning. Not only was it good experience for him, but he also found it rather entertaining.

Isabella was in a predicament. The CIO obviously

knew the maid had come up to the house. And to make matters worse there was the *assegai*. It was still leaning up against the gun cupboard. If they found it she'd be in real trouble. Because of this, she decided to remain firm and stand her ground – anything to prevent them from entering the house.

But then what other option did she have?

'You have no jurisdiction to come here with your insults and accusations. Where is your search warrant?'

'Search warrant?' The young policeman laughed sarcastically. 'In case you have not heard, lady, we have the authority to enter any premises at any time we wish – especially if we suspect a crime.'

'I'm sorry, but you are not entering my house without a warrant,' Isabella countered, knowing her assertion to be legally bound, but fearing its lack of power in this lawless land.

The sergeant turned to look at his superior. Still chewing on the grass, he gave a barely perceptible nod. Confident he now had the officer's approval, the sergeant proceeded with the interrogation, eying the woman like a predator.

'Well lady, we seem to have a problem here. A bit of *mzungu* aggression, hey? Not to worry; we have interesting ways of dealing with you insolent *umfazis*.'

Images of the brutal attack on Gazelle Farm flashed through the woman's mind. She had seen the pictures in the papers. Was this to be her fate? Then she remembered Robert Doyle's rifle. Although she had shot and killed animals before, like the vicious leopard that she and Joe had tracked above the Honde Valley, Isabella had never been faced with a situation anything like as dangerous as this before. She wanted to appeal to the belligerent policeman's superior, but seeing the insolent grin on his face, she knew it would be futile.

She retreated towards the door. Another few paces and she would reach the weapon. She'd never used an FN before, so quite what she was going to do with it she did not know.

'Where are you going?' the sergeant shouted, running towards the steps.

Isabella froze briefly before turning to reach for the rifle. Her hand had barely touched the FN when she heard the scream.

From the overhanging shadow of the clapboard porch, Shamari leapt onto the unsuspecting African, the sheer weight of the animal propelling the hapless man to the ground. Powerful jaws locked onto his throat, tearing away at the soft flesh, as the African tried desperately to pry away the ferocious teeth. The blood was everywhere.

Before Isabella could control the dog, the sound of a rifle echoed through the air and she watched helplessly as Shamari audaciously tried to maintain her grip on the policeman's throat. Then she heard the second shot and saw the dog jerk violently under the impact of the bullet before falling to the ground.

'No!' Isabella screamed, running down the steps and throwing herself in front of the animal, oblivious to the injured policeman gasping frantically for air as he crawled away across the yard.

Her entire focus was now on the officer covering her with his Kalashnikov.

His smile had disappeared, along with his nonchalant attitude. 'This is your dog?'

The woman was unable to speak.

'You will be held responsible for the attack on my sergeant. You are under house arrest and you'll stay here until we have made our inquiries. Do *not* try to leave the farm.' This was an irrelevant order. Having already instructed his soldiers to block the farm entrance with a tree trunk, he knew it would be impossible to leave Ingombe.

It took all of Isabella's effort just to nod.

'Do you understand what I am saying?' the officer shouted aggressively.

Before she could reply his attention was diverted by his comrade's muted groans. Turning his back on the woman, he slung the sergeant's rifle over his shoulder and lifted the stricken man into the Land Rover. 'We will deal with you later,' he shouted, before driving off.

Isabella's eyes were fixed on the track where the dust had now settled. The dog lay motionless at her feet in a pool of blood. How strange that Shamari would have nothing to do with her, and yet when she sensed the woman's life was in jeopardy, she had come to her rescue. Isabella reached down and placed her hand on the dog's head, softly stroking the rough fur. The touch brought a flicker of recognition. Shamari opened her eyes which, once so ferocious, were now just feeble brown pools, and she struggled to move her head in a vain attempt to lick the woman's hand before she died.

Isabella looked helplessly at the old, grey, whiskered face and then at the wiry fur and then at the bullet holes. It was more than she could endure. The worn blanket, still impregnated with the dog's smell, was on the *stoep* and this she used to cover the body.

She had to call Sally. Her fingers were shaking as she

tried to dial the number. 'Please God, find Robert and send him back,' she whispered to herself while waiting for a reply.

'Ngozi Cottage.'

'Sal it's me,' Isabella said, trying to keep her voice calm. 'Is Robert with you?'

'He went across to Wayne's – I don't know where he is now.'

'Can you find him please Sal? And ask him to get back here as soon as possible.'

'Whatever's the matter Isabella?'

Oh God, what do I tell her? she thought. 'There's been an accident, Sal.'

'An accident?'

'It's the dog. I need you to find Robert – *please* Sal, it's urgent.'

None of this was making much sense but the gravity in Isabella's voice told Sally to accept the situation without further explanation. 'Hang on Issy. Samnaya – hey Sam, where are you?' Sally shouted through the open door.

'*Nkozikazi?*'

'Find boss Robert! Try the hotel – *haraka, haraka,* hurry, and tell him to come here!'

'Thanks Sal.' There was relief in Isabella's tired voice. 'I'll explain everything when we get to South Africa. And as soon as we are settled we'll come back for Shazi and the kids.' She looked down at her watch, suddenly conscious of the time and how much there was still to do. But somehow it all seemed so irrelevant with Shamari lying in the yard.

Robert Doyle had been right all along – this part of Africa was dead.

35

There was no traffic on the main street when Robert Doyle drew the vehicle up outside Juliasdale Motors. Wayne, a thin-featured man with a face tanned like crinkly boot leather, emerged from under the chassis of a rusty old Series 2 Land Rover, dressed only in a pair of faded blue oily denim overalls and a peaked cap that advertised Valvoline oil. He extended a greasy hand. 'Hi! I guess you must be Robert.'

Robert Doyle clasped the friendly, outstretched hand without hesitation. The grip was firm. 'I'm a friend of Isabella's. I don't know whether she explained but I need a gasket making for the water pump. Any chance of dropping onto it? I'm in a bit of a rush.' The urgency in his voice conveyed the message and he decided to leave it at that. This was small-town Zimbabwe and he was the stranger – any loose talk would be up the high street soon enough, with assumptions made and conclusions drawn.

The mechanic nodded easily. A man of few words, he had lived long enough in Zimbabwe to understand the predicament. 'No problem,' he said, in a strong South African accent. 'I'll get onto it right away. The job shouldn't take any more than a couple of hours. I know it's a bit early but there's the hotel up the road if you want a beer – it's about all you can drink in this heat.'

Their eyes met briefly across the vehicle. 'I appreciate it Wayne,' Robert Doyle said, handing him the keys and turning towards the hotel. Although it was still only mid morning, the bar seemed like an easier option than explaining the events of the last few days to Sally. And then his mind returned to Shazi and the drama in the kitchen and he knew there was still a long way to go before they were away from Ingombe. A suspicion, which he tried to dismiss as absurd, clouded his vision. It was the same premonition he'd had when leaving the farm. What, if anything, should happen to Isabella? No, he thought, what could possibly go wrong now? It was all so straightforward – he just needed to repair the gasket and head for the border at Bietbridge. They would be in South Africa before midday tomorrow. In spite of his convictions, misgivings still lingered in his mind and he stopped mid stride and turned back towards the mechanic. 'Excuse me Wayne – would you happen to know if there's a solicitor in town that I can see at short notice?'

The mechanic poked his head out from under the bonnet of the Land Cruiser, spanner in hand. 'Ya, you're in luck – Dick Simmonds comes down from Mutare three times a week. He uses the building society office next to the Kwik-Save supermarket. Just call in, he's never that busy. If he's not there, he'll be in the pub.'

Robert Doyle raised his arm in appreciation. There was a glimmer of a smile on his face when he imagined the local solicitor solving legal disputes across a crowded bar, but he decided to try the office first.

When he emerged an hour later the street was deserted. The midday heat was intolerable and even the dogs were playing dead, lying wherever they could find a patch of shade, on or beneath the sidewalk. He passed the garage and waved to Wayne who, on noticing him, shouted across the street. 'About another half hour or so should see the job done!' Robert Doyle acknowledged him and continued on to the hotel, where he climbed the dilapidated steps to the wooden porch. Swinging the barroom door open, he then stepped into the room.

The coolness of the air-conditioning rolled out across the floor like an Atlantic wave on a Skeleton Coast beach. Considering the time of day, the bar was doing a roaring trade, but then what else was there to do in this one-horse town? Old men with tired faces, red from too many years in the sun, sat at the beer-stained bar drinking lager, the froth from the liquid settling on the stubble that covered their dishevelled features. Above them a large overhead fan swirled the smell of stale beer, tobacco and sweat around the room.

Robert Doyle ordered a Castle lager. The bleary-eyed barman pulled the top on the bottle and left it on the stained work surface. The beer was both cold and refreshing and satisfied his thirst immediately. From his position at the corner of the bar he was able to observe the crowd and he wondered whether the locals had any inclination who he was or where he was staying. No one showed any sign of recognition, but then why would they? Few people in Juliasdale knew of his existence.

A couple of farmers, wearing serious looks, were in deep conversation about the state of the country. Public houses made for good venues to eavesdrop on local gossip and the absence of any Africans brought a degree of freedom to the dialogue.

'I tell you, Jim, it's never going to get any better while

that bloody dictator Mugabe is still around. But what chance do we have if we leave and where do we go?'

Jim downed his glass of beer before replying. 'The easy option is to cross into South Africa, but I often wonder how long it will be before we'll have to move on again from there. I heard last week that they are already starting to reclaim farms in the Transvaal. Ach, Pete, I reckon the whole of Africa has gone to the bloody dogs.'

'I was born here and I guess I will die here.' The despondency in Pete's voice shocked Robert Doyle. 'You know, Frik,' he said, turning to speak to the man behind the bar, 'all I ever wanted was to be a part of Rhodesia and now I don't even have that.'

Although barmen are good listeners, they tend to be reluctant conversationalists. The old Afrikaner publican had heard too many stories over the years that he had tended bar in this small town to form an opinion one way or the other and he simply nodded in agreement.

'You heard what happened at Rusape last month?' Pete continued. 'You know, when they killed Ronnie Walker and his family at Gazelle Farm?'

'You mean up at Headlands?'

'Yeah, well, now the murderous bastards are camped out at Ingombe.'

'Look Pete, we've been telling Issy for ages that she needs to get out before they invade the farm, but she keeps saying it won't happen to her.'

'Well sometimes I wonder if she's living in the real world since Joe died. And her friend Danny up at Rigby's Creek is just as crazy. They both think that they are immune to the violence and that the *kaffirs* are playing games.'

Jim nodded. 'I guess it's not that easy,' he said, picking up his fresh pint of beer. 'She's lived at Ingombe all her life and everything she has is up there on the farm.'

'Is it that important next to her life?' Pete asked. 'And those bloody *tsotsis* don't give a shit that she's a woman. In fact they would enjoy it even more if she put up any resistance. And you know what Isabella is like.'

'That's what happened at Gazelle,' Jim replied. 'Look what they did to Andrea and her mother after they killed Ronnie and Tom. The black bastards are like animals.'

Robert Doyle was aware of the incident. Although the attack had happened some time ago, papers were still running the story and he'd seen the latest report splashed across the front page of the *Rusape Herald* when he'd stopped at the Troutbeck bottle store the previous Saturday. But he wanted no part of the subversive gossip so he ignored the discussion and looked away.

As he did so he caught sight of his gaunt image staring back from amongst the whisky bottles in the fly-speckled mirror behind the bar and he wondered once again what a woman like Isabella wanted with a drifter like him. They came from such different worlds. Then he saw in the reflection the bar room door swing open and the noisy hustle and bustle of the drinkers died a sudden death.

Slowly, Robert Doyle turned around to face the room.

An African child stepped into the bar, his apprehensive eyes searching the crowd. Eventually he spotted who he was looking for and rushed across the congested room to Robert Doyle, hostile, inquisitive eyes following his progress. Cast in this role, Samnaya looked nervous, but Robert Doyle immediately put him at ease by placing a hand on his shoulder. 'It's OK kid – what's wrong?'

Only those in the immediate vicinity heard the whisper.

'Miss Sally needs you urgently please, *nkozi*.'

Robert Doyle squeezed the boy's arm reassuringly and placed the empty bottle onto the wooden bar top with a Zimbabwe note. Then, without waiting for the change, he put his arm around Samnaya's shoulder and walked with him through the room. The crowd parted and when the pair reached the heavy old wooden door, Robert Doyle pushed it open and together they stepped out into the blazing sunshine of the street. Behind them the hustle and bustle of voices quickened to a crescendo, with questions thrown to and fro across the stunned bar room.

It would not be long before they would all know why the stranger was in town.

36

The tracker lay concealed in the branches of the marula tree next to the farmhouse. After seeing the maid and her children flee from the compound, and the soldiers forcing a group of villagers to drag a tree trunk across Ingombe's drive, effectively blocking the entrance to the house, he realised that today was the day the *wazungus* would lose their farm.

A sense of urgency had prevailed. After hurried farewells from the *umfazi*, the *mzungu* had bundled the African family into the Land Cruiser and had set off across the farm on a narrow disused track. Sengamo smiled to himself. This was a clever one, he thought – he must have figured out that the compound at the crossroads was dangerous, so he was using the old track. But then, thinking about it, would the white man know that the entrance to Ingombe was barricaded and guarded by soldiers? Probably not.

For the moment all was quiet and Sengamo examined his options. Sooner or later the *vanamukoma* would come to the house and then perhaps he would get the chance to kill two birds with one stone. He decided, therefore, to wait.

The white woman walked out of the house and stood for a moment on the *stoep* watching a flock of purple starlings settle in a flame tree. The scavenger birds were becoming a nuisance – there was no food around here for them so he hoped they would move on to the fruit trees further down the valley. And then he saw the dog exit a shadow near the building, perhaps disturbed by the starlings. He'd assumed that the animal would have travelled with its master, so he was relieved he'd taken the precaution of avoiding the house. At least he was safe in the tree, and the canopy of green leaves provided respite from the stifling heat.

It was the sound of a vehicle screeching to a halt in the yard that had stirred the tracker. Alarm bells rang when he saw the CIO Land Rover – what were the secret police doing here? There was much shouting between the *umfazi* and the policemen, yet the woman stood her ground. This was indeed a proud and strong *nkozikazi*, he thought. But this business was not his concern and he felt no inclination to compromise his position. Neither had he any problem with the land allocation, rather only the fairness of the distribution. For too long his people had worked for the *wazungus* for a pittance and in conditions that were deplorable.

Before he had time to contemplate his next move the *imbwa* had attacked the aggressive policeman and then he'd heard the shot that killed the dog and saw the hurried departure. But Sengamo knew they would be back. And when they returned they would bring with them many more soldiers. It was the farm they wanted and they would eliminate the *umfazi* to get it.

This was the opportunity he had been waiting for, his chance for retribution. Not only would he be able to repay his debt to the white soldier, but he would finally avenge the deaths of his family – his two birds with one stone.

The *umfazi* sat with her head in her hands, staring at

the dog. What was it about the *wazungus* and their sentimentality? To him the *imbwa* was a threat and he was relieved that he no longer had to worry about the animal.

For perhaps an hour nothing happened. And then in the distance Sengamo saw a plume of dust on the old track, long before he heard the vehicle.

The *mzungu* had returned.

37

The Land Cruiser approached the house from the west, up the disused dirt track.

Robert Doyle parked the vehicle behind the wooden barn, a derelict building that had once been a useful storage facility but was now, like much of the farm, merely abandoned. Concealed by the barn, the Toyota would be impossible to see from the yard or the front drive, but it would be easy to access when the time came to leave.

Everything appeared normal at first glance. The Isuzu was parked in front of the kitchen door as he had instructed, although it did not appear to be packed. There had been a confused message from Sally and now the empty vehicle. He tried the kitchen door. It was locked and there was no sign of life.

What was happening? And where was Shamari?

Suddenly he was alert and on his guard, as he cautiously approached the side of the house. But it was only when he turned the corner of the building that he saw the dog lying in the yard and the woman sitting on the step.

And then Robert Doyle was running.

Isabella sensed his presence before he reached the steps. He lifted her up and into his arms. The smell of stale beer and cigarette smoke had impregnated his clothes in the Juliasdale Hotel bar and at any other time the nicotine would have been nauseating; now it was almost a comfort.

'It's OK Isabella,' he said, gently, 'it's all over now.'

'Oh Robert, it was awful, just awful!'

He looked at the dog lying in the dust and then at the woman who had stopped crying. 'OK now?'

She nodded her head.

'Can you tell me what happened?'

As he held the woman in his arms, exhausted from recounting the tragic events, Robert Doyle silently cursed his actions. Why hadn't he disposed of the *assegai* instead of throwing it in the bushes? But then everything had happened so quickly that night and he had acted instinctively without thinking of the consequences.

'She saved my life Robert. Why? She didn't even like me.'

'You are wrong,' he said, nonchalantly. 'She's been trained to attack Africans at the first sign of intimidation.'

'I don't understand why you are like this,' Isabella cried hysterically. 'Don't you care?'

'Look,' he said, in a harsher tone than intended, 'we all have to die one day. You have lived on a farm all your life, so you know animals. Shamari was rather like an old elephant when they lose their eyesight and their teeth go rotten; they are rejected by the herd and driven into the bush.'

'But she was not a wild animal.'

Robert Doyle's arm was resting comfortably on her shoulder. 'I guess that's a matter of opinion.'

All of a sudden Isabella understood why he was treating the death lightly. It was the only way he could accept it without breaking down. 'She tried to lick my hand.'

Robert Doyle closed his eyes and said nothing.

'Why didn't we go yesterday, Robert – why?'

He felt her anguish. As a soldier he should have anticipated the *tsotsis* would come looking for the maid and he should never have left the woman alone at the farm. Another balls-up. But it was not too late – they still had a small window of opportunity to escape before the CIO returned. 'We have to get out of here,' he said. 'We'll use the old track again.'

'Why didn't I listen to you?'

Robert Doyle frowned. He knew the woman was still in shock but he didn't need this – not after having spent so long trying to persuade her to leave. And now, ironically, it was her fiery temperament that was forcing the issue. Yet it was exactly this spirit that had attracted him to her in the first place and he would not have it any other way. 'Right or wrong, Isabella, there is no going back. We can all be clever in hindsight. What we may or may not have done yesterday is of no relevance today. Now we need a plan.'

'Do you really think they will come back?'

'Yes, but I have no idea how long we've got . . . it all depends on what happens to the injured policeman.' He looked down again at the body of the dog covered by the faded blanket. He would miss Shamari and perhaps grief and recriminations would come later, but he knew that if he had taken the dog to Juliasdale, the woman would have been in a serious predicament – perhaps even raped and killed. Then he recalled the day he found Shamari lying emaciated beneath an acacia bush. Had this been her way of finally settling old scores?

'Isabella, we need to move quickly. But first I must bury Shamari.'

'Can I help you? I don't want to be alone.'

'We'll do this together,' he said, taking hold of her hand and leading her to the msasa tree.

When the hole was prepared, Robert Doyle wrapped Shamari in the blanket and laid her in the grave before covering it with soil. He then built a mound with the rocks that Isabella had collected. When the soil and grey stones finally obliterated the colourful blanket, Robert Doyle stood up and reached for the woman's hand. 'That should keep her safe from scavengers,' he said, anxiously looking around. Because of the rocky ground, the grave had taken longer to dig than he had anticipated and he was restless to leave the farm.

But the woman held his hand tightly, reluctant to let go. She was crying. 'Oh Robert! I dread to think what might have happened if Shamari had not been here. There was so much hate – I'm sure they would have killed me if it was not for her.'

He looked at the woman. 'Perhaps,' he said softly. 'But then you are worth dying for.'

They were standing beneath the wide embracing branches of the msasa tree when Isabella heard the words and they sent a shudder through her body.

***

At last, after all the years of uncertainty, Isabella was finally able to distance herself from Ingombe and the past and escape her mountain fortress. Most of the packing was complete and while she moved the boxes towards the back door, Robert Doyle loaded them into the Isuzu. Her whole life lay before her in ten boxes.

'Is the Drakensberg really so beautiful Robert?' she asked, handing him her mother's old guitar and looking for one last assurance.

He smiled. 'You will see for yourself tomorrow.'

'All I want is to be with you.' Her eyes wandered around the kitchen where they had spent so much time together over the last couple of days. And yet now she was leaving she felt strangely remote from the room and all its contents, almost as if she had walked into someone else's house. She turned to look out of the window that overlooked the valley. For so long it had been her whole life, where so many memories had been captured in the simple wooden frame. And she realised that after tomorrow all of this would cease to exist.

Robert Doyle stood beside the woman and watched her deal with her memories. Dark brown hair framed her pale olive skin and for the first time that day it showed a hint of colour. And her eyes, which only short moments ago were filled with despair, now conveyed a faint hope.

Soiled dishes filled the sink and coffee cups lay scattered around the table. They were insignificant objects, but they nevertheless caught Isabella's attention and she managed a smile. 'Why don't we leave the washing up for the *tsotsis?*'

He laughed, taking hold of her hand. 'OK, let's go,' he said at last.

38

The sound of vehicles labouring up the hill caught Robert Doyle by surprise – he hadn't expected this, and certainly not so soon.

Isabella was in the process of dialling Danny's number to let him know they were leaving when she heard the Land Rovers. Dropping the receiver back into its cradle, she saw Robert Doyle turn away from the kitchen door, his eyes mirroring her concern.

'It looks like our friends are back.' They needed to leave right now: absconding down the old track was one possibility, but he knew it was futile – they would be stopped before they had any chance of escaping the farm. Then the thought came to him; this is exactly what you were trained for during the war – deal with it.

The woman could taste a sickness in her throat, driven by a fear that was almost tangible. 'What are we going to do?' she cried, looking at Robert Doyle for an answer.

He picked up the FN rifle and smiled calmly. 'Listen – we don't have much time. I want you to go out to the *stoep* and meet them.' His manner was cool. 'They are not the brightest guys on the block. I reckon we can bluff our way through this – just play it straight.'

'*Play it straight* – I can't do that – they terrify me!'

Robert Doyle held his hand up to signal her to listen. The vehicles were close. 'You have to buy us time, Isabella.

Agree to whatever they say – offer to give them the farm – anything to appease them! But if they want to interrogate you about Shazi, tell them you will take their questions at the police station. Above all, stay calm and *please* don't antagonise them, if that's possible.' A barely perceptible smile fleetingly crossed his face.

'Robert this is serious. Why are you making fun of it?'

'I'm sorry – it will be all right. Whatever you do, don't let them into the house. It's easier dealing with them outside where I can see them.'

'I don't know whether I can do this.'

'You can do it! Just don't show them you are afraid. They get a kick out of frightening women.' The automatic rifle was hanging by his side. He unclipped the twenty-round magazine and checked the gas system before pressing the trigger. The sound of the firing pin hammering onto an empty chamber sent shivers down the woman's spine. Adjusting the gas regulator down, so there was less chance of it jamming, he then moved the selector switch from single shot to full automatic. At close quarters, the firepower was awesome. 'Remember; they can't see the Land Cruiser from the front yard so they don't know I'm here. These guys can be unpredictable, but don't worry – if it gets nasty, I'll be covering you.'

Isabella stared at him with a blank look. What did he mean by covering her? From the way he had assumed control with that funny little smirk on his face, he probably relished this rush of adrenalin. Joseph had once told her of fellow soldiers who got a kick out of 'living on the edge'; they felt flat if they were not close to death, to the point that they would spend their free time base jumping off mountain tops. Did Robert Doyle live on the edge?

But there was one consolation: Isabella knew he would protect her. She pulled herself together and assumed a brave face. 'OK Robert: I'll get rid of them. If it's the farm they want, they can have it.'

'That's what I wanted to hear. Just try not to lose your temper with them.'

She was sceptical. 'We will be all right – won't we?'

'Yes. You *must* trust me.' He still held the cold black weapon loosely in his right hand. The stock was worn from constant use and the woman shuddered when she thought of how many people it might have killed.

Robert Doyle noticed her tremble and he walked up to her and put his free hand on her shoulder. 'Be strong and we'll see this through.' Then he brushed her lips with a gentle kiss. 'I will never ever let anything happen to you – you must believe that.'

There was a question on her lips, but time was not on her side – Robert Doyle had disappeared through the back door with that quiet air of indestructibility and he was once again the stranger. She looked out beyond the open frame of the kitchen door and wondered if they would ever be able to put all this behind them. Then she turned away from the empty doorway and for just a brief moment there was nothing – no soldiers, no Robert Doyle, nothing. And the silence was deafening.

The screech of the vehicles coming to a halt in the yard brought Isabella back to reality and she walked out to the *stoep* to meet them. There were two open-top Land Rovers and perhaps twenty or more soldiers, most of whom were crammed into the back of the vehicles. Isabella gasped, amazed to think that it was necessary to bring this many troops to arrest one woman.

The same obnoxious CIO officer from their earlier encounter had returned. This time he was in no hurry. In his right hand he held a machete and he was savouring the moment, confident that he had the situation well under control. Two soldiers from the notorious Fifth Brigade were by his side. They held their AK-47s loosely, almost as if they were toys. But from the looks on their faces there was nothing playful about them.

'You are Mrs Isabella George?' The words were slurred, but it was the way he ran his fingers threateningly across the steel blade of the machete that really frightened the woman.

'Yes,' she replied politely.

'You remember me from earlier this morning?'

'Yes. What is it you want?'

'*We* will ask the questions, Mrs George,' he said, and then turned to confer with his aides. The thin smile on his lips was devoid of any warmth and his demeanour seemed bolstered by *mbanje*. Why, Isabella wondered, did they need drugs to accost a woman living on her own, or was there some other sinister reason?

Then the officer turned to face the woman. 'My sergeant is dead.'

The words stunned Isabella and she tried to apologise. 'I'm sorry, how—'

'I told you that *we* will ask the questions! Do not speak until we tell you to do so!' He conferred again with his aide before continuing. 'One of the brigade soldiers is missing. And we have also found the body of another one in the *nganga's* hut. His rifle, ammunition and grenades have gone. So what do you know about all of this?'

The accusation shocked Isabella. 'Do I look like a

woman who creeps around in the dark killing soldiers and hiding them in *nganga* huts?' she asked in a fit of exasperation. 'And what am I going to do with your rifle and grenades – start a war?' She was aware that her impetuousness could prove to be her downfall and yet, in spite of this, she refused to be bullied.

Robert Doyle had not anticipated that they would bring this many soldiers and he grimaced at the outburst. Here she was again, once more putting their lives in jeopardy. '*Shit*', he cursed under his breath. 'What the hell are you doing Isabella?'

Sengamo also heard the *tsotsi's* words, delivered with fire, which carried clearly across the still morning air to his new position, on the ground behind an old msasa tree trunk and barely yards from the army vehicles. He smiled when he heard the woman's reply. 'Ah, you are a brave *nkozikazi!* Or perhaps a little foolish.'

The soldiers standing around the Land Rovers in the yard sniggered. A threatening look from the officer silenced them and he turned his attention back to the woman. 'You *wazungus* think you are very clever, don't you, making fun of us? Three of my men are dead and you stand here and treat us with contempt, like we are *rubbish.*'

'I'm afraid I don't understand.'

'You don't understand? Really? Then I will explain. With your superior voice, you address us as if we are uneducated "*kaffirs*" or "*munts*" – isn't that what you call us?' The officer spat a ball of phlegm at the step below where the woman stood, frustrated at how the interrogation had stalled. And then, realising he was making a spectacle of himself in front of his soldiers, he adopted a different approach. And in this composed state he was all the more menacing. 'For a clever person, you do not seem to know much, Mrs George. Let us try an easier question. If you do not know where the soldiers are – or your maid – perhaps you can tell us where your friend is, the one with the scout vehicle? And maybe *he* can tell us who killed my soldiers.'

How did they know about Robert? Had someone seen him arrive at the farm? And *three* dead soldiers? Isabella knew about the policeman that Shamari had killed, but what about the others? Then she recalled the *tsotsi* with the *assegai* and for just a brief moment the mask of complacency slipped from her face. Yet in spite of the revelation, she hid her surprise well. 'He went back to South Africa yesterday,' she said calmly, the abhorrence still faintly perceptible in her voice.

'Don't lie to me. Do you think we are *stupid*, Mrs George? Your friend cannot leave – the entrance to the farm is blocked and guarded.'

Isabella didn't know what had shocked her most – the belligerent language, or the realisation that she was now a prisoner on her own farm. Then, just at that moment she remembered Robert Doyle's advice. 'I refuse to be called a liar. If you have any further questions, I will answer them in the police station at Juliasdale, in front of my lawyer and responsible officials.'

As she turned away the officer's voice lashed at her like a whip. 'Don't walk away from me when I am speaking to you, you arrogant woman! I am a criminal investigation officer, what you call a responsible official, and you talk to me like I am a monkey.'

The words stopped the woman in her tracks, but it was indignation rather than fear that drove her. 'You might be an investigation officer, but you are the rudest man I have ever met and I have had enough of your intimidation!'

This was more than the officer was prepared to tolerate. 'Mrs George: you are under arrest for obstructing the police in their enquiries. And don't think you will get preferential treatment by ringing a white policeman in Juliasdale – those days are gone. It is about time you white trash were taught some respect for the laws of Zimbabwe.'

'*Your* law is *not* the law of Zimbabwe. It is bullying.' Isabella realised that once again her fiery temper had put her in a precarious position. Yet she was beyond caring; her chance to accommodate them had all but dissolved. And then she wondered if it was ever really there.

All vestiges of self control that the officer might have had disappeared, replaced by a rage that showed no concern for consequences. He now sought a way to rebuild his credibility which would not only serve to teach this insolent *umfazi* a lesson, but also provide his men with some entertainment – the sort of fun they'd had with the *umfazis* at Gazelle Farm. Just the thought of this caused him to break into a smile.

'So, Mrs George, you think we are bullies do you?' he said slowly, having regained his composure. 'Then maybe we should act like bullies!' He patted his manhood with the *machete*. 'Perhaps we can show you how good we Africans really are!'

This immediately brought a chorus of jeers from the soldiers. At last the chief was making a good decision and they held their rifles aloft in delight. 'Ah *induna*, let us have fun with the *umfazi!* Let us show her what she has been missing with the *wazungus!*'

'You are *disgusting!* How dare you make these suggestions! I'm going to phone the police immediately.'

The woman's outburst brought further laughter from the officer. 'We *are* the police, lady – and the army. And the only law and order. You are the one who is being obstructive by refusing to answer my questions. My men here can testify to your insolence.' He turned to the soldiers for assurance.

'Yes, we can testify,' they chanted. 'We can testify. Let us have some fun *induna!*'

'So you see, lady, *you* are really the guilty one,' the officer said nauseatingly. 'You need to be taught a lesson and,' he grinned, revealing a mouth filled with tobacco-stained yellow teeth, 'we are the ones to teach you some respect.' He laughed again, revelling in the woman's discomfort. 'By the time we have finished with you, I think you will have told us everything we want to know.'

Isabella's skin crawled. 'I have told you what I know! *Please* – you must understand!'

'There you go again Mrs George, you are just not cooperating. But do not worry; my men are trained to help white women. They have *very* interesting ways of getting their information.' The lecherous remarks were greeted with another round of barracking.

Isabella saw the anticipation on the faces of soldiers and she suddenly felt very alone. In spite of Robert Doyle's instructions, she retreated towards the front door.

'Ah! So you want to go into the house . . . a little privacy perhaps,' the officer sniggered. 'That is understandable.'

The soldiers' uproarious laughter encouraged their leader. Excited by the chase, the pack could smell blood. 'Give us the *umfazi!* Give us the *umfazi!*' they shouted in unison.

Then, just when the intimidating barrage had reached a crescendo, Robert Doyle stepped out from the shadows. 'I think I am the man you are looking for.' The words were calm, but they penetrated the deathly silence. The FN rifle was pointed directly at the officer and his two aides and the laughter abated immediately, leaving the soldiers frozen in their tracks. Confronted by the cool deadliness of the *mzungu* with the rifle, the police officer's confidence evaporated immediately. The *vanamukoma* by his side were itching to start a fight but were sensible enough to wait. Then the officer turned to face the new enemy, whilst nervously licking his lips. 'Ah ha! So here we have the missing man!' he said in an attempt to disguise his weakened voice. 'We thought you were in South Africa.'

'I guess you just thought wrong.' Robert Doyle continued to cover them with his rifle.

'Ah yes! Yes! It looks that way,' he said slowly. The officer knew that the odds were stacked against the solitary *mzungu* and he regained his composure. 'Well, this business is between the police and Mrs George. I don't need to remind you that threatening police officers with a rifle is a very serious crime.'

A thin silence prevailed. Then Robert Doyle was speaking again. 'You were asking about me earlier. Now you can talk to me directly instead of picking on a helpless woman.'

'I told you: my business is with the *nkozikazi*,' the officer shouted. 'Put down your weapon at once.'

Robert Doyle smiled. There was absolutely no chance of him acquiescing – there were too many dead soldiers and he had no intention of spending the rest of his life in Chikurubi. His only option was to force the enemy's hand; this supposed officer was a coward – it wouldn't take much to make him back down. 'I have seen your business and what you want. But what you want and what you will get is not the same thing. You have a choice: walk out of here now and perhaps we might just be able to forget your disgusting manners.'

The officer was amused. 'That is very kind of you. But it is a long walk back down the hill – what if we do not want to go?'

'That is up to you. But whatever you decide to do, you and your men leave your guns and the vehicles here.' He nodded towards the valley. 'You just walk back down the hill with what you are wearing.'

'With what we are wearing, hey? That is not much!'

'It is more than you deserve. And at least that way you get to keep your life.'

Isabella watched Robert Doyle from her elevated position on the *stoep*. What was he playing at? Why wasn't he just letting them drive away?

And then she remembered: he was living on the edge and actually revelled in the confrontation.

Sengamo was out of sight behind the tree trunk, yet he had heard every word. The *mzungu* was in a tricky situation, but he understood his actions. If he were to give up his rifle they would arrest him – perhaps even kill him – and then they would rape the woman before killing her too. They had already made up their mind about that; it was the farm they were after and the woman was in the way. The nonsense with the maid and the missing soldiers was just an excuse to rape the *umfazi* and then get rid of her. Or they would have arrested her earlier and taken her to Mutare for questioning. The *mzungu* had no option but to force the soldiers to walk back to the compound – then he could escape down the old track.

Although the white man was outnumbered, the police officer was in charge and he would make the final decision. But with an assault rifle pointing at him, it was not a difficult choice for the CIO.

Nevertheless the *mzungu* from the mountain needed his help. The odds were not stacked in his favour.

The time had come to take action and repay the debt. He centred the adjustable iron sight of the AK-47 onto the soldier standing to the right of the officer, the more aggressive looking of the two aides. A burst from the Kalashnikov would take out both men. Then he would need to move position to confront the troops next to the vehicles. He was about to squeeze the trigger when the officer started to speak again.

'So, you want us to leave our weapons and our vehicles and in return you will give us our lives? That is very generous of you. Yes, very generous,' the officer smirked. 'There are many more of us, so why should we listen to your stupid demands?'

A slow smile spread across Robert Doyle's face. 'As I said, my friend, you have a choice. And the numbers do not really matter, because you will be the first one to die.'

The impact of the words struck the officer like a slap across the face. Used to giving the orders, he was now being pushed into a corner. And it was not to his liking.

His tongue licked nervously at his dry lips but there was no longer any saliva. 'You will not get away with this! We will come back for you and find you wherever you are! This you can be—'

'You only have any courage when you are threatening women,' Robert Doyle said, cutting the officer off in his stride. 'Either drop your weapons or use them.'

Isabella tried to shout 'Robert, this is not the war. Just let them go!' But the words were stuck in her throat. He was pushing the Africans beyond the point of no return, and the tension was unbearable.

The police officer understood the implications of the situation. He may have lost this round but he would be back with reinforcements. Reluctantly, he dropped his machete to the ground and the two soldiers by his side followed suit, lowering their rifles. He was in the process of issuing the order for the remaining soldiers to drop their arms when a shot shattered the silence, its recoil reverberating across the valley.

And the words were left unsaid.

Over the years, whenever Isabella's thoughts returned to Ingombe, she would try to piece together a picture of what had happened that day. Yet no matter how many times she ran it through her mind, it always ended in confusion.

It was as though the clock had stopped and each second was broken down into a millisecond as the drama played itself out in slow motion. Another one of those bad dreams. Her mouth was dehydrated and there were no words there, only a brittle dryness.

'Please God, don't let this be happening.'

Then she heard the shot.

Her eyes were on Robert Doyle and him alone. She saw him reel from the impact of the bullet and a red stain appear above his belt. Then she saw the FN rifle come up and a blinding flash illuminate the barrel as he fired a long burst on automatic from the hip. But, because her eyes were still on him, she did not see the officer and his aides fall to the ground.

Strange thoughts danced through her mind as she watched the scene unfold. He had only come to Ingombe for water. And then she heard the words he had thrown over his shoulder as he'd walked out of the kitchen, his last words before the *vanamukoma* had descended upon them. 'I will never let anything happen to you Isabella.'

Suddenly the air was wrenched by the sound of gunfire. From the lea of the corner post, Robert Doyle's automatic rifle spurted death across the yard. Then another bullet found its mark on his shirt pocket and at almost precisely the moment he collapsed to the ground, a stray round hit the wooden beam above the woman's head, and she threw herself onto the floorboards.

And then all hell broke loose.

Sengamo, shrouded in the bushes behind the msasa tree, opened fire at close range, raking the area with his AK-47. Soldiers standing out in the open scattered for cover behind their vehicles. But there was no hiding place. The tracker pulled the pin on the phosphorus grenade and threw it in a long arc towards the nearest Land Rover. It rebounded off the vehicle and exploded in a blinding flash. The white phosphorus cloud obliterated the vehicle and its radiance dazzled the immediate area. And then he threw the second grenade. Three soldiers leapt from the burning cab as the first Land Rover disintegrated in a ball of fire. Before Sengamo could take further action, a grenade on a soldier's webbing belt detonated, killing all those within the vicinity of the blast. The explosions rocked the house, accompanied by the rattle of Sengamo's Kalashnikov, which only ceased firing when he changed magazines. Then the second vehicle's petrol tank exploded, its blast drowning out all other sounds as sheets of flame reached for the sky. In the aftermath of the fighting only two soldiers had managed to escape the killing zone and they were running frantically down the hill when Sengamo ruthlessly gunned them down.

Isabella hugged the floor. Pressed face down onto the smooth planks as if they were her protector, she lay motionless. Within minutes the gunfire and explosions had abated, followed by a deathly stillness that was punctuated only by the smell of burning flesh. She opened her eyes and, turning her head cautiously, she looked up. The blue sky was still there, albeit clouded with a dense black smoke from the burning vehicles. But her attention was on a butterfly that had settled on the rail above her head. The yellow patterns on its translucent wings caught the sunlight and held her fascination; an apparition of pure beauty that seemed to transcend the violence.

Then a shadow obliterated the sunshine.

The butterfly fluttered away out of reach and when Isabella looked up, she was confronted by a face. A black face. She was terrified – unable to move or scream.

The tall African was dressed in a camouflage jacket. He carried an AK-47 casually in his right hand, its steel-blue barrel pointed down towards the floor. All of the woman's concentration, all of her being, was projected onto the figure standing over her as she waited for his next move. Is this where it all ends? If it is, please God let it be quick and don't let him touch me, she cried to herself.

But when the man spoke his voice was gentle. '*Kunjani nkozikazi*, how are you?' The question was asked in a tone that belied the savagery that had just transpired.

Isabella was apprehensive – who was this man? She looked up into eyes that carried concern rather than hate. 'I am well, I think,' she replied warily in Shona, not knowing who she was speaking to. And then the confusion returned and with it the last image of Robert Doyle crumbling slowly into the dust. With what seemed like a monumental effort, the woman forced herself off the floor. The African was quickly by her side, his stout, sinuous arms supporting her and helping her to her feet before guiding her to the rattan chair.

He put his hand on her shoulder. 'I'm sorry *nkozikazi*. This was not how it was meant to be,' he said, searching for the right words. 'I did not see the soldier who fired the rifle. He was standing behind the Land Rover.'

Isabella stifled the horror and forced herself to stand and walk to the front of the *stoep*. There before her lay Robert Doyle's body, where it had fallen. The stain on the ground was the colour of the soil and it was a while before she realised it was his blood mingling with the earth. She could see him again in the kitchen, letting the soil sprinkle through his fingers onto the pine table. And she could hear his words: 'This is the colour of the sand because it's stained with the blood of Africa.'

Oblivious to the mutilated bodies and the burning

vehicles in the background, Isabella somehow found the strength to stagger to the corner of the house where Robert Doyle lay. She lifted his head and cradled it in her lap. Surprisingly he was still breathing, but life was fast ebbing away from his frail body.

'Robert, speak to me!'

The red stain on his shirt was spreading, washing the khaki fabric with its odious colour, and her tears were a light rain falling softly on the wound. But he did not feel them. She saw his pale blue eyes trying desperately to communicate with her. There was a brief flicker of recognition.

'I'm sorry, Isabella. Not how . . . I . . . ' The stain now covered most of his abdomen and his eyes, once so intense, were glazing over as the colours changed to monochrome and started to fade.

In the distance a voice was shouting and it was a while before the woman realised it was her own. 'No Robert! No! Please don't leave me, please Robert . . . please!'

Robert Doyle briefly opened his eyes. For just a moment there was no pain. He could see her again as he saw her in the kitchen, the sunlight catching her profile, and he inhaled deeply, trying desperately to finish the sentence. 'I will never leave you, Isabella . . . just try not to . . . forget me . . . '

'Robert, I love you! I will always love you! Don't go, *please* don't go! *Robert – Robert – Robert,*' she said in prayer, as if in doing so, she would be able to awaken him. And all the time she was crying uncontrollably. But Robert Doyle did not hear her. His eyes were looking out over the valley towards Inyangani, but he did not see the mountain. He would never see it again.

And then she was aware of huge black hands, reaching down and gently closing his eyelids. The words in Shona floated above her head.

'*Yena file, nkozikazi.* He is dead, I am sorry.'

The woman looked up through tear-stained eyes at the silhouette of the tall African standing above her. But her thoughts were in the Drakensberg. She would never go there with Robert now. And then, looking down again at his face, his eyes closed as if in sleep, she understood at last what he had been trying to tell her.

She must take him with her, in her thoughts, wherever she went. If he could be with her in this way, then she would never forget him.

The Land Rovers continued to smoulder, sending signals to the squatter camp below. Isabella could not comprehend the chaos that surrounded her because a lullaby played in her head and she hummed softly along to it while she thought of the man lying in her arms.

Love was not meant to die like this, in the dust of a dirt yard. Nor was it meant to be like the desert flower which blossomed but once in a lifetime and remained for just one day. Delirious thoughts filled her mind. Had he not said they would be as one? But would their love really have survived if a bullet had not ended it? Would it have lived through the routines of normality?

She would never know.

Her mouth was dry through both thirst and fear. Exhausted, she cradled Robert Doyle's head, feeling more alone than she had ever felt before in her life. There were so many questions, but none of them mattered now – except for one. Tearing her eyes from his face, she looked up at the African waiting patiently beside her. The weapon was slung over his bandolier and the last of the grenades hung from his dark green webbing belt. Although he looked the epitome of aggression, she sensed he was not one of *them*.

'Who are you?'

His voice, in contrast to his appearance, was kind and gentle. 'I am Sengamo. Your man once spared my life. I tried to repay the debt today.' He shifted uncomfortably from one leg to the other before continuing. 'I'm sorry for the way it happened, *nkozikazi*.' And then, as if to justify himself, he added 'But they paid heavily.'

'*Paid heavily*.' Isabella looked out over the yard of Ingombe. It was unrecognisable. Bodies lay scattered where she had once thrown stones into the little hopscotch squares and black acrid smoke obliterated the valley.

Yes, they had indeed paid heavily. But the words were scant consolation. She would have given a thousand of their lives in return for Robert Doyle.

But it was not to be.

39

The cry of a fish eagle called from the distant river; a sound of Africa that was so evocative to Isabella. It was the stench of burning rubber that was repulsive – a smell that reminded her of a long-ago bonfire. Then she heard Sengamo's deep voice

'We must go *nkozikazi*. It is too dangerous to stay here any longer.' He spoke slowly, aware that the woman was still in shock. 'If they catch us they will kill us.'

'Will they come back again?' Isabella was confused. She had asked Robert Doyle the same question when he had returned from Juliasdale.

'*Yebo*, they will come. But they have a problem which will delay them. They are no longer mobile – I have destroyed both their vehicles and they only have one truck left at the camp, and that is also broken.'

'Surely when nobody returns to the camp they will be suspicious and radio for help?'

'It is possible. But their brains are riddled with *mbanje* and when they hear the explosions and the guns they will assume it is their soldiers taking the farm. By the time they figure it out we will be far away from here,' he said, watching the drive. 'That is why the sooner we go, the better. And there is still much to do.'

The African was right, yet she was reluctant to leave Robert Doyle amongst the *tsotsis*. She looked up at the man. 'Please – will you help me bury Robert?'

Sengamo was restless. In spite of his misgivings, he lifted the body up from the ground and cradled it in his arms. Perspiration settled in droplets on his forehead. '*Tafadhali nkozikazi;* show me where to dig the grave.'

The woman climbed slowly to her feet. 'Will you wait a moment while I fetch a blanket to wrap him in?'

'You must hurry *nkozikazi*.'

Isabella nodded. She knew where she was going and what she wanted and yet when she walked into the bedroom, it overpowered her. The bed sheets were still infused with the faint scent of their love and she shuddered when she stripped the linens.

Sengamo had laid the body on the patio table and was waiting patiently when she returned with the bedding. There was an uneasy question in his eyes. '*Nkozikazi*, the keys to the Land Cruiser. Do you have them?'

'No,' she said, casting a worried glance towards the African. 'They must be in Robert's pocket. Please . . . I cannot do it.'

Sengamo understood. Running his hands lightly over the blood-stained jacket, he found them in an inside pocket, next to a wallet and a small leather pouch. After handing the contents to the woman, he covered the body with the sheet, leaving just the face exposed.

Isabella glanced down at the man she had come to love and thought again of his last request: 'Try not to forget me'. He hadn't needed to tell her this. She leaned over the table and gently kissed his face. Eyes that once carried the teasing smile and compelled her to want to hold him were now closed. And his skin was not as warm as she remembered it. How peaceful he looks, she thought, how much like a child.

He was on his last journey – alone again, but where would it take him? Then the realisation hit her; she would never see him again – it was the final goodbye.

She nodded imperceptibly to the African, struck dumb by the soldier; how odd it was to see him dressed like the *vanamukoma*, with an AK-47 strapped across his back, carrying out this sensitive task.

Sengamo folded the sheet over Robert Doyle's face. Then securing the body with short lengths of rope, he looked at the woman. 'Can you show me the way *nkozikazi?*'

Isabella picked up the spade and walked purposefully out onto the rocky path leading up the *kopje*, a path trampled by thousands of tiny feet. The African followed her, perspiration soaking his thin cotton shirt as he struggled with the weight of the body on his shoulder.

Walking up the narrow path, Isabella suddenly had an overwhelming urge to escape from Ingombe and its tragic past and leave behind the *swikwiros*, the evil spirits. Perhaps there really was a curse on the farm, because everyone she had ever loved was buried there.

The first thing she saw when she came over the ridge was a purple-crested lourie perched on her father's grave. The bird was extraordinarily beautiful with its contrasting shades of red, green and glossy purple.

Sengamo noticed the woman looking at the bird and he understood her confused mind. 'It is the *mhondoro*, the spirit bird, *nkozikazi*. When it sits on a grave it's a good omen.'

The woman had never heard such a saying, but because she wanted to believe the words, she clung on to them and watched as the bird took to wing, its magnificent arc of scarlet feathers still visible in flight.

Just above the little burial ground there was an overhanging rock that supported a small flamboyant tree, somehow surviving in the harsh environment. Its branches would offer Robert Doyle a modicum of shade and she pointed to the spot.

Sengamo gently laid the body on the ground. The sun mercilessly burned the rocks on the barren hill, its heat stifling the African's movements. Removing first the rifle and the bandolier from his chest, he then took off his jacket and shirt, now soaking wet from perspiration. The first task was to clear away the rocks at the base of the tree. The woman then handed him the spade and watched him dig the shallow hole beneath the shelter of the flamboyant tree. His lean, strong body handled the spade as it had the Kalashnikov: it was a tool like any other tool, in the hands of a man who knew how to use it. And what a strange man he was. Yet, in spite of her reservations, she was grateful that he had taken charge.

Sengamo worked swiftly, labouring in the relentless heat without taking a rest. Sweat ran in rivulets down his chest. When he was satisfied with the depth of the hole, he man-handled the shrouded corpse into the shallow grave and covered it with the soil he had extracted, before starting to heap rocks over it.

He was conscious of the weight of the woman's eyes on his back.

'Can I help?'

'Please *nkozikazi*. We need more stones. If you can bring them to me, I will cover the grave. Just be careful because they are very hot.'

They worked silently together. Some of the rocks were heavy and the exertion was burning the woman's throat, but she laboured on, knowing it was essential to protect the body from wild animals. When they had completed the cairn, Sengamo stood up and looked at the woman across the unorthodox monument in much the same way one looks at a stranger across a room.

'*Nkozikazi*, what is his name?'

The woman held his stare.

'His name was Robert Doyle.'

Sengamo breathed deeply. To the Ndebele, it is good to know the name of the one who has given you a life. He only wished he had known it on the mountain in Mozambique all those years ago. Looking up to the sky, he shouted to the *mudzimu* in a language that the woman did not understand. Then he was speaking again in Shona and there was a damp mist in his deep-set, brown eyes. 'Sleep well *induna*.'

The woman took hold of his hand; two people united in a shared grief, regardless of colour. In times like this it did not matter. Perhaps someday it would be this way across all of Africa.

For a moment her thoughts drifted back to the last time she had been beside the graves. It seemed like a lifetime ago now and yet it had only been the previous day – her in the black dress, with Robert Doyle by her side. He had known the *vanamukoma* would come back – that was why he'd tried to persuade her to leave. The worried face she'd seen through the camera lens should have told her that. So why couldn't she just have trusted him?

Now he was just a part of the earth; a part of Africa.

A light gust of wind carried the pugnacious scent of wild honeysuckle across the *kopje*. The woman closed her eyes and in her dreams the stones were no longer piled up over the graves. They lay scattered on the ground, as they had been for a thousand years, in this same spot where she and her parents had once sat together to watch the sunsets. Long before it was a burial ground.

Then Isabella was crying. And as the tears sprinkled the dust at her feet she could see the grass growing in front of her eyes and her mother's voice floating above her. In desperation she tried to catch the words. But they were as elusive as the wind and it was a while before she realised that they were only in her mind.

Sengamo's voice cut across her thoughts. 'We must go now *nkozikazi*.'

The woman opened her eyes and the graves were as they were before the hallucination. All her dreams had now died. Here, on this little hill, where there were no shadows, where there was no tomorrow, where everything was once seen through the eyes of a child. Even her beloved distant mountains were now on top of her, towering over her like the impenetrable walls of a prison. She released her hand from Sengamo's grip. 'Thank you for all that you have done.'

'*I-ni hakuna kitu*, it is nothing.' Embarrassed by the gratitude, the African turned away to replace his shirt and bandolier before slinging the Kalashnikov nonchalantly over his bony shoulder. Isabella gasped when she saw the transformation from bare-chested farm worker to killing machine and she stepped back to allow the African to lead the way off the *kopje*.

40

When Sengamo reached the farmhouse, he waited for the woman. There was an uneasy look in his eyes. 'It is now very dangerous on the farm *nkozikazi*. The soldiers could come back at any moment. We must leave as soon as possible by the broken track. And I think that maybe we take the Land Cruiser because it is a more practical vehicle than the Isuzu.'

The woman was confused. She did not understand any of this; after all, her plan was simple – to ring Danny and then drive down to South Africa when it was dark. Quite what they were going to do there, she did not know. She turned to face the African. 'Sengamo, you have done so much for me already. There is no need for you to help me any further. Robert and I had already decided to go to South Africa; in fact, we were about to set off for Bietbridge when the soldiers came.'

Sengamo slowly shook his head and his next words shattered any last illusions. '*Nkozikazi*, this is where you need my help more than ever. You cannot go by road to South Africa. When the soldiers see what has happened here they will be looking for you all over the country. They'll alert every airport and border post and block all escape routes; you won't get far before they find you. This is a very serious business.'

The words drained the colour from the woman's face and turned it ghostly white. 'I didn't realise . . . I'm sorry,' she stammered.

'That is why we cannot take the Isuzu,' Sengamo said patiently. 'It is your *bakkie* they will be looking for. And when they catch you they will put you into Chikurubi. Killing CIO men in Zimbabwe is the worst crime because they are the ones who are in charge.'

The woman shuddered at the words. There was no escaping the fact that she'd be imprisoned for life for her involvement in the massacre of so many soldiers. Isabella could not even begin to imagine what it would be like languishing for the rest of her days in the hellhole that was Harare's maximum security prison. But then life expectancy in the harsh, deplorable jail would be short. She remembered once, years ago, seeing a newspaper article exposing the cruel and terrible conditions. Thirty people were crammed into a tiny cell, no more than two metres square. Murderers, rapists and robbers slept in their own excrement, vying for space on the bare concrete floors, stifled by the heat and plagued by the mosquitoes, a place where they did not segregate men from woman and where most of the inmates suffered from AIDS. Prisoners were expected to survive on a daily diet of *sadza* and a cup of bracken water in the rat infested concrete block, where beatings and torture were a daily routine. It was too frightening to even contemplate. Isabella glanced around the yard at the devastation and realised the African was right.

'What will we do?'

'Cross into Mozambique. I thought about the Skeleton Pass, in the Chimanimani Mountains – we used it to slip across the border into Rhodesia during the war. It is a quiet post, but it will still be manned.' Sengamo paused to look out over the distant mountains. 'It is also a long way south through Mutare where there will be road blocks.'

'How can we leave Zimbabwe without going through a border post?'

The African smiled confidently. 'There is a way, *nkozikazi*, through the Mtarazi.'

Isabella was hesitant. The Mtarazi lay above the Honde Valley, a vast area where only the odd corrugated track penetrated the bush. 'I don't understand.'

Sengamo addressed the woman patiently, as an elder would speak to a *msichana*. 'There is a small disused track off the road to Aberfoyle.'

'Aberfoyle? But there isn't a border post there. And how do we cross the mountains?'

'I know this area well, *nkozikazi*. You are right – there is no border crossing so they won't expect us to take this route.' The African smiled like a child with a secret. 'But in the Honde Valley there is a pass that very few people know about. Even the *wazungus*, with their whirly-birds, could not find it in the war.'

Sengamo's interpretation of a helicopter amused Isabella. And for the first time there was a glimmer of hope in her worried eyes, put there by this strange man. The plan was so bizarre that it might just work. And what alternative was there? Then she thought of Chikurubi again and she shuddered. '*Tatenda induna*, for all your help.'

The African was unused to words of kindness from a white woman. 'We must reach the Honde Valley before the soldiers discover what has happened here. It will be at least three hours before we are safe.' The camouflaged jacket he had commandeered from the dead soldier was draped over his shoulder and he noticed the look on the woman's face and smiled, the wide reticent smile of an

African. 'If they do find us then maybe with these clothes and the Land Cruiser they will think I am one of them. Do you not think so?'

Isabella nodded her head and smiled faintly. 'I thought so when I first saw you.'

The act of acknowledgment was the encouragement the African was looking for.

Suddenly Isabella remembered Danny. How could she forget him? 'My friend at Rigby's Creek Farm, my neighbour – he was coming with us!' The woman's voice was hesitant when she noticed the apprehension on Sengamo's face. 'Will this be . . . all right?'

'Is he ready? *Nkozikazi*, I am worried – we have very little time now.'

Isabella stammered. 'When we were leaving,' she paused, her speech interrupted by an image of her standing in the kitchen with Robert Doyle. It all seemed so long ago now, before all the killings. 'When we were leaving, I was trying to call him – to arrange to meet him on the old track. Then the soldiers came.'

The African was reluctant to delay their departure any further, but he could not bring himself to demolish the woman's plans. And thinking about it, a second vehicle would give him options. Yes maybe, just maybe, it would work. 'Make your phone call,' he said, holding out his hand. 'I will move the bags and some of the guns to the Toyota – please *nkozikazi*, the keys.'

Isabella looked at his finely chiselled face. His rugged features were strong but the years of violence they had been subjected to showed clearly in the deep-set lines around his eyes. She handed him the keys.

'I still don't understand why you are doing this for me.'

The African hesitated only briefly. 'It is my debt,' was all he said as he turned to go. She watched him stride purposely across the yard, a fearsome figure, but not to her. He was so much like Robert Doyle – watchful and alert and totally aware of his surroundings.

When he'd disappeared round the corner of the barn, Isabella walked slowly back into the kitchen. Everything was just how she'd left it before she'd faced the *vanamukoma*. But there was a presence in the room that frightened her. She felt she was not alone. For a minute she stood perfectly still, hardly daring to breathe, her bare arms covered in tiny goose pimples. Was it her imagination or could she see Robert Doyle striding through the doorway, a smile lighting up his face while he bantered with her in that husky voice of his?

It was not to be.

The only tangible part of him that remained were the dregs of that morning's coffee, in the bottom of the cups that lay unwashed in the sink.

The sound of the Land Cruiser shattered the illusion and Isabella was reminded of the task in hand. She picked up the receiver, dreading the silence that would indicate that the telephone lines had been cut. But the tone was as clear as a bell and she began dialling the number. There was no reply. She closed her eyes. The loud ring of the outside bell at Danny's farm could be heard all over the yard, so why wasn't he answering? 'Danny, where are you? Please God, let him be there,' she mouthed softly into the receiver. Suddenly, Isabella realised that she could not leave Zimbabwe without Danny. It would waste valuable time, but they would have to go via his farm. She was on the point of hanging up when she heard his voice.

'Rigby's Creek,' Danny gasped between deep breaths.

He must have been running for the phone. 'Danny, it's me,' she whispered.

'Issy! I heard the explosions. I tried to ring but there was no reply. What the hell is happening over there?'

'I can't talk now – we don't have much time. Please just listen carefully,' she said, speaking rapidly into the mouthpiece. 'Can you meet us by the waterhole on the old track as soon as possible? You must be quick. We are leaving here in ten minutes.'

'Issy, I–'

'Just trust me Danny.'

Although he was hungry for the details, Danny understood the gravity of the situation from the urgency in her voice. He knew exactly where the waterhole was – they'd played there together as children. 'I'm packed and on my way,' he said, with a forced camaraderie.

That's what she loved about her friend – no big inquisition, no questions asked. She was about to hang up when she heard him speak again.

'Issy, no matter what has happened . . . I just want to be with you.'

Her friend's intuition never failed to amaze her. And Isabella knew that he meant what he said as being more than just good friends, and it brought tears to her eyes. 'Thank you Danny,' she said, not realising she had already replaced the receiver.

For a minute she stood perfectly still and looked at the kitchen for one last time. There was the old pine table, at which she had sat with her parents, her husband and her lover. And now they were all dead. She shuddered when she thought of the *tsotsis* invading the house, rifling through all of her belongings. The idea of them sitting at her table, their women wearing her clothes, suffocated her. Removing her light khaki jacket from the clothes hook beside the larder cupboard, Isabella walked out into the sunshine without bothering to close the door.

Sengamo was busy destroying the mechanics on the Isuzu when she reached the vehicle, the concern written plainly on her face. He raised his head from under the engine compartment and put the hammer down. Isabella flinched at the vandalism, knowing he had made it impossible for anyone to use the vehicle again. But then, wasn't that the idea?

'What is on your mind *nkozikazi?*'

'There is too much pain,' she said, after choosing her words carefully, 'when I think of the *tsotsis* living in the house that my father built.' Although it sounded like a racist remark, this was not how she intended it to be, and she hoped the African would not interpret it as such.

Sengamo remembered the squatters at his former employer's house on Gazelle Farm. It would have broken Tom's heart to have seen it in the state he had found it. 'I understand *nkozikazi*. If you wish, I can destroy the house?' He scratched his head. 'Perhaps the soldiers will think you have died in the fire if we place two of the bodies inside the building.'

The woman could not comprehend what he was talking about, but she was happy to leave the arrangements to him and she nodded in agreement before climbing into the Land Cruiser. Suddenly overwhelmed by the smell of Robert Doyle, impregnated in the worn pseudo-leather seat, she closed her eyes and tried to picture his every movement. She saw again the faded leather bush hat pulled down low over his eyes as he squinted in the bright glare of reflected sunlight, constantly scanning the surroundings. And the big hands: one on the wheel and the other on the gear lever. 'Oh God, Robert, God! What have I done?'

The thought of the *vanamukoma*, the gunfight and the grave was just too much for her. Opening her eyes, she wound down the window and breathed deeply to steady her nerves. Then she noticed the brown envelope in the open-top glove compartment. Her name was written on the front of it – it was from Robert; she recognised his lazy italic script from the note he'd left her before driving Shazi to Juliasdale. The envelope was partially covered by an old *Zimbabwe Times*, almost as if the bearer had wanted it to be discovered. She was about to open it and investigate the contents when the driver's door opened. The appearance of the African convinced her to change her mind and she hurriedly buried the envelope in the inside pocket of her jacket.

Sengamo started the diesel, a boyish grin of excitement on his face. He nodded casually to the woman and drove the Land Cruiser a safe distance from the house before killing the engine. 'Are you sure this is what you want *nkozikazi?*'

She nodded. The thought of leaving the farmhouse to a bunch of criminals was overwhelming and Isabella closed her eyes again. Although she was still not entirely sure what the African was up to, anything was preferable to having the squatters invade her home. She heard the Land Cruiser door close and when she opened her eyes, Sengamo was gone.

Through the windscreen the woman watched the

African drag the bodies of the two soldiers lying next to the officer up the steps. Man-handling them inside the hall, he then closed the front door.

The officer lay in the dust where Robert Doyle's bullets had ended his life. Horse flies were already settling on his body. In the skies above, the vultures hovered on enormous outstretched wings, waiting their turn. They had left their teeming roosts for this site of feasting, where the air was putrefied with death. She imagined the sinister birds pecking out the policeman's eyes, yet she felt no horror; it was no less than he deserved. Then she saw the African retrieve the five gallon Gerry-can of petrol from the back of the Isuzu and disappear into the kitchen. And all at once she understood the plan.

It was some minutes before Sengamo reappeared in the yard. The smell of fuel was overpowering. When he was a safe distance from the building, he unhooked the last of the grenades from his webbing belt and, pulling the pin, threw it at the kitchen window. The glass shattered and Isabella suddenly remembered Robert Doyle's warning: 'All you will hear is the sound of breaking glass.'

Then the grenade exploded, destroying the serenity that had been imposed on Ingombe in the aftermath of the fighting. It ignited the petrol and an enormous ball of fire erupted from the kitchen window before ripping through the building. In the time it had taken for the grenade to detonate, the African was back in the Land Cruiser, smiling, his brilliant white teeth contrasting vividly against his black skin.

The house that had held all of Isabella's dreams was engulfed in flames.

Sengamo was still laughing when he started the engine.

Selecting first gear on the Land Cruiser, he then turned around to take one last look at the blaze. 'When they eventually manage to put out the fire it will be difficult to identify the bodies,' he said, with grim satisfaction. 'I hope it will give us the time we need to cross the Honde Valley.'

As he was speaking, another huge explosion blew the boiler room door off its hinges and sent the woman diving for cover beneath the dashboard.

'That's the gas,' Sengamo said, laughing hysterically. 'There will be nothing left when the soldiers arrive!'

Nothing left. Isabella looked up through the smoke to the house that had taken so long to restore. It had been built and demolished twice, but it would never rise again.

41

Sengamo drove as quickly as possible down the rough terrain of the old track, conscious that this second explosion would surely alert the soldiers at the compound. He hoped that, by his actions, they would have the time they needed to reach the Mtarazi Plains and make their escape.

Occasionally, where the track disappeared, he would stop and search the bush. For much of the way he was able to follow the fresh tyre tracks that Robert Doyle had drawn in the sand when he'd driven to Juliasdale.

It was early afternoon and there was perhaps four hours of daylight left. Sufficient time, the African assured himself, to cross the Ruda River.

Isabella had not spoken since leaving Ingombe. Sengamo understood her silence. He'd experienced the same feeling when he'd left his family in the graveyard beside the *kraal*. Strange how nothing really changes, he thought; how the violence destroys lives without any regard to the colour of a man's skin. He glanced across at the woman and saw her perhaps for the first time. That is, saw her properly. For a *mzungu* she was very attractive, he thought. Her hair shone and smelled of summer streams where wild lilac touched the water. And its colour was that of the deep burnt elephant grass that blew in the wind. Her cheek bones were high, like those of a young Masai *msichana*, and Sengamo imagined that when she smiled it would bring her face to life. But it was her large brown eyes that held him, when she looked at him full in the face and spoke to him, as she was doing now.

'My friend is at the waterhole.'

'Where is this place *nkozikazi?*'

Her reply was barely audible above the noisy diesel engine. 'At the bottom of the hill there is a small overgrown track on your left – that will take us there.'

Waterhole was hardly an apt description. What little of the water that remained after the previous year's drought had been transformed into a brown sludge. Nevertheless, it was one of the few places in the immediate area where animals could still replenish their thirst. On the steep bank a couple of dirty looking Marabou storks, spindly legs anchored in the mud, waited patiently for fish, crabs or a frog to appear in the shallow water. They all seemed oblivious to Danny's Land Rover, standing in the shade of an umbrella thorn tree, the roof rack stacked with Gerry-cans, boxes and spare tyres. He appeared to have loaded most of Rigby Creek into the back of the vehicle. Quite remarkable, the woman thought, in the short time he had available to pack. But then Danny was the most practical of men.

'This is your friend, *nkozikazi?*'

'Yes. That's him.' He was opening the door to exit his vehicle when she wound down the window and shouted urgently to him. 'Danny, we can't stop. Can you follow us? I'll explain everything when we are safe.'

Sengamo turned to the woman. 'You know the area around Ingombe, *nkozikazi* – perhaps it will be better if you travel with me for the first part of the journey,' he said, manoeuvring the Land Cruiser out of the soft sand near the waterhole. 'We will try and make the border before it is dark.'

When they reached the gravel road, Isabella instructed the African to turn right and away from the army camp. Tyre tracks, clearly visible in the soft sand where both vehicles had exited the bush, did not concern Sengamo. They would be well away from the farm before the evidence of their escape was discovered.

'Please *nkozikazi*, I need to find the track to the Honde Valley,' Sengamo said when they eventually reached the corrugated road in the Mtarazi Park.

Isabella reached over to retrieve Robert Doyle's faded Ordnance Survey map from the glove compartment. She passed it to the African. 'Is this what you want?'

'*Tatenda*.' He pondered over the grid references, many of which he recognised from the early days of the war, searching for the obscure, disused track that would take them down into the Honde Valley. 'Ah *nkozikazi*, it is further south than I thought,' he said, handing the woman the map. 'We need to be off the Mtarazi Road before we are seen.' Fortunately there was no traffic in either direction and when they eventually discovered the track, it was heavily overgrown and hardly distinguishable from the surrounding *veld*. Easing the vehicle carefully off the old corrugated road, Sengamo felt vindicated in his decision to take the Land Cruiser; it was built to meet the rigorous demands of the wild, off-road terrain, but – even more importantly – its twin tanks were full of diesel and there were sufficient spare tyres on the roof rack. He hoped the Land Rover was as well equipped.

The track through the bush was deserted and apart from the occasional tribesman or bare-footed *piccanin*, they were alone. His only concern now was to avoid the Hauna tribesmen in the south of the valley. These tribal villages had been infiltrated by the Rhodesian Special Forces during the war and, as such, even hardened freedom fighters gave them a wide berth. The tracker's mouth settled into a grim line when he thought back to the border raid with Manjaro. But he said nothing. It was all such a long time ago now.

In the silence the woman felt herself drawn to this curious man. So much had happened in the last few hours that she was unable to comprehend the enormity of it all. And yet there was a comfort in knowing that Sengamo was here beside her and that Danny was following behind. The African had mentioned an obligation he owed Robert Doyle. What was that all about? What had Robert Doyle done that had brought this man to Ingombe, involved him in the fight and put him in this perilous position? Isabella was unable to contain her inquisitiveness. Her voice, now steadier, was nevertheless soft as she spoke for the first time since handing him the OS map. 'Tell me Sengamo, why are you doing this for me?'

The escarpment was falling away towards the open plains, an awkward route that led them down into the Honde Valley, where the broad girth purple-trunk baobab trees mixed easily with the acacia bushes. Red-billed buffalo weavers' nests hung bedraggled off the crooked branches amongst the fruit. Elephant country, Sengamo thought – plenty of food here for them. The thought of the fruit made him thirsty, since when it was brewed with mlala plums it made his favourite drink.

Eventually the vegetation flattened out and at last Sengamo was able to speak. '*Nkozikazi*, I was a *gandanga*, a guerrilla fighter. You understand? But I have to go back to where it all started. It was not far from here, in the mountains, that we fought for eight years, living in caves and eating roots like animals. We were tired and wanted an end to the struggle. Sometimes I would wake up in the mornings and look at my small band of comrades and wonder what we were doing. Then I would think of Zimbabwe and the injustice – and the fight would go on.'

'How many deaths does it take until somebody accepts they are wrong?' Isabella asked, a disturbed look on her face. 'And how do you put it right?'

Sengamo shrugged his shoulders. 'We talked only about the war and rarely of what was to come. At some point the realisation hit us that there probably was no future, so we accepted this and just took one day at a time. We lived like vermin.'

'I'm sorry,' Isabella whispered softly, when she thought back to the way the natives had been treated. But it was not a regret that the African acknowledged.

There is a hot wind that blows through the Honde Valley in the summer. Isabella could feel it burning the skin of her arm, resting on the windowsill, and its heat brought a dryness to her throat. It is an ill wind that comes before the rains. She had seen it blow amongst the Africans. It drew lines on a man's face in the tobacco fields and took years off his life. When the rains came it was a relief, like manna from heaven. It watered the natives' crops and enabled them to feed their families. And she whispered again. 'I'm sorry for the way you have been treated.'

'It was not of your doing, *nkozikazi.*'

'But I still don't know why you are helping me.'

In the distance an old bull elephant, a solitary male, stood and contemplated the approaching vehicle. Sengamo instinctively positioned the Toyota to the left of the trees, giving the bull a wide berth – they could be unpredictable when rejected by the herd and consequently they were prone to attacking anything that annoyed them. His hands were on the steering wheel and his eyes vigilantly searched the plain. But his mind was somewhere far away, back in the mountains of Mozambique.

'Your man was leading a small troop of Special Forces soldiers. I don't know how they found us. Maybe somebody talked. They knew we were in the area and by chance they stumbled onto one of my men.' The bitterness was tangible in the African's voice. 'We ended up slaughtering each other. When the fight was over, there were only the two of us alive and I was without a weapon. The *mzungu* should have killed me – it is what I would have done had the roles been reversed. I was the *gandanga* responsible for the death of his men and there was a price on my head. Yet he told me to go home to my *kraal*. I did not understand this.' He glanced briefly at the woman. '*Nkozikazi*, I have thought about it many times since but I have never found an answer.'

Isabella was relieved at the revelation that there was no animosity in Robert Doyle's heart. Because where there is hate, there is revenge and where there is revenge there is no rest. Or perhaps his weariness had removed the hate and he was seeking an end to the relentless conflict. Was that the reason for sparing the African's life? She knew he wasn't a ruthless killer – the man she loved was gentle and compassionate. 'I know Robert – he is a soldier, not an executioner. He would never be able to bring himself to kill an unarmed man in cold blood.'

Sengamo nodded unobtrusively. 'That is my debt *nkozikazi.*' There were beads of perspiration on his forehead. Absentmindedly, he wiped them away with the dirty edge of his worn shirt sleeve. 'He told me that there had been enough killing. That sooner or later one or the other of us must stop. When we parted he held my hand with respect, like we were equals. No *mzungu* has ever done this to me before.'

Isabella gasped. This was the man Robert Doyle had spoken of, the man who had changed his perspective on the war. There were so many questions she wanted to ask to fill in the missing pieces of the puzzle. She looked across at the quiet man with the proud features. He was different, strangely so from any other African she had ever known, and she wanted to help him with his hurt. Perhaps by listening to him it would help her too. 'So how did you come to be at Ingombe?'

'I returned to Zimbabwe to see my family. I was at Ingombe to find the people who murdered them. It was a big shock when I saw your man at the farm.'

'He came by chance just three days ago – he wanted water and I asked him to stay.' The woman's face twisted, like that of a child about to cry, and she found it difficult talking about Robert Doyle and that first day. 'I wish now he had never come.'

'You must not think like that,' Sengamo said. 'Even minutes are worth keeping. This much I have learnt in my short life.'

Isabella smiled at the African. Robert Doyle had been right; they were equals – not *bwana* and labourer, *mzungu* or black man, but the same people. She wanted to know more. 'Please tell me about your family.'

'It is a long story *nkozikazi.*'

'Do we not have time?'

'*Yebo*, we have time – it is still some way to the border.'

The bush was changing to an open *vlei* with the occasional tamboti tree now dotted amongst the acacias that covered the plain all the way to the mountains. The driving was easier through the sea of thorn bushes, which allowed Sengamo to relate his story. He talked about his childhood, the earliest memories of his simple life in the *kraal*, waking up to the sound of chickens squawking in the yard and falling asleep with the noisy cicadas. He told her about his schooldays and the path across the bush at Gazelle Farm that eventually became his playground, and of his friendship with Tom. But it was when he related Andrea's story – the betrayal that set in motion his entire journey – that Isabella shuddered. Although she found it difficult to condone the girl's behaviour, she had come across such racism in the school playground at Juliasdale where many of the children talked callously of the Africans, as if they were monkeys not long down from the trees. Nevertheless, despite the girl's cruelty, she and her family did not deserve the horrific deaths they had suffered at the hands of the *vanamukoma*. Was the African aware of what had happened?

She decided it was not her place to tell him.

Finally he recounted the war years and his coming home. Isabella's attention never for a moment wavered. She had to blink her eyes to clear the tears when she pictured him standing beside the graves of his family and at last she understood the hate that drove these men to do what they do – to embark on a cycle of relentless revenge against their fellow man.

'Is it not tragic, the way we are brainwashed into

believing that every member of ZANU is a terrorist?' She looked at him cautiously. 'What *were* you Sengamo?'

The tracker laughed at the woman's forwardness. 'An American journalist once asked me the same question, many years ago. But he asked it in a different way.'

'How?'

'It was after a FRELIMO patrol had destroyed a white farm in Rhodesia. I was not with the patrol but I was in the camp when they returned. And so was the journalist. He assumed that I was one of the guerillas who had murdered the *wazungu* family and he asked me if I thought of myself as a terrorist or as a freedom fighter.'

'And what did you tell him?' It was something Isabella desperately wanted to know, her father having been killed in the same pointless manner.

Sengamo was looking straight ahead across the wide open *vlei* to the distant mountains of Mozambique where the guerrillas had once been based. 'I told him this was a question to ask his newspaper readers; that perhaps the answer lay with whichever side you supported. I was fighting for my freedom, but this did not include the killing of innocent women and children.'

'Perhaps our people should ask themselves the same question,' she said, putting her hand on his arm. 'The *vanamukoma* that attacked Ingombe are nothing more than animals. I am glad you are so different to them.'

'We were once all the same people during the revolution, when we were fighting for our freedom – now we fight amongst ourselves and our tribes.' There was a worried look on Sengamo's face when he glanced across at the woman. 'We all have our pain and our cross to bear. It could not have been any easier for you in the war.'

'No,' she said, going on to tell her story that, in many ways, was not too far removed from that of the African's.

'I am sorry about your family,' Sengamo said when she'd finished speaking. 'We are really all the same people – Africa's children. You know, *nkozikazi*, this land is like a snake, so beautiful and yet so dangerous, and it strikes when you least expect it to.'

Hearing these words, Isabella finally had no regrets about leaving behind the hate and the petty tribalism that would eventually spiral Zimbabwe into oblivion.

She did not want to see that day.

It was late afternoon when they reached the small tributary. A light trickle of crystal clear water meandered through a line of tree fuchsias, their dark red flowers producing a magnificent display of intense colour. A scarlet crested sunbird, seemingly attracted by the nectar dripping to the ground, hovered above them, its iridescent feathers sparkling in the sun. Brown pods carpeted the floor beneath the deep green foliage, while in the open *bushveld* delicate impala lilies grew like wild flowers, splashing the savannah grass with a palette of red, white and pink. The landscape that nature had sculpted so delicately left the woman breathless. 'Oh God, Sengamo . . . it's so beautiful.'

'We call it Africa's garden, *nkozikazi*.' He stopped the vehicle in the shade of the overhanging branches. 'It is the only place I know where the river is low enough for us to cross; when the rains come it is impossible.' He opened the door of the Land Cruiser and removed an empty water bottle from its holder on the dashboard. 'We need to take a short break,' he said, looking at his watch. 'Ten minutes?'

Isabella nodded her head. 'I could stay here forever.'

The African smiled and set off through the tall grass to the stream. A light breeze fluttered his faded shirt sleeves and the woman thought again of how much she owed him and what her fate might have been if he had not come to Ingombe.

When was there ever a day like this? It had started with the morning sun washing the bedroom. Robert Doyle was not at her side when she had opened her eyes but he had come back to her and given her hope that their fledgling love would survive. Then Shazi had appeared at the kitchen door with her story and, in that moment, everything had changed.

The African did not look back nor did he beckon her to follow. Perhaps he felt that she and the *mzungu* needed their time together. Removing his boots, he sat on a blanket of fallen leaves and dangled his bare feet in the cool waters.

Isabella's eyes were still fixed on him when she heard the passenger door open and Danny's smiling face greeted her. She rushed towards him – how heartening it was that he was always there when she needed him. And right now she needed him more than ever. Her arms were pressed tightly against his chest and she could smell the freshness of his clean khaki shirt, in sharp contrast to the rags Sengamo was wearing. 'Oh Danny, what is going to happen to us?' She shuddered as she spoke the words for it was the same question she had asked Robert Doyle just that very morning. And the answer was the same.

'It will be all right Issy,' he said gently, still oblivious as to why they had been forced to abandon their farms in such a hurry.

The previous day's fragrance still lingered on the curve of Isabella's neck. Danny wanted to kiss her. Instead he just held her tightly, her feet barely touching the ground. She was crying and what remained of her tears dampened the fabric of his thin cotton shirt. And then Danny found the words he had always wanted to say, words that had been so difficult until this moment: 'I love you Issy,' he whispered, into the soft strands of her sun-bleached hair. 'I've always loved you. It's just that I've never been able to tell you. And even if you don't feel the same way now, I will wait for you to change your mind.'

Isabella caught the sob in her throat and she held her breath, unable to speak. She stared with swollen eyes over his shoulder towards the African sitting on the river bank and then beyond him to the distant mountains that symbolised their freedom. And the only response she could give Danny was to hold him.

And for now, that was enough.

The wind picked a leaf off the tree fuchsia and carried it gently into the pale blue sky before laying it down placidly on the soft grass at the water's edge. And in a sudden burst of affection, Isabella dug her nails into Danny's arms. One day she would tell him everything. Perhaps that day was coming sooner than she realised. And when she thought this way, Isabella knew there was indeed hope beyond the mountains; it lay with the tall man sitting by the river. Releasing herself from Danny's arms, she watched him stride purposefully back up the river bank. He knew what had to be done and he wasted no energy in accomplishing the task.

'It is time to go, *nkozikazi*,' he said when he reached the Land Cruiser.

'Sengamo. This is Danny.'

'It is good to meet you at last,' Danny said, extending his hand towards the African.

'*Habari, nkozi.*' The handshake was firm and brief.

'What happened at Ingombe?' Danny asked, desperate to know who, and where, Robert Doyle was.

The African was restless to go. 'The *nkozikazi* can explain everything if she travels with you. I am sorry to be rude, *nkozi*, but I have to find the pass before nightfall. Or before they send out the helicopters.'

42

The Land Cruiser moved slowly towards the river. Danny engaged low ratio and followed cautiously, staying in the African's tracks as he forded the slow-running stream. The water lapped against the bottom of the door and occasionally the tyres lost their grip on the smooth river-bed stones. Using the power of the four-wheel drive, Danny stamped his foot hard on the accelerator and the vehicle surged forward out of the river and up the shallow bank. To the south were the open plains of the Honde Valley and to the east the purple-headed mountains that formed the border to Mozambique.

The African turned south and Danny followed.

'Issy, you mentioned South Africa,' he said, snatching a quick glance across at the woman. 'Is that where we're going?'

Isabella's gaze was fixed on the Land Cruiser. This would be the first of many questions and she realised she owed him the truth, but it would have to wait until she could get her thoughts into some semblance of order. 'Yes, to the Drakensberg,' was all she said. Not that she knew much more – an address and a brief description of the farm was all Robert Doyle had given her. And then she remembered the envelope she had found in the glove compartment and wondered whether this would be any more illuminating.

Danny understood her need to be alone. His thoughts

returned to the river and the words that had been spoken; words that had long been buried. Where had the courage come from to dig them up? He had tried on so many occasions to say what he felt in his heart – he'd even tried writing the words down, but each piece of paper had been discarded to the waste bin. And yet it had happened so easily by the river. Was this the desperate action of a man frightened of losing the woman he loved yet again?

A thin film of dust coated the windscreen and momentarily obliterated their vision. Easing his foot off the accelerator, Danny flicked on the washers and they were once again able to see the unbroken path of trees that indicated the trajectory of the river, an undulating thin green line meandering its way across the savannah.

If there ever was an Eden, then this was its garden, Isabella thought, trying to imagine the journey with Robert Doyle. But no, it would have been so different. Had he survived, they would be travelling in convoy on a tarmac road heading directly for the border at Biet Bridge.

Then she recalled how frightened she had been the first time she had seen the Land Cruiser at the crossroads. The man and the strange dog had come out of nowhere, out of a past that she knew so very little about. Robert Doyle had fed her fragments in their few days together, but how much more was there? She would never know. And did it really matter now? They had been destined to live a lifetime together in just a few days, like the dragonflies hovering above the pool in the mountains.

Danny's voice broke her thoughts. 'Issy . . . '

She glanced at him, acknowledging that she owed him an explanation. It would have to wait. Like brother and sister, fate had entwined them as one. But perhaps one day it would be different. Perhaps one day she would love this compassionate, life-long friend in another way. 'Please Danny,' she said, cutting him off, 'just give me time.'

Termite hills that resembled the pyramid mounds of some lost civilisation covered the vast open plain, pointing up towards the sky like ancient phallic symbols. Isabella imagined the millions of little insects all rushing busily through the vast network of tunnels and chambers. Here there were soldiers who would lay down their lives in defence of the community and protect their queen. Were Robert Doyle, Shamari and now Sengamo any different?

Isabella's hands were red from clutching them together. In her pocket was Robert Doyle's wallet and the strange leather pouch. The wallet could wait until later, she decided, when the moment was more private. Perhaps within its folds there would be names of friends or kin, something to link him to his past. Then her hand touched the little pouch and she removed it from her pocket. The faded leather was tied with a piece of *rympie*. No longer able to contain her curiosity, she unpicked the knot and withdrew the simple gold band with its unusual moonstone. She knew immediately that it was Emily's ring. 'Oh God, this Africa . . . this bloody Africa! It is killing us all. Get rid of the ring,' she cried. But the words were only in her mind and she realised that she would not obliterate the past by discarding the moonstone.

Then she cursed her impetuousness in the face of the *vanamukoma*. Why had she upset them? Robert had told her to stay calm, not to antagonise them. The answer lay in her temperament, but she knew Robert Doyle would never have allowed her to grovel to a bunch of lawless thugs high on *mbanje*.

And then she saw him walking from the shadows, hopelessly outnumbered, to kill or be killed. But there was another side to the man; the soul of a poet living an African dream. He had loved life and lived it freely without a thought for the consequences.

And this was the reason she had loved him.

Finally she remembered him standing in the kitchen, looking across the valley, and his words: 'You cannot change the way you are.'

Robert Doyle had tried, but he had lost, that day he came to Ingombe.

The savannah of the Honde Valley was constantly changing and Danny's concentration was riveted to the deteriorating track. He saw nothing of the leather pouch and was not privy to the woman's thoughts. And yet he understood the battle that was raging within her mind. Still he said nothing, and when the opportunity arose, he reached across and touched her arm reassuringly.

And as the vast plain unfolded towards the mountains of Mozambique, it slowly changed colour from the burnt yellow of the savannah grass to the purple hues of the rocky hills. Isabella felt she could almost reach out her hands and touch the mountains.

And beyond them was the horizon.

Was this really an end to the violence and a start of something new? If it was, then perhaps this was the time to tell Danny about Robert Doyle, but where did she start when the words remained locked in her mind?

The brake lights on Sengamo's vehicle flashed dimly

in the bright sunshine and the vehicle came to a standstill. A lone African buffalo stood defiantly in their path, surrounded by oxpecker birds. The long gash down its flank was evidence that it had been in a mating fight, and in this state it was extremely unpredictable. This was certainly a day for meeting outcasts, Danny thought, as he watched Sengamo calmly reverse the Land Cruiser back along the recently formed track, before manoeuvring it away from the buffalo and down a dried river bed.

Danny had known Isabella since she was a little girl, and he knew she would talk when she was ready. And once she started there was no interrupting her. 'I'm sorry Danny,' she finally whispered. 'What happened . . . neither of us had the inclination to stop, nor did we want to.'

This was a time to be truthful. If she was to move on, then there were to be no lies.

Danny listened quietly, his jaw set grimly, as Isabella recounted the details of the affair. He kept telling himself that the past no longer mattered. After all, today was the first time he had ever found the courage to voice his feelings; to tell the woman he had known all his life that he loved her. Reaching over, he kissed her gently on the cheek.

She made no motion to either stop him or encourage him. It was a small step on a long road Isabella would need to walk slowly and it would, in time, become easier.

43

The little convoy had now reached the outer edge of the vast plain. It was dry, but in spite of the fact that the area had seen very little rain, the mixed woodland was dense.

Blindly and obediently, Danny followed the African into the evening sunset, where the landscape was painted in tranquil colours. Then Sengamo changed direction towards the east and half an hour later a small steep pass appeared between the towering granite cliffs. The rocks, fashioned in the shape of ancient castles, formed a seemingly impenetrable barrier.

The Land Cruiser slowed to a crawl and eventually stopped at the entrance to the pass. A luxuriant mopane tree stretched its branches, like arms, over the travellers, bestowing a sense of calm and a feeling of being cut off from civilisation. Sengamo stepped down onto the dry yellow grass growing in abundance at the entrance to the gorge. 'Welcome to the Mozambique border post!' There was a broad grin on his face and he was unable to keep the laughter out of his voice. 'It is the only place I know that has no customs or immigration.'

'I'm amazed Sengamo!' Danny shook his head in astonishment. 'How on earth did you find this place?'

'It was an accident – during the war we used it to cross the border into Zimbabwe. It is very good because we do not need *stoepas*.'

Danny's laughter was spontaneous. 'No passport, no

roads, no border, just Africa. Wonderful! I can understand now why our forces could never find you guys.'

' The African ignored the comment. He did not want to talk about the war. The woman, too, said nothing. She was looking back across the plain they had crossed, like shadows, from Ingombe. It was true – there were no roads or border posts. All that stood between them and freedom was an overgrown track that wound its way up through the mountain. And it looked impassable with a vehicle.

The site Sengamo had chosen was beside a slow-moving stream that meandered through a grove of exuberant sycamore fig trees. In the fading light he laid the map out across the bonnet of the Toyota. 'This is the route through Mozambique,' he said, his finger tracing a line across the chart, 'if we can get over the mountain.'

'Will we stay here the night?'

'*Yebo nkozi*. It is not possible to travel through the pass when it is dark. It is difficult enough in the day but at night it is impossible. And the lights would be seen from miles away when we reach the top of the hill. We will leave at first light.'

Danny nodded in agreement.

'Good. Then we'll sleep in the vehicles tonight – the baboons like very much the fruit of the sycamore tree.' Then he laughed again. 'The figs are very ripe so we may have company.'

The woman shuddered. 'Don't worry Issy,' Danny said, putting his hand on her arm to reassure her, 'it'll be fine – I'll be right next to you.'

'You will have to be or I won't be able to sleep.'

'Early tomorrow morning we will go through the pass,' Sengamo said, ignoring the small talk between the man and the woman, 'and pick up a small gravel road that will take you south to Chimoio.'

Danny was intrigued. He studied the map, following the African's wide finger as it devoured the miles like a time traveller. It all sounded straightforward enough. And then, just when they were feeling confident about their escape, Sengamo shattered their illusions.

'Once we find this road, I will leave you to go your own way.'

Isabella's thoughts were still with the baboons. When she heard the words 'go your own way', she felt the sense of euphoria drain from her body.

'Sengamo – what do you mean "leave us"?'

The African smiled patiently. 'You will have no further need for me, *nkozikazi* – once you are on the tar road, it is an easy run to Maputo; from there you can either cross the border into Swaziland or South Africa. Your passports will get you into either country.' His smile faded. 'I do not have that luxury.'

'Of course.' Isabella suddenly remembered Robert Doyle had explained this to her some days earlier. 'But what will you do? Where will you go?'

Was this an end to his obligation? Had he finally repaid his debt to Robert Doyle?

There was a lost look in the African's watery eyes. '*Nkozikazi . . .* out there,' his long sinewy arm swept across the landscape to Zimbabwe, 'out there are my people.' He paused to gaze at his beloved mountains. 'They are a people who have nothing except the clothes they stand up in. They have been enslaved, beaten, abused and segregated just because of the colour of their skin. Can you imagine being a second-class citizen in your own country? Maybe at last they have a chance.' He turned and looked directly into the woman's eyes. 'This is why I have to go back.'

Although Isabella understood what he was trying to say, she persevered. 'You cannot possibly do this on your own Sengamo.'

Again the lazy half smile, so much like Robert Doyle. 'I know this *nkozikazi*. But I will go back to Zimbabwe because I have something the opposition needs.' He reached over and touched the Kalashnikov leaning against the side of the jeep. 'Maybe one day we will have a land that is free of persecution where we can all live together.'

They both knew deep down that it was just a dream.

Danny had listened attentively to the conversation. Now he spoke. 'Isabella has told me your story. I hope that someday we will be able to come home and share this land with you – perhaps when your enemy is asleep.'

Sengamo nodded sadly in agreement.

Isabella's eyes never left the African's face. She saw him standing alone in the shadow of the mountains, dressed simply in a camouflage jacket that was a size too big. The coat was draped over ragged trousers, the frayed cloth resting on worn boots which were tied with string. He was a man alone, with no family or friends, and her heart went out to him. 'Please come with us to South Africa Sengamo.'

His eyes gave her the answer before she heard the words. 'It is not possible *nkozikazi*. I am a black man – I cannot live in a system of apartheid.'

He was right. Nevertheless, the woman felt like an imposter when confronted by the humble simplicity of this honourable man. His movements were slower, tinged with tiredness, and she noticed the first signs of grey on the edge of his temples. Not yet thirty, he was already an old man. Yet within his dark eyes burned a fire, a flame that carried the same intensity she had seen in Robert Doyle's eyes. His brow was lined with deep furrows that told tales of a weary journey through life; a journey that had been short in miles but long in hardship, on a path where only young men walked – a path that led nowhere. And she thought briefly of the wars and the cenotaph on which she had seen the inscription 'They grow not old as you or I'. How many of them were left; the real freedom fighters that crossed the borders like shadows, men like Sengamo, Samora Machel and Sithole, disillusioned or dead, their places taken by the scum Mugabe called the *vanamukoma*?

Would Mama Africa cry for them too?

And the woman realised then that before her stood one of the last of the true *gandangas*, the last of that breed. They were all gone, their lives now obsolete, their skills no longer required. Or were they? Perhaps they were the warriors that Africa would always need until man learnt how to live in peace with his fellow man.

Isabella walked up to the African and kissed him lightly on the cheek and a barely perceptible flush crept across Sengamo's ebony face.

They ate simply that night – cold rations out of tin cans – before retiring to their vehicles. There were no fires to alert anyone of their presence and in the inky darkness the woman lay awake, cramped in a sleeping bag on the cloth seat of the Land Rover. In the distance the roar of a lion occasionally silenced the barking baboons.

Danny was fast asleep by her side and yet she wasn't scared because Sengamo, in the Land Cruiser, would sleep lightly, his ears tuned to extraneous sounds while he held his rifle. How sad that the Kalashnikov was the only companion he really trusted.

Looking at the stars, twinkling like glow worms above the mountains, Isabella prayed that the African would one day find his destiny away from the killing fields.

Her mind was in turmoil. She had told Danny nearly everything there was to tell of Robert Doyle and yet he harboured no ill feelings or bitterness, only a deeper commitment to want to help. Was there ever a man quite like him, fed on scraps and yet unfailingly loyal? His humbleness struck a chord in her heart and when she closed her eyes, she recounted snatches of the conversation they had shared that evening in the fading light of a candle.

'Issy, I'm sorry I was not around when you needed me.'

Why was he apologising? Isabella asked herself. After all, none of this was his fault. How many times had he offered to come over and she had rejected him?

'Danny, I tried to phone you on numerous occasions,' she said, taking hold of his hand, 'but somehow I could not go through with it. I didn't want to endanger your life. Can you understand that?'

'Yes, but I still wish you had called me.' There was a pain in his eyes that she could not see in the dim candlelight. 'I haven't been trained for this work, but I could have helped. Issy, I know I can never take the place of men like Robert Doyle or Sengamo but I want to try to be like them, I want–'

'Don't Danny.' She gripped his hand tighter, an urgency to her voice. 'Don't try to be like them. Just be yourself. There have only been three men who have meant anything to me since my father died. You are one of them. And you have qualities that neither of the others has.'

'Why are you saying this?'

'Danny – oh Danny, how can I make you understand? Robert Doyle and the African are Special Forces soldiers; what they have seen and what they have done has made them what they are. I would never wish that on anyone, especially you Danny. Please,' she reiterated, 'just be yourself.'

The candle on the metal dashboard flickered and then died. The woman closed her weary eyes and the dream she'd had the night before Robert Doyle came to Ingombe interrupted her sleep again, only this time something had changed.

On the edge of the darkness stand five men. Only now there is a log lying on the ground. When Isabella places the wood on the fire she is able to see the faces of the men in the shadows. One by one they step forward – her father, Joseph, Robert, Sengamo and then Danny.

When the embers die the figures disappear.

Then out of the gloom a man appears with his arm around a child. But there is no more wood and the apparition fades, leaving her alone in the darkness.

Isabella awoke with the dawn, bathed in a cold sweat. High above her in the sycamore trees, a Heughlins robin screamed 'don't do it, don't do it', ushering in the new day.

In the semi-darkness she moved her aching muscles to revive the circulation. The dream was now as clear as if she was viewing it on celluloid. The men standing on the edge of the darkness – those she had been unable to recognise in the first dream – were the men in her life. But who was the man with the child? And why was she not able to see him?

If there was a message in the dream, what was it?

She recalled her mother had told her of a gypsy in Spain, a vagrant that had read her fortune at the fairground in Seville. The old lady never did disclose what she had read in Francesca's palm but Isabella often wondered if the Romany traveller had seen the malaria that had taken her mother's life. She shivered. Was it a figment of her vivid imagination or the early morning wind blowing through the gap in the Land Rover door that touched her skin? She pulled the sleeping bag tighter around her body. It was all so silly, she told herself. And what are dreams anyway? Most of it could be explained away but, although she was unable to understand the implication of the men standing in the darkness, it was the last image of the man with the child, lingering in the shadows, which frightened her.

The first strains of daylight touched the vehicle interior. Isabella looked at the luminous dial on her wrist watch – it was 5 a.m. and Danny was still soundly asleep. In another hour the sun would rise above the trees and its heat would eventually kill off the last of the inclement haze.

And then they would be in the pass. Ahead lay Mozambique and whatever future there was in South Africa.

Suddenly Isabella remembered the letter in her jacket pocket. The words 'Only to be opened on the advent of my death' were written on the front. What a strange message – it was almost as if Robert Doyle had predicted that events would turn out this way. She stared at the script for some time before slitting open the envelope with her fingernail. Inside were two white foolscap pages.

She unfolded the first page.

Isabella,

If you are reading this then I am not with you.

Her tears made it difficult to focus on the writing.

There will come a time when everything will be quiet – a great peace, when the years can no longer take anything from me. When I found you, I was living a life in the past with retribution as my companion. You showed me another way and taught me to love again.

Remember those days, for they were precious.

There is only one more thing that I can do for you now.

I have taken the liberty of making this official. You will be familiar with the young man in Juliasdale who I understand is your solicitor. I have obtained his promise of confidentiality on this matter. The farm in the Drakensberg is called Shateen, because it was once a wilderness. I have no one left in the world so all I wish for now is that you will be happy there.

I will always be with you; in the trees that whisper in the wind that sweeps down the escarpment, in the brook that babbles its tune and in the swallows that fly free.

Me acompañas a casa?

I love you, Robert

Isabella read the page and read it again. He must have sworn the will when he was in Juliasdale, waiting for his truck to be repaired. This was obviously his way of ensuring she had a future should anything happen to him. He *must* have known.

The time they had spent together flashed before her eyes again. And yet it was the letter that finally brought everything home. It was all over and she could no longer control the anguish that racked her body.

In the first grey light of dawn, Danny woke to hear her uncontrollable sobbing. He reached across and pulled her gently towards him. It was not a time for questions.

Her head was on his shoulder. And when there were no longer any tears, Isabella looked up into Danny's gentle face and knew at last that there would be a tomorrow.

44

October is the hottest month of the year. The waterholes were dry and the animals were desperate. In another month the rains would transform the Highlands. They would arrive in the late afternoon and the days would be clear. Until then, both man and beast would suffer.

The early morning sunrise bleached the *veld* with a delicate shade of pink and for just a brief moment the austere bush was transformed into a vibrant landscape. Then the sun rose above the horizon and obliterated the soft colours.

Isabella occupied herself with preparing breakfast from the dry rations while Danny repacked the boxes and cases from the Land Cruiser into the Defender. Suddenly a thought occurred to her that they may encounter problems at the border.

'Don't worry,' Danny assured her, 'many white Zimbabweans are now entering the Republic and carrying whatever possessions they can. South African customs officers are so used to seeing their plight that they'll wave us through without so much as a second glance.' He closed the rear door of the vehicle and turned to face Isabella. 'There is still a fragile spirit of comradeship between the old Rhodesia and South Africa.'

'What about Mozambique immigration?'

'They just view us as another bunch of *wazungus*. Shoot us or deport us, they are happy to be rid of us.'

'He is right, *nkozikazi*,' Sengamo said, returning from hacking saplings at the entrance to the pass and overhearing the conversation. 'They do not want you.'

They ate the simple meal of dried biscuits and cold tea before the men carried out their final checks on the vehicles. The woman looked at the roof rack holding the lashed-down boxes that contained their few personal possessions, the foundations of their new life. 'Danny, I would like to travel through the pass with Sengamo.'

Danny understood her intentions. 'OK Issy. I guess I'll see you in Mozambique – just make sure Sengamo takes it easy. The old Rover is carrying a heavy load so I'll have to stay in low ratio most of the way. Don't lose me.'

How she loved his exuberant mood. Did nothing ever bother him or did he hide his feelings where nobody could find them? She had known Danny all her life and yet she still thought of him as an enigma, the little boy who had never grown up.

'I won't ever lose you again.' She was looking at him the way a woman looks at a man she has found at last. 'I can never repay you for everything you have done for me.'

'I don't understand.'

'Where do I start Danny? When I think of the pain I have caused you over the years and yet you are always there whenever I need you.' She remembered the little church in Juliasdale that she had walked out of with Joseph as her husband, and seeing Danny on the edge of the crowd in the sea of faces. 'It could not have been easy for you,' she said softly, her hand on his arm.

How many times had he watched her from afar, wanted her from afar, yet he'd never been able to cross the divide? And how many times had he seen the laughter in her eyes and wanted to share it, or the tears and wanted to comfort her? And yet he had only managed to tell her the day before. 'The moments I have shared with you have more than compensated – even if you only thought of them in terms of friendship.'

Over her shoulder, Danny could see Sengamo watching them. 'It really is nothing Issy,' he repeated, trying to avoid any further discomfort.

Isabella reached up and kissed him on the lips before turning to go. The old jeans hugged her slender body and Danny's eyes were still on her when he raised his arm in a friendly wave to the African.

Sengamo acknowledged the gesture. Letting out the clutch of the Land Cruiser, the vehicle lurched forward with a sense of urgency, negotiating a shallow stream before hunting a way through the lower entrance to the gorge.

Danny tried to follow the same track as it wound its narrow way up through the pass. His thoughts were still with the woman. Then his deliberation was broken when the suspension caught a rock. It jerked the steering wheel out of his hands and forced the vehicle into the bushes. Fighting to regain control, he finally brought the Land Rover to a stop on the edge of a deep gulley.

Sengamo was out of sight and it was some minutes before Danny could regain his composure and restart the engine. He silently cursed the country he was leaving, the land that had destroyed so many of his aspirations. They had lost the war, lost the country, and now, having lost his farm, there was nothing left in Zimbabwe. But when he thought of what lay ahead, he knew it was infinitely more precious than what he'd left behind.

In the rear view mirror there was a picture of a landscape

falling away, a country fading into the distance. For a moment it attracted Danny's attention and then a low branch splattered against the windscreen and an eland broke cover and dashed in front of the vehicle. He braked sharply, just managing to avoid hitting the large antelope. Eland normally preferred the mopane plains, so what was she doing up here in leopard territory? 'Pay attention, you idiot!' he remonstrated with himself and yet, in spite of the two near misses, he found himself once again thinking of Isabella.

Sengamo must have been waiting for him because in the distance he could just make out the faint outline of the woman's hair being blown gently in the breeze through the open window of the Land Cruiser. There was something wildly delicious about her, something that he had grown up with and always taken for granted, and something that he had so very nearly lost. He thought back to what she had said, about the day she married Joseph. It had broken his heart and he had not been able to bring himself to go to the ceremony. Instead, he had stood lost amongst the crowds on Juliasdale's main street. When she came out of the church, she had leaned forward to kiss a guest and a wisp of brown hair had fallen across the freckles on her face. Danny had never forgotten how excruciatingly beautiful she had looked.

The route through the gorge was tortuous, much of it heavily overgrown with saplings and small bushes, and it required all of Sengamo's concentration to avoid the sharp rocks and keep the Land Cruiser moving slowly up the hill. At any other time this would have been a stupendous drive across some of Southern Africa's most beautiful and unspoilt scenery.

Today, in their quest to reach the Mozambique plains, it was a drive for survival.

In the prevailing silence Isabella remembered the letter from Robert Doyle. It had contained two pages, and she had read only one. She removed the envelope from the inside pocket of her jacket and withdrew the second page. It was an official document, signed, sealed and witnessed by Dick Simmons, her solicitor, confirming her rights to the inheritance of Shateen. She read the form slowly and then once more to digest it, but the more she thought about it the more it confused her.

There were no simple answers.

Two hours later they reached the highest point of the pass where the view onto the escarpment was unforgettable. The African and the woman stood together and gazed down in silence over the dappled green treetops to the arid brown *veld* of the Honde Valley. Far away in the distance they could just make out the silhouette of Inyangani rising above the neighbouring mountains, like a tsunami sweeping across the *bushveld*, and in her shadow lay the green hills of the Aberfoyle tea estates.

This was Isabella's Zimbabwe, all she had ever known. She looked at Sengamo and spoke for the first time since they had left the camp. 'Have you ever seen anything like this?'

The African laughed. 'Many times in the war I have stood here looking back into my country. When the sun lies on the mountain it is even more beautiful. But I am sorry; we do not have time to wait for this.'

'Can we have just a few more moments – please?' There was a child-like quality in the woman's petition. 'While we wait for Danny.'

'*Yebo nkozikazi*. This is not a view you will see again. We will take a short break and wait for your friend. It's just that I need to be back over the pass before it is dark.'

'Oh God! I forgot you were returning to Zimbabwe.' For a moment the sense of loss enveloped her. Then she thought of the bizarre journey through the Honde Valley and her escape from Ingombe, which would never have happened were it not for this unassuming man standing beside her; her guide to freedom.

'It is me who should be apologising, Sengamo – for my thoughtlessness.'

A tiny dwarf gecko caught her eye. It stood immobile on a warm rock, as it searched for insects, its camouflaged skin rendering it almost invisible in the sun. The slightest movement from either of them would send the lizard scurrying away into the crevices beneath the rocks. In a strange way the gecko reminded the woman of Robert Doyle lying alone on the *kopje* with her folks, under a pile of stones just like those the lizard sat upon. It could all have been so different if they had only left those few minutes earlier, if the soldiers had only arrived a few minutes later, if they hadn't stopped to bury Shamari. There were so many ifs.

But it was not meant to be.

The African knew nothing of the woman's thoughts. His eyes were focused on a distant valley beyond the Mtarazi Plains that was home to the farm they called Ingombe. 'I think by now the *tsotsis* have discovered what we did. They will be very angry to find the house has been destroyed.' Realising the implications of what he had just said, Sengamo grinned. Then, the more he thought about it the more he burst into a giggle until finally there was no holding back a deeply infectious belly laugh that seemed to carry right across the yellow escarpment and into Zimbabwe itself.

That was how Danny found them. 'What's the joke?' he asked, walking over to join them at the top of the pass.

Sengamo's eyes were still fixed on the distant horizon. 'I was thinking of the *vanamukoma* returning to Ingombe and finding a heap of ashes.'

Danny was unable to share the humour; it was too painful to think of Ingombe as a heap of rubble.

Isabella noticed his concern. 'It is better this way, Danny. We are never going back,' she said, trying to imagine the soldiers entering the yard. Then she turned to Sengamo. 'They will know we have escaped, won't they?'

'Maybe *nkozikazi.*' There was no longer mirth on his lips. 'But it will take them some time to work out what has happened.'

'And then they will be looking for us?'

'It is no longer a problem – you are in Mozambique.' The African hesitated, choosing his words carefully before continuing. 'But if they realise you have escaped, you will not be able to return to Zimbabwe for a long time. Perhaps not until Mugabe has gone.'

'There is no reason to go back and live under a dictator.'

Sengamo nodded in agreement, in a way that transcended any racial barriers. 'It will not always be like this *nkozikazi.*'

The little band of fugitives stood alone on the mountain. There was a silent bond between them that would always prevail. It was left to the African to break the quiet. 'We must go now.' His eyes scanned the horizon below the pass. In the distance was a thin brown ribbon which was the gravel road to Chimoio and it was with mixed relief that they noted the road was empty of dust.

'It is very quiet,' Danny said, his eyes on the landscape of Mozambique.

The African nodded. 'This is a good sign. The track down the pass is easier but stay in low ratio. We will wait for you at the bottom of the mountain.'

'OK,' Danny said, turning away towards his vehicle. 'Take care how you go.'

The African's right foot hovered above the brake pedal as the vehicle slowly descended the pass, its tyres slipping on loose rocks. Occasionally Isabella caught sight of the distant gravel road running south through Mozambique, where she knew they must part. She looked across at the African and she thought again of how none of this would have been possible without him. She might well have been lying raped and dead beside Robert, or languishing in some hellish prison. And because of this she hunted carefully for the words.

'Sengamo, my friend Sally lives in Juliasdale. This is where Shazi is staying. Can I give you her address? She will help you.'

Sengamo wanted to laugh. Did the woman not know the soldiers and the police would be out looking for him? Or would they? Apart from the young girl he had slept with at the compound, all those that had seen his face were dead, and dead men do not make good witnesses. Either way, he was not going back to his country to hoe some *mzungu's* garden. His life was fragile and uncertain and work was the last thing on his mind.

There were too many scores to settle first.

Isabella tried to picture the *kraal* where he would have spent his younger days. It was not difficult – his home would have been similar to the compound at Ingombe. While he drove she talked to him. She told him that she could understand the past because she had lived it, all the horror and the killing. She talked of the ugliness and of how the cruelty had become the justification for the cause. 'But there has to be another way,' she finally said.

The African could see her hands gripping each other, nails digging into flesh. 'What other way is there, *nkozikazi?*'

'I don't know the answer.'

The African almost felt sorry for the woman. The treatment of his people was not of her doing. But then she was a *mzungu* and, as such, she was part of a system that was the reason for all the fighting. However, it had been a long time since anybody had talked to him like this, and his eyes were misty in the sun filtering through the trees. Maybe this *was* his opportunity to walk away from the hate and the revenge. The woman beside him held the olive branch and if he did not take it, he knew he would drown. '*Nkozikazi*, I will go to Juliasdale.'

Isabella smiled. It was another small step towards the future.

At the bottom of the gorge the vegetation thinned out and they dropped onto a flat scrubby plain. Sengamo deselected low ratio and turned towards the gravel road that was hidden from view by the acacia bushes. At the angle they were driving, the light caught the woman's profile and reflected it onto the windscreen, a face on glass washed by the sun which reappeared each time they exited the shadow of another tree.

With his attention enraptured by the mirrored image, he did not see the small klipspringer that darted across their path. Braking sharply at the last moment, he narrowly missed the animal. The dainty little buck, that was able to leap intrepidly across sheer rocks, was far from her home in the mountains and a thin smile crossed the African's lips. We are both a long way from home klipspringer, he thought.

The gravel road was deserted. Fierce fighting in the long, drawn out civil war had devastated much of Mozambique. It was not just the people that had perished; many of the animals had shared a similar fate, gunned down to feed a desperate and starving population. Once the eastern plains around Gorongoza had been alive with the beat of thousands of hooves and vast herds of animals roamed freely between Mozambique and South Africa's Kruger National Park, crossing a land without fences or borders. Now the lowland was almost uninhabited.

Sengamo stopped the Land Cruiser beside the gravel road and cut the engine. The ground here was hard and barren and there was little evidence they had crossed it.

'This is where I must leave you,' he said simply.

Isabella reached over and put her arm around his shoulder.

Sengamo flinched, taken aback by the affection. The last time anything like this had happened with a white girl was on the farm with Andrea. Then came the betrayal and the years condemned to the wilderness. However, this was different. No *umfazi* had ever shown him such kindness and he wondered how one repaid this compassion. It was much easier to react to violence – he could fight evil with an AK-47 and this was and had always been his solution. Africans do not blush easily, but he could feel the heat in his head.

Isabella gently ran her hand over his ragged shirt. Beneath the cotton his arms were skin and bone, the emaciation caused by years of surviving on very little food. She took a last look at the face where youth had flown, where sadness now mapped contours that were aged beyond their years. 'I am proud to have known you Sengamo,' she said, 'and I will never forget what you have done for us.'

The African let the words linger in the air. An inner voice told him to catch them and hold them; that way they would not escape. On the front windscreen the remains of a locust were trapped in the windshield wipers. Perhaps the dead insect reminded him of what he wanted to say. '*Nkozikazi*, there is one more thing I can do for you. The graves at Ingombe . . . I will look after them. They will be like my children and I will care for them until you return to Zimbabwe.'

There were tears in her eyes. How could she repay such kindness? Hadn't he enough of his own problems without tending to her graves?

But then she realised there was one *shamba* on the *kopje* at Ingombe the African would never forget – the final resting place of Robert Doyle.

'*Tatenda induna.*'

The long goodbye was over. Conscious of the African's awkwardness, Isabella did not want to prolong the agony. She reached over and kissed him on the cheek.

Danny watched the scene unfolding through the dusty windscreen and he knew what this meant to her. Eventually the driver's door opened and Sengamo stepped out to be met by a multitude of mopane flies, which he angrily swatted away with the back of his sleeve.

'*Nkozi*, now your journey is easy,' Sengamo said, spreading the large-scale map out on the bonnet of the Land Rover. 'We have come over the border here.' His finger rested on the dotted black line. 'You must continue south to the tar road. This is the main road between Zimbabwe and Mozambique so there will be more traffic. When you reach Inchope take the coast road to Maputo. Cross the border at Moambo and you are in South Africa.' Sengamo glanced up to determine whether the *mzungu* had understood his instructions and then turned his head back towards the mountains and contemplated the pass. He was about to say something, but decided against it.

'Is there anything we need to look out for?'

'*Hapana*. Much of the fighting in Mozambique is now over. Just stay on the road; there are many land mines in the bush.' Acknowledging the woman who had walked over to join them, he then continued with his instructions. 'Once you are on the tar road you should make good time to Maputo. Head straight to the border; the sooner you are in South Africa the better.' Then, removing his hand from the map, he folded it up and handed it to Danny.

Danny took his hand. He understood why he was going back. There are some things a man has to do, things he cannot run away from if he is going to be able to live with himself. He'd felt the same way after he had lost his own family. The ghosts must be laid to rest before he could live in peace.

'Sengamo, you know the *vanamukoma*, you know what they are capable of doing. If you return to Zimbabwe and they find you, they will kill you.'

The strangest of smiles flirted across the African's face. 'Death,' he said, looking back over the mountain to Zimbabwe, 'is like a faceless man. It is a man who has no friends or enemies. I have walked with this man by my side many times in the Bush War, never knowing when he would call me. I saw him go to many others, but he left me alone . . . no, he does not frighten me, *nkozi*. And first they have to find me.'

Danny had never encountered anyone quite like the African. His roots lay deep in a Zimbabwean valley, and from there they had been moulded into a formidable fighting machine through circumstances beyond his control. What they owed Sengamo was beyond comprehension. He had brought them to this place of freedom, and it had not been without cost.

'Goodbye my friend.'

The African held his gaze without flinching. '*Kwa heri nkozi*.' Then, turning to the woman, he looked into her misty eyes. '*Nkozikazi*, it is time to leave.'

Isabella felt the stubble on her lips when she kissed his cheek.

Sengamo was both reluctant and restless to go. Then the empty awkwardness that prevailed was broken by the harsh shriek of a starling and the African turned away. The woman was crying but he did not see the tears. Turning around one last time to acknowledge the *wazungus*, he closed the door.

The last sound they heard was the Land Cruiser's diesel engine turning over slowly as if disinclined to want to start. And then it fired.

'Till we meet again *nkozikazi!*' Sengamo shouted above the noise of the engine.

Then Robert Doyle's Land Cruiser began to move off slowly towards the bush, back the way it had come, leaving Danny and Isabella standing alone by the side of the road. Sengamo's arm rested on the windowsill and Isabella caught a brief glimpse of the silver catch on the black leather bracelet, almost indistinguishable against the dark shade of his ebony skin. And then his arm vanished back into the cab.

The seconds ticked away, each one increasing the distance between the white farmers and the last of the freedom fighters. When the vehicle reached the tree line it stopped and Sengamo's arm appeared briefly out of the window, raised in a final farewell. Then, as if impatient to return home, the vehicle surged forward and the thick bush finally devoured both man and machine.

It had been less than four days since Isabella had first seen the strange vehicle coming up the dusty track to Ingombe.

Four days and how many lifetimes?

In the distance a pair of impala danced across the *veld,* hurriedly avoiding the dust cloud that dispersed into the tinder-dry atmosphere, a khaki rain that covered the leaves of the acacia bushes, changing their colours from a light shade of green to a dirty brown.

Isabella could taste the dust. Then she remembered the shroud that had first brought the Land Cruiser into her life.

It was this same dust cloud that had now taken it away.

Finally, there was no longer any dust; no longer any manifestation to distinguish the path of Robert Doyle's Land Cruiser.

It had vanished completely from their lives.

EPILOGUE

Shateen is just how Robert Doyle described it, nestling in a valley at the base of an enormous escarpment. Dainty klipspringers play amongst the rocks in the desolate granite hills that form the edge of the dome, while shy slender-legged steenbok roam the floor of the valley. Man is the only predator here.

The log cabin is basic. But like everything that Robert Doyle built, it is solid. Everywhere I go I feel his presence, like a shadow that constantly follows me around both day and night. Danny understands that there will be difficult times but once again he is my rock, my support and my companion, nursing me through the melancholy days.

In the brief period I knew Robert Doyle, he was the love of my life. Nothing will ever change that.

I cannot erase him; cannot just rub him out like he never existed. In our new world we all have to learn to live together. And each day, life becomes a little easier. We no longer think of the past, of Juliasdale or Zimbabwe – only of today and sometimes tomorrow.

That is enough.

Danny and I spend endless hours talking about Winterton, the small town on the edge of the escarpment, and Shateen, our Drakensberg farm. We talk about the prospects of having a small game park one day, perhaps trying to replicate our childhood dreams, the fantasies we had of being the big game hunters of Ingombe. And we talk of a horse riding school and a future, one that we can see at last. We are happy together – as happy as two people have the right to be after what we have both been through.

When we first arrived at Shateen, something still bothered Danny. There was a question on his lips and a reservation in his eyes. 'What is it, Danny?' I asked one evening, as we sat on the new *stoep*. 'Come on; remember . . . we said no secrets.'

'It's the ring Issy,' he blurted out. 'I've never seen you wear it before.'

For perhaps a few minutes, I said nothing, just looked down at the moonstone on my finger. He was right. When we'd arrived at Shateen I'd put Robert Doyle's wallet and the inheritance papers in the bottom of the old wooden blanket chest, under all the sheets and clothes. I was about to do the same with the little leather pouch when an idea struck me. Why hide the ring? Why not wear it? After all, it did not detract from my relationship with Danny.

'Sit down, and I will tell you where it came from.'

So I told him Emily's story.

For a long while Danny had been silent and I wondered if I'd upset him. And then he took my right hand and slipped the ring off my finger. I was about to remonstrate when his voice cut across my protests. 'Isabella, I don't ever want to lose you again.'

That was the first time ever that I'd heard him call me Isabella. And I guess it was also the nearest he had come to a proposal.

He then reached for my left hand. Without further hesitation, he slipped the narrow gold band onto the third finger, next to Joseph's wedding ring, and kissed me. 'I know it's not my ring, Issy, but it was conceived in love and that is good enough for me.'

When I looked into Danny's face, I saw first my childhood friend, then the young man I sat next to on the Juliasdale street bench beneath the jacarandas and finally the shoulder I cried on when Joseph died. This was the man who had helped me to not only rebuild Ingombe but also my life after the war. Now here he was doing it all over again.

Why can we never see what is in front of our eyes?

Finally, I thought of the words I had whispered to myself when we were crossing the Honde Valley and at last I realised that this was the man I wanted to share my life with.

I guess that's nearly the end of my story.

Or perhaps it's just the beginning.

Two months after arriving at Shateen, I woke up with a nauseating feeling. It was a sickness I had never felt before. Danny was away for the day working on the fences down in the valley. The horses for the new riding school were being delivered a few days later and we had to get the grounds ready for their arrival. The last thing Danny needed was to be bothered with a silly hypochondriac so I jumped into the Land Rover and drove into Winterton. Doctor Hennie Du Toit, our local general practitioner, is an Afrikaner from Boer stock and his gentle smile matches his temperament. After the consultation he sat behind the old mahogany desk with a puzzled look on his face, while I waited like a little schoolgirl for the results.

'There is no medication I can prescribe for you, my girl.'

He didn't have to say another word, because all at once I knew.

It could only be Robert's child.

The dream that had reoccurred on the mountain pass suddenly struck me like a bolt of lightning. At last I knew the identity of the man with his arms around the child.

That evening the drive home was the longest journey I have ever made.

What would Danny say? Would he accept the child? Would he still love me?

I need never have worried because the light shining in his eyes said it all.

It was our child.

The day our son was born was one of those African days when everything stood perfectly still. Eagles soared gracefully in the thermals off Cathedral Peak, their spirit the spirit of Africa. In the wind their cries echoed across the valley above the cold clear waters that cascade off the ancient mountains. And as the waters fell they cast rainbows across the sky.

It was on such a day that Robert Doyle came home.

ACKNOWLEDGMENTS

There are many people you have to thank when writing a book but initially my appreciation goes to Bill Maxwell, friend and creative writer, for all his advice. Next a special thanks to Nel Luyendyk for her wonderful, enigmatic painting that she so kindly allowed me to use on the front cover – your magic has captured Sengamo perfectly. Thanks also to Jane Leadham for her talent in bringing the artwork together. But it is to Lucy Beevor, my editor, to whom I give my most heartfelt thanks. Her inspiration, structural insight and professional approach over three years has been nothing less than remarkable in moving the book forward.

Thanks also to all my friends who continually supported me throughout the dark days. No note of thanks would be complete without acknowledging my deep gratitude to my family, Mat and Laura and James and Efe.

Last, but by no means least, I am deeply indebted to Angie, my wife, who always listened to my ramblings and responded with constructive criticism. Thank you for all the times you read and re-read the story, never once doubting it would one day come to light.

ABOUT THE AUTHOR

In 1947 Michael Anthony's mother fled to Africa with him, to escape his father. They settled in Rhodesia and sixteen years later Michael joined C Squadron, SAS. After three years of operations in the bush he left to travel the world, eventually returning to England where he now lives.